ENEMIES OF MERCIA

BOOK 6 THE EAGLE OF MERCIA CHRONICLES

MJ PORTER

B

Boldwood

First published in Great Britain in 2024 by Boldwood Books Ltd.

Copyright © MJ Porter, 2024

Cover Design by Head Design Ltd

Cover Photography: Shutterstock

Map Designed by Flintlock Covers

The moral right of MJ Porter to be identified as the author of this work has been asserted in accordance with the Copyright, Designs and Patents Act 1988.

All rights reserved. No part of this book may be reproduced in any form or by any electronic or mechanical means, including information storage and retrieval systems, without written permission from the author, except for the use of brief quotations in a book review.

This book is a work of fiction and, except in the case of historical fact, any resemblance to actual persons, living or dead, is purely coincidental.

Every effort has been made to obtain the necessary permissions with reference to copyright material, both illustrative and quoted. We apologise for any omissions in this respect and will be pleased to make the appropriate acknowledgements in any future edition.

A CIP catalogue record for this book is available from the British Library.

Paperback ISBN 978-1-83751-214-0

Large Print ISBN 978-1-83751-215-7

Hardback ISBN 978-1-83751-216-4

Ebook ISBN 978-1-83751-213-3

Kindle ISBN 978-1-83751-212-6

Audio CD ISBN 978-1-83751-221-8

MP3 CD ISBN 978-1-83751-220-1

Digital audio download ISBN 978-1-83751-218-8

Boldwood Books Ltd
23 Bowerdean Street

This one is for Elizabeth R Andersen, Kelly Evans and Eilis Quinn – my writer friends on this mad, crazy journey. Thank you.

Designed by Flintlock Covers

CAST OF CHARACTERS

Icel, orphaned youth living in Tamworth, his mother was Ceolburh
Brute, Icel's horse
Cenfrith, Icel's uncle, brother of Ceolburh and one of the Mercian king's warriors, who dies in *Son of Mercia*
Edwin, Icel's childhood friend, in exile with Lord Coenwulf
Wine, Cenfrith's horse, now Icel's alongside Brute
Wynflæd, an old herbwoman at the Mercian king's court at Tamworth

The Kings of Mercia
Coenwulf, king of Mercia r.796–821 (died)
His son, Coenhelm, murdered before his father's death
Coelwulf, king of Mercia r.821–825 (deposed), father of Lord Coenwulf
Beornwulf, king of Mercia r.825–826 (killed)
Lady Cynehild, King Beornwulf's wife before marrying Lord Coenwulf, now dead
Wiglaf, king of Mercia r.827–829 (deposed) r.830–

Queen Cynethryth, Wiglaf's wife
Wigmund, Wiglaf's son, married to Lady Ælflæd, sister of Lord Coenwulf
Wigstan, Wigmund and Lady Ælflæd's young son
Ecgberht, king of Wessex r.802 onwards, r.829 in Mercia

The Ealdormen/Bishops of Mercia
Ælfstan, one of King Wiglaf's supporters, an ally to Icel who is a member of his war band
Ælflæd, Lord Coenwulf's sister, married to Lord Wigmund, the king's son
Ælfred, ally of Lord Wigmund
Beornoth, one of King Wiglaf's ealdormen
Hunberht, an ally of Lord Wigmund
Muca, one of King Wiglaf's ealdormen
Sigered, a long-standing ealdorman who's survived the troubled years of the 820s
Sigegar, Sigered's grandson
Tidwulf, an ally of King Wiglaf
Wicga, ally of Lord Wigmund
Æthelweald, bishop of Lichfield
Ceolbeorht, bishop of Londonia
Ceolnoth, archbishop of Canterbury
Heahbeorht, bishop of Worcester
Eadwulf, bishop of Hereford
Hunbeohrt, bishop of Leicester

Rulers of Other Kingdoms
Athelstan, king of the East Angles
Ecgberht, king of Wessex
Æthelwulf, Ecgberht's son, king of Kent, under his father
Ealdorman Hereberht, ealdorman of Kent

Ealdorman Ælfstan's Warriors
Cenred, Mercian warrior
Godeman, Mercian warrior
Kyre, Mercian warrior
Landwine, Mercian warrior
Maneca, Mercian warrior
Ordlaf, Mercian warrior
Oswy, Mercian warrior, once an ally of the queen
Uor, Mercian warrior
Waldhere, Mercian warrior
Wulfgar, Mercian warrior
Wulfheard, Mercian warrior, Ealdorman Ælfstan's oath-sworn man, brother of Wulfnoth
Bada, Wulfheard's horse
Bicwide, Icel's horse
Flêotan, another horse

Those Living in Kingsholm
Coenwulf and Coelwulf, the sons of Lord Coenwulf and Lady Cynehild
Eadburg, living in Kingsholm, protector of the children, her mother was their wet nurse
Lady Cynewise, sister of Lord Coenwulf
Eadbald, Mercian warrior
Deremann, Eadweard, Forthgar, Mergeat, Wulfred, oath-sworn warriors of Lord Wigmund, now all dead

In Hereford
Hywel, living in the forest
Æthelbald, now dead
The Wolf Lady, forest dweller

In Northumbria
Wulfnoth of Eamont, now dead, brother of Wulfheard

Those Living in Tamworth
Cuthred, training to be a healer with Wynflæd
Eahric, commander of the king's household warriors
Gaya, previously a slave woman with a talent for healing, now freed
Theodore, previously a slave man with a talent for healing, now freed
Wynflæd, a healer
Brother Sampson/Heca, a member of Bishop Æthelweald's community

Traders
Benedict, trader
Eardwulf, trader in herbs and spices
Giric, fur trader
Morgan, trader
Durcytel, a Norseman, trader in stone
Heanflæd, horse trader
Wulfthryth, Heanflæd's assistant

Those Living in Winchester
Freawine, goat herder
Heardlulf, Wessex warrior, brother of Heardred
Heardred, Wessex warrior, brother of Heardlulf
Brihthild, sister of Brihtwulf
Brihtwulf, brother of Brihthild

Places Mentioned
Canterbury, home of the archbishop in the kingdom of Kent, was

Mercian but claimed by the king of Wessex in the 820s. Built on the Roman ruins of *Durovernum*

Eamont, in the north-west, the site of a famous meeting in 927 (if you look at maps of Saxon England, you'll find precious few names on the north-west side of the country)

Hereford, close to the Welsh borders, in Mercia

Island of Sheppey, part of Kent, where the Viking raiders held Lord Coenwulf captive

Kingdom of Wessex, the area south of the River Thames, including Kent at this time, but not Dumnonia (Cornwall and Devon)

Kingsholm, associated with the ruling family of King Coelwulf, close to Gloucester, home to the exiled Lord Coenwulf. Lady Ælflæd, his sister, is now living there.

Lichfield, close to Tamworth and one of the holy sites in Mercia

Londonia, combining the ruins of Roman Londinium and Saxon Lundenwic

Tamworth, the capital of the Mercian kingdom

Winchester, the capital of the Wessex kingdom, built on Roman ruins

THE STORY SO FAR

Lord Coenwulf has been banished from Mercia for seven years for his believed treason in approaching the king of Wessex, Ecgberht. While King Wiglaf hoped to be forgiving, with the connivance of the queen of Mercia, Cynethryth, and her son, Wigmund, the king was left with no option but to exile him. Lord Coenwulf's exact whereabouts are unknown, although it's believed he's sought refuge at the court of the West Frankish king. He was forced to leave his young sons behind. His sister, Lady Ælflæd, married to the Mercian king's son, has taken responsibility for their care.

In the meantime, Icel has wounded himself protecting the children of Lord Coenwulf, and the now dead Lady Cynehild, from their abductors. He's held true to the deathbed oath Cynehild extracted from him while informing him of the truth of his parentage. This knowledge has left Icel conflicted and unsure of his place within Mercia. Does he wish to pursue his claim to the kingship? Does he hope no one else ever discovers the truth? The similarity of the position he and Lord Coenwulf's children find themselves in is apparent to him.

Still, despite rescuing them, and the death of all those who held the children in the north, the true power behind the movement to kill the children has yet to be discovered. Icel fears the involvement of the queen, and her son, married to the children's aunt.

Icel is far from fully recovered from the beating he experienced while hunting down the children, which left him for dead. Eadburg, the daughter of the children's wet nurse, yet lives, but has been badly wounded. Her mother died attempting to escape their captors.

Wulfnoth, the man behind the attack is no more, and the men of Lord Wigmund's war band, who were also implicated, are dead. But Icel is yet to understand what happened between Wulfnoth and his brother, Wulfheard, a man who has long looked after Icel and made him the warrior he is today.

Recovering, and aware Wulfheard and Ealdorman Ælfstan are as invested as he is in discovering the truth, and protecting Mercia's future, Icel is by no means assured that anyone else even cares.

THE MERCIAN REGISTER
AD834

In this year, Lord Coenwulf of the Hwicce was banished for his treason.

1

AD835

The woodlands close to Hereford

'You shouldn't have come.' Her words reach me, and I wince over the snap of the twig beneath my foot. I've almost forgotten when I could move with the litheness of my youth. The wounds I took trying to fight off Eadweard and his allies have been slow to heal and have scarred me. I know that I'm not the man I used to be. Some of those injuries are more than skin deep. With twenty, nearly twenty-one winters to my name, I'm not the warrior I thought I was.

The Wolf Lady emerges in the gloom before me, a wraith-like creature coated in the grey of the coming night. I'm not the only one to rear backwards. Brute lets forth a startled neigh, which doesn't surprise me.

'I wanted to thank you,' I begin, but she's already turned her back on me, making her way through the gloom. Brute and I hasten to follow her. I allow him to walk unaided. It's me who really needs the comfort of his smooth back to keep me upright. 'For saving Eadburg's life after she was attacked by the bastards who stole the children,' I continue, raising my voice for fear she won't hear me. The winter has passed, giving me time for my wounds gained from fighting to heal. I was resolved to rescuing the children from what their abductors planned to do, fulfilling my oath to Lady Cynehild. But it's not yet Eastermonað. There's a bitterness in the air tonight.

'That she lived was thanks enough.' Her words are suddenly much closer, yet she's far from my side, way out ahead, where her footsteps over the rustling forest floor reach my ears.

I feel my forehead furrow, and there's a soft breath at my side only for eyes to shimmer before me. I startle again, almost swallowing my tongue in confusion. I was sure she'd walked ahead, but clearly not.

'Young Icel,' she exhales. 'You didn't need to find me. In fact,' and now she's the one looking puzzled in the dim glow from the moon and stars overhead, her long hair showing in a glossy sweep down her back, 'you shouldn't have been able to.' These words are much softer, almost as though she's talking to herself.

'I brought you gifts,' I offer. 'From Kingsholm. Lady Ælflæd begged me to thank you in person. She was one of those who agreed I should make this journey alone and as soon as I was able.'

'Did she now?' This reaches me from far away. I turn once more, but she's no longer where she was.

'How do you do that?' I demand, feeling uneasy at these strange occurrences.

'Do what?' And she's back. Now we walk side by side through a more familiar landscape, for all I've only been here once before. From close by, I can hear the shuffling of hens and the soft snores of something else. Animal or human, I'm not sure.

'There's nothing to fear,' she breathes from beside me. Her

hand runs over Brute's back, and I'm disconcerted when it rests on the mostly patched-up injury inflicted by my enemies. She surely can't see it in the gloom. 'Not the smoothest repair,' she whispers to Brute. 'But you won't mind now, will you?'

I feel my mouth open in astonishment. How does she know Brute was wounded in that exact spot above his front leg? Despite everything, has word reached her here of what befell me?

'Come, Icel, inside. I need the heat from my hearth. It's a cold day. Place your horse in the stables with the other animals. There are hay and oats for him. And close your mouth, Icel. Guests should always be welcome. I'm sure you know that.'

All the same, my mouth doesn't close, not even as I make Brute comfortable and allow him to eat the offered oats and drink deeply from a bucket of water. I glance around in the murkiness. There are no other horses here, not even a donkey. How then did she have the oats and hay to hand? I don't think the few hens and goats need those foods. The only explanation is that she did, indeed, know I was coming and had prepared.

'We won't be here long,' I murmur to Brute, but he's not listening. I appreciate the words are more to settle me than him.

I loop the saddle from his back with a wince, the sacks he carries thump to the ground with a dull thud. The reins are harder to remove, forcing me to stretch my healed belly wound. I feel tears prick my eyes at the reminder of all I've endured. Perhaps Wulfheard was right. I should have waited to fulfil this task. I shouldn't have been in such a hurry to declare myself fit and to venture out alone. But I needed to do this. I needed to prove to myself that I could, and with Ealdorman Ælfstan's warriors at Kingsholm, I'm confident that nothing will slip past their guard. The children are safe in my absence. And their aunt, who I once suspected, is as determined to keep the children safe as I am, and she encouraged me to come here. And of course, Eadburg is at

Kingsholm as well. She's already nearly died for those children. I'm sure she wouldn't hesitate to do so again.

Perhaps I should have spent the night in Hereford and come here in the morning. Maybe then I'd feel less uneasy. I thought I had nothing to fear from the mysterious woman who healed me and Eadburg last year, but now I'm less convinced.

I leave Brute unencumbered in the building before emerging into the ever-deepening dimness of the coming night. The sacks I carry are heavy. I'm weighed down with supplies and some coins for the Wolf Lady, provided by me, Lady Ælflæd and Wynflæd. Wynflæd too knew of my intent before I did and sent her gift to Kingsholm with a baggage train from King Wiglaf for his grandson. When, I think, did I become so predictable?

I'm directed more by my nose than anything else, wobbling towards the glow of the fire, a sullen red in the night, as the smell of a cookpot encourages me onwards.

The door's been left open, but I stop and close it as I move inside. Not that I see her. I expect to find her by the hearth, as she said, but there's another figure there, hunched over, perhaps ancient. I startle again. I thought she was alone.

'No need to fear, Icel. I think you'll remember Hywel from last year.'

At the name, a head jerks upright, and shocked eyes greet mine. If she knew of my arrival, then her guest wasn't informed.

'Hywel's been ill, but I've cared for him, and soon he'll be well enough to leave if he chooses.' Although the words are softly spoken, I detect an element of menace to them. Will she cure anyone? Even those who don't deserve it. But then, Hywel might have held me captive, however he also helped me escape in a roundabout sort of way. He told me who was behind the conspiracy – well, the parts he knew about – and was much kinder to me than that bastard, eaten by the wolves, Æthelbald.

'Good day,' I call to him, attempting to stride with more confidence, despite the niggles from my healed leg wounds. But the sacks are too heavy. I'm forced to drop one or risk falling over.

'Ah, my thanks, Icel,' the Wolf Lady mutters, opening the first and dipping her head low to explore the contents.

'These are from Lady Ælflæd of Kingsholm and Wynflæd from Tamworth, amongst others.'

'Then they have my thanks as well.' A soft exclamation of delight, and I see she's poured forth one of the larger pottery jars encased in soft fleece to ensure its contents aren't disturbed. 'Honey,' she exclaims, removing the lid and sniffing appreciatively. 'From Wynflæd?' She arches an eyebrow. How does she know this item is from Wynflæd? It could have been from Lady Ælflæd.

'Yes, she said you need it.'

'I do, yes.' But she offers nothing further, although whispers of happiness greet her foray through the gifts I've brought for her. I stand, unsure what to do. Hywel, sensing my unease, jerks his head towards me in what I take as a gesture to join him in holding my hands towards the heat from the flames.

'You look like you've had a beating,' he offers, his words as faint as the Wolf Lady's, almost as though this is hallowed ground, and they both fear to wake the spirits that might claim this place. I feel a cold shiver down my spine that not even the heat of the leaping flames can dispel.

'I did, yes, no thanks to you and your friend.' I don't mean to voice my complaints, but they follow the twinges in my belly from hefting the too-heavy sack of supplies.

'Yes, well, I've been punished enough for that,' he mutters unhappily. I catch sight of him in a flicker of bright flame and realise his face is twisted, perhaps scarred. It's not easy to see. I don't know how it's become dark so quickly, but it has. Aside from the gentle crackling from the stone circle inside which the flames leap, there are only two candles, reeking of pig fat. They're both close to the Wolf Lady as she continues sorting through the offerings I've brought with me. I intended to make an elaborate game of presenting each item to her, the herbs, the exotic spices, the sharp knife that Lady Cynewise insisted on sending to her, in imitation of my intentions to get her one, but my explanations aren't needed. I can hear the pleased murmurs with each new discovery and, after it, the names of those who sent them for her. I shake my head, perplexed by how the Wolf Lady knows such things.

'The woman?' Hywel asks. 'She's well?'

Recalled to the here and now, I stretch my booted feet towards the heat, hoping to dispel my chill and unease. 'Eadburg's physically healed, yes, but perhaps not in her mind.'

'The bastards,' he murmurs, a roll to the word. 'They left her to be eaten by the wolves.' He shudders, no doubt remembering the fate of Æthelbald, the pair of them keeping me tied up in the woodlands not far from here.

'You found her?' The pieces of the riddle as to how Eadburg was healed start to fall into place.

'I did, yes, unconscious and bleeding, well, what blood was left. I brought her here. Best thing I could do.'

'I thought you were scared of the Wolf Lady.'

'I might be,' he mumbles defensively, 'but that doesn't mean I don't appreciate her skills. She's a good woman. A pity about everything.'

'And what was everything?' I press. I'd like to know the mystery of the Wolf Lady, but Hywel smiles, showing me a mouth with fewer teeth than I expected.

'Not for you to know, young warrior. We all have our secrets and pasts. Some more than others. Just be grateful she was here to help you and your young friend.'

He leers at me then. I smell the sweat of a man who's been fighting for his life but is now recovering, if slowly. He needs to bathe. I'm surprised he's not been forced to dunk his head in one of the water barrels. The Wolf Lady made me do that when last I was here. Admittedly, I stank of the latrine ditch, and Hywel's smell isn't quite as offensive.

'Not for you to know,' the Wolf Lady echoes from close behind me. I jump again, thinking she's proved I'm about as alert as a sleeping hound with a belly full of pork. If I was on guard duty against the Wessex warriors or the might of the Viking raiders, my warriors and I would be long dead.

'Apologies,' I feel quelled into saying. She nods and resumes her inspection. I watch her. It's impossible to tell much of her shape beneath the thick cloak she wears. But the fact she hums and sways as she decants the contents of the supply sacks makes her seem much younger than I thought her to be. She's no Wynflæd, wizened like a long-stored summer apple, but what she is, I'm unsure. I'm grateful for her skills, however, or why ever she's found herself living alone in the woodlands close to Hereford.

'Are they dead?' Hywel recalls me to the plight of Eadburg.

'Yes, all of them, Eadweard, Deremann, Forthgar, Mergeat and Wulfred, and many others beside. Ealdorman Ælfstan and his warriors journeyed north and ensured they died.'

'And those little lads you were looking for. You found them?'

'We did,' I confirm with a firm nod of my chin. 'It wasn't easy,' I murmur more softly. The fact he doesn't reply makes me think Hywel knows some of what I've suffered. Or perhaps, he can see that I'm changed from the man he captured last year. Can he determine how wounded I was? Does it show in how I walk and speak?

'That's good, the lady whimpered for them in her sleep when she began to recover. Terrible business.' When he speaks again,

I'm torn away from my memories of all I suffered at Eadweard's hands, only to be recalled to what I endured at Hywel's. Does he forget he held me captive at the bequest of these people? But then, he was after coin and food. Perhaps I shouldn't be so angry with him. What would I do to feed my belly and my horse if I was a desperate man? 'I didn't like them,' Hywel speaks as though this forgives all. 'And I liked that bloody Wulfnoth even less.'

'You met him?' This surprises me. I wish he'd told me about Wulfnoth when I spoke to him after my escape. I could have done with knowing about Wulfnoth's involvement before I left Hereford. Perhaps I'd have been less rash in my attempts to recover the children and waited for Ealdorman Ælfstan to arrive.

'I did. He was well known in these parts. It's been a quiet winter without him causing problems with his stealing and whoring. There have been many fewer graves dug as well.'

'Who was he?' I can't get Wulfheard to speak about his traitorous dead brother. Ealdorman Ælfstan won't tell me either. He says it's not his story to tell and that Wulfheard must be the one to speak about Wulfnoth. I'm surprised by how many people have told me that during my recovery.

'A bastard.' Hywel nods slowly, the flames casting his face in shadows again. 'He took what he wanted. He had men who did his bidding no matter how horrific the crimes would be, and they did far worse than I ever did.'

'But he lived to the north?' I'm confused by this. Wulfnoth had a home close to Eamont.

'He did, but he came from here. Him and his brother. His name begins with Wulf as well. I don't know what became of him. The whole family thought a lot of themselves. The two of them were inseparable once, when King Coelwulf was king, over a decade ago. But Wulfnoth was an ambitious bastard. He wanted to be more than just a warrior in an ealdorman's war band. He took the coin from anyone who'd pay and didn't care about the rightful paths of kings and their sons.'

'Do you know who his immediate allies were?' Hywel's mentioned many names already, but does he know more?

'Anyone who'd pay him over the odds,' he complains, wincing as he stretches his back, curling in on himself. But from the depth of the movement, he does speak. 'Eadbald was one of them. We heard he was involved in what happened to Lord Coenwulf two summers ago. Wherever he is, he'd be worth talking to if you want to know more about Wulfnoth. He's a bastard as well.'

Behind us, the Wolf Lady remains occupied. She doesn't interrupt my conversation which makes me think it's acceptable to ask the questions that tumble freely from my mouth. It's nice to have someone answering my questions, for once. But then she does speak.

'Wulfnoth had no love for wolves,' she finally comments, her words sharp. I can imagine the purse of her thin lips as she recalls that. 'He was badly named.' There's a sourness to her tone that almost makes me smile. 'Although perhaps not the second element. Noth means daring, and he was certainly that.'

'Wulfnoth had no love for anyone but riches and all that glitters and shimmers,' Hywel continues, as though she's not spoken. 'He would have killed kings if he could. He certainly ensured others had the opportunity.'

'So it's true he was involved in casting King Coelwulf aside?'

'Yes, and more besides. Not that he was alone in that. There were many who thought King Beornwulf would make a better king than Coelwulf. Wulfnoth was certainly happy to be part of Lord Beornwulf's movement against the ruling family. But Wulfnoth believed he received little reward for his involvement. He was sullen about it. When King Beornwulf died, and there was such uncertainty within Mercia, he thought to capitalise on the turbulent situation. Some even say he provided support to King Ecgberht when he stole Wiglaf's kingship. And the old king's son, Coelwulf's brother. He certainly had a hand in murdering that young man. Named Coenhelm, I recall.'

'You know a great deal?' I offer, trying not to consider the implications of my father's name being associated with Wulfnoth's. Or the knowledge that Wulfnoth had long been intent on decimating the line of Mercia's kings.

Hywel smirks, the tightness of his shrunken cheeks revealing themselves. 'It's well known in these parts. We all knew to fear Wulfnoth, and his ambitions. I shouldn't have become involved with Æthelbald, but I was a desperate man.'

'Why did Wulfnoth concern himself with such things?' I'm hoping there's more of an answer than just 'coin'.

'Because he could,' the Wolf Lady confirms, finally settling beside the hearth, her hands filled with the cloth sent by Lady Ælflæd to make clothes or put to whatever use she wants. It's not priceless silks but thick and well-spun cloth made from fine flax. Eadburg was adamant that such things as silks would be useless to the Wolf Lady. Indeed, she suggested sending more livestock and not the herbs and spices. I'm pleased she didn't win the argument on that score. It's been difficult enough to find my way here without sheep, goats or cows to cajole as well. Admittedly, I could have brought more of Ealdorman Ælfstan's warriors with me. But I chose against that. This, I needed to do alone. I've passed too much of the last half a year ensuring I was always with others. It's time I spent time with myself and learned to reconcile what happened to me. If I don't, I'll end up scared of a butterfly, just like Brute in the kingdom of the East Angles.

I've found enemies in the past where there should only have been allies. I won't make the same mistake again. But, until I know the truth of the conspiracy, I must be wary. Or, as wary as I can be when everyone else knows so much more and they refuse to tell me all of it.

'And you know nothing else?' I query.

'Oh, Icel, I know all there is to know, but you don't need to be aware of that. There's already enough for you to think about.' Her dismissal of my questions irks but then Wulfheard will tell me nothing either, so why expect more from her? I half expect her to make reference to who my father was, but she doesn't. Hopefully, she doesn't know that. I need it to remain a secret. 'Now, I hear rumours of a book of healing?' She swiftly changes the subject, making it clear I'm to receive no more answers, even if Hywel might know the truth.

'Yes, Ealdorman Tidwulf and his healers.'

'The former slaves you liberated from their master in Londinium,' she interjects. She chuckles at my confusion. 'Icel, where such matters are concerned, even here, hidden as I am, word reaches me. All know that I'm a healer who can be employed if I'm found. Hywel here might tell you my skills are lacking, but then, he was very ill and doesn't seem to realise that the body can't be cured in one night's sleep.' Her tone's acerbic. I detect some unease between the two.

'Then yes, a book of healing, to be in the hands of those who need it.' I reconcile myself to the fact I'm not going to discover more about Wulfnoth. I've learned more than I did know.

'And not the monks,' she finishes for me with satisfaction. There's a gleam in her eye. I realise she's holding one of the heavier items in her hands, running it between the two as though it's a ball.

'What's that?' I demand.

'A thing of beauty and potency,' she assures me, only to turn and wink at me, showing me her true face, with its terrible scarring that merely serves to make her more beautiful. I blink and look away, ignoring the stirring in my belly. I'm not here to bed her. I'm here to bring her such gifts and, if possible, learn more about last summer's conspiracy.

With the children safe at Kingsholm under the guardianship of their aunt and with Ealdorman Ælfstan's warriors in attendance, I feel as though I'm the only one still seeking answers. Certainly, King Wiglaf hasn't demanded to know more, nor has Lady Ælflæd, as she sits within Kingsholm, refusing to leave even when summoned by the king's wife and her husband, who've both taken themselves away to Tamworth.

'But what does it do?' I persist.

'Icel, there are things in this world that you don't understand and even more that you don't need to know about. I'm surprised that Wynflæd didn't ensure you knew about that.'

'So, it's a form of charm?'

'No, no charm. A talisman, perhaps, but no, I've said too much. I assume this is from Wynflæd?'

'Yes, she was most insistent,' I grumble. A sad smile touches her lips.

'Then rather than sitting here, complaining, young Icel, you should be with her. The time she has left grows short, and you and her have words that must yet be shared.'

'She's well, I know it for a fact,' I counter quickly, horrified by the idea that Wynflæd might be sick. It's only been a week since I last received word she was hale and hearty.

'She is for now, yes, but a woman such as her knows when the end's close. She's been trying to make provision for such ever since she took you under her wing. Of course, that didn't end quite as she hoped.'

'There's Cuthred,' I argue, wishing my voice didn't wobble at the thought of Wynflæd no longer being at Tamworth whenever I have need of her.

'Yes, and he'll do what he can. But I think Tamworth will be lost without her. No one can truly take her place other than you, and that isn't to be your wyrd.'

I open my mouth to dispute that and then snap it shut. I can't deny that her words shock me, and yet I've been aware for many years that Wynflæd has survived far longer than her contemporaries. There's no one who can recall as many winters as her within Tamworth. Not since the death of Beornwyn. I stand, only to feel a firm hand on my forearm.

'A single night won't make any difference, and you should rest.'

Uneasy, I settle again, aware that Hywel's watching the exchange between us eagerly.

'Tomorrow, you'll travel to Tamworth, and I've something for you to take with you and give into Wynflæd's hands. But you must not look at it or even think about what it is. It's a gift from me to her. It's not for one such as you to interfere with.' Her words are hard and edged with iron. 'You must promise to do this for me.'

I don't deny that I'd like to say no, but if I'm going to Tamworth anyway, on her command, then I'll carry whatever this mystery item is.

'Very well,' I confirm, and she nods, satisfied.

'Now, it's time to eat and then sleep. It'll be an early start tomorrow before the rain comes.'

I'd ask how she knows this, but it's not any great art. I've been watching the clouds form throughout my journey here. There's a dankness on the wind that means it'll rain. I hope I make good headway before I get drenched with the freezing water.

2

Drenched and bedraggled, I moan about my predicament to Brute. It's too bloody wet to canter, let alone gallop, and rain drips unceasingly onto and inside my cloak, leaking into and then out of Brute's black and white coat.

I'm grumpy and angry. I went to the Wolf Lady for answers, but I didn't receive the ones I wanted. I know more about Wulfnoth, but not everything. Indeed, I worry I have more questions. And now I fear for Wynflæd. Will she truly die this year, or was it just a means employed by the Wolf Lady to ensure I didn't linger? She was expecting me, and yet my presence was unwelcome, or so it feels.

Hywel still slept when I made my departure. I could see, in the brighter daylight, that he had indeed been very ill. He seemed to be all skin and bones. There was certainly no muscle or fat on him, which surprised me with the quantity and quality of the food the Wolf Lady shared during the evening. Not only can she heal, but her meal was one of the most flavoursome I've ever eaten.

'He's lucky to be alive,' she confirmed as I mounted Brute. 'He should have come to me sooner, but he didn't. Bloody fool.' There was a fondness to her words, which made me consider if she and Hywel were perhaps lovers or family. Maybe family. Perhaps a wild brother or an erratic uncle. Not lovers. I find the Wolf Lady too ethereal to have such a thing as a lover. She has a certain allure, and yet I doubt anyone would think it a good thing to actually kiss her.

As the daylight grew, although hazed with heavy, rain-filled clouds, I eyed her carefully. She's certainly not as old as Wynflæd, as I had suspected, but it was impossible to tell her true age. Even the tendrils of hair showing beneath her head covering were bright with no streaks of grey threading them.

'Tell your healers they're welcome to visit if they'd like to know more of my methods. I should like to know others could make use of them.'

Now, with the day almost at an end, I muse over my futile visit to her home. I desired to thank her, and understand more about her, but I still know little more than Hywel's hints.

I was perhaps more successful in learning about Wulfnoth. From what Hywel told me, and which the Wolf Lady didn't refute, I can, admittedly, understand why Wulfheard thinks his brother a traitor and doesn't want to speak about him. But, if Wulfnoth was the man who took the children, who ordered him to do so? Was he truly so important that he would conspire against Mercia's æthelings alone? I don't believe so. And, if he truly felt himself poorly repaid for his involvement in my father's usurpation of Mercia's kingdom, then why would he think to meddle even more? Time and time again, my thoughts turn to Wessex. If Wulfnoth was known to King Ecgberht, then perhaps the answer lies there.

I watch the sodden ground passing beneath Brute's hooves. It's almost as wet as the river I can hear churning in the distance. I shudder inside my cloak and run my cold hands over my wet face and drenched beard, hoping to clear some of the water away. But it's futile.

Not for the first time, my mind turns to the item pressed into my hands by the Wolf Lady. I wish I knew her name. It was heavy and unwieldy. I had to pack it tightly to ensure it doesn't disturb Brute, her scrutiny intense as she watched. She must have known how much I wanted to unwrap it and see what was inside. I stop my hands from reaching for it.

No doubt this is some sort of stupid test, and I won't be a part of it. Instead, I consider her warning with regard to Wynflæd. I can't imagine her not being there, in Tamworth, waiting for me, but it seems there will soon come a time when that will happen. The knowledge sits uneasily with me. I've been a petulant child of late, and I've also been too often absent. I thought she'd always be there. I hoped, despite everything, that she'd somehow learned the secret to eternal life.

Who, I consider, will be the healer in her place? I don't think Cuthred will be allowed to tend to the royal family as Wynflæd has. Maybe Theodore and Gaya will be called upon. Perhaps another healer from one of the other royal sites. But no. Healers know the herbs and plants close to where they live. They know what does what. If another healer came to Tamworth, they'd struggle to understand the changing seasons and the ingredients to hand. That would never work.

My mind tumbles onwards considering if I should be the one to be Tamworth's healer. Certainly, I believe that was Wynflæd's intention, although perhaps it wasn't. I shake my head, dislodging the water that runs into my eyes and into my black beard and moustache. If it was warm rain it might be pleasant, but it's icy and heavy, sinking into my clothes, my horse and me. My body judders with the chill, and all of my wounds, healed now on the surface, make themselves known once more. I recall when I thought I'd die, my coldness now an unwelcome reminder of then. I believed, in that quarry, somewhere close to Watling Street, that my pain would only end with my death. I don't wish to be reminded of that moment in time.

I grimace. Since my injuries, I've had too much time to think, and I've spent too little time being active. I believe that what I need is an enemy. One I can overpower but with my old skills built upon by Wulfheard, Ealdorman Ælfstan, my time in the shield wall and inside Londinium. I want to feel strong once more, not weak and pathetic. I want to be a warrior of Mercia and not a man who fears he's been broken by Eadweard. I could curse them all, but they're dead, so what good would that do?

I flex my right hand, feeling the tight leather of the glove as a resistance against the movement. Beneath the glove is my eagle scar. I imagine I can see it even through the thick leather layer that covers it.

I reconsider the options I have for the future. I'm a warrior of Mercia, but I could be much more. I have just as much claim to rule Mercia as the young children of Lord Coenwulf, as well as King Wiglaf's son, Wigmund. Perhaps more for I am a man grown and with the reputation of a fierce and loyal warrior. The children lack my age. Wigmund has a dearth of military experience.

If I intend to reveal the truth of my parentage, I need to build a collection of allies who believe in me before Wynflæd and her knowledge of my birth are gone forever. No one would dispute Wynflæd's claim. No one.

Only I don't want to do that. I'm more or less sure of it. I've seen what such a high birth can do to men, women and children. I've witnessed what ambition can make people do. I've watched too many kings fall beneath the blades of Mercia's enemies. I don't want that. I'm almost confident.

I don't want to be Tamworth's healer, and I don't want to be

Mercia's king. And yet I might not be a warrior of Mercia any more, either.

I recall the beating I took from Oswy before my journey here. I cautioned him against going easy on me, and so the bastard didn't. I have the black and green bruises to prove it and also the knowledge that I'm weak. I remain fragile even after a winter of good food, being warm and working on overcoming my wounds.

I refuse to accept that Eadweard's beating has taken away my warrior's instincts, but the doubt remains. What if I can never defend Mercia again? Would I step into the fray with a Viking raider with as much relish as in the past? Would I journey into enemy land to rescue a wounded Mercian? I'm unconvinced, and that knowledge haunts my dreams. Time and time again, I've seen myself trying to fight for my life, only to come up against an enemy that can best me while I fumble to pull my weapons clear from my belt, or to adopt the stance I need to counter the blows and hold firm. I've always been too slow. I've woken gasping, drenched in sweat, heart pounding, to find myself asleep amongst my fellow warriors, their snores and farts assuring me that no one else is as crippled by dread as I am.

These worries infect me now. I'm alone, somewhere between Hereford and Tamworth, shrouded by the heavy rainfall, aware that I'm vulnerable should anyone think to attack. Not for the first time, I reach for my seax, ensure my shield's close to hand, and wish I'd stayed with the Wolf Lady. I've not even told my allies at Kingsholm of my intentions to travel to Tamworth. They expect me to return in a few days. They'd never think to find me on this road. I should have thought more before blindly following the Wolf Lady's instructions.

I hope to be safe from Wessex warriors so far north. No news of war with Wessex has been sent to Kingsholm. Neither have Viking raider attacks been reported. Not that I think either of

Mercia's enemies has given up. At least, I console myself, I'm unlikely to see warriors beholden to the king-slayer of the East Angles, Athelstan, this far west.

I loll in my saddle, growing colder and colder, the rain pressing in against me, as unsettling as my thoughts. Brute, head down, picks a careful path without my aid. I imagine he knows the way better than I do. His body heat keeps my arse warm but little else. My eyes close unbidden, exhaustion from my journey to Hereford taking its toll on me. When I open them again, I've no idea where I am, but voices reach me. I curse my stupidity. I might have thought myself safe here, at least from the Wessex warriors, but another enemy is close to hand.

The harsh cries of Viking raiders resound through the sodden air as Brute comes to an abrupt stop, his head coming up, his ears moving as he too hears what I do.

Ahead, the sound of the river, in full flood, is loud, the rain no doubt making it run deep and wide. For now, I'm hidden beneath spreading tree branches and also high above the steep riverbank. I listen more intently, turning my head as though it'll aid me in catching the words I can hear. I can determine the accent far too easily, but not the words themselves.

On cold legs, I slip from Brute's saddle, wishing my boots didn't squelch on hitting the overwhelmed ground. The movement jars my teeth. I grimace against the fear snaking down my back, flinging my cloak to one side, eager to ensure I can easily reach my weapons belt without hindrance. Brute dances away from me. Luckily, the sucking noise of his hooves lifting and falling is masked by the thunder of the river. I try to remember which one it is. The landscape close by is filled with rivers. It might be the Wye or the Severn. I'm not entirely sure because I've been allowing Brute to lead the way, dozing in the saddle. I don't know how far we've travelled. What a bloody fool I am.

Gingerly, I slide the shield from Brute's saddle and, tying his reins out of the way of his legs and hooves, move him to one side. I slip beneath another branch, the tendrils of wintry, wet leaves adding to my general misery as they brush my cold face. My heart thuds in my chest, my breathing ragged. I should run from here, but I can't. This might well be the opportunity I need to stop doubting my abilities.

Although the day is dank and grey, the path I follow grows steadily brighter, even as it dips lower, my knees and thighs straining with the movement after sitting in my saddle for two straight days, one to reach the Wolf Lady and then the next to here. I wince as the leather on my boots creaks, and my feet slip inside them, my sock snaking down my ankle. The incline is steep.

The voices remain indistinct, but the Norse accent is obvious.

The roar of the river quickly drowns out all sounds other than its thundering mass. I see it and then hastily take cover behind a thick tree trunk filled with bores. This tree has stood for decades, if not centuries. It provides me with some welcome cover as I try to make sense of what I can see ahead.

There's certainly a ship, and people close to it where it's been pulled clear from the torrent. They have a fire that splutters fitfully under the onslaught of the rain and a single canvas beneath which at least three men stand, their faces almost blue with cold. They laugh and joke, busy playing some sort of game. But it's not one of them who speaks with the accent of the Viking raiders.

No, that falls to a man who stands on the riverbank, his hands above his head as he shouts to be heard. I watch him, unsure what he's doing. It's obvious this isn't something new. The other men are entirely oblivious to his actions. I allow my thudding heart to slow and my breathing to return to normal.

There's nothing to fear here, although it's very strange.

Only then, I feel a cold blade at my throat and turn, meeting startling blue eyes, forgetting I have my shield to hand with which to defend myself.

'Who the hell are you?' an outraged voice demands.

'A warrior of Mercia,' I splutter, swallowing against my renewed terror. Bloody hell. I came here to prove myself a warrior, and instead, I've allowed another to sneak up on me.

'Then you're welcome.' The man bows his head, stepping aside, lowering his blade and looking me up and down, a wry smirk noting the shield hanging lifelessly in my hand. 'You look like a drowned dog. Come to the tent.' His resounding menace has bled away. I eye him.

'Who are you?'

'A trader, as are my fellow drowned rats. We're on our way to Worcester, but we've been caught out by this bloody storm. Ignore old Durcytel.' He indicates the shouting man with a jerk of his chin. 'He's "communing" with his gods, as he calls it.'

'He's a Norseman?'

'Aye, a bloody good sailor, but strange with his demands on his gods. Come on.' The man hastens towards the shelter, his fellow traders glancing at me with disinterest as I step closer. I take some solace in the knowledge they don't fear being set upon within Mercia, even by a man with a shield and seax.

'Good day for ducks,' a tall man calls, his lank hair falling into grey eyes. 'The bloody weather here is always shite,' he mumbles, while the others variously agree or tell him to shut up. 'Who've you found?' he continues, looking not at me but the thin man beside me.

'A Mercian warrior,' he calls. 'And his horse.' At that I startle and turn, seeing Brute, head down, coming towards us.

'I told you to stay where you were,' I complain. Brute hastens to the shelter, but the men eye him, aghast.

'There's no room for him,' the first man I met says. 'Take him to the trees.'

Brute glares reproachfully, but there's no choice in the matter. It's either him beneath the canvas or the traders.

Emerging once more into the gloom, I eye Durcytel and his thundering voice, which echoes that of the rushing river. He doesn't seem as fearful as the Viking raiders I've met, but then, he's a trader, not a warrior. The thought perplexes me as I secure Brute beneath a thick tree branch, removing his saddle but not his reins, which I loop around a branch, and leave my shield leaning against the tree trunk.

'Stay here. I won't be long,' I urge him.

Running back through the rain, head down, I'm surprised by how such a small amount of exertion makes my cheeks puff. Wulfheard's told me to rebuild my strength and stamina, but I haven't fully appreciated it's fallen so low despite my beating from Oswy before leaving Kingsholm. If I came upon an enemy now, say the Norseman and his strange words, I'd have to beg for my life rather than fight a battle.

'Fine horse,' the initial man compliments.

'A gift,' I confirm quickly. Men always make assumptions about my wealth based on Brute.

'From who, the bloody king?' he chortles, disbelief evident in the way he speaks.

I'm too slow to rebuff that, and now he observes me with renewed respect.

'So yes, a gift from the king,' he muses. 'It seems we've found ourselves a man beloved by Mercia's king, for all he looks like something found in the bilge water.'

'I'm Icel,' I offer. 'One of King Wiglaf's warriors.' I hesitate to say more. I could explain why I'm here, but that might make me vulnerable to these traders. They look affluent enough, but a good trader always has an eye for profit.

'I'm Benedict, and my fellow traders are Eardwulf, Giric and Morgan. And that there is Durcytel, as I said.' The larger man is still out in the rain. He must be drenched. 'We're travelling to Worcester with herbs and spices.'

'Which will be ruined,' Eardwulf, or at least the man Benedict pointed to when saying that name, complains.

'Furs.'

'Which will be sodden,' Giric interjects.

'And fine inks.'

'Which might survive,' Morgan offers hopefully.

'And stone.'

'Stone?' I feel my forehead furrow at that. I'm sure Mercia has no end of stone. It has many quarries. I know this only too well. I nearly died in a quarry.

'For carvings. The church at Worcester has retained our services to assist with the carvings the bishop has requested.'

'Stone?' I murmur again, perplexed by that. But then, I've never given much thought to the carvings in and around the churches. I know some of them are elaborate. Some are crosses left outside churches, but it seems there's a lot more to it than that.

'Not only is Durcytel a fine shipman, he knows his way around good stone as well. He creates the designs.'

As the large man lumbers towards the dubious safety of the shelter, I watch him. I was dismayed to hear his Norse words, thinking him an enemy. But certainly, these traders show no fear in his presence.

'Tomorrow,' Durcytel announces without preamble. 'Tomorrow, the River Severn will quiet, and we can continue our journey.' He notices me, but only briefly, and turns to slump onto a wooden chest that creaks alarmingly under his weight.

Benedict smirks at my expression.

'And where are you going on a day like this?'

'Towards Tamworth,' I mutter without thinking about it. I want to stand by the fire, and absorb some of its heat, but that would involve returning outside in the rain, which would mean I'd only get wetter even while getting dry. The result of which would be that I'd actually be no dryer or wetter. I shake my head and dislodge more rain down my neck.

'Off to see his mate, the king,' Morgan comments. I incline my head towards him.

'No, a healer woman friend of mine.'

'The great Wynflæd?' Eardwulf questions, his gaze suddenly intense.

'Yes, Wynflæd.'

'Then you know of this Mercian endeavour to write a book of healing.'

'I didn't realise it was so well known,' I admit, surprised in the space of two days by those who know about it. I also didn't realise Wynflæd was so well regarded. To me she's always been a grumpy older woman, keen to slap my hands for mistakes and to order me to carry buckets of water for her. It's obvious she's much more than that. I'm a foolish man to only just begin to realise that. No wonder she slapped my hands and berated me for being sloppy with my work.

'Oh yes, the traders in spices and herbs are determined to bring the best of their cures. I've something you can take to her. No charge. I'd hoped to visit her myself, but we're running late. We must get to the market at Hedeby in the land of the Danes as soon as we've visited Worcester. If not, I'll miss the opportunity to gather more supplies from the east.'

He turns to a pile of sacks while speaking, and he gabbles

something so that a figure rises from amongst those sacks, one I'd not realised was there.

He's no more than a boy, perhaps Cuthred's age. He watches me with dull eyes, and I consider who he is. Is he their slave?

'He's my son,' Eardwulf offers quickly. 'I'm teaching him all I know. I can't say he's very receptive.' He laughs, even as the boy hastens to hand him one of the sacks. They seem interchangeable to me, but Eardwulf's pleased with it. He peers inside and pulls forth a small wooden box. The smell of whatever is inside it fills the tent with the promise of sunlight and heat, and my juddering pauses.

'Take this saffron to her. She'll welcome it. They say it's used for treating women's afflictions and diarrhoea, as well as making the most difficult of patients fall asleep.'

I take it hesitantly. There's little weight to it. Whatever it is, it must be needed in small quantities.

The boy quickly thuds back down amongst the sacks, dismissing the talk of the older men. I smirk at his complete disinterest. His father will have a hard time with him, I'm sure of it.

'My thanks. I'll see she gets it,' I assure him, unsure what to do with it now I'm holding it.

'Here, keep it out of the rain,' Eardwulf chastises, taking it back from me and placing it back where it was.

I stare out at the gloomy rain, my belly rumbling.

'We're low on food,' Benedict mutters unhappily. 'The ship tipped as we brought it out of the water. Lost all our bread and cheese. The fishes can feast on it.'

I know he's asking me to share what I have. I've no problem with that. I'd enjoy a hot meal, but bread and cheese will suffice when it's stopped raining.

'I have enough,' I confirm. 'But we'll wait a while. Tell me, to what use is the stone being put?'

Benedict shrugs and turns to Durcytel. 'What design have you devised this time?'

Durcytel looks sullen for a moment. No doubt the tone in Benedict's voice didn't help, but then he shrugs his massive shoulders and meets my gaze. 'It's to feature holy men, your saints,' he confirms. 'And then, beside it, I've devised a scene that will show my gods' animals cavorting, a snake, a wolf, even a cat.' He smiles, describing the scene. 'It'll take a truly skilled stonemason to bring forth the pattern. I'm merely the designer. I have it prepared on vellum, and they'll pay me handsomely for it.'

I confess I'm astounded by this news. I never considered that someone designed the statues. I realise I've been foolish. And that turns my mind to my mother's gravesite and the statue that lies above it.

'Tell me, have you ever designed grave markers?'

'I have yes, once for the king of Mercia.' And now Durcytel's face clouds, his eyes losing focus, his tongue poking through thick lips. 'Not your current king. I forget his name. It was a thing of beauty, made of the best I had available. He wouldn't tell me who it was for, but I believe it was a woman he'd loved long ago.' A wistful note enters Durcytel's voice. I swallow a sudden spurt of grief. I've never considered that my father loved my mother, only that he abandoned me when she died.

'Was it made of onyx?'

'It was, yes.' Now he looks at me in surprise. 'You know of my fine skill,' he preens, while the others laugh. Benedict shakes his head and slaps the huge man on the back. I'm glad they don't ask me how I'm aware of the grave marker. I wouldn't wish to explain further.

'He has the pride of one of his gods.'

I chuckle along with them, but the sound is off in my ears. Durcytel designed my mother's grave marker, and it was commissioned by my father years after her death, when he was king. Beornwulf showed more care for his dead wife than he did his living son. I taste the bitterness of that knowledge.

Abruptly, the hammering of the rain ceases. I don't believe it will last. Hastily, I dash towards Brute, ensuring he's well and not tangled in the branches. I return with my remaining bread and cheese to share with the men just as the thundering rain resumes once more.

I distribute what I have, and they offer me ale and a wine that tastes as though it's been warmed in the hearth, although it clearly hasn't.

'Tell me, have you visited Londonia recently?' I ask later when we're sitting on sacks and other stray items, anything to ensure the rain doesn't seep into our trews. The shelter above our heads is trying to keep the rain off us. It's not as effective as a thatch roof.

'Last summer. They were on high alert for the Viking raiders, but I think they've more to fear from Wessex,' Benedict muses.

Durcytel's face clouds. 'Not all Norse men are Viking raiders,' he mutters darkly. 'They give good, honest traders a bad name.'

'Durcytel, it little matters if we're turned away from some markets. There are others who'll pay handsomely for your skills.' All the same, the Norseman's face shows his fury.

'So, the attacks aren't just centred on Mercia, Wessex, Northumbria and the East Angles?'

'Of course not. Their ships can go where they like. Some of them are sleek and quick. We've encountered a few in our time. Durcytel's a useful lump to have around on those occasions.'

Durcytel's face is still troubled. Then he speaks once more. 'They could be honourable traders. The north is well connected to the lands of heat and spices, where that little box that Eardwulf gave you came from, but these men have no thought for that. They wish to make money, but they only have the skill to steal it. They should trade their furs and amethysts. There are many who would pay far too much to have the smallest piece in their hands, but they're foolish and weak.'

I notice Benedict rolling his eyes at this and realise Durcytel has argued this many, many times before. All the same, I'm intrigued by his words.

'But they must be wealthy to have swords and byrnies? Helms and mail coats?'

'They steal them. They take a ship. They thieve food to take on their journeys. They take what's not theirs at the end of their journeys. Then they return to their homes, filled with tales and other damn fools then purloin their ships and do the same. They leave behind a furious man without a ship, who must then filch another one, and who in turn left another behind before. So there are feuds and fighting, and then men spend all their money on warriors, and so the whole thing begins again. They're all damn fools.'

'Can the rich man not build another ship?' I'm perplexed by his argument.

Durcytel laughs at my words, but the sound's sour. 'They could if they employed skilled shipbuilders, but such takes time. The wood must be cut, seasoned, and forced into shape. The sail must be made from good cloth, which has first been spun from wool. And these men thirst for new riches and have no time to build. And anyway, those they stole from in the first place desire revenge, and so there's war and fighting, and everything gets burned.' He sighs deeply. 'Better to be an honest trader than a dishonest Viking raider. Better to come to Mercia and deal in our spices, inks, furs and stones, and perhaps, a few amethysts.' He grins at the end of this. I notice his fingers are entangled in a chain around his neck. 'See, wouldn't you trade for one of these?' The item he shows me is a silver hammer. A valuable item in itself, but a shimmering yellow globe sits at its centre.

'Is that amber?' I question, intrigued by the stone that glows as though fire sits at its core.

'It is, yes. And a damn valuable one. But it's mine, and no one dare take it from me.' He hides it quickly. I grin at his evident pride. He must think of his gem as I do my uncle's seax. Men might look like ruffians but we all, it seems, possess items of value.

We eat the rest of the food, which is little when shared amongst us all, and come the morning the rain has indeed stopped, much to Durcytel's satisfaction. While they bicker amongst themselves, I bid them goodbye, thanking Eardwulf for his gift for Wynflæd, and resume my muddy journey to Tamworth. Brute knocks my side as I mount him, unhappy at being left outside all night, but at least he had some comfort from the branches above his head. I shiver, rubbing my hands together, and welcome Brute's heat along my legs.

3

Two days later, Brute and I arrive in the Mercian capital of Tamworth at noon, the sky hazed, the sun glinting sullenly. Our journey has been beset with difficulties, thanks to the heavy rain. I sigh with relief on seeing Tamworth and imagine Brute doing the same. I still carry the wooden box for Wynflæd containing the saffron and also whatever it is that the Wolf Lady gave into my keeping. I hope she's appreciative of its contents, which I've endeavoured to keep dry from the continual downpour.

'Hail, Icel.' It's Commander Eahric who calls a greeting. I'm surprised he sounds happy to see me. 'King Wiglaf will welcome speaking with you once you've sought out Wynflæd, of course.' He smiles. I'm so unused to it that I grimace away from him.

'All is well in Tamworth?' I question. I really want to know of Wynflæd's health, but hope he'd have warned me of any problems with less joviality.

'All is well amongst the people of Tamworth. Those who rule, perhaps not so. King Wiglaf bids us all be vigilant.' I think Eahric's confiding in me, but his words elicit no surprise from the other guards who hear them.

'And I will be,' I confirm, taking in the sights of the place that was once my home. The blacksmith, Edwin's stepfather, raises his arm in greeting. He tries to entice a horse closer to him, although the animal, wild-eyed, looks no more biddable than Brute would at the thought of fresh shoes for his hooves. I glance towards the well, expecting to see Cuthred there, but of course, that's only a small part of his daily routine. I take Brute to the stables and tend to his needs in the familiar surroundings before venturing towards Wynflæd's workshop.

Cook fires elicit enticing smells, and my belly rumbles. Having shared my supplies with the traders by the side of the River Severn, I've gone hungry more often than I'd like. I feel a little shaky as I walk. I really do need to take better care of myself, and I crave some food. But first, Wynflæd.

Walking past the king's hall, I peer inside the open door, wondering why it's open when it's far from warm outside. But the servants are busy at their tasks, scrubbing the wooden floorboards and generally removing the dust and filth of a winter spent beneath the blackened beams of the roof. I catch sight of Ælfthryth or, rather, she does of me, and a squeal of delight pours forth from her mouth. I'm reminded of the catcalls from my fellow warriors. I've yet to bed Ælfthryth, but it's clear she still hopes to pursue me. I think she'll come towards me, but instead, I hear a voice hailing me and turn aside, grateful to escape her attentions. From all Wulfheard and my allies have told me, Ælfthryth's far too experienced for someone like me. I'd sooner wait to find someone else to share a bed with who might not object to fumbling hands.

'Icel.' Wynflæd's sharp voice recalls me, and I turn. She stands before her workshop, resting heavily on a stick for support, its sheen blackened with charcoal and shining in the bright daylight. Her wispy hair peeks beneath a thick cloak, and I eye her, looking for any sign that the Wolf Lady was right.

'Come inside,' she commands. I hasten to obey, for all I have to slow at the doorway to allow her to proceed before me. I inhale deeply, the smell of home flooding my senses, the warmth welcome. I take in everything. The workshop is in a good state. It's clean and tidy, the fire burning merrily, with a blackened cooking pot suspended over it and other pots positioned close or far from the heart of the fire, depending on what's needed. Cuthred swivels to say something to Wynflæd, but his questioning face clears on seeing me.

'Icel, welcome,' he calls. 'I'm sure you've grown,' he complains, which makes me chuckle, for he's the one that's grown. His brown hair hangs down his back in a neat braid, and it nearly reaches his waist. His head almost brushes the dangling spiders' webs that Wynflæd allows inside her workshop.

'He eats more than you did,' she growls, settling herself before the hearth on a raised stool and with a grunt of satisfaction. 'I gave the old boot the potion. I doubt it'll work,' she offers gloomily to Cuthred.

I consider who ails within Tamworth. But I don't have time to ask the question. It's possible, given my many absences, that I wouldn't even know whom they spoke about. Not any more.

'Why are you here?' Wynflæd asks quickly as Cuthred hands me a beaker of boiled water infused with some dried berries. It promises spring, for all the damp weather of the last few days does entirely the opposite. I cup it gratefully, allowing my hands to warm up. He also spoons another mixture into a bowl and I take that gratefully as well. I need to eat, even if it's only porridge seasoned with some honey.

'The Wolf Lady sent me. She said you had need of me.'

'Did she now?' But there's a glow of triumph on Wynflæd's face at my explanation. I consider what it means. 'And along the way, I met a trader who wanted me to bring you this.'

I pull the small wooden box from inside my cloak, and she reaches out small, clawlike fingers to grasp it.

She sniffs appreciatively and fixes me with a stern look.

'He gave you this saffron?'

'He did, yes. I didn't waste my good money on it.'

She nods, satisfied with my response, and opens the box, a glow of delight on her face.

'Then he was indeed a friend to me.'

'He was, yes, keen to be written into the book of healing,' I offer. She nods and snaps the box shut, although the smell lingers in the workshop, even over the pleasant aroma of last summer's berries in my drink.

'And why did the Wolf Lady bid you come here?'

'She said you had need of me. She implied, well, that you required assistance in ensuring who would be healer in time. She also gave me this.'

'Did she now?' Whatever look of delight had been on her face vanishes as quickly as the snapped lid on the wooden box, even as her frail hands take the next offering from my hands. 'She was always too interested in other people's affairs,' Wynflæd harrumphs.

'Who is she?'

'It's not for me to say,' she murmurs. I curse, thinking her anger towards the woman might have allowed her to tell me more. 'But, she's right. You were supposed to take my place, and that's not going to happen now, is it?'

I can see the confusion on Cuthred's face as she speaks. And I also know Wynflæd must sense his scrutiny. But she continues all the same, even as she opens the parcel from the Wolf Lady, a soft smile on her lips that disappears as quickly as it arrived.

'It needs to be someone the people of Tamworth trust and have known for a long time. It can't just be anyone.'

I try not to look at Cuthred with his open mouth, knife suspended in mid-air, where he cuts old garlic to Wynflæd's exacting demands.

'And it can't be some young snippet who most only know for falling from trees they shouldn't be climbing.'

I nod along as though I agree with her, and then she scrutinises Cuthred.

'And he can't be so lanky that he won't fit in most people's homes, either.'

I laugh at the outrage on Cuthred's face, but Wynflæd whips around to face me once more.

'This isn't a time for amusement,' she castigates.

'But surely you'll allow Cuthred to do this? He knows more than me now.'

'No, he doesn't. And anyway, and I'm sorry, Cuthred, I don't believe the queen will allow it. The king has murmured he'll have Theodore or Gaya here.'

'Well, if it's them, I can still aid them,' Cuthred retorts, his face flushed with suppressed fury.

'You can, lad, you can. And in time, people will come to accept you. Anyway, despite what the Wolf Lady's told Icel, I'm not going anywhere. Not for a long time yet. By then, you should be a man grown, and perhaps one who's learned to bend down when he walks inside an unknown building, as opposed to knocking himself out.'

I notice the livid bruise on Cuthred's forehead, just before he reaches up to run his hand over it. I wince. 'That must have hurt,' I sympathise. But he gets no time to reply.

'And he cracked the other side as well. No use was he to the poor miller with his griping stomach when Cuthred was the one rolling around on the floor with an aching head.'

Once more, I chuckle at Cuthred's discomfort and laugh even more when Wynflæd's bright eyes rest on mine.

'Not that you came for news of that. No doubt you need to know about affairs at court, and I want to know how everyone fares at Kingsholm, including you. I've heard of your wounds. Now show me. The one on the belly concerns me the most. I can see that the one below your eye is healed. The mark on your chin will need to be covered by that great bush of a beard you insist on growing.'

Unwillingly, I lift my tunic and wait for the laughter to come to an end. Wynflæd's fingers probe at Oswy's terrible sewing. I eye Cuthred. Oswy, the bastard, has ensured I always remember his work. The scar, now it's all but healed, benefits from a collection of marks that are far from straight. I'm only grateful that the pattern hasn't quite become what he planned. He meant to mark me with something akin to a giant cock. I'm pleased that can only be seen if I look at it from a certain angle.

Wynflæd sucks her lips and tuts, moving the flesh around. I wince to realise I can hardly feel her fingers. My flesh is always cold there now.

'A passable attempt,' she grudgingly admits as I lower my tunic. 'I mean, he probably saved your life, but never inform him of that. Tell him he needs to practise more if he means to sew anyone else together. And that he should concentrate more on knitting the wound together than drawing a cock in a man's flesh.'

I grimace, and Cuthred laughs. I glower at him, but he doesn't stop. Not even Wynflæd castigates him which infuriates me all the more.

Wynflæd speaks again. 'The children are well?'

This surprises me. I thought she had little love for Coenwulf and Coelwulf.

'Everyone is well, even Eadburg. It's taken all winter, but she's recovered.'

'Good, the king's intent on determining who was behind last year's attempts on them. He's had word from Lord Coenwulf, via a messenger from Frankia, demanding to know why he's not been caring for the children in his absence, and threatening to involve the Frankish king to ensure the children are protected. I can tell you that didn't go down well. The Frankish king has long been an ally of Wessex. King Wiglaf berates himself for not doing more last summer, and secretly, he wishes he'd not listened to his wife and son. Of course, the queen doesn't share his concerns, but she, thankfully, is rarely within Tamworth. The pair are far from united. I think the king suspects her involvement. I hope he means to use it as a means of setting her aside. If she were found guilty of trying to harm the children, then that would be adequate grounds for them to divorce. In the meantime, the queen prefers any of the king's royal properties to Tamworth.' I consider where Queen Cynethryth might be. I thought she was at Tamworth, but if she's not, and she's not at Kingsholm or Winchcombe, then where is she?

'How does he mean to find out who was behind the children's capture?' The news that the king means to seek the truth surprises me. I thought he'd wish to ensure the truth was never known, especially if it involved his wife and son. But Wynflæd interprets his actions differently. I consider where the truth might be. Does the king fear his wife and her ambitions?

'I don't know,' Wynflæd admits, only to lean forward and lower her voice. 'I think that might fall to you.'

'Oh,' I expel, thinking she might have known more than that. 'Then where am I to start?' But my thoughts have already tumbled to Eadbald and his part in all this. It was he who denounced Lord Coenwulf to the king. It was he who said he knew of Lord Coenwulf's interactions with the Wessex king because he was the go-between. Eadbald's not been at Kingsholm all winter, but I've not heard he's dead either. It was his testimony that was so damning for Lord Coenwulf. Perhaps he's with the queen. That wouldn't surprise me. 'Did Edwin send word, alongside Lord Coenwulf?'

'I forgot to say, but yes, he did. And some trinkets for Eadburg. It sounds to me that they're enjoying themselves more in exile than if they were within Mercia. His mother has the gift for the girl.'

'Then I'll ask her if she wants me to take it to Eadburg,' I comment quickly.

'I'd see what the king intends first. You might not be going to Kingsholm.'

'But I must. I've left my fellow warriors there to guard the children, but Ealdorman Ælfstan won't allow that for long. He means to have them returned to him as soon as possible.'

'You'll have to ask the king about that as well,' is her immediate response. 'After all, you are the king's sworn man.'

'I am, yes, and how fares the king's son?'

Lady Ælflæd has ensured her husband, Lord Wigmund, has stayed far from her side all winter. It's been pleasant without him and his petulance. No doubt, it's not been as pleasurable for Wynflæd if Lord Wigmund has been within Tamworth. She doesn't like him. I don't think anyone does.

'The two are so different,' she muses without rancour. 'It's often that way. The son is nothing like the father. He's a devious toad. He has allies everywhere, especially that Lord Beorhtwulf. I don't like him at all. He's been gifted land and wealth by the king, because Lord Wigmund petitioned for it, and the king is keen to keep the ætheling loyal to him and not his mother. But there's some good news.'

I doubt that, but I wait expectantly all the same.

'Ealdorman Tidwulf and his book are progressing well.'

That pleases me, for all I thought Wynflæd was going to speak to me of politics.

'Now, seek the king before he comes looking.' And with that, Wynflæd heaves herself upright with the use of her stick. I hear the slap of her hand on Cuthred's arms. 'Smaller, I told you smaller.'

I smirk and leave. I hope the king doesn't intend to send me away to seek out the truth of last summer's attempt on the children. I'm not at all convinced I have the stamina or the desire to travel alone after everything I endured last year. Wynflæd is right. My wounds have healed, mostly, but they were many and painful. I'm not yet the warrior I once was. I might not be the man to discover who Mercia's enemies are.

4

'My lord king.' I bow low and wait for King Wiglaf to acknowledge me when I finally discover him, of all things, admiring Brute in the stables. My stallion takes the acclaim as his right, preening under the king's inspection.

'You've worked wonders with him.' King Wiglaf's words are filled with respect. 'He was always so difficult to control.'

'Indeed.' I'm still bowed, waiting for the king to bid me rise.

'Oh, stand up,' he eventually commands. 'There was no need.'

But I can tell from the eyes of those who surround the king, including Ealdorman Sigered, who holds his cloak high to avoid the horse shit steaming on the ground, that I very much needed to be respectful.

'Saddle him up. We'll ride,' King Wiglaf announces, and I don't miss the swift look of fury on the ealdorman's face. I'd ask why, but there's no need. Ealdorman Sigered is the queen's man. Ealdorman Sigered doesn't like me, and I despise him as well. He's survived decades at the side of whoever is king of Mercia, but he's never lifted a blade to defend Mercia from her many enemies. He's a snake. I've no idea why he's even allowed to attend upon the king. Perhaps the king merely means to keep him close.

'But, my lord king, I can't accompany you, not at the moment. I'm unable to mount with my, well, my problem,' Ealdorman Sigered mumbles. I eye him. He does look pale. Perhaps he's unwell. Or perhaps he's just inflicted with that well-known problem of being unable to sit for long due to piles. I hope it's that. It really couldn't happen to a nicer man.

'Indeed, my lord, but I must exercise my horse.'

So spoken, there's a flurry of activity as the king's horse is prepared. The animal is a rival for Brute, but not as conceited. I hasten to saddle Brute, who watches me with disbelief at being removed from his warm stable. I'm unsurprised. He knows that I'm likely to make him travel huge distances with little to no time to rest.

'It's just a walk,' I murmur to Brute when he tries to evade me. Backed into a corner, I finally manage to fasten his harness and reins, but I don't miss the chuckle of two men who watch me.

I turn, eyeing Ealdorman Sigered, and Lord Beorhtwulf. Their proximity to one another assures me that Wynflæd is correct not to like Beorhtwulf. I've never been introduced to him, but he attended the trial in which Lord Coenwulf was exiled.

'Are you accompanying us?' I ask the other man. Again, I find myself seeking something in him. I want to know if he might have been related to my father. But I see nothing. Admittedly, my memories of King Beornwulf are hazy. I try not to think about him too much. Even my uncle is difficult to visualise any more, although I can hear him speaking to me if I try hard enough.

'Lord Beorhtwulf will be,' Ealdorman Sigered's quick to reply.

I incline my head to him, trying to be respectful. It's either that or punching him. I already know I don't like him.

'Then he better hurry,' I murmur, leading Brute past them and outside, where the king's also mounting. I see Commander Eahric called to accompany his king and other familiar faces from Tamworth, including a man he calls Eadred. I have very vague memories of him. But the king's son is missing, and so, it seems, is Lord Beorhtwulf, who's not yet readied himself. The king glances at me, then peers into the stables, and immediately encourages his horse onward, a jaunty cry over his shoulder at escaping both Ealdorman Sigered and Lord Beorhtwulf. I share his joy.

'I'm not waiting, Lord Beorhtwulf. I am your king,' Wiglaf calls to the missing man.

And so we erupt into the countryside around Tamworth. The clouds have turned white, as opposed to grey. I hope we might enjoy riding without getting wet. My cloak's still damp as the cold wind bites against my face. Not for the first time, I can feel the scar on my chin in the cool air. Wynflæd might bid me grow my beard to cover it, but there's nothing like a biting wind to get right through it.

'Icel, ride with me,' the king demands, sometime later, when we're far from Tamworth, able to look down on the settlement from the rise close to the road that leads towards Lichfield. If not for the trees in the forest, we'd no doubt be able to see both settlements, twisting our heads from side to side to determine which is the biggest.

'My lord king,' I murmur, bringing Brute to him.

'I would speak with you about the affairs of last summer. I owe you an apology for not doing more. It seems I must be grateful to you for ensuring those children survived. I see you were gravely wounded.'

I swallow around the sudden thickness in my throat. Thinking of my recovery pains me. It's taken too long, and I'm still weak. It frustrates me how slow my progress has been. 'The children are safe. That's what matters.'

'Indeed, yes, it is. But tell me, Icel, why were you so suspicious?'

I open my mouth to shrug away a response but then stop myself. He's my king. I must tell him the truth of why I was so concerned. 'There are many who think to cause problems within Mercia, my lord king. Your son, Lord Wigmund, isn't much liked. He surrounds himself with aggressive men who'll do anything for money. The children could be an alternative to your son, and so I feared he might wish them dead, especially with your grandson so weak throughout the first year of his life.' I'm astounded by my candour, but Wiglaf merely nods. It's a relief to speak aloud my fears to the king.

'Yes, Wigmund's done himself no favours. And I should have sent him to war rather than allowing him to remain with his mother. He's no warrior, and I fear never will be. His son grows stronger, I know that. But, would he truly jeopardise his wife's nephews?'

I lick my lips then, running my hand through my beard as our two horses walk sedately, side by side. I don't know if the king wants me to reply, or if he merely speaks aloud. I distract myself from answering by focusing on my horse. I'm astounded that Brute's not played one of his usual tricks, but grateful all the same.

'What will you do?' I eventually speak into the silence.

'My son must have firm allies, like Ealdormen Ælfstan and Tidwulf. Like you. Not like Ealdorman Sigered.'

I'm grateful the king knows the truth about Ealdorman Sigered and his ambitions. I hope he also suspects Lord Beorhtwulf, but he doesn't specifically mention him, which does concern me.

'I'll do all I can for him to build a set of alliance, but in time, I hope his son will rule with a firm hand when he's a man grown. All I need to do is live a good many winters yet and ensure the youngster becomes king, not the father.'

I consider Wiglaf. He's ageing, but I suspect he'd do better than I would if we met an enemy right now. He fought for his kingdom. I think he'd do so again. Indeed, he's fought more than once. Wigmund. Well, I fear he'll never do anything like that. He wouldn't even fight for a fine cask of ale.

'Of course, I hear the rumours that some wish to see him replaced, and myself as well. People have short memories when peace is established.' The words are filled with tightly suppressed fury. And then Wiglaf fixes me with a quelling look. 'I have a task for you, Icel, and one you won't appreciate, but one you must carry out regardless.'

'My lord king?'

'You've long had a habit of being the one to rescue me, tell me information I must know, or just been there to be useful.'

'My lord king?' I'm unsure how to reply. Repeating myself seems like the right thing to do.

'My son's unloved, but it's my wife who causes me problems. It's better that we live separate lives now, but she also has more potential to meddle in matters that shouldn't concern her. She had me banish Lord Coenwulf. I was unhappy to do it but he wouldn't defend himself. I could only act on the evidence presented to me, which I've always suspected was devised by my wife. So, Icel, I order you to journey to Winchester and determine if Eadbald, the man who provided that damning evidence, truly went to Wessex, as he stated, or if it's all lies.' King Wiglaf hisses as he speaks, spittle flying from his mouth with his fury. 'Go to Winchester, find the truth, and then, if it's all fabricated, as I suspect, I can summon Lord Coenwulf home, and he'll bolster my support base, and work as a counter against my wife and any ambitions she might have. It'll also mean Ealdorman Ælfstan's warriors can leave Kingsholm and return to other duties. Not that I take exception to their involvement in this. Those boys must be kept safe. If something happens to my grandson, there must be alternatives suitable to the ealdormen and bishops of Mercia. The grandsons of King Coelwulf will be acceptable.'

I open my mouth to speak. 'But—'

King Wiglaf shakes his head, denying me the opportunity to refuse. 'You must do this for me. For the future of Mercia. With Lord Coenwulf returned to me, the unease that runs through those I rule will dissipate. I'll have them see that my wife doesn't command the kingdom, that I'm Mercia's king. I can set her aside once her involvement is known, as opposed to suspected. I'll make reparations to Lord Coenwulf when the lies are proven.'

I try once more. 'But...?' I don't deny that the thought of venturing into enemy territory isn't as terrifying as it might once have been, despite my fears about defending myself. But all the same, Winchester is the heart of the Wessex king's power base. I'll be noted as a Mercian before I even open my mouth. And then when I do open my mouth, they'll hear that my words are formed differently. People say we speak the same tongue, and we do, but there are differences, as I know only too well from my time in Londinium.

'I'm sending Commander Eahric alongside Mercia's bishops to this meeting of holy men in Canterbury, as ordered by the archbishop. If there are problems, make your way to them. Despite all the difficulties you've caused Eahric in the past, he won't denounce you.'

'Then why can't he go to Winchester?' I finally manage to get a word in.

'Because King Ecgberht knows who he is.'

'But he must know who I am as well. I fought at Londinium.'

'But King Ecgberht didn't.'

'But I chased him to the River Thames?'

'With helm and byrnie, yes. I hardly think he took a good look at you. But enough, Icel, I need you to do this. As you say, there are enemies circling my royal helm, and they're not from Wessex or from the cold northern lands but within my own kingdom. And they threaten small children. I can't allow it. How can I devise new laws when something so base as murdering children seems acceptable to the powerful few?'

I don't want to agree to this... this crazy idea, and yet, I would welcome having Edwin returned to me. And if Lord Coenwulf was back inside Kingsholm, then he could care for his children and not me.

'You must go alone,' the king continues. 'Ealdorman Ælfstan's warriors are much better known than you. Some of them fought at Ellendun, for King Beornwulf, against King Ecgberht, and so might well be recognised. The battle was only a decade ago, and men who tried to kill one another tend to have very good memories.'

'Very well, my lord king.' I bow my head, my mind already swirling. He might think it best for me to go alone, but I have other ideas.

'And don't take Brute with you. Men will know him for a certainty.'

The thought of going anywhere without Brute fills me with disquiet, but he is instantly recognisable. Even those who don't know me acknowledge the quality of his breeding.

'I'll leave him in Londonia,' I confirm. 'Or perhaps at Kingsholm. It'll depend on how I decide to travel into Wessex.'

'Whatever you do, Icel, do it quickly. I don't want you returning to me when my kingdom is already lost.' The bleakness of those words astounds me. I can't believe it's become so imperative so quickly, but the queen is devious. Perhaps she's grown tired of her husband and thinks to place another under Mercia's warrior helm. I've never liked her. The king might be regretting his union as well, although it was many years ago. Becoming Mercia's queen has made Cynethryth ambitious. She wouldn't be the first Mercian queen to believe she knew better than her husband.

In the near distance, I see a horse and rider hastening to catch us, even as Commander Eahric moves to intervene. As Lord Beorhtwulf's features come into focus, I notice the scowl on his face and hear the king laugh at having evaded the man who is such a close ally of Ealdorman Sigered, even as Lord Beorhtwulf calls to him.

'I'll return as soon as possible,' I confirm, watching Lord Beorhtwulf trying to evade Commander Eahric's men. Eahric moves closer to the king, hand on his seax. Although he doesn't look at me, I imagine he knows what the king has asked me to accomplish for him. At least, I hope he does. Perhaps that accounts for why he was almost pleased to see me. It's a long way from Winchester to Canterbury, but if I have to get there to be assured of my survival, then I'll do that. But I hope I won't need to. I have an idea. If it works.

5

'You're doing what?' Wynflæd hisses at me as I make my goodbyes. I've told her of the king's intention, but now I think I shouldn't have done. She's furious with me. 'There are more boys than just you that can carry out such instructions for the king,' she complains, both hands resting on her walking stick because the left one shakes without cease.

Not for the first time, I berate myself for readily accepting the king's command, but I've given it now. I can't retract it, and probably had no option to anyway. Despite her words, she knew what King Wiglaf intended, I'm sure of it.

'Take Cuthred with you,' Wynflæd announces, much to my surprise. 'Don't tell him where you're going, but take him. I'm sure you've got some idea how to hide your identity, taking along a herb boy will make it much easier. Him I trust not to get himself killed.' Her stubborn jaw shows that I'm unable to argue my way out of this.

'Cuthred?' I think of the tall youth and shake my head. I don't want to be burdened with him on such a dangerous journey.

'Take him, and he'll aid you. You know how resourceful he can be.'

I shake my head again. Wynflæd opens her mouth to continue her argument, but I suddenly nod. Perhaps this will fit perfectly with my thinking. 'Very well, I will, but you must send for Gaya or Theodore, perhaps both of them. You need help here while we're gone.'

'I need no such thing,' she expels, but it's without the usual venom. If she doesn't do so, then I will, and she knows that. I might even summon the Wolf Lady, although I don't know if she'd obey such a request. For once, I hope Wynflæd will take an instruction given to her, as she's so fond of handing them out. 'Do it, or I'll order the king to.'

She harrumphs, but nods unhappily. 'They'll be more help around here than two useless boys,' she capitulates.

I hide my smirk.

'Cuthred, get yourself ready for a journey.'

I startle. I didn't realise he'd entered the workshop. Again, I curse my warrior's instincts, which seem to have deserted me since being set upon by Eadweard and his allies. I should be spending my time ensuring my skills are sharpened, my strength returned and my warrior's instinct renewed, not travelling to Winchester on what I suspect will be a hunt for something that never happened but which I won't be able to prove either way. The king asks me for proof, but makes no mention as to what that proof might be. How I'm supposed to determine if Eadbald went there is beyond me. I'll do what I can. I've toyed with the thought of saying that Lord Coenwulf was innocent and Eadbald lied. But I'd like to have more to present to the king. I need something irrefutable, especially if it's to tarnish the queen's reputation, and that of Lord Wigmund as well. The fact King Wiglaf shares my suspicions reassures me. It must pain him to realise his enemies might once have shared his bed.

'Where?' Cuthred queries, forehead furrowed, as he places a bucket of water close to the fire without sloshing any over the side.

'You don't need to know where, you just need to go,' Wynflæd grouches at him. I consider if she's just realised that she'll be without his aid while we're away. 'With Icel.'

'With Icel?' Cuthred's eyes are rounded now, his mouth open in surprise.

'Yes, now stop nattering and get yourself ready. I assume you mean to leave immediately?' Wynflæd directs at me.

'Um, yes, I am.' I can't think my way out of this, even after a good night's sleep in the king's hall. 'I'm heading to Worcester.'

'And what's in Worcester?' Cuthred questions.

Only Wynflæd nods, a slow smile spreading across her face. 'A good idea,' she agrees. 'But be quick. These traders don't tend to wait around for long once their business is transacted. I'm sure they'll have other markets to visit.'

Cuthred's busy behind Wynflæd, dragging items into a sack and hunting for a thick cloak. I consider how he'll travel. I have only one horse, and while the king bid me leave Brute behind, he means in Mercia, not in Tamworth. Will I be able to borrow a horse for Cuthred? I hope he can ride. Apart from the times he exercised Wine for me, in my absence, I'm unsure if he's ever ridden a great deal. I need to make haste. I can't be encumbered with someone who's slow.

'Ask old Alhred if you can have one of his horses. A good one, mind. Tell him that I've made the request and I know things he would sooner others didn't.' I gasp at the relish in those words. Wynflæd and her secrets. I didn't know she used them against others, but it makes sense that she does.

'Very well.' I stoop and plant a kiss on her wrinkled cheek.

She smells of garlic and rosemary. She smacks my face, and I'm not sure if it's affectionate or not. But Cuthred, she sends a steady stream of instructions towards, so much so that he turns pained eyes my way.

'We'll be fine,' I eventually expel. 'We can only travel with so much,' I clarify. Cuthred's already struggling to hold the sack he's been bidden to fill. I don't want to weigh down the horse or the ship I plan on taking to Winchester.

'Very well. You may leave, but if something happens and you don't have the supplies you need, I won't be held responsible.' Her harrumph of petulance brings a smile to my face. Perhaps she's more uneasy about this than I suspected, but all the same, we can't take every unguent from her workshop.

'We'll be back soon,' I offer quietly, striding towards the door.

'You better be,' she calls. I hear soft words exchanged between her and Cuthred. Then his footsteps hasten to catch me. It's early. I slept in the king's hall last night, my mind a riot of complaints and questions, but now I have Cuthred to contend with as well, I find I'm more concerned with him than with anything else. I could curse Wynflæd for sending him with me. I should have refused. But he might just prove useful.

Alhred grumbles and groans as I pull him from his bed, but quickly, he offers us one of his good horses without so much as a word said about Wynflæd's threat. Cuthred and I emerge from Tamworth as a gentle breeze cools the air. We call murmured greetings to the men on guard duty. Commander Eahric isn't there, but I'm aware that there are other riders preparing their mounts for a journey. I must assume these men are collecting Mercia's bishops to travel to Canterbury. The smell of damp's ripe in the air, but the day holds half a hope that it'll remain dry.

'Why are we going?' Cuthred, silent until now, finally asks as we crest the bridge over the river, and head westwards.

'To meet some traders, I hope,' I reply.

'And what do we need from these traders?' he prompts when I offer nothing further. I eye him. How far has he travelled from Tamworth in the past? He was born here, I know that. He's visited Lichfield before, but further than that? I don't know.

'It's not what we need from them. It's what we need to do with them,' I explain. Unsurprisingly, Cuthred still looks perplexed, but I don't elaborate. Cuthred's attention is taken up with trying to control his horse. The animal's a good one, but Brute has already tried to take a bite out of its neck, and strangely, it's unwilling to get too close to him.

It's going to be a long day. I can't encourage Brute to his normal speed for fear Cuthred will fall. Not that I say that to him. With his sack of supplies banging and clattering behind him and his uneasy seat in the saddle, he's going to be black and blue with bruises even if we never get above a canter. What with his bruised forehead from knocking himself out on a low rafter, he'll be far from happy.

I pity him. He had no idea he'd be leaving Tamworth today. Indeed, until yesterday, I didn't know I'd be going to Wessex either. But that's where we're going. I hope we both make it back to Tamworth with the intelligence that the king wants to prove Lord Coenwulf's innocence. What will happen then I'm unsure, but surely, the queen won't survive if she's been found to be meddling against Mercia's king. Maybe, I think, with Lord Coenwulf's return, she'll be banished in his place. Although what the king means to do about his son, is unclear. He's made it evident that his hopes rest on small Wigstan's shoulders.

* * *

We ride all day. Cuthred slowly manages to gain his balance on the horse, named Flêotan, and we make good progress in the end. As the daylight wanes, I pull us away from the road into a thick line of trees as the clouds glower once more with the menace of rain. The ground's both dry and wet, depending on where we stand. I carefully select a place that's covered in last year's fine pine needles. Cuthred does the same. We face each other. His face is pink with exertion, and yet he seems to be walking well enough, considering the time we've spent riding.

Just before he sits, Cuthred drops his trews, much to my surprise, and pulls forth a bundle of soft wool.

'I took precautions,' he chortles. I laugh along with him. I should have realised he was clever enough to appreciate the potential for problems. 'But tell me, Icel, why are we going to Worcester?'

'We're going to Worcester to try and catch up with the traders I met, in the hope they'll let us on board their ship, and we can get into Wessex.'

'Wessex?' he gasps, the colour draining from his face. We've not yet lit a fire, but I'm aware we need one.

'The king has bid me go there,' I offer, my words very soft, my ears straining to ensure no one can hear us talking. After all, we're not that far from the roadway.

'Why?' Of course, Cuthred is Wynflæd's assistant. He doesn't know all the politics of the court.

'To find a liar, or a truth-speaker, we won't know until we get there.'

On his knees, Cuthred fiddles with the sticks of wood, ready to try and light the flames, but his silence tells me he's thinking.

'Is this about Lord Coenwulf?'

'Yes. The king wants to recall him.'

'Then he means to go against the queen?'

I laugh softly at that. I've just dismissed Cuthred as Wynflæd's assistant, but of course, she knows more than I do about what happens inside Tamworth. 'If we can find the proof that's needed, although how we'll do that, I don't know.'

With the flames catching, Cuthred moves back to sit more comfortably. 'I'm sure you'll find a way, Icel, you normally do.' His words are strangely reassuring.

'But, we mustn't speak of this to others, not even the traders when we find them. If we find them.'

He nods. 'And if we don't find them?'

'There'll be another way. We just need to think what that might be.'

'If we go in a ship, don't we risk Viking raiders setting upon us?'

'Perhaps, but the traders seem well skilled, and one of their numbers is a Norseman anyway.'

'And you trust him?'

'I know that the others do, and that'll have to suffice. Better than trying to make our way over the River Thames or through the Wansdyke. If we can get a ship to the coast of Wessex, then we can walk or ride from there.'

'What about the horses?'

'We'll leave them behind. I've been told that Brute is a bit familiar to some people.'

A groan greets those words. 'So I'll have to carry Wynflæd's bloody sack,' Cuthred complains, and I nod, lips curved in amusement.

'Yes, or leave it behind. And you know what she'll say if we fall ill and we have no cure.'

Muttering to himself, Cuthred makes himself busy with the fire, although we eat bread and cheese, not warm pottage. Hopefully, we'll be in Worcester tomorrow. One night without a hot meal is more than survivable. Not that Cuthred thinks so. He moans and complains about the poor food. It's a relief when he finally falls asleep. Looking through the canopy overhead, many of the branches only just starting to bud, apart from those which keep their needles all year round, I consider just how I'm going to accomplish the king's demands. I genuinely have no idea, but as Cuthred says, we'll find a way. I hope this expedition provides the king with the answers he seeks. I pray that Cuthred and I both survive to return home to Tamworth with the intelligence the king requires. And that Wynflæd is still well when we do so. Although, if she's not summoned Theodore and Gaya to her side, I might just threaten her life.

6

Worcester is a hive of activity when we arrive early on the third day of our journey. Cuthred might have taken precautions to ensure his arse doesn't get sore, but he's still not a skilled rider. To push the animal onwards would have also stretched him. Instead, we've travelled somewhat more slowly.

The cries of market traders reach my ears almost immediately and account for the press of men and women, raucous children and stray animals that have lost their owners. I hold out hope that the traders we seek will have lingered to take advantage of the influx of people.

We stable the horses in the local inn, the owner nodding to show he knows who I am, while Cuthred heaves his sack of supplies onto his back.

'Can't you leave that here?' I ask him. 'I'm sure most people won't know what to do with a bunch of limp nettles.'

'But they'll take the honey,' he's quick to counter.

'Then you're carrying it, not me,' I advise, having removed the saddles from both horses and left them to eat. In separate stalls, of course. Flêotan remains unhappy with Brute. I'm not surprised. If we find the traders, I'll have to ask someone to take Brute to Kingsholm for me or even Budworth. I'm not sure which location would be best. Probably Kingsholm. At least that way, I can send word to Ealdorman Ælfstan and Wulfheard. If I don't return from Wessex, they'll know that something's befallen me. I've learned from my time alone in the northern lands. I don't plan on being so incautious again.

Once more outside, having pressed good Mercian silver pennies into the hands of the innkeeper and the stable boy to ensure the horses are cared for, I eye the mass of people. The markets are busier than I anticipated. There are also grain sellers, although they have little to offer at this time of the year. There are leather workers with the output from the winter to sell. There's even a silversmith displaying his wares, while a beefy-looking individual keeps an uneasy watch over the treasures on display, growling low in his throat if someone he deems insufficiently wealthy takes too much interest.

I eye the items displayed on the silversmith's stall with curiosity. The eagle-headed sigil I wear around my neck reminds me that someone, somewhere crafted it for my uncle or my father, I'm unsure for whom it was made. But the goods on show aren't anywhere near as well made. The pieces look highly polished but more iron than silver. All the same, the proprietor's making a good trade in other pieces with twisting animal shapes or holy crosses. He doesn't glance at me, and the guard offers me no complaints. Perhaps my clothes, made from fine flax, are good for something after all.

I turn and gaze over the heads of the busy visitors to the market. There are many more people here than live within Worcester itself. I recall what the traders sold, although I'm not at all convinced that stone on display will draw much of a crowd. But then I remember the furs, the inks and the herbs. The fur seller will be the easiest to find amongst the press of bodies because his goods will be the biggest.

'Look for a fur seller,' I urge Cuthred, who remains close to me, although his sack keeps banging into others. They round on him angrily when their arms and backs are knocked. I've glowered at any number of them, and so far, it's not come to more than angry words, but it might do. I can't exactly tell them it's Wynflæd's fault and not the boy's at all.

'Over there,' Cuthred eventually calls when we've made our way along one side of the marketplace. I look to where he points and pick out the familiar face of the bored youth who escorted his father on their travels. He handed me the precious wooden box containing saffron for Wynflæd. I consider why he's tending the fur stall and not the herb one.

'That's them,' I agree, but now we need to move against the flow of the crowd, and it's hard work, even with Cuthred's height, his sack, and my warrior garb. More than one person glowers at me. I'm minded to growl just like the guard at the silversmith's. In the end, I forge a path through, pulling Cuthred behind me. Better to get this done as quickly as possible. 'Good day,' I call to the youth.

He eyes me sullenly and then perks up. 'You,' he offers. 'Giric's busy in the inn, talking with some local lord about something,' he mutters hurriedly.

'And you've been left here to watch his wares.'

'Yes, but everyone just looks, and no one's buying,' he complains. 'Giric will be angry with me.'

I can see the problem. The furs are high quality, ranging in colour from almost white to deepest brown, but it's about to be the summer. Few will be thinking of trying to keep warm under their bedding or cloaks when the promise of the warmer weather beckons. All the same, they're fine quality.

'What animal?' I question. I should have asked this before.

'All sorts. Wolves, bears, seal, not that anyone around here seems to need such to keep them dry on board a ship.'

But I might, I realise. 'I need one, and so does Cuthred, and we need to speak to your father or one of the other men.'

'Giric's busy talking. I'm not sure where Benedict has gone, but my father's over there and Durcytel's with him.' I look where he indicates and realise the men are only two stalls down. I don't know how we missed them.

'Cuthred, stay here and help find two seal cloaks that will fit us. I'm going to speak with Eardwulf and Durcytel.'

I shoulder my way through the crowd once more, aware that with my and Cuthred's interest, there are people stopping to look at the furs and cloaks. Ahead, there's a queue surrounding Eardwulf's stall, but Durcytel seems to have little to do, what with his few pieces of carvings on display and a lump of shimmering stone resting on the ground. Perhaps, I think, he should try carving it. Maybe then people would pay more attention to him.

Durcytel eyes me as I arrive before him, recognition quickly showing on his face.

'The man from the river, Icel,' he booms in his distinctive voice while Eardwulf flashes me a quick look from where he's encouraging someone to part with the price of a goat for some unguent that's horse-shit green.

'Good day,' I call to them both, reaching out to run my hands over Durcytel's carving of a wolf. It looks so lifelike it takes me back to my time in the woodlands when I thought the wolf would eat me. Even the teeth look as though they drip with gore.

'You like?' Durcytel questions.

'I don't like, no, but it's a very good likeness.'

'Yes, it is.' He takes the acclaim without false modesty, and I find I like that. Oswy would accept someone calling him a great warrior in a similar way. 'You've returned from Tamworth quickly,' he continues. By now, Eardwulf has pocketed his coins and joined us, his eyes appraising, just like when he checked the weight of the coins and the moneyer's name stamped onto their obverse side.

'I have, yes. I've something to ask you, but perhaps not here, where all can hear.'

Eardwulf understands immediately and beckons me away from the stall and down a small alley, cut off at the moment by all the traders' supplies that block it.

'We've no more of the saffron if that's why you're here,' he's quick to assure me.

'No, it's not that at all. From here, you're heading to the land of the Danes and Hedeby, aren't you?'

'Yes,' he says slowly. 'Durcytel needs to get there quickly.'

'And along the way, you'll be stopping in Wessex.'

'Yes.' He nods along with my questions.

'Where you'll be welcomed as traders?'

'We will, yes.'

'I want you to take me and Cuthred with you.'

'What?' Eardwulf gasps and then remembers to keep his voice low as a too-interested head appears from further along the alleyways. 'Why do you want to go to Wessex? They hate the Mercians more than they do the Viking raiders.'

'Yes, but as a trader, we'll be able to move around more easily.'

'Well, yes, but again, why do you want to go to Wessex?'

'I have to find something,' I prevaricate. I don't want to tell him more than that. 'I can pay you well.'

'No matter how much you pay us, we won't be coming back this way. How do you mean to return to Mercia?'

I pause then. I've not considered that. 'We'll find a way,' I announce. 'Perhaps another trader coming to Mercia.'

'Possibly,' Eardwulf mutters. 'But traders are a funny lot. They won't want strangers on their ships.'

'You could vouch for us.'

'I could, yes, but I don't really know you either.'

'Look, I'm Wynflæd's old assistant, and Cuthred's her current assistant. Surely that speaks for something? She trusts us with all her knowledge.'

'Yes, she does. Did she appreciate the saffron?' he queries.

'She did, yes, and sent thanks.'

He nods and falls silent, and I realise this isn't going to work.

'I'll speak to Benedict and Giric,' he says after some time. 'If he agrees, then we'll do it. But if not, then we won't.'

'Please ask him somewhere no one can overhear,' I caution him. 'This needs to be done without anyone knowing what we're doing.'

'Which fills me with enthusiasm for what you have planned,' he grumbles, and I can tell he's far from happy at the request.

I return to Cuthred where he's found us two seal cloaks, which cost much more than the price of a goat. With our business transacted and the fur stall heaving with men and women keen to see why I've spent so much of my coin there, we force our way through them, picking up a few items, including more cheese and bread for the journey. Only then, my belly rumbles, and so we forge a path to the inn and sit outside, on two stools, watching the crowd swirl for much of the rest of the day. Slowly, the traders sell their wares, so that whatever stall they have, if they have one, clears, great empty spaces opening up, even amongst the blacksmith's wares. People begin to depart from Worcester. Some happy with their purchases, others gloomy. When there's enough space to see, I realise that Eardwulf's son has managed to sell more of the furs and cloaks than I thought he would. Giric's still absent, though. I consider what would be more important than making a profit for a trader. Whatever it is, I hope he hurries to complete it. I'd like to know whether we're going south on their ship or not.

Durcytel and Eardwulf have also sold a great deal. Even the wolf carving's gone. I consider whether I should have purchased it for the Wolf Lady, but with my trip to Winchester, I'd have no means of taking it to her. I certainly don't intend to haul it around after me, as Cuthred has done with his sack of supplies from Wynflæd.

'Here you are.' Eardwulf hastens towards us as though we've been the ones missing all day and not Benedict and Giric.

I stand to shake his hand, and he returns it and leans in towards me.

'I've convinced them to take you and the boy. But no horses. We leave in the morning.'

'My thanks,' I offer. He grunts, and I can't tell whether he's happy about it. And then I get my answer.

'There'll be nothing but trouble for you there, but you look like you can probably contend with that.' His words are far from reassuring. Still, we're one step closer now.

'How long does the voyage take?' I think to ask.

'It depends on the weather and how many times we stop. It won't be the quickest journey, but as you say, perhaps the safest. Be by the ship for sunrise tomorrow. And don't be late. Durcytel's fractious to be away from here. And the river's still running high with the rains. He means to take advantage of that.'

'My thanks,' I repeat.

He steps away and races back towards his stall, checking on his son along the way. I can't hear the words, but it's clear they're arguing about something. I turn to Cuthred. His eyes are focused elsewhere, and I smirk at the bubbling laughter from a group of young women playing with a small, vicious-looking dog, its teeth dripping with slobber. Cuthred is indeed growing up.

'We need to send the horses away,' I announce. This is a problem. I could approach Bishop Heahbeorht, but he'd want to know what I was up to and why I needed to abandon my horse in Worcester when Kingsholm isn't far away. As Bishop Heahbeorht's also going to Canterbury, it's possible he won't even be in residence. I don't want to argue with the monks. They can be a pestilent bunch.

I'd hoped to see someone during the market day whom I might have trusted with my horse, perhaps some of the Kingsholm inhabitants who'd come to buy something specific, but there's been no one. And Brute is a particular animal. He needs to be handled by someone who knows him. In all honesty, it would be easiest to take him by ship as we're going to pass Kingsholm anyway, but Eardwulf made it clear horses weren't welcome on board. But that does give me an idea.

'Wait here,' I instruct Cuthred.

Turning, I make my way inside the heat and stink of ale and cooking, wrinkling my nose at the harassed-looking innkeeper. He might have made a small fortune today, but he's evidently earned it.

'Good man,' I begin. 'A favour, if I may prevail upon you.'

He eyes me, a complaint on his lips that dies as he recognises me once more. Worcester isn't far from Kingsholm. A good horse could make the journey in a day. Even an ox could do it in three.

'Anything, my lord,' he murmurs.

'My horses? Can they stay here for two or three days, and I'll send someone from Kingsholm to retrieve them.' His eyes boggle at the request, but I'm quick to place good Mercian silver pennies in his hands – more than enough to cover the expense of keeping two very high-calibre horses in his stables.

'Of course, my lord, of course,' he splutters.

'And you're to make sure the man who comes is entitled to

them. I'll give a word to say to you.' I lower my voice further. 'Wolf, that's the word. He'll tell you he's come to collect two wolves. Don't give the animals into anyone else's care.'

The innkeeper nods again, biting his lip. I can see questions he wants to ask.

'If they don't come, keep the horses here. I'll return and collect them myself and pay you for the keeping of them. But don't try and ride my mount. If he needs to be removed from his stall, do it with his reins and nothing else. Hopefully, he'll behave himself.'

Once more, he nods, and I pray I've not just left him with my tetchy horse for the entirety of my trip to Wessex. If I have, I doubt there'll be much of the stables left when I return. And that'll cost me a great deal of Mercian currency to rebuild. Perhaps not quite as much as the cost of a horse, but not far from it.

'And a bed for the night,' I also request, but he's already shaking his head to deny me. 'No problem, I'll sleep in the stables.' I turn aside before he can argue with me about that. Tomorrow, I leave for Wessex, and I'm curious to know what the experience will be like. The only other time I've been on board a ship, I had to pretend to be a fisherman, and the old man who aided us was not impressed by my skills or any of the men with whom I shared the boat close to the Isle of Sheppey. I hope masquerading as a trader is at least less smelly.

7

Yawning and stretching, I discover that Cuthred isn't a morning person, and that certainly counts double when the sun has yet to start climbing. But we need to be on our way. With a few shakes of his arm, which is flung over his eyes, I eventually haul him upright and then leave him to stand or fall, depending on how awake he is. Such actions are somehow enjoyable. No wonder Wulfheard has always taken delight in punishing me when I transgressed.

Brute watches me with dull eyes as I say my farewells and demand he behave himself. I've slept poorly, regretting my choices repeatedly, but I need to get to Winchester. I can't take Brute. I could, I realise, have journeyed to Kingsholm and then found a trader at Gloucester, but I'd rather go with men I know as more than a business transaction. Yes, I've only met them once before, but the fact Eardwulf knows of Wynflæd fills me with assurance that he'll keep me safe, or as safe as possible heading into enemy territory.

As we make our way to the quayside, Cuthred yawns continuously. I can't see that he gets away with such in Wynflæd's workshop. She always had me awake before cockcrow. Perhaps he's just exhausted. I sympathise with that. He's been dragged from the safety of Tamworth on a horse he doesn't know, riding for nearly three days, and now he needs to take ship to Winchester.

At the quayside, Benedict and Eardwulf seem engaged in some sort of argument, but they break off their cross words on seeing us.

'You look strange without your horse.' Eardwulf offers half a smile, but a sense of unease makes my returning smile less than effusive.

'I do, but he'll be well cared for. And Brute wasn't always my horse. Before him, I had my uncle's mount, Wine.' Why I feel the need to explain, I don't know. Perhaps I shouldn't speak of my wealth in horses. I certainly shouldn't mention that I'm the lord of Budworth.

Durcytel's busy in the ship, tying and untying ropes in an apparently random way, but the craft is watertight, despite the flooding it was caught in when I first encountered them. That reassures me as I assist Cuthred into its hull. His eyes are wide as he struggles to maintain his balance against the gentle surge of the river. That doesn't bode well for later when we reach the open sea. I have some fears about that as well. I don't think that fishing off the coast of the Isle of Sheppey really counts as having experience in the seas that surround my island home.

'We'll be calling in at Bristol,' Benedict tells me, 'if you'd rather come ashore there.' But I shake my head. It might be quicker, avoiding the dragon's tail of Cornwall and Devon, but I need to get to Winchester and not be forced to make my way overland towards the capital of Wessex. Thanks to Wulfheard, I know that Winchester isn't far from a port. If Lord Coenwulf spoke the truth, then the men and women close to the Wansdyke know to be wary of Mercians. I'm amazed at my knowledge of Wessex.

'My thanks, but no, as close to Winchester as possible,' I reiterate.

'Then you'll have to pretend you know what you're doing when we call in at the other markets and watch your accents. Stress your "ash"s not your "a"s, or they'll know you for a Mercian before you can disembark.' Eardwulf grunts. I appreciate they're fearful of being discovered with a Mercian on board in the Wessex kingdom. I look at Durcytel and find it somewhat amusing that they're content with a Norseman in Wessex but not a Mercian, or rather two of them.

'We will, and young Cuthred's a clever lad. He'll pick everything up quickly,' I reassure them, hoping I'm correct.

And then there's no more time for talk as the ship enters the current in the direction of Gloucester. I sit and watch the landscape glide past, surprised by how much more quickly we appear to move with the river's flow. The stained sail glints overhead, and the traders seem to do little but find somewhere to sleep or count their proceeds. The lull of the river sends me to sleep, and when I wake, I'm stiff and sore, and it's the thud of the ship against the side of the quayside at Gloucester that's woken me. It's much later in the day. I'm not the only one yawning and stretching.

'We stop here tonight,' Eardwulf informs me. 'We leave early, with the tide; don't be late,' he cautions me. I can already see men and women flocking to see what goods the traders might have for sale, but Cuthred and I force a path through them all. Stretching our cramped legs, I direct our path to Kingsholm.

I keep my head down and my cloak over my head, feeling naked without Brute at my side. I don't truly want to be noted, not without my horse. That would occasion far too many questions. Cuthred is eager at my side, much more alert than when I woke him this morning. He looks at everything with wide eyes, absorbing this change from all he's known at Tamworth. It takes surprisingly little time to reach Kingsholm, into which we slip just before full darkness falls. I find Cenred watching the gateway. One of Ealdorman Ælfstan's warriors, and a man I trust implicitly. Cenred asks no questions, but his forehead furrows as I arrive without Brute and with Cuthred in tow.

'I'll tell you later,' I inform him as he allows me to enter. He nods and resumes his warrior's stance, ensuring only those known to him are permitted inside Kingsholm during the night. I find my steps taking me towards the stables. Only at the last moment do realise I need to go to the hall, not the stables. Cuthred almost walks into my back with my abrupt change of direction, but he merely squeaks in alarm and resets himself. I can hear the voices of many talking from inside. The smell of good food fills the air. Kingsholm is a jollier place with the children of Lord Coenwulf returned to it. Certainly, it's far more welcoming than when I first visited the place, but the absence of Lord Coenwulf is felt. Some of the laughter is too forced. The giggles of young Coenwulf and Coelwulf reverberate, a good attempt to banish the spectre of their dead mother and banished father.

Inside the hall, my eyes adjust to the glow of candles and the flames from the blazing hearth. I seek out Wulfheard and find him sitting with Eadburg and the two children, eating a bowl of meaty pottage, scooping huge chunks of meat into his mouth. The children are fed much smaller pieces, with bread dipped in the juices. I don't miss that Lady Cynewise notes my passage, but she's forced to sit with her sister, at the front of the hall, dining in comfort. She can't just come and ask me where I've been.

Wulfheard's eyes narrow on seeing me. He quickly glimpses Cuthred. I can see the questions forming on his lips.

'Well met,' I greet him. He nods, although I can tell he's not sure today is a good day. His face is half-shadowed, somehow making his old wounds more prominent.

'Cuthred.' He inclines his head towards Wynflæd's young helper.

I speak before he can question my extended delay and why I've clearly been to Tamworth when he thought I was only venturing to Hereford. 'This is Eadburg, and these are Coelwulf and Coenwulf.' I introduce the two boys to Cuthred. Coenwulf's much more interested than Coelwulf, who grips a small wooden ball firmly in his pudgy hand. He's a determined boy.

'Hello, Cuthred,' Eadburg speaks softly. If Cuthred notices her scars, he's too used to tending to the sick to show any unease. I lean over and offer the gift from Edwin, which I did thankfully remember to collect from his mother before I left Tamworth. Eadburg takes it with less enthusiasm than I expected. Perhaps her ardour has cooled, although I rather suspect she fears Edwin won't find her attractive when he returns. We've spoken of this before. My reassurances fall on stone walls. She'll only believe it when she sees Edwin. If I can find what's needed in Winchester, that'll be much sooner than she might think.

'Sit, eat,' I urge Cuthred, pushing him down while a servant brings us both bowls of pottage. 'And Wulfheard, I'd speak to you, please, alone,' I cajole when I think he'll be too stubborn to realise the request isn't for everyone's ears.

'Very well.' He stands abruptly, and another wooden ball appears from inside his huge hand, as he returns it to Coelwulf, who shouts triumphantly at seeing it.

I can well imagine the game that Wulfheard has been playing with him. I often think him too rough with the youngsters, but neither of them seems to object. Indeed, their cries of delight show they don't mind being thrown high in the air, with Wulfheard always appearing too slow to catch them, although he manages all the same.

'Well,' Wulfheard mutters when we're standing on the ramparts, gazing down at the few stragglers hastening to get inside before the gates close. 'It seems to me you've been to more places than just Hereford.'

I nod. 'Yes, I went to see Wynflæd. The Wolf Lady was cryptic about it. I feared she was dying, but instead, it was the king who wanted me.'

'And now you're back with Wynflæd's lad, so where has the king sent you?'

'To Winchester. I'm to determine if Eadbald lied about Lord Coenwulf's intentions. He wants to invite him back to Mercia. He needs Lord Coenwulf's support against his queen, and so I'm to decide if Eadbald went to Winchester or not.'

'Bloody hell,' Wulfheard expels. 'Why doesn't he just ask for your stones and have done with it?' I can tell he's as unhappy as I am. But I'm the king's man. I must do as I'm bid. He'd do the same, and he knows it. 'How will you get there?' he asks abruptly, gazing towards the stables, for all he can't see through wood.

'Ship. I met some traders. They'll take me to Southampton.'

'Why not Bristol?' he counters quickly, his forehead furrowed as he considers possible routes.

'It'll be too far to travel over land. I'd rather spend as little time as possible on Wessex soil.'

'Hum,' he muses. 'And where's your bloody horse? I've not heard a commotion from the stables, so he's clearly not here.'

'Worcester. I'll ask Pega to go and get him and Cuthred's mount as well. We borrowed him from Tamworth.'

'Ealdorman Ælfstan won't like this,' Wulfheard murmurs after a few moments of silence.

'The ealdorman isn't the one who has to go.'

'No, but he won't like the thought of you there, and I agree. There are more than enough warriors whom the king of Wessex has never seen, and they would be better sent than you. They would also be able to defend themselves, if the need arose.'

'No doubt, but the king trusts me.' I ignore the complaint against my ability to fight. I'm not going to argue that I've regained my strength when I know I haven't.

'He does, yes. The king also knows you can think on your feet. All the same, it's dangerous. Getting there's perilous, let alone walking through Wessex to bloody Winchester.'

'The king says if there are problems, I'm to make my way to Canterbury. The bishops are meeting there, and Commander Eahric will vouch for me.'

'It'd be quicker to return to Londonia than try and get to Canterbury,' Wulfheard growls. His knowledge of Wessex doesn't surprise me. Mercia was powerful underneath the brother kings of Coenwulf and Coelwulf. It's only since my father claimed the kingship that Mercia has faltered and lost more and more of her possessions, starting with Kent.

I nod. 'I know that.' I don't add that I know it because Wulfheard taught me about it when we first travelled to Londonia.

'Then I wish you luck, Icel. I'll inform Ealdorman Ælfstan of this. He'll be angry about it but will know better than to seek out the king and complain until after you return. We can't allow anyone to know of the king's intentions. His wife won't think twice about sending someone to ensure you don't return home.'

The thought's far from comforting. A deep sense of foreboding shudders through me as I look out at the familiar landscape around Kingsholm and towards Gloucester. And with it, a stray thought. I've trusted the king, but what if this is his wife directing him? What if she already knows I'm going to Winchester? I need to be alert and ensure that Cuthred has the means to escape and defend himself.

'Your horse better behave himself,' Wulfheard continues. 'He's a bloody menace at the best of times.' And with that, he grasps my forearm and pulls me close. 'Keep safe, young Icel. I don't want to have to kill everyone in Winchester to avenge your death. Although, admittedly, Oswy will take pleasure in doing just that.' His words are an attempt at humour, but they ring hollow. I can tell he's as uneasy as I am about my immediate future. I consider telling him that if he'd only speak the truth about his brother, then I wouldn't need to go, but no doubt Wulfheard understands that. Perhaps there is much he doesn't know of his brother's treachery. If I had a brother, I wouldn't want to know more than that he was a traitor.

I swallow against the dryness of my mouth and follow him back to the hall, where the hubbub of people talking after a day's work fills the space. I notice Lady Ælflæd's look of interest but merely lift my hand in greeting and evade her questioning look. Luckily, young Wigstan demands her attention and I escape her immediate notice.

I'd sooner know I only needed to remain here, where I can keep the children safe, but there's much more at play within Mercia. And I need to ensure that the king is kept safe, as well as the children.

If there was ever a choice about whether to venture to Winchester or not, seeing the children again and noting their similarities to their mother and father ensures that I'll do anything for them. If Lord Coenwulf was safely back in Mercia and not in Frankia, then it would be his responsibility and not mine. And, of course, Edwin would also return with him. That would please Eadburg and, I admit, me as well.

But there's much I must do before that. I don't welcome

another journey into Wessex-held land. I'll be marked as an enemy and a Mercian, and that's provided no one recognises me from Londinium, which I helped to undermine and return to Mercian hands when the Wessex warriors claimed it. King Wiglaf does ask a great deal from me, and I'm powerless to deny him. I hope I'm not powerless to defend myself should the worst befall us.

8

Pega assures me he'll collect Brute and Cuthred's horse, although he offers with a downturned smile, aware there might be difficulties. Still, he's tended to Brute for me before. I hope my stubborn horse recalls that. I remember to tell him my code word, which he acknowledges with an amused shake of his head. A man such as him sees no need for the precautions I've taken in ensuring no one steals my horse.

While it's still more dark than light, Cuthred and I return to the quayside. The ship isn't quite ready. Evidently, some late-night trading means that items need to be put on the ship and others removed. Eardwulf's unhappy about it, but Giric moves swiftly to remove sacks filled with furs, replacing them with barrels of something else with the aid of Durcytel. I'd look at what was inside, but they're sealed tight.

'Ale,' Eardwulf complains. 'And a barrel of salted fish. Let's hope he sells them on quickly because they both stink.'

I wrinkle my nose, mindful of the smell of the river and other less pleasant aromas. Eardwulf winces as one of the ale barrels falls heavily into the hull, and he's not alone in hoping the ship stays watertight. I don't wish to get into the wider estuary and find we're taking on water.

'And you?' I ask him. 'Did you trade last night?'

'Always a few little transactions to make a trader keen to return again,' he chuckles when we're finally allowed on board ship and can begin the journey away from Gloucester. I've been warned it will become rougher as we enter the wider estuary. I keep an eye on Cuthred, but he seems to have discovered how to stand in the ship so as to absorb the sudden surges that rock it from time to time. He's learned that more quickly than he's become a good rider.

I keep alert as we make our way south, so that water seems to be all around us. My eyes are drawn to where I know the steep hill we climbed last summer on our way to Londonia should be visible if only I weren't so low in the water.

I gave Cuthred a seax last night. He wears it on his belt, close to his sharp blade used for slicing herbs for Wynflæd. He looked shocked to be given such a weapon.

'It might be needed,' I cautioned him. 'We'll be Mercians in an enemy kingdom. No one will be pleased to see us.'

'Perhaps.' He shrugged his narrow shoulders. 'But I'm sure the common people won't care whether we're from Mercia or Northumbria.' He made a fair point, ensuring he spoke with less of a Mercian accent, and now I consider that.

When we went to the Isle of Sheppey to retrieve Lord Coenwulf, the fisherpeople were keen to help us. Perhaps the same will happen in Winchester. I could disembark at Bristol and make my way towards Winchester over land. But surely, taking the sea route will ensure we arrive more quickly?

I'm still debating with myself as we arrive at Bristol later that day. Bristol is part of Wessex. From here, Cuthred and I must remember not to be too Mercian. The journey has been calm, the roll of the water gentle beneath the hull of the ship. Durcytel spent some time regaling me with tales of how difficult the waters around here can be, mentioning the bore tides, but just as I began to fear, he assured me it wouldn't rise for some days yet. I know of the bore tide, only from dry land, not the river and estuary. As Durcytel secures the ship to the quayside, once more men and women flock to the side of the trader's ship to see what they have on offer.

I know there are still inks, stones and spices for sale. The furs have all sold. The ale and salted fish remain, but they're not even mentioned.

The first thing I notice is the accents of those calling to the traders. The words are understandable enough, but some of the letters roll more than I expect. I can see Cuthred, eyes narrowed, listening carefully to the cries of those all around. He's been practising his accent, and now he means to absorb more of the Wessex dialect. I remember when I was trapped inside Londinium, fearful that the way I spoke would mark me out too easily. I managed then, but I did have iron at my side.

'You can stay on the ship,' Eardwulf informs me. 'It's probably better if you do. Just follow what we do and try not to arouse any suspicion,' he orders. If it's meant to reassure, it has the opposite effect, and where before I was only worried about the way I spoke, now I'm concerned about everything. Cuthred, of course, shows no such caution. Because he knows the spices and herbs as well as Eardwulf, he's quickly on the quayside, helping the man with his sales, and earning himself a foul glare from Eardwulf's son. I linger towards the rear of the ship, wishing I could somehow make myself smaller.

I've removed my warrior's garb, other than a more commonplace belt and eating knife around my waist, but while my clothes and weapons are hidden in a sack, I realise it's much harder to hide my size and strength. Despite my long recovery, I've not lost the bulk of my warrior's body, even if I feel as though I'm weak. When Durcytel sells his barrel of salted fish, despite me thinking it wasn't for sale, I find myself lifting it easily to the quayside, my arms almost stretching around its girth. I don't even wince. I don't miss Eardwulf's appraising gaze, and curse my foolishness. I shouldn't have taken such delight in being able to lift it alone.

'A fine slave you have there,' a rotund, squat little man calls to Durcytel. 'I'll give you thirty silver pennies for him. He's as strong as an ox. I'll pay you the price of one.'

Durcytel laughs at the request, although the man making the offer looks petulant at such a response.

'He cost me three times that, and I'll not release him.' Abruptly, I realise it might be good if these people think me a slave. Admittedly, in the fading daylight, it's impossible to see the quality of my garb, but perhaps I should find myself some less well-made clothes. However, I dismiss the idea just as quickly. As only Cuthred and I are going from Southampton to Winchester, he's hardly likely to have control of a slave such as me. After all, he's merely a boy. Perhaps, then, I could make him my slave?

Eventually, Durcytel manages to redirect the squat man's demands, offering him some fine amber for his wife's necklace. I duck low, using the darkness to cover my presence.

When there's little more than the cry of the traders left on the quayside, I think it safe to move around more freely, stretching my back from where I've been cramped behind the rolled sail.

Cuthred's grinning as he and Eardwulf search through the remaining supplies. I'm pleased that Cuthred's fitting in so much more easily than I am.

'Thank you for not selling me,' I call to Durcytel.

He turns and grins. 'It was a fair price he offered, but no, I thought it best to keep you.' His Norse-accented words remind me of earlier.

'How come no one complains about you being a Norseman?'

'They know I'm no Viking raider. I bring coin with me,' he counters quickly. 'Although, most Viking raiders have some coin as well. Trading is for those with the intelligence to turn a profit. A trader need only visit Gnezdovo, and suddenly, the world is open to them. The Volga, Don, Donets, Seim, and Kama. There are peoples who wish to have what we have just as much as we wish to have what they have. I hear there's a particular preference for beaver furs from the far northern lands. And the coins they trade in have great value, although most seem to melt them down to make ornaments. Still, the silver content's high. And of course, again, there are those intelligent enough to masquerade as traders, and then when they've gained the trust of others, they kill them and take what they want. They think to make more profit that way.' Durcytel's dismissive tone makes me smile, despite my hatred of the Viking raiders.

'So, the Viking raiders are too stupid to do what you do?'

'Indeed they are, my friend, indeed they are.' I chuckle along with him, but still, such knowledge surprises me. I thought the Viking raiders were vicious warriors, determined to destroy all before them, but according to Durcytel, not only are they vicious, they're also stupid. Maybe, then, it should be easy to dispatch them by employing one or two tricks.

* * *

We sail once more with the glow of the sun a haze on the horizon.

'Watchet,' Benedict informs me, 'will be where we stop next.'

'And what's there?' I query. I've been tasked with winding in the rope usually employed to secure the ship to the quayside.

'More of the same,' Durcytel offers me. 'It's another place not truly beholden to Wessex, although there are those within Wessex who think it is. And from there, while we'll stay close to the coastline, you'll get a glimpse of the wide open sea.'

'So, this isn't the sea?'

'Well, it is, but there's land to the north and the west. If you went overboard, you'd no doubt drown, but if you can swim, you could make it to one of the Welsh kingdoms.'

'I'd not be welcome there, either,' I assure Durcytel.

He nods, his lips turning downwards. 'It seems to me you're not welcome in many places,' he taunts, grinning to take the sting from his words. 'Your king isn't well loved, is he?'

'My people aren't well loved,' I counter quickly, amused despite myself that a Norseman casts such slights against me. 'Mercia was once as aggressive as Wessex is now.'

'And now she isn't?' he queries.

'No, she's been weakened, by a succession of kings who died fighting the kingdom of the East Angles.'

'Ah, well, they're fierce warriors in that kingdom. I'm unsurprised that Mercia's kings should fall beneath their blades.' Once more, he chuckles, but the words bring an unwelcome remembrance of my father. I don't wish to be reminded of him. I've almost banished the knowledge from my mind, but then, every so often, it reappears, and I don't appreciate it.

'And where then, from Watchet?'

'It will depend on where the sea takes us. There are smaller markets until we round the dragon's tail, but the larger settlements are when we turn to run around the south of your island. There we'll visit Exeter and Corfe before reaching Southampton.'

'And from there, where you will go?'

'We'll visit Selsey, Pevensey and a few more places before we turn and run towards the north and Hedeby in the land of the Danes.'

'You'll trade with Frankia?'

'No, they're tight with their coin. I'd sooner travel to Hedeby, take my chances with my fellow Norse, and then make a return journey to this island. The East Anglians, people of Wessex, Mercians and the Welsh are much easier to turn a profit from than the tight-fisted Danes.'

'And where do you spend the winter? Do you have homes to go to?'

'I have a wife and four sons in Hedeby,' Durcytel confirms.

'And another three in Pevensey,' Eardwulf pipes up.

'And I'm sure another two or three along the way,' Giric mumbles, and while Durcytel grins, looking proud of himself, I consider that. He has no problem admitting his many families.

'And so you have many wives and sons. Do they know about one another?'

'Of course not, to tell them as such would cause me no end of problems,' Durcytel announces with satisfaction, but I feel uneasy at that. As the child of a man who never claimed me, I don't think Durcytel's quite the man I once thought. 'It does no one any harm. They all live well, and one day, perhaps, I'll introduce my sons, but never my wives. They'd scratch one another to death with their carding combs.'

'Or take half of your goods and divorce you,' Eardwulf counters, 'as Mercian law says.'

'Well, yes, if they all took half, I'd be left with nothing,' Durcytel confirms grudgingly. 'So,' and he grins once more, 'it's better that they not know about one another, isn't it?' He fixes me with a firm look, and I nod against the implied threat.

'I'll never visit these places, so I can never tell,' I admit.

'Then we understand one another,' he grunts. 'And next time someone asks to buy my "slave", I'll be sure to say no.' But the menace remains, all the same. He's portrayed himself as some sort of gentle giant, but he's a strong man. Perhaps not as strong as I once was. Or maybe he is. I don't wish to find out.

9

Seven days later, we arrive at Southampton. My face has been wind-whipped and sunburnt, and I'm grateful that Cuthred brought some ointment with him and then made more with Eardwulf's supplies to stop it from hurting every time I smile.

'Well.' Eardwulf offers me his hand to alight from the ship. 'This is where we say goodbye.'

I nod and grip his forearm. 'My thanks for getting me here,' I offer. 'And for exchanging my Mercian coins for Wessex ones.' That, I realise, would have been a terrible oversight had Durcytel not commented on it last night.

'We were coming anyway.' He shrugs, but I don't think they were. The intention was for the traders to make it to Hedeby as soon as possible. They could have taken to the open sea long before now. I've certainly delayed them, and in offering me the opportunity to swap coin for coin, they've been left with more Mercian than Wessex currency. At least, as traders, that'll be acceptable for them. It wouldn't have been for me.

'I wish you luck with your endeavours.'

'And you with yours. Perhaps I'll see you all soon. Send to

Kingsholm when you next visit Gloucester,' I offer, but my eyes are already on the view before me.

This is Southampton. I know it's an important port for the kingdom of Wessex. I seem to recall Wulfheard told me that, like Lundenwic, this was once a wic, called Hamwic, or something like that. Southampton is certainly a much bigger mouthful.

It's thronged with activity. There are at least twenty ships bobbing on the sea, all of varying sizes, and even a ship that must belong to King Ecgberht, proudly displaying the Wessex wyvern. I hope I won't stumble into the path of the shipmen. The closer and closer we've come to this point, the more and more nervous I've become. Cuthred has taken everything in his stride. I wish I could have done so as well.

'We will, now go before we're overwhelmed with those keen for a bargain. Slip away carefully and avoid the port reeve and the king's warriors.' With Cuthred beside me and without a backwards glance, we do just that.

I've retrieved my sack containing my warrior's garb, and Cuthred has his supplies from Wynflæd. By the time we're clear of the press at the quayside, I'm not alone in regretting the weights we carry. It's so much easier to transport everything when I'm wearing it.

Cuthred's jovial, his eyes taking in all around him, whereas I'm keen to keep my gaze down and not draw attention to myself.

What we need to do is find some horses to buy so we can ride towards Winchester. The swell of the inhabitants of Southampton is all around us, their accents more pronounced here. Yet I don't miss that there are also many who speak with a Mercian dialect as well as with a Frankish or Norse one. Perhaps it won't be as difficult to mingle. Although, well, Cuthred has once more shown his quick thinking, and with the aid of Eardwulf, he carries a collection of herbal supplies that will mean he can pretend to be a healer or trader. I should have thought of that. The ones he carries aren't Wynflæd's more specialised knowledge, but instead concoctions he can sell to aid digestion, bad skin or a woman's failure to get with child. I've sniffed some of them. They're not likely to do any of those things, I'm sure of it.

'Over here.' My young companion grips my arm and pulls me clear from a gaggle of people making their way along the roadway. In their midst is a holy man, and I realise this is some sort of religious festival.

'What day is it?' I ask Cuthred, but he shrugs.

'I've no idea.'

I try to recall the passage of days. 'Easter Sunday?' I mutter, but I'm not sure. No doubt I'll discover soon enough and if it's important.

Cuthred stops in front of a stable, from which I can hear the raucous cry of an old crone, berating someone. I wince at the sharp slap of flesh meeting flesh. I don't call a welcome. Instead, I examine the horses I can see through the open doorway.

None of them are anywhere close to Brute's breeding, but then, there are few who would have a hundred and twenty silver pennies to purchase a horse such as him. The animals available all look well-cared-for. There are at least three that would be suitable for Cuthred's slim build and long body, but I don't see an animal that could take my weight.

I shift the bulk of my sack once more and reach for my money pouch. It remains heavy with coins, Wessex silver pennies, not Mercian ones, but for how much longer, I'm unsure.

'What do you want?'

I rear backwards as a small, squat woman appears before me. Her cloak's the finest bear fur I've seen. She's a rich woman indeed, even for a trader.

'Two horses, one for me and one for my friend here.' It's

Cuthred who speaks. He's managed to adopt the accent of a Wessex-born lad more easily than I have.

'Who's asking?' she screeches, her eyes never leaving my face. I don't appreciate the scrutiny when I've only just disembarked and feel disorientated. I still need to reach Winchester.

'A healer and his assistant.' Cuthred effects a small bow. I try not to chuckle. He really does have a gift for speaking with people.

'You don't look old enough to heal a worm,' she scorns, but her temper has lessened.

Cuthred eyes her appraisingly. 'More meat in your diet would aid you,' he offers, having assessed her quickly. 'It would make you as strong as when you were young. And that tremor in your hands, you should take some betony boiled in ale.'

'Now,' she hisses. 'You shouldn't be saying that sort of thing to a woman such as me.'

'I don't know who you are,' Cuthred retorts. 'I don't know what sort of woman you are. Now, do you have two horses?' he continues, not at all concerned. I'm pleased he's managed to redirect her gaze towards him.

'Easy for you. That great lout, I'm not so sure. And if I do, it'll cost you.' I don't miss that she still doesn't tell us her name.

'I've good coin. Or, I can provide you with something to ease the burning in your belly when you eat if you prefer that?'

'Now, how do you know about that?' she complains, but Cuthred's not alone in smelling the sourness of her belch.

'I'm a healer,' he reiterates, eyes sparkling with mischief.

'I might have something for him.' And she juts her hairy chin towards me. 'Doesn't he speak?' she asks again.

'Only when asked a direct question,' Cuthred opines. I glare at him, but he winks. He's enjoying himself far too much.

'Come this way then.' She shuffles back inside the stables, which is well-repaired and smells of fresh hay and clean water.

I notice a shadow lurking in the corner and fix on the sobbing figure, but the horse trader makes no indication that she knows the person is even there. She's a hard woman then, or the youth deserved her ire. I don't know which it is.

'Here he is.' I look where she points and see a horse, much taller than she is, its head entirely covered by a feed sack. 'He likes his food, so you'll have to ensure you feed him well.'

He's a huge old horse, black as night, apart from where some silver threads his mane. I can tell from his crunching that he has good teeth. He stands tall and proud with no sign of a bowed back. But he's not any sort of horse I've seen before.

'Where did you get him?' I find myself asking in surprise at being presented with such an animal, contrary to Cuthred's earlier words, which I've forgotten about.

'None of your business,' she retorts, appraising me with a knowing look. A slither of worry worms its way along my spine, but the horse is the only one that'll suit me. I take offence to being termed a lout, but I am a well-built man. Two Cuthreds could stand side by side in front of me, and part of me would still show.

'What's his name then?'

'Whatever you choose for him,' she growls. I'd shake my head at her contrariness but realise I'm showing too much interest. 'He's yours for only a hundred pence, and I'll give you his saddle as well,' she offers, almost eagerly now, eyes alight with profit as she waits beside the animal. He doesn't fix her with doleful eyes, but the look of hope in them has me realising I'll pay the cost, no matter what. I feel some affinity with the horse. I don't know why. I really should stop gathering horses.

'A hundred for two horses,' Cuthred rejoins. I'm grateful one of us has kept our heads.

The woman tilts her head from side to side as though giving it serious consideration.

'A hundred and twenty for two,' she eventually announces, 'and another twenty for the saddle.'

'Ninety for two and twenty for saddles for both of them,' Cuthred is quick to respond. 'It'll save you that not to feed the big bugger,' he cajoles.

'Fine, fine,' and she spits into her hand.

Cuthred shows no squeamishness in sealing the bargain.

'Wulfthryth, get here and untie the two horses for the gentlemen.' She stands expectantly, and I realise I must hand over the coins. Turning my back on her, I root through my supplies. A hundred and ten Wessex coins isn't an insubstantial amount, but I have much more. I just don't want her to see that. I'm hoping by the time I've been to Winchester, I'll have managed to spend all of the Wessex king's coins. I don't like having them close to me. It reminds me too much of the pennies we found in the kingdom of the East Angles. King Ecgberht and his head get everywhere.

With the aid of Cuthred, I count out and hand over the coins. In no time at all, we have a horse each and make our way to the northern gateway.

'If you're going to Winchester, you need to go that way,' is the least unhelpful reply to Cuthred's request for directions, but it's easy enough to find. A vast quantity of people swarm into and out of Southampton. I turn and gaze back the way we've come, noting the blue sea in the distance. We're on Wessex land, and we're alone, but we were always going to be, I realise. Mounting the old horse I've named Bicwide, because he's huge, I lead the way, trying to take my ease in the purchased saddle. Evidently, it was made for the horse, but it's far from comfortable. It needs its stuffing removing and replacing. There's a hard edge to one side. I consider what's caused it. I hope it doesn't affect Bicwide. I wouldn't want him to rub a sore on his shoulder. Cuthred follows on behind, kicking his stubborn mount onwards.

Eardwulf promised it wasn't far from Southampton to Winchester, a journey of a day at most, and yet we need to be wary and careful while also appearing as though we belong. It'll not be easy. I'm sure of that. As the cries of Wessex-speakers fill my head, I realise just how out of place I might sound. While we remained with the traders, we could pretend to any accent we liked, even that of the Norse, but here, in Wessex itself, it's not going to be possible.

Once we're free of Southampton, Bicwide lumbers to a gallop. He astounds me by managing to go even faster so that I'm left bouncing around in the saddle, struggling to match his gait but knowing that if I don't, I'll be black and blue in the most personal of places.

Cuthred finally manages to encourage his horse to join Bicwide. He doesn't ride with a great deal of skill, but once the animal realises which way we're going, it seems content enough to follow Bicwide. I consider if they knew one another before this.

I absorb my surroundings. As with our venture to the Isle of Sheppey, there's little about Wessex that's different to Mercia. The fields are just waking from their winter slumbers. The animals are sleepy where they've been released from their winter captivity.

We don't talk for much of the morning, too intent on what's happening around us. But then I call a halt, aware we need to eat and that this is a good opportunity to decide what we'll do when we reach Winchester.

Cuthred jumps to the ground with a thud and a shriek combined.

'As comfortable as riding a bloody sack,' he complains. I take it more slowly. Even as tall as I am, I feel high up. If I fall from here, it'll bloody hurt and might even reawaken some of my old hurts, especially around my belly and leg wound. The journey here has tanned my skin but I've not had time to work on building my strength. I'm getting stronger every day, but it's not fast enough.

I shake my legs on hitting the ground, trying to get some feeling back into them and lead Bicwide towards a gurgling stream of clear water. He drinks thirstily and then barely steps back before unleashing a gush of bright yellow piss into the grass. Cuthred grimaces, and I do the same. It would have been better if he'd done that away from the stream.

I drink thirstily from my water bottle and chew on a piece of cheese that Eardwulf offered to us as we parted. The wind's gentle, the sound of the stream pleasant. I could almost forget that I was in an enemy kingdom. Cuthred's grin tells me he feels the same.

'We need to be more wary,' I warn him, thinking of my weapons and byrnie, hidden and tightly rolled in a sack sitting on the back of Bicwide.

'I am,' he assures me, but I can tell he's not. I can hardly berate him, when I'm no better.

'When we get to Winchester, we must be even more on our guard.'

'And you need to keep your mouth shut,' Cuthred offers, an eyebrow arched into his hairline. 'You can tell you're a Mercian from the way you say "day".' I wince. I know he's right. I remember it from Londinium.

'Then how should I say it?' I ask.

'Like this. *Daay*.'

I furrow my forehead. 'I sound like that,' I complain.

'You don't,' he rejoins quickly. 'You sound like this. *Day*. But it should be like this. *Daay*.' When he says it, I realise the 'a' is elongated.

'So like this. *Daay*,' I reply, making the 'a' longer, and he inclines his head from side to side, as though trying to decide.

'It's better than it was, but probably, keep your mouth shut,' he cautions. 'And I'll do all the talking. Even the trader woman wasn't convinced by our story, so better if we don't have to revert to it again.'

'And what will you say, then, when we arrive at Winchester?'

Cuthred lapses into silence, his mouth opening and closing. 'I'm a healer looking for a miracle at the church for one of my ill patients.'

'Why would a healer need a church and which church?'

'Whichever one they spoke about.' He shrugs his narrow shoulders. 'Everyone knows healers need the help of Our Lord God and His saints to aid with tending to the mortally sick.'

I consider his suggestion. It's not a bad idea. 'That might work,' I admit.

Cuthred nods more vigorously. 'Of course it'll work. Perhaps the miracle will be to make you speak again.' He grins.

I growl low in my throat. 'Look, I survived inside Londinium with a host of Wessex warriors, I'm sure I'll be fine within Winchester.'

'Yes, but you were with warriors. And we all know they only think about two things: their weapons and their ale.'

I reach out to slap him on the cheek, but he runs from me, laughing. I merely growl once more. After all, Cuthred might have the right to it. We'll have to see what happens when we reach Winchester. And I hope I can get my *day* and *daay* correct, or I'll be known to be Mercian before I can find the truth of Eadbald's lies.

10

The number of people journeying towards Winchester swells the closer we get to it, and in the near distance, I can see the shimmer of a river. No doubt there are ships along it as well, but we're not quite close enough to pick out the details. And then, when I'm convinced I can smell the cook fires of Winchester, darkness falls, and I realise that everyone's making camp.

Cuthred, with his determination to be the one who does all the talking, has made short work of making an ally of three men travelling with a herd of goats. The animals are being coaxed by sticks, and three dogs who sniff us and then decide we're no threat.

I don't much appreciate the inquisitive wet noses, but once the beasts leave me alone, I understand they accept me. Perhaps Mercians smell no different to those from Wessex.

The men remain mostly silent, apart from whistles and clicks with their tongues which send the dogs running all over the place, while the goats just about remain under control. The smell of the animals is neither pleasant nor unpleasant, and I'm grateful it's not a herd of cows we follow.

'Big market day tomorrow,' Cuthred informs me softly when

we're settling for the night with a slight rise at our backs and the view of where we're going turning black before us. The horses haven't been tested. I didn't allow Bicwide to gallop once the roadway became busier, instead walking with the other market-goers.

We've shared a fire and some food, but it's only really Cuthred and the one man, Freawine, who seem comfortable in one another's presence.

'He says the gates will be open from early until late, so we should be able to get in and out without any problem.' Cuthred's words are as muted as mine. 'The holy men don't approve of the market taking place the day after the celebration of Christ's resurrection, but the people are eager to trade and buy goods they require.'

I nod, pleased to hear that. I'm astounded by how many people are heading towards Winchester.

'How big is the place?' I muse.

He shakes his head. 'No idea. Big enough?' he questions and laughs. He's in a good mood, almost as though he's forgotten the peril we're in. I don't think to remind him. The more natural he acts, the less likely he is to say something we'll both regret. 'Freawine says all the lords and ladies will be there, perhaps even the king. They'll pretend they've come to pray but really, it's an excuse for a feast and a market day.'

This does give me pause for thought. I chased down King Ecgberht beside the River Thames. My face will be known to his son if he's also in attendance. Lord Æthelwulf's now king of Kent, under his father. Will he have any recollection of a youth he met only briefly when Wessex lost its foothold in Mercia?

'I hope not,' I retort, already fearing the many possibilities for our endeavour to go wrong, having somehow managed to convince myself all will be well. But Cuthred laughs.

'I've discovered the names of all the churches,' he informs me, reminding me that he hasn't entirely forgotten our purpose. 'I think it was St Mary's we need to visit, which is the one that Eadbald said he'd been to when he came to speak to King Ecgberht, or rather Ealdorman Wilfhardi, on Lord Coelwulf's instructions. Unlike Tamworth, there are more than one church, there's also St Peter's, and Saints Peter and Paul, where the kings say their prayers.' His eyes gleam. It's clear he's happy with all that's been uncovered. I admit, it will make it easier for us. I try to recall exactly what Eadbald said about Winchester and St Mary's, but I can't move aside from the way the queen seemed to prompt him to even mention St Mary's when he was giving his testimony to the king at Kingsholm. I'm convinced Eadbald has never been to Winchester. I'm equally unconvinced that the queen hasn't been. Although, how or why that might have happened, I'm unsure. But Cuthred's still talking. 'There are seven gates, I think. Freawine told me their names, but I can't remember them all. Should we just follow them tomorrow, and make our way to the market?'

'Yes, and from there we can mingle, especially if there are more people than usual inside the settlement.'

So decided, Cuthred curls into his cloak and is soon softly snoring, but I lie awake, a sense of unease making it difficult for me to sleep. We're surrounded by people and bloody goats, but I feel as though we're alone and that our Mercian heritage is stamped upon us in more than just the way we say 'day'. Hopefully, tomorrow, we'll learn what we need to and will be able to leave. I feel as though Bicwide could take me to Mercia, provided I can determine why his saddle is uncomfortable. Maybe we'll even find some traders heading towards Mercia and be able to travel with them.

It's been less than a day on Wessex soil, and already, my skin is itching and I'm desperate to be back in Mercia.

Not, I realise, that I quite know how I'm going to be able to confirm either way if Eadbald truly came to Winchester. I just have to hope that something proves he did or didn't. I'm hoping that someone will remember him, or something like that, but it will involve speaking. I'll have to give that task to Cuthred. Perhaps he can pretend to be Eadbald's son or maybe we could say that Eadbald recommended we seek out someone inside Winchester. My thoughts swirl. So many possibilities and none of them seem to be good ones.

Eventually, I must sleep. I wake with a goat asleep across my feet and the growl of one of the dogs at my ear as it tries to encourage the animal to leave my side.

'Stay still,' a voice calls to me harshly.

I do just that. I can smell whatever the dog had to eat yesterday, and I can feel its saliva on my cheek.

'Come here.' The cry's sharp. The dog whines and moves away, as does the bloody goat. Cuthred's watching, wide-eyed. I can imagine the stories he'll tell Wynflæd when we return to Tamworth. 'Sorry about that,' Freawine shouts when he has his goats and dogs under control once more. 'Stupid animal is always running away.' Sitting upright, I glance around. There's a layer of dew on the grass. I slick more moisture from my face, hoping it's not all saliva. Most people are awake, and many are already encouraging animals onwards. It appears the market day has an early start as Cuthred and I scramble to ready the horses that have been tied up for the night. They've fed hungrily from tall grasses and the oats we purchased alongside them. Before the sun has fully risen, we're queuing to gain entry into Winchester even as the monks' morning prayers ring through the air. I doubt few will be thinking of God and prayer today, but only of profit and buying a bargain. I hope that even fewer are fearful that two Mercians walk amongst them.

* * *

I dismount to gain entry into Winchester, as everyone seems to be doing. It's congested and unpleasantly busy. I've never seen Tamworth so full of people, even when it's market day, but Tamworth doesn't seem as big as Winchester. The haze of smoke over the settlement speaks of many people living inside.

We shuffle forwards. Luckily, the size of Bicwide means we're given room. Even the guards – yawning and scratching themselves where they stand, just outside some ancient walls that remind me strongly of those found at Londinium, although not as high – pause to gaze at him. They allow us entry without questioning Cuthred. But I don't miss a look that passes between two of them. I'm not sure what it means. I wish I had my byrnie and weapons belt in place. I'm wary already. If I thought it was busy outside, inside we're more tightly packed than the salted fish in the barrel that I helped Durcytel get on and then off the trader ship.

'We need to find somewhere to leave the horses,' I murmur to Cuthred. He's dismounted as well, but even as tall as we are, it's not easy to see where we need to go. The guards would have done well to let fewer people inside at once. I don't think Commander Eahric would have just opened the gate on a market day and allowed this many to flood inside. It would overwhelm all the free space inside Tamworth.

We're funnelled along the street with no option to turn left or right. To the right of us, I see the familiar walls and exterior crosses fastened to the wooden beams that depict a church. But I can't get Bicwide over there quickly enough before we're swept along in the flood of Wessex people. Angry cries greet my attempts to stop, not helped when Bicwide pisses over the feet of some market traders. I keep my head down and stay shuffling forward, hemmed in by goats and carts and all manner of items, including some chickens, which squawk so loudly it's hard to hear my thoughts. Eventually, we're disgorged into a wider area. The traders hasten to their site of choice allowing Cuthred and I the chance to take a deep breath. I realise then that I can see two churches, not just one. I wish I knew what they were called. Are these St Peter's, St Mary's or Saints Peter and Paul?

'That way,' Cuthred informs me, pointing onwards.

'But we need to leave the horses somewhere. We'll find an alehouse.'

Slowly, I turn in a circle, eyeing the few streets that lead from the market street. There are buildings everywhere. I feel hemmed in all over again. The buildings, like the church I've seen, are wooden, coated with wattle and daub, although I think some might have stone at their bases. No doubt a few have stolen the stone from the standing walls encircling the settlement. The walls must also have been built by the ancient people who lived here, those giants Wulfheard once told me about. If the stone continues to be robbed, they won't be standing for much longer.

The trading area's claustrophobic, with the usual sellers opening their shopfronts and shouting as loudly as the itinerant traders. I watch, in amusement, as a baker sets up his stall in front of the couple who are clearly resident in Winchester. If I were to venture over there, and let drop my Mercian accent, they wouldn't care, their anger too focused on one another, both vying to sell their baked goods.

'This way,' Cuthred shouts, heading onwards. I trail him, and only just in time. Another swirl of people enter the market street. Now I can hear the cries of men and women eager to make early sales and spend their afternoon asleep, or in the alehouse. Maybe they even hope to return home with a pocket full of Wessex coins.

Cuthred leads me down a wide street. As I try to avoid the liberal splatters of horse shit, I realise he has indeed found an alehouse, a banner flying in the scant breeze, showing what the owners must think signifies an alehouse. I'm not so convinced that the bee truly looks like a bee. At least, not any more. And, I hope they have more than just mead for sale, or there'll be an almighty fight in short order between those unable to hold such a strong drink.

There are benches outside, for all it's cold enough to welcome a fire's warmth. There are youths already helping travellers with their horses.

'Two, my good man,' Cuthred negotiates. I'd laugh, but the boy he speaks to is no older than him. Both of them stand there as though they're world-weary as they discuss requirements and their cost. 'Ten pennies for the daay, and we get to eat in the alehouse as well,' Cuthred confirms. The more he speaks to the people of Wessex, the more he sounds like he belongs. He was right to caution me. My Mercian accent would stick out like a sore thumb here, and while it's a market day, the accents that reverberate around the place are predominantly West Saxon, with the roll of certain words. I'll have to be mindful.

'What brings you to Winchester?' the boy asks just before he takes Bicwide's reins, a perplexed expression on his face that I don't miss. I suspect Bicwide's well known here. I wish I'd had more choice from the horse trader at Southampton. It's almost as though I've brought Brute with me; for all I know, he's safely in Mercia.

'A cure. He's a healer. We seek out a miracle from the churches or, rather, from the holy men. One that's written in their books and not known in our settlement,' Cuthred answers for me.

This brings a downturned smile to the boy's face. He seems entirely indifferent to the many others waiting to leave their horses with them. His interest concerns me. 'I wish you luck with that. The monks and priests are all querulous gits. They'll be about today, casting their appraising eyes over everything for sale and trying to run off with the best of it, even while they mutter we should all be on our knees praying. But tell me, where did you get this horse?'

'A trader in Southampton,' Cuthred replies quickly, clearly not thinking much of divulging the information. But the boy's lip curls. I'm reminded of the guards' reactions at the gate. There's something about this horse, I'm not sure what, that means more to these people. Perhaps it's merely his size?

I want to ask the question, but mindful that I'm a Mercian and sound Mercian, I clamp down my lips.

'He doesn't say much, does he?' the boy murmurs as I reach for my sack of supplies, trying to ensure my seax doesn't clunk against my sword or byrnie.

'No, he doesn't.' Cuthred cuts him short, finally realising we're being asked too many questions. 'Tell me, how do I get to St Mary's?'

'Back to the market street and follow it towards the river. You won't miss it,' he confirms, and I can't help wishing that Cuthred hadn't asked him for directions. And that he'd not told the stable boy the almost truth about the reason for our visit. He's too interested in us already.

With misgivings, I allow the horses to be led away. Cuthred and I retrace our steps and force a path through the busy marketplace. If possible, there are even more people here now, and more than once, I lose sight of Cuthred, only for him to reappear some steps ahead. It's a relief to emerge into the quieter roadway, that I hope will lead to St Mary's. I've still no idea how to discover if

Eadbald truly came to Winchester or, rather, didn't. I'm convinced from his description of Winchester that he didn't. Surely, he'd have mentioned the market street and the commotion of the many hundreds of people visiting it. Surely he'd have known to talk about the river, the view towards the sea, even the strange accent of the West Saxons.

'He was a bit too nosy,' Cuthred comments when we can hear ourselves.

'He was, yes. And the horse? I noticed the guards eyeing him as well when we came inside Winchester.'

'Well, Bicwide's a big bastard,' Cuthred offers, but I can tell he's as uneasy as I am. Only then the wooden church appears before us. St Mary's. The one that Eadbald specifically mentioned or, rather, the one that Queen Cynethryth prompted him to mention. I note with a sour look that I can't see the king's palace close by. But I don't actually know where it is, and I'm sure that Eadbald doesn't either. He's just been lucky on this occasion.

I resolve myself to what must be done. I need to find out if a Mercian visited the church, and how we're to achieve that, I still have no idea. It's not as though Eadbald has any distinguishing features. His brown hair was long, without grey threading it. He had the stance of a warrior, but then I imagine many people here do.

But there must be some way of finding out. Surely?

11

There are four of them. I've noted them as Cuthred and I have made our benedictions and bobbed up and down inside the wooden church, as we should. I'd have preferred the arrival of the monks, not the men who might or might not be warriors. I'd like to have convinced myself they came to pray, but I know men intent on causing mischief. I can tell in the way they're too alert, too eager, and too tense.

I keep close to Cuthred, aware I need to protect him, but the men do nothing while we're inside. Perhaps they're respectful of their God after all and merely come to pray on this holy day. But after we've lingered for as long as possible inside, with nothing presenting itself to us to reveal whether Eadbald might have come this way or not, and even Cuthred's trying to ask me why we don't leave, we're forced outside by the arrival of the monks once more, ready to celebrate terce. I can tell we're unwelcome while the monks pray, and so, unwillingly, I make my departure, turning to bow my head low before I do so. I use the opportunity to seek out the men. There are two of them still lingering as we do, but the other two, I realise, are outside, no doubt waiting for us.

Despite the hum of prayer, it's quickly swallowed by the raucous cries of the market taking place not far away. I finally get a good look at two of them, aware that the other two have followed Cuthred and me outside. They stand like warriors, tall and well built. How they hold themselves assures me that these men know how to fight.

'Why do you have Heardred's horse?' The question's directed to me, although I won't be the one answering it. I consider if they see beyond the clothes I wear to the shape of my body. Yes, I've been beaten within an inch of my life, but I'm recovering. My strength's returning. I might not be as robust as this time last year, but I hope I can beat these bastards all the same. The thought of my encounter with Oswy has me considering how I can overpower them. Not with brute strength, but maybe I won't need it. They're very sure of themselves. I can use that against them.

Cuthred, quickly alert to the danger, stands before me, arms on his thin hips, eyeing the warriors before us.

'We have no one's horse. The horses we have are ours, paid for with our silver pennies.'

'A likely story,' the one who speaks dismisses contemptuously. He's a big man, but not as big as me. Mind, he has three others with him, and I have Cuthred. The West Saxon's face is lopsided, although I can see no scar to show it's been caused by a badly healed wound. Perhaps he was born like that. His hair's cut short to his face, making his bulbous nose appear even rounder. A round nose, on a round face. He's not a good-looking man.

'Go and ask the old crone we bought him from in Southampton.'

A quizzical look passes between the men. I wish I knew what this was all about.

'Heardred had no business in Southampton. He'd not have gone that way,' the one muses to the other. I'm eyeing them up, trying to decide who's the better warrior and whether I should remove my seax from my sack now. I don't want to start the fight, but I do want to be prepared for it.

'They've killed him and stolen his horse,' an outraged voice shrieks from behind us. I keep my eyes on the two in front, but the menacing tone makes Cuthred flinch. I'd tell him to be calm, but that would no doubt alert them to my Mercian heritage.

'Shut up, Heardlulf, I'm trying to think,' the spokesperson growls.

'Who's Heardred?' I'm glad Cuthred thinks to ask.

'My brother,' the voice from behind screeches. I can sense this could quickly escalate, or it might just dissipate, provided we can prove we don't know who Heardred was, and that buying his horse, if Bicwide is his horse, has occurred by chance.

'We don't know Heardred, and as I said, we bought that horse from a trader in Southampton. And he wasn't bloody cheap,' Cuthred menaces.

'Why doesn't he speak?' another of the men asks, jutting his chin towards me.

'Mute,' Cuthred offers. 'We come seeking a miracle to cure him.'

'Hah,' he chuckles. 'If you believe in all that shit, then you're touched.' Not that I truly believe in miracles, but he'd do better not to say as such just outside the church where the monks might hear. Or God.

'He's a big bugger,' the first man muses. 'I can see why you have Heardred's horse, but as you say, you bought him. We need to seek out the horse trader,' he informs the others. I think they'll walk away, only the man behind, I assume it's Heardred's brother, launches himself towards Cuthred. I sense it more than see it and thrust myself before Cuthred, turning as I do so. I might want my seax in my hand, but I can use my fists as well as the next man.

Heardlulf's hand is bunched in a tight fist, and if he'd struck Cuthred, he'd be on the floor, but instead, my chest absorbs the impact. My fist hits him in the face, knocking his chin upwards, although not without affecting me. I'm already panting at the exertion. I curse my frailty and Eadweard both for wounding me so badly. I'm glad he's bloody dead.

The impact sends a shudder through my arm as I follow through with a jab from my left fist. Heardlulf's face fills with fury as he staggers backwards, not anticipating my response. Suddenly, he's punching me, the blows landing well but without a great deal of force. I focus on him, but I can hear the dismay shuddering through his fellow warriors and brace myself to be set upon by the other three as well.

I don't have time for this, I think, punching with my right hand with so much power that Heardlulf staggers backwards and then crumples to the floor. I'm breathing heavily, Heardlulf's blood in my beard, as I face the next warrior. He's of medium build and height, his eyes switching from me to Heardlulf's unmoving body. I doubt he has it in him to take me on. But one of the others has no restraint.

Sharp stabs on my back have me turning to face him. It's not the man who spoke, but the other one who asked why I didn't speak. I'll show him I can do much more with my fists than with my tongue.

He's grinning broadly, and I realise that while I might have no blade, he has two held in his hands. Already, I can feel the burn of cut flesh. The git has bloodied me. What sort of warrior is he to attack a man from behind? A Wessex warrior, I glower to myself, but I'm more angry with myself. I shouldn't have allowed myself to be caught unprepared.

Despite his blades, I reach out and grip his clenched hands with my hands. One of the blades falls to the ground beneath my feet at the unexpected pressure. I don't allow myself to be distracted by reaching for it. Instead, I focus on the other hand. His face has clouded. What he thought would be an easy win is anything but that. Damn fool.

I step closer to him. I could squeeze him between my arms, and then he'd drop his remaining blade. But now the first man inserts himself between us. His face is filled with fury and, I think, not directed at me.

'You'll have the king's commander down on us, you bloody fools,' he glowers, bending to pick up the discarded blade and swiping the other one from his ally's hand. 'We came to ask questions, remember?' And with that, I can hear the thud of booted feet coming our way. The three men hasten to run away, leaving the one on the ground, Heardred's brother, Heardlulf. He's an ugly brute.

I look to Cuthred, and he nods. We don't want to be found here either.

Following the path the three unwounded men took, we run between the church and the building closest to it, the path is narrow and only just wide enough for me to fit through. There's an unpleasant smell. I decide not to think too carefully about what it might be as I hurry to catch Cuthred.

I don't risk looking behind me, but I am forced to yank my sack through the space, wincing at the metallic scrape of my blade or helm. I hope they're not dented. And then we're back amongst the milling crowd at the marketplace.

Cuthred's quickly at my back, his fingers reaching for my sack.

'Put your cloak on,' he hisses. 'It'll hide your cut tunic.' I bat him aside and pull the cloth clear much more quickly than he can, mindful that curious eyes are watching us. We need to get this done before the running steps come any closer.

'Go back towards the tavern,' I urge Cuthred in an undertone.

If anyone saw us, they'll be looking for two men together, not a man and a youth going about their business separately. With the cloak around my shoulders and a wince for the blood I see on my hand from running my fingers along the wounds, I merge into the crowd. I direct my path towards someone with clothes on display. I doubt they'll have a tunic that'll fit me, but I decide to look anyway. I don't want to get blood on the ones in my sack.

There's a company of women sitting behind the makeshift stall, their fingers and hands busy as they pull thread through tunics, cloaks and dresses or use spindles to work the raw material into yarn suitable to create clothes. This, I imagine, is where men and women who lack the skills can get their clothes repaired or buy new ones, ready-made. A collection of tunics, folded and lying on the table, assures me that my assumption is correct. I'm not the only one to be looking at them, either.

There's a gathering of men and a few women. I recognise the men as warriors, who need tunics because they lack wives to do it and their lord's wife and servants don't provide enough. Others are clearly wealthy, fingering some of the more expensive fabrics, some thrice-dyed, not just dyed, and also made perhaps from nettle, not flax. They'll be expensive to buy. Both take a long time to produce, but nettle provides a much finer fabric. The rich colours of some of the fabrics also assures me that only the finest ingredients have been used to produce the dyes. But there are also others, barely holding a shade of green, that might just have been plunged into a vat treated only with random pieces of green grass.

I just want something serviceable, pale and only dyed once. I don't need the tunic I determine on to mark me as a wealthy man, just one who can afford to have his clothes made by others. I have some Wessex coins in my hand, from where I retrieved my cloak. There certainly won't be enough to pay for the tunics thick with embroidery, or bright with colours.

My attention's drawn to the woman who uses square pieces of bone to twist and turn the lengths of wool she's threaded through them, weaving a pattern that moves from side to side through the thin ribbons that are being produced, the line a pleasant red colour. It will make someone a fine belt, perhaps for a woman or a ribbon to hold a wimple in place.

Beside her are two younger women, girls really, who have a loom, and are clearly learning how to weave the weights to make a small piece of cloth. The clack of the loom weights is a reminder of my childhood, when Edwin's mother used to care for me. She might well have been the blacksmith's wife but making clothes was her responsibility for me, Edwin, herself and her husband.

Aware I'm staring, my eyes fasten once more on the tunics and I suddenly become conscious of a conversation taking place between a man and a woman who don't seem to be together but who are clearly talking to one another to the rear of the stall. The woman's dress is covered in soft fibres from her endeavours, but the man wears a dark cloak, a dark tunic and boots that look as though they've only just been stitched. They're incongruous together. Why would they even know one another, let alone be speaking as they are? The dark colour of his clothes speaks of wealth, whereas she's a market trader.

'Disappeared.' I catch the tail end of their conversation.

'He came himself, in person, to ensure all was done as it should be.'

I can't think the words are relevant to me, but I listen all the same as I wait to complete my purchase of the thin pale-green tunic. It's easier to focus on them than on the cries of West Saxon warriors seeking out Cuthred and me in the swelling crowd, or the shrieks of those they disturb.

'They say Wulfnoth's dead,' the woman murmurs. The name sparks my interest. I manage to stop myself from looking up.

'Well, even if he is, he was never the one behind it all,' the man murmurs. His words, I'm convinced, lack the roll of the Wessex-speakers. If he said 'day', would he sound like me? Is he Mercian? I try to catch a glimpse of him but only observe an idea of an unusual dull-brown beard and moustache, sharp eyes beneath a mop of hair before I'm bargaining for my tunic.

It costs me the price of a goat, but at least it'll keep me from ruining the tunic I have with me. I didn't truly anticipate getting into a fight, but I did worry that if I had to journey to Canterbury, I might need a good tunic to blend in with the nobility and holy men and women.

As I hand over the two pennies, complete with King Ecgberht's face on them, I turn aside, listening to the woman's voice.

I fix her image in my mind. She's far from young, a cloak covering the back of her hair, but I don't miss the unusual shade of her eyes, that flash bluer than the sky and the ocean, as though warmed from the interior by a fire that blazes forth.

Then, before she can sense my scrutiny, I dip away from the stall, my tunic to hand, my sack bashing against others who crowd too closely. Slowly, stopping here and there as though I'm interested in the hens, fresh-caught fish and other items for sale in the marketplace, I allow myself to seek out the tavern.

I need to find Cuthred, and then I must find the woman and the man. I came here looking for proof that Eadbald either visited or didn't visit Winchester, but it seems there's more at work here after all. There can be no coincidence that they spoke of Wulfheard's brother, Wulfnoth. The man behind the children's kidnapping. A shimmer of unease ripples my wounded back, making me gasp in pain. But, at the same time, I feel a thrill of excitement. There's something here that I can discover. With that knowledge, Lord Coenwulf will be allowed to return to Kingsholm and his children, and I can relinquish my responsibilities to them.

12

I find Cuthred with the horses in the stables. His face is pinched with worry that clears on seeing me.

'Where have you been?' he demands.

'Looking in the market,' I reply in a harsh whisper. While it's busy all around us, I'm aware, after the conversation I overheard in the marketplace, that anyone could eavesdrop, and I'm supposed to be mute. The stables are busy, horses and donkeys everywhere. It's hard not to step in shit or piss. The stable boys are entirely overwhelmed, and Bicwide's space is getting smaller and smaller, and he doesn't like it.

'Let me look at your back,' Cuthred demands, turning me and pulling my cloak over my shoulder. I can feel his fingers prodding at the cuts. 'Two of them,' he announces. 'Not deep. In fact, they barely cut the surface of your skin, but they've bled a lot. I've already got hot water, although it'll be cold by now. You'll have to remove your tunic. It'll hurt because it's stuck to your cuts. You should have got here quicker.'

I grimace at the thought of that but realise I just need to get it over and done with. Bracing for the stab of pain, I pull my tunic clear, a sheen of sweat on my forehead. Cuthred quickly begins the repair work.

'It doesn't need stitching,' he confirms. 'But you'll have to be careful with it.' Once he's finished examining my fresh wounds and bound a poultice into them of moss soaked in honey, I force myself into the new tunic, wishing it wasn't quite so tight around my arms. If I have to clench my fists, the wrists will burst open, as will the shoulder element of the cloth. For all that, it's a good weave and feels comfortable over the dimming burn of my cuts. It might have been reasonably priced, but I can't fault the skill of the craftspeople. 'We need to seek out the other churches,' Cuthred whispers to me as he packs away his precious supplies. I'm shaking my head. I've been thinking about this.

'No, he said he went to St Mary's, or rather, the queen told him he went to St Mary's. There's no means of knowing whether he did or not, although I can't imagine he did. But, I heard Wulfnoth's name in the marketplace.'

Cuthred's eyes open wide at that. 'It's just a coincidence,' he replies eventually, lips having twisted in thought. 'Wulfnoth would never have come to Winchester.'

'But what if he did? And they knew he was dead. And they said it didn't matter if he was because others were involved in it.'

'Icel, we came to seek out the truth of Eadbald's claims, not interfere in anything else. We need to find that proof so that Lord Coenwulf can return to his children.' I grimace at that. Cuthred's right to remind me, but I can't help thinking there's more to be found within Winchester. The horse is a mystery to me. I almost wish I'd asked those warriors more about this Heardred, and why he was missing. Was he, perhaps, somehow involved in all of this as well?

'Did you see anything at the church?' I clamp down on my speculation focusing on Cuthred.

'No, but we also need to visit St Peter's and Saints Peter and Paul, and not be found by those West Saxon warriors in the process. There might be something at those churches to resolve the king's questions.'

'Agreed, we'll do that then.' I stifle a yawn. We started the day early. It's still a long time until evening will fall. We should do as Cuthred said. 'Come on then.' I slap Bicwide on his wide shoulders, wondering what Heardred called him, if he was Heardred's horse in the first place, and follow Cuthred outside.

Overhead, clouds are forming, the bright morning fading away. No doubt that's why the market was so busy; the locals knew to expect rain. Hunched inside my cloak, I follow Cuthred, trying to ignore the occasional burn of my wounded back and the throb in my fists. When I return to Mercia, I'm going to have to put more effort into returning to my former level of fitness.

For someone who's never been to Winchester before, Cuthred has a good grasp of the layout, and in no time at all, we're standing before another church.

This one is surrounded by a burial ground, unlike St Mary's. I'm sure it's the one we passed on the way into Winchester. It's much bigger than St Mary's and appears far more popular, enclosed behind stone walls, again, no doubt stolen away from the exterior walls. I hope they don't have cause to regret that decision. It's unusual to find a burial ground within the walls of a settlement like this. Whoever is buried here is important.

While we heard the monks in St Mary's, here there are priests, monks, and what look to be wealthy individuals as well. I see someone sobbing over an open grave and appreciate there's a burial this day. Not the best timing, with the market in full swing and the cries of traders reaching my ears. Who wants to know about the best-priced goats as they bury their loved one? But Cuthred hurries on, his eyes on the building. Again, I'm struck by the surroundings of the church. As at St Mary's, if I was the one asked to describe the place by my king having said I'd visited it, I wouldn't be able to stop myself from adding some little details, the colour of the darkened wood, the grey-white stones used in the construction, even the fact the thatch on the roof seems new and glows in what sunlight there is beneath the grey clouds.

I'm growing ever more convinced that Eadbald has never stepped foot inside Winchester, which I've long suspected anyway. But what if it was never Eadbald at all? What if it was Wulfnoth who came to Winchester? And if it was Wulfnoth then whom did he come to meet, and who's involved in this and able to cast their net so wide that it includes Wessex and Mercia? I can't see anyone being able to move too freely between the two kingdoms, not even the traders. Benedict and his companions were happy on the coastal sites, but they didn't even ask to come to Winchester itself, contenting themselves with Southampton.

I worry about the problem, even as Cuthred gains admittance, bowing and offering a small fee to the monk guarding the doorway. I follow him inside, body tense, and alert to who might be watching us. Ideally, I want to seek out the woman with the blue eyes from the market stall or the man with his indistinguishable features, although I'm sure I'd recognise his voice if I heard it again. But Cuthred's focus is elsewhere. And then we finally have some luck.

'Your name?' An elderly monk stands to the side of the door, assisting the one who takes our alms. I appreciate that here, at least, they like to keep a record of those crossing the threshold. Now, I just need to look at the book and see if Eadbald, or Wulfnoth's name, is included.

'Cuthred,' he offers without guile. 'I come seeking a miracle cure for my friend here. A man such as he shouldn't be mute.' The monk eyes me with some surprise, his mouth half-open, revealing few teeth left to protrude from his gums. He's old but has evidently led a good life if the wobbling of his chin is anything to go by.

'Then you've come to the right place,' he replies quickly, all the same. 'Prayers, and of course gifts, ensure our Lord God looks kindly upon all who come before him.'

Cuthred bows once more, and while he does that, I circle behind the monk, gazing down at the neat letters that cover so much of the page. Cuthred's a quick lad, and soon realises my interest.

'Tell me,' he asks quickly. 'Of those who've obtained a miracle before. Are they listed in your book?'

'Yes, yes,' the monk offers even more quickly. I can tell he's greedy for more riches, although it won't be going into his pocket, or at least, I hope it won't.

He pores over the vellum book, the pages filled with tiny writing, almost impossible to see in the dim glow inside the building. But his eyes seek something in particular. I hope he goes back to last year. After all, how many people can visit here in one year? How many can say a miracle has occurred? And then I see it. I thought to look for Eadbald's name, but as the monk tells a seemingly enraptured Cuthred how a tithe of thirty pence, equivalent to purchasing an ox, brought one person the gift of sight when they were feared blind, I see the name Wulfnoth of Eamont, depicted in a clear, square script, the sum of a hundred pence beside it. Now what, I consider, was Wulfnoth trying to buy that made gifting a hundred pence to the church within Winchester worth such an expense? He could have had our two horses for the same cost.

I thought Wulfnoth's involvement was – as his brother, Wulfheard, commented – only because he'd do anything for coin but while that might be the case, it seems that there's more to it than that. He's spent much here as well. He must have been assured of earning far more.

Wulfnoth came to Wessex from his holdings in north Northumbria to meddle in affairs in Mercia. Who then was paying his bill? Whom was he seeking within Winchester? And why did they meet in a church?

Cuthred has far outdone himself in holding the monk's attention, but now the tale's told. I move aside, follow my young friend, and join the queue of those coming to offer prayers and exhortations to their God. I consider how many people here are praying for riches as opposed to performing a selfless act. Not that I blame them. We all believe our lives would be better if only we were rich. Just as I'm about to bend and whisper what I've discovered to Cuthred, I feel eyes on me and look up to see one of the men from that morning assessing me. Not the ugly one.

I incline my head towards him. He does the same. He's alone. And I think he's arrived after us, for he's not progressed much beyond the monk with his scratching quill and request for a tithe to enter the church. The monks have set up their stall, just as surely as those in the marketplace, although they're selling hopes and miracles, not goats or tunics.

He walks towards me. I watch his approach.

'I've been looking for you,' he whispers to the pair of us. If Cuthred's startled at the man's arrival, he doesn't react.

'What do you want?' Cuthred demands. The Wessex warrior runs his eyes over my frame, hesitating even now, but then he steps closer. I brace, expecting an attack, but it doesn't come.

'My friend's angry and bereaved. He can be a fool sometimes, but I am his ally, and his brother's horse was dear to him, so I'd ask you to give him to me. In recompense for whatever's happened to his brother.'

'And how much will you pay me for the horse?' Cuthred questions.

'Pay you?' the man drawls. 'I won't pay you anything. Merely let me have the horse, and we'll leave you to your business.'

Cuthred meets my gaze. I shake my head. I'm not about to give up Bicwide for nothing. That would surely arouse far too many suspicions in the man's mind. Why would we willingly relinquish a horse unless we were up to no good?

'I don't think so, and I don't believe this is the correct place to discuss this,' Cuthred counters. I'm impressed by his quick wits. 'Meet us later, in the marketplace, before the market closes for the day. Then, we can discuss your request more fully. But I suggest you bring coin with you,' Cuthred offers as the man turns aside to leave us. 'A horse such as that is worth good pennies.' I think the man will react but, clenching his fists, he merely forces his way through the crowd waiting to enter, occasioning shouts and cries from those he disturbs. I wait for the monks to complain, but they wisely hold their tongues as the foul-faced warrior leaves the sanctity of their church.

Cuthred and I continue on our path toward the shrine. The closer we get, the more and more fervent the prayers being uttered become. There are many desperate people here. Some sightless. Some without limbs, and even a mother weeping over a small child she cradles in her arms, its body limp for all I can see it breathes.

I swallow my horror.

These are people desperate for a miracle, but I don't believe they'll find one within the church. There's nothing that can aid some of these people. But still, there are things that Wynflæd could do to help them. The babe could be given a pottage filled with meat juices to strengthen it. The sightless woman, if she is indeed sightless, could be made a lotion of celery and wormwood.

It might help. It certainly stands more chance than a miracle within this church, where it seems to me the monks are more interested in making coins from those desperate for assistance than in aiding them. I'm reminded of Bishop Æthelweald of Lichfield. He's another who isn't a holy man because of belief but because of what he hopes to gain from it.

I lift my eyes to gaze at the cloth laid out over the altar, the wealth of gold stitches assuring me, after my visit to the market stall selling and mending clothes, that these would have been expensive and far beyond the reach of most.

I turn to murmur to Cuthred that we should leave. I feel I have my answers. But he's not there. Squinting into the gloom and trying not to choke on the expensive, cloying incense, I see he's taken himself to where a woman bends over someone else. I can hear coughing and also Cuthred's soft words to them. I shake my head and force my way towards them.

Cuthred doesn't notice my arrival, but the woman does. Mouth open, she eyes me with unease. I don't smile, but I try to set my face so I don't look as fearful as she thinks. It's difficult to tell much about her in the gloom. She seems swathed in dark hues, but her face is angular, even a little haunted. She's known loss and now she fears for whomever she's come to pray for.

'Icel,' Cuthred hisses to me. 'This man has a bad chest, but it's perfectly treatable. There's no need for a miracle here.'

I gaze down at the figure and jolt with recognition. I know this man. I fought with this man. His black hair is thick and shaggy, the pretence of a moustache playing above his lips. Only then I blink, and I realise it's not Brihtwold, the youth I killed in Londinium. But it could be. I try to recall what family he said he had, if any, but I draw a blank.

I search his body for some sign of a wound, but there's nothing, not that it's that easy to see inside the gloomy interior, and my actions are starting to draw the unwanted attention of the monks.

I walk to Cuthred and whisper what I want him to do, before ambling my way towards the church's exit.

Behind me, I hear the sound of people following on and hope that Cuthred has done as I asked. If we try and aid the ill man here, the monks will complain. I'm sure that too many people know of our presence, even if they don't know who we are. I anticipate some of the king's guards arriving at any moment to apprehend us for the fight outside the first church, St Mary's.

Outside, it's still daylight, which surprises me, but I realise we've not been inside for that long. The day is becoming one of the longest I've ever endured.

Yet the queue of those waiting to enter Saints Peter and Paul stretches onwards. I think of St Mary's, and wonder why these people aren't there. Perhaps, I realise, the monks have ensured the legend of their church grows to the detriment of all others. Either that, or the king ensures that happens.

I move aside. I don't want to be the focus of more attention. I bid Cuthred ask the woman to bring the man to the tavern, but I don't know its name. I do, however, know the way. And without too much haste, I retrace my steps. My mind's ablaze with questions. I know Brihtwold's dead. I remember witnessing that only too well. But if this is his brother, or son, or related somehow, I can make no mention of that. It would mark me as Mercian even without opening my mouth.

But I could aid him. Cuthred is right to think there's a chance to do so. From what I glimpsed, the man isn't dying, but he could, without the correct treatment.

As I try and move towards the tavern where we left our horses, the push of people coming the other way intensifies just as the first heavy drops of rain fall, hitting the ground and me with enough force to make me wince. People scurry all over the place, seeking shelter where they can. There's a general groan of unhappiness. I hunker down, pulling the hood of my cloak over my head, wincing as my wounds tug with the movement, but in moments I'm drenched, and worse, the rain's cold. It's not warm summer rain, but wintry rain that chills immediately.

I look up, holding my hand above my eyes, and spy the tavern ahead. But before I can get to it, I need to work my way through a huge press of bodies. Just as I'm about to make it, the stables in sight, I feel a heavy hand on my shoulder, and turn, mouth open to argue about it, even though I need to keep my mouth shut and clasp eyes on someone I didn't expect to see here, in Winchester. In Wessex no less.

Oswy.

I point towards my destination and move onwards, having been jostled more than enough by those still seeking cover from the rain. A hundred questions rush through my mind, but I keep them tight inside. Only when I round the tavern and find myself inside do I seek out Oswy once more. I startle, for Oswy isn't alone, Wulfheard and Cenred accompany him, and now I can't help myself.

'What are you doing here?' I hiss, mindful of my Mercian accent.

'We came to find you,' Oswy growls, but then Wulfheard's close enough to whisper.

'Your whereabouts are no longer a secret. Ealdorman Ælfstan fears for you as you did the children of Lord Coenwulf. We've come to take you home. This foolhardy request from King Wiglaf is entirely that.'

Again, I open my mouth and then clamp it shut, catching sight of Cuthred and the two people he's escorted from the church. He's busy talking to them and finding somewhere for the man to sit. I can feel the woman's eyes on me, and it's as if she knows who I am. Her gaze switches between me and the rest of Ealdorman Ælfstan's warriors. Then, when I least need to be under the scrutiny of someone else, Heardred's brother confidently walks into the tavern, his face a welter of blood and bruises: vengeance, no doubt, on his mind.

13

I look from Heardlulf to Oswy, and then to Cuthred, and the woman. I don't know what to do but turn my back so that Heardlulf won't immediately recognise me.

'Come on, we need to leave,' Wulfheard hisses once more. 'The rain will allow us to hide. Men and women don't want to be outside in this.' He indicates the raging storm with a jerk of his chin.

Neither do I.

'But Cuthred. He's helping someone.' I don't say that I want to know the man's identity and determine if he was related to Brihtwold, whom I killed in Londinium.

'Then bring them along.' This surprises me. Wulfheard doesn't have a soft heart. It speaks to me of his worry about our safety, which only increases mine. He doesn't want to take the time to argue about this. He's simply capitulated. Perhaps we should leave the man and woman. Although, well, I confess, I'd like to assist him if I can. If he is truly Brihtwold's brother, then I owe them that much.

'And that man there needs to be avoided.' I nod towards Heardlulf.

'Your handiwork?' Wulfheard mutters, his eyebrows high.

I nod, but I'm looking at my Mercian allies and realising that they don't wear their usual clothes, but cloaks that allow them to blend in easily. Unlike me, their cloaks are fastened with plain silver, or probably iron, brooches. It would have been good if someone had mentioned that the brooch I use to keep my cloak in place is of a particularly Mercian design. It would have helped a great deal.

'And I need to go and meet someone.'

'Yes, yes, whatever, just get Cuthred, and whoever's with him, and meet us in the stables. I'll have a little chat with your friend over there.' Despite the press of bodies, a passageway seems to open up for Wulfheard and he easily diverts Heardlulf.

Cenred has moved towards Cuthred. The boy jerks upright and then, with a warning hand on his shoulder, settles once more, although his eyes seek me out across the space between us, confusion in them.

With Oswy standing beside me, it's not as if Cuthred can doubt Cenred's words.

'Come on then.' I dip my head and begin to force my way to the doorway, against the press of tightly packed bodies. I think I'm going to make it. Wulfheard and Heardlulf are talking, with some animation on Heardlulf's part. I consider what Wulfheard says to him, I assume with a Wessex twang. But I don't much mind provided Heardlulf doesn't see me.

I was fearful when I was one of only two Mercians within Winchester, but now there are five of us. I feel as though we're even easier to identify despite the others changing their dressing habits to blend into the Wessex populace.

It doesn't help that, no matter what we do, all of us, apart from

Cuthred, have the build of warriors. Here, amongst farmers and traders, artisans and bakers, we look like what we are. Warriors. We eat well and train often – unless we're all blacksmiths or woodspeople, we have no real reason to be as big as we are.

I try and make myself smaller, once more huddling inside my cloak, aware that Oswy isn't directly behind me but instead follows on, attempting to appear to a casual observer as though we're not together.

We're nearly at the door when Heardlulf looks up, meets my eyes and glowers at me.

'That's him,' he calls. Heardlulf's no longer alone. I offer him a smile, and see where Wulfheard expels a long breath so that his shoulders sag. Then all hell breaks loose.

Heardlulf has brought at least six men with him. One of them, I notice, is the warrior I spoke to within the church. Damn the bastard. Beneath their sodden cloaks, they're armed with seaxes, war axes and swords. They didn't come here with the intention of making peace. Whatever it is about Bicwide, or whatever it is they think I've done to Heardlulf's brother, they mean to leave me with some pretty injuries.

'Hurry up,' Oswy urges me. He's right to do so. Here, in a room filled with people sheltering from the rain, isn't the place to have a great big, bloody fight.

I hasten my steps, trying not to smack people with my sack of weaponry, even while I skirt around them. People lying on the ground, taking a nap, are jostled awake as I run over them.

Ahead, I can see the doorway. People have become alert to the fact that something's not right. While a few still try and push their way inside, most have stopped. And indeed, some of them are quickly trying to make good their escape. If I were them, I'd prefer the rain against the potential trouble brewing inside the tavern.

I'm preparing to rush through the doorway only for it to crash shut in front of me. I all but plough into it, just coming to a stop before I'm impaled on the seax blade of the three warriors who stand there. That means that Heardlulf has nine men. There are five of us, and one of that number is Cuthred, who can chop garlic cloves with great skill, but not defend himself from an enemy Wessex warrior.

'Damn,' I mutter, backing away slowly. I allow my hand to drop into my sack, which has remained closed all this time. The two cuts on my back throb, but it's not enough to stop me from fighting.

My hand grips a hilt, no doubt my seax. I pull it forth, eyeing the men before me. Oswy's joined me. It's a relief to know he'll fight at my side. Heardlulf only bettered me because I remained unarmed when we fought. The same won't apply this time.

'I want my brother's horse.' Heardlulf stalks from where Wulfheard's been delaying him. He sounds furious and nasal, from where I punched him.

'I told you, we paid a good price for him.' From somewhere close by, Cuthred's words ring with more conviction than my seax. He's a brave lad. He really is.

'You killed my brother and stole his damn horse.'

I meet Wulfheard's gaze, where he follows Heardlulf towards me. I can see what he's thinking. In the heart of Wessex, far from home, I've managed to pick a fight over a bloody horse. Perhaps I should have just let them have the horse, but that would have aroused even more suspicions. I'm sure of it.

'A hundred pennies,' Cuthred counters quickly. Again, I admire him for standing up to the Wessex warriors, even if Heardlulf looks less than fearsome with his broken nose.

'I want to know where my brother's body is,' Heardlulf counters.

Now Cuthred shrugs and shakes his head. 'Ask the woman who sold us the horse, you damn arse.'

Heardlulf's on Cuthred in less than a blink of an eye, his hand snaking out to grab his tunic and try and pull him close. Cuthred bucks backwards, and by then, I've had enough.

I pivot into Heardlulf, my seax blade facing down, but in no time at all, it's prodding at Heardlulf's back. I can smell his foul stink.

'Put him down,' I growl, keeping my voice low, trying to mask my accent.

'Make me,' Heardlulf defies belligerently. The sourness of ale on his breath greets my words. I close my eyes briefly, aware of all those close by. There's no way to do this without injuring others. I meet Cuthred's glower. It's fiery and filled with fury.

'He'll do it,' Cuthred cautions Heardlulf. 'And he's a bloody better warrior than you are,' he squeaks as Heardlulf's grip grows tighter and tighter. I can see where he pushes his blade closer and closer to Cuthred's face. Cuthred's almost cross-eyed with looking at it. All sound in the tavern has died away. Everyone holds their breath.

'Have it your way.' I hope Cuthred's caught my look and that Wulfheard knows what to do. I thrust my head forward to knock into the back of Heardlulf's even as my seax runs around his midriff, front to back. I don't force it as deep as I can, just enough of a score, like my back, that'll be itchy and uncomfortable as it heals. If he has the skills to keep it clean it won't kill him.

Wulfheard's there to grab Cuthred and pivot him out of the way while Heardlulf roars with fury, his weapon clattering to the ground. He rounds on me, fists ready to punch.

His thrusts are heavy, impacting my chest but not my face. I defend with my seax, as well as my left fist, purposefully aiming for where I've wounded him, a thin line of blood already staining his tunic, running from his back to his belly. I think he'll give in. I believe it'll only be a matter of a few moments before I have my blade at his throat and can bring this to an end. The damn arse. Cuthred was right to name him as such.

Heardlulf repeatedly punches. As he does so, I watch Wulfheard move to shoulder his way through the collection of warriors blocking the door, but it seems they're all arses in Winchester.

They stand, weapons to hand, and while I counter Heardlulf's noticeably weakening jabs, Cenred joins Wulfheard. Pulling Cuthred behind them, they lay into the three men at the door. Any moment now, I'm expecting the others with Heardlulf to get involved, but they don't. Not yet.

Another slice of my seax over Heardlulf's face, and now his fattened nose is missing its tip. Blood pours down his face and into his mouth. He breathes wetly into my mouth.

'Hurry up,' Oswy complains.

'I'm trying to ensure only he gets hurt,' I huff, trying not to give away my Mercian accent as another of my blows knocks him sideways. He careers onto a wooden table with a loud shriek of wood over the floorboards. He spits blood into the face of one of the women drinking her ale. Her scream pierces the silence broken only by the thud of flesh meeting flesh. Suddenly, everyone's panicking.

I kick out. Heardlulf's balance fails him again. I don't want to gut him like a fish, but he's being particularly belligerent about accepting defeat.

I jab my elbow into his face. His blade wavers before my eyes, I imagine, because he can't see very well. But that's not going to stop him. I feel a burn on my left arm and realise he's torn a hole through my new tunic. Now I've had more than enough.

I advance on him with quick steps. He progresses to meet me.

'I didn't kill your damn brother. And I paid for his bloody horse,' I counter.

His eyes narrow. His mouth opens. I fear I know exactly what he'll say. With my efforts, I've forgotten to moderate my accent to ensure I sound as though I don't come from Mercia. Wulfheard and Oswy have managed to cover their origins much better.

'Bloody hell,' I glower, coming ever closer. His mouth opens again, blood-filled. He sucks in a deep breath, his seax once more coming for my face. I let it. I can't have him shouting to his allies.

A rush of rain-scented air assures me that Cenred and Wulfheard have the door open. I just need to finish this. Then, we can pay our dues to the tavern keeper and be gone from here before anyone else knows I'm Mercian.

'M—' The single letter forms, but my seax is in his mouth, stabbing down, while his blade scores my face.

With my blade in his mouth, he can't speak, although he tries to, his mouth opening and closing, his thin lips hot on my hand so that I grimace. As the letter 'e' comes forth, I ram my blade even deeper, until his eyes close and his hot breath expels, hot on my hand, but the last sound he's ever going to make.

I pull my seax free. I turn, aware Oswy's beside me, while the others have gone. I look at the shocked faces of those inside, of the men who said they stood with Heardlulf but have done nothing to assist him. I glower.

'I bought the damn horse from a horse trader in Southampton.' I put all my effort into sounding West Saxon, not Mercian. With a thud of coins onto the table where the bloodied woman has finally stopped shrieking, I turn and scamper into the deepening gloom.

'Well, that went well,' Oswy offers conversationally as he runs with me to the stables. I grunt, mounting Bicwide, having flung his saddle over him. This horse has caused all that trouble, but I don't regret my decisions as I encourage him to follow the others into the rain-drenched night.

None of the three Mercians have their own horse. They've bought spares as well. As the rain sheets into my eyes, we hurry through the deserted, rain-soaked streets of Winchester.

It was never a good idea to come here. I should have said no to King Wiglaf, even though I am his oath-sworn man.

14

It's hard to see, with the rain stinging my eyes, but I follow Oswy, who appears to know where he's going. As with when we ventured to the Isle of Sheppey, I consider how often these men have been to Winchester before, if at all. If they'd previously made the journey, it would have been better for King Wiglaf to have sent them, not me. I've done nothing but stumble my way from one problem to another. And then I'm reminded of the conversation I heard between the woman and the man at the market. There's certainly something going on. And it's not all seaxes and warriors. There's political intrigue as well.

'Where are we going?' I huff to Oswy, when I manage to catch him and his borrowed horse.

'North,' is his only reply. The others stretch out ahead of me. We made our way, with some haste, to the gate, which I think must face the north. We were allowed to leave Winchester without any arguments from the guards, sheltering beneath the eaves of the gates, the ruins of the enclosing wall visible in the glow from their braziers. Perhaps if we'd hurried, allowing the horses to gallop through the streets, we might have aroused more suspicion, but Cenred, who led us, barely had the animals above a gentle trot.

'And what's north?'

'The road that leads to Canterbury?'

'What?' I feel my forehead furrow at that, but Oswy allows his mount to stretch his legs, despite the thudding rain. It's all I can do to get Bicwide to keep pace. He's no Brute, that's for sure, but he's not a bad horse. Out of practice from a winter spent eating in the stables, I imagine. I consider what befell Heardred, who once owned Bicwide. Perhaps it's better if I don't know. His brother believes I was involved. Why he'd think Heardred had been murdered, I'm unsure.

'Well, towards the River Thames first, but we're going to Canterbury,' Oswy clarified, no doubt so I'll shut up and just get on with our escape. Sometime later, we slow with the deepening advance of night. It won't be long, and we won't be able to see anything. I consider if we're being chased. I can't see any lit brands behind us, but if we're being followed, they're no doubt sensible enough not to use them.

'Why?' I query, recalling our earlier conversation about our destination, but then remember King Wiglaf's words to me when he tasked me with visiting Winchester. 'We're going to the meeting of the bishops?'

'That we are,' Oswy confirms, but there's no joy in his words.

'With Bishop Æthelweald and Bishop Heahbeorht?'

'With the Mercian bishops, yes, not just Æthelweald and Heahbeorht. We've been bid to protect them all, but we took a small diversion to come and get you first.'

'So, I'm not going back to Mercia?'

'Not yet, best to keep you where we can see you. Ealdorman Ælfstan believes you're in danger. If you're in Mercia and we're not, anything might happen to you.' The words are far from reassuring.

I consider why Wulfheard came to get me. Does he suspect his brother was in Winchester as well? Or, does he mean to undo all the harm his brother's caused? I wish he'd speak to me about Wulfnoth. He needn't fear I'll think any less of him. After all, as I now know, my father was a treasonous bastard.

I've done little but add to the tangled web of lies and deception. But still. The woman and the man at the cloth stall. I keep thinking of their conversation and how Wulfnoth's name was mentioned. And Eamont. It can't be a coincidence.

Eventually, we emerge onto what seems to be a more permanent and well-built road.

'This'll take us towards the River Thames,' Wulfheard announces, bringing the line of riders almost to a stop.

Cuthred, eyes wide, looks from me to Wulfheard. I can sense the man and woman he thought to help doing the same. The man's doubled over, certainly in pain, and the woman looks scared and angry. Yet I can't help suspecting her after I saw her watching me in the tavern with such an appraising gaze. I suspect she knows me. I feel we need to keep the pair close. Perhaps it wasn't happenstance that they came to Cuthred's attention. I've not actually asked him how he realised the man's plight.

'You said you'd help us,' she directs to Cuthred, the words flecked with fury. 'Not that you'd kill him more quickly by having him rush into a bloody storm.'

'We can help him,' I interject. 'Or, I think we can. We just need to stop somewhere, and then Cuthred can examine him.' I don't add that I'll be helping him. It's better if she hates me rather than Cuthred. It's better if I keep her attention on me and make the promise. I think we can keep it, but whether we can or not, I want her close.

'You're Mercians?' the man puffs, his words laboured. This is the first opportunity he's had to voice his concerns on our dash from Winchester.

'We are, yes, what of it?' His face is even more hate-filled than the woman's.

'A Mercian killed my brother, Brihtwold. Inside Londinium.'

'And a Mercian will heal you outside Londinium. Or you can die, as he did.' There's no sympathy in my words, even though it hurts to have my fears confirmed. I was responsible for his brother's death. But I can't tell him that. It does explain why the woman hates Mercians so much.

'I don't want you touching me,' he puffs angrily. I peer at Cuthred. He looks uncertain.

'Then you can stay here. We won't force you,' I offer more gently than I'd like. I don't intend to argue with them when we're escaping from Winchester in a hurry. I would sooner they stayed with us but Wulfheard answers before I manage to determine how to say what I'm thinking.

'You can keep the horses,' Wulfheard mutters.

'We don't want your damn horses,' the man cries through tight lips. I fear if I could see him better in daylight, they might be tinged with blue. He's not well, but it should be possible to help him. If he listens to anything that Cuthred and I have to say. 'Brihthild and I don't need your bloody pity.'

'Then leave them and walk back to Winchester. But if you tell anyone about us, we'll hunt you down and gut you like your brother.' I wince at the words, pleased that Wulfheard growled them.

'No, no, you said you could help him.' Brihthild's words are filled with worry now. No doubt she fears he'll die and leave her to fend for herself.

'And I can, Brihthild.' Cuthred's more assertive. 'He needs rest and to inhale certain herbs to heal.'

'And we can get these herbs anywhere?' Brihthild retorts.

'Perhaps, but you were the one in the church, praying for a miracle. That miracle can only happen if you use these treatments.'

'Then tell me about it, and I'll find someone who can provide them.'

Again, Cuthred looks uncertain, but I nod to show he should do so. I'm wary of my and Wulfheard's intentions towards them. They know we're Mercians. They know we've been in Winchester. They know we're heading towards Canterbury. I killed Heardlulf for having half of that knowledge. Will we really allow them to leave?

'You need to make a pottage. It should contain betony and white horehound, wild carrot, radish, wood sage, carline thistle, radish and celandine.'

'What?' Brihthild sounds furious as well as bewildered.

'You need to make a pottage,' Cuthred repeats more slowly, his eyes bright as he considers the problem.

'Stop, stop, I don't know what those things are. I mean, yes, I know what carrot and radish is, but the others?'

'Then seek a healer and tell them what to include,' Oswy counters aggressively. He's eager to press on.

'There are no healers who know how to treat him, not in all of Wessex. Don't you think we've tried? They said there was a man, in Winchester, but he died in Londinium, as well as my other brother.' Her words are bitter. I think of Ecgred. He was an evil bastard who would have done nothing to help her brother unless she'd had the money to pay him. 'You'll have to make it for us, and then we can let you go on your way without telling anyone about you.'

'You don't need to threaten,' I begin, but Oswy snarls low in his throat. I turn to him with a quelling look, which he ignores.

'Look,' Wulfheard counters. 'We sleep here tonight. We'll do whatever we can in that short time, and then in the morning, we go our separate ways. And if you do think of telling others of our presence here, then I can assure you, we'll hunt you down, and a slit throat can't be healed with any bloody herbs. Now, Cenred, you have the first watch, Icel the second, and I'll take the third. And don't try and do anything stupid during the night,' Wulfheard comments. 'We'll just kill you and think nothing of young Cuthred's wounded sensibilities.'

'Now wait a moment, we didn't ask.' The man speaks only to descend into a racking cough, and Wulfheard rounds on him.

'And neither did we. Now dismount and get on with caring for that horse and getting some rest. Cuthred has work to do.' Cuthred dismounts eagerly. His horse, head hanging low, picks at the few long grasses sprouting upwards. I follow him. I don't know if we have everything that's needed, but we can make some efforts to produce the healing pottage. The vapour needed will be more problematic. It needs to include incense, and out here it's not going to be possible to find any, although, if they came with us to Canterbury, it would be abundantly available. Not that it would be inexpensive. But nothing about the church is cheap.

I leave Bicwide with Cuthred's horse and go to his side. Cenred has already begun building a small fire just to the side of the road, beneath some sheltering branches overhead. The drumming of the rain is growing weaker, but in its wake a chill wind is blowing through, disturbing the rain-drenched leaves overhead so that cold splatters touch my face, chilling me all over again.

'What do we have?' I murmur to Cuthred. He looks at me for a moment without comprehension. I'm not surprised. It's been a very long day, filled with no end of peril.

'We have betony and wormwood, carline and some dried radish.'

'So, we need to find wild carrot and wood sage?'

'Yes,' he replies quickly, understanding what I'm asking. I'm impressed he has so many of the ingredients. But then, they're common enough, and Wynflæd was adamant he had everything we might need to treat, it would appear, any ailments from the yellow disease to a thorn stuck in our thumb. I shouldn't complain. I've already used the moss and some of the honey on my back. I should perhaps also do something about the cut on my left arm I received in the tavern fight. 'And horehound,' he quickly adds. 'We need horehound as well.'

'Then, I better look for them. You start the process. And I'll see what I can find.'

'I have more honey,' he confirms, as though I need the reassurance.

I nod and turn to make my departure.

'Don't go far,' Wulfheard cautions me, half an eye on the man and Brihthild. They've both dismounted with some groans and complaints. The man is almost bent double, coughing and spitting aside phlegm, which I imagine will be dark in colour.

'Make him a hot drink, and sweeten it with some berries,' I instruct Cuthred, but he's already busy with his task. Brihthild hovers closer to him. I can't see them well enough in the gloom to know her thoughts. I would be angry if I were her. But someone desperate enough to seek out a miracle in a church will surely be welcoming to spending time with healers, even if they're trying to evade the fight they started in Winchester. It's at moments like this that everyone reconsiders their thoughts about their enemy. If, as Brihthild says, no one in Wessex can save her brother, then it's unsurprising she'll accept the help of Mercians.

I move along the roadway, seeking out some hedgerows and places where the horehound might grow. It's really too early for horehound. It's a summer plant. But perhaps there might be some. It's also much too early for wood sage. I can't see we have much chance of finding any of the items that Cuthred doesn't have, but

I'll look all the same, using the light of the moon, when the clouds allow, to guide my steps through the damp undergrowth.

Perhaps, I reason, there might be some mint that would make a replacement for the horehound. I don't deny that it's frustrating. If Cuthred were at home in Tamworth, then these items would be available readily, if not fresh, then at least stored throughout the winter months in Wynflæd's vast array of clay pots.

I return to the small campfire with a collection of herbs in my hand. I've found a stray collection of wild carrots, flowering far too early, but not the horehound or wood sage. I have some substitutes. They'll suffice for now.

I stroll towards Cenred, who stands, face in shadows, his cloak wrapped around his body, as I smell pottage cooking and hear the soft murmurs of Oswy and Wulfheard. It's clear they're arguing, but about what, I'm unsure. No doubt they're angry with me. Not, I think, that this is all my fault. Well, not all of it.

'Here,' I offer to Cuthred. He nods his thanks. In the glow from the fire, he sets to work adding the items to the pot he already uses. We don't have butter, so we can't complete all of the recipe for the pottage, but we're working with what we have.

The man has subsided into a tired heap, alternating between snoring and coughing. He's sitting almost upright, my sack behind his bag. I remember then that I have my seax in there, and it needs cleaning, the blood of Heardlulf still stuck to it. It'll give me something to do when I'm on guard duty later. Brihthild continues to glower at me as she hovers close to Cuthred, watching all that he does, and when not watching him, glaring at me.

'Well, isn't this pleasant?' Oswy offers sarcastically as we shovel hot food into our mouths a short while later. 'I've always liked eating outdoors at this time of year.' I meet his blazing eyes and wince away from them. 'And in such pleasant company as well.'

'Shut up,' Wulfheard growls. I sense Brihthild tense, reaching out to grab the man's hand, for all he's asleep once more.

'What's his name?' I ask her.

'None of your damn business,' she counters.

'Who is he, your husband, your lover?'

'All you need to know is that he's my brother, you bloody oaf,' she counters angrily. 'The only member of my family left to me. Brihtwold, my other brother, was killed fighting the Mercians. Fighting you.'

I try not to think about that too much. Brihtwold died poorly. He should have had a better death. I doubt she actually knows I had a part to play in Brihtwold's death. She means 'me' as in the Mercians.

'So, you live in Winchester?'

'No, we travelled there from the southwest, from close to Exeter.'

'For the miracles?'

'Hah,' she growls again. 'It wasn't much use to him, was it?'

'You met us?' I offer, and Brihthild grumbles again and lapses into silence.

Cuthred has been busy in my absence. Now he adds some more items to the separate pottage he's cooking for the ill man. I watch him. His movements are careful and precise, his tongue poking through his lips. I see so much of myself in him that it hurts. He shouldn't be here, but all the same, he's focused on what he can do. Not what he can't do.

Eventually, the man is woken and encouraged to eat Cuthred's concoction.

He does so eagerly, but then his eyes cloud.

'This is just pottage.'

'A healing one,' I reiterate. 'It's not just meat and onions, I assure you.'

I think he'll argue with me, but instead, he resumes scooping it into his mouth. He's desperate to live.

Only when everyone has eaten, and Cenred is standing his guard watch, do Oswy and Wulfheard direct me away from the camp. I've been curious to know more about Oswy's caution to me, perhaps now I'll find out what I need to know.

'A bloody mess,' Wulfheard begins. His eyes gleam in the bright moonlight. The clouds have thankfully been blown away, taking the rain with them, but it's still cold.

'The king,' I begin, determined to defend myself.

'I know what the king wants you to do. And I agree with it. But the king doesn't act alone. He thinks he does, but he doesn't.'

I narrow my eyes at that and wait for him to say more.

'The queen has spies everywhere. She knows what the king intends. And she doesn't want Lord Coenwulf to return to Mercia. She fears that if he does, the king will grow even more distant from her. She's a desperate woman.'

'So, she means to prevent me from succeeding in discovering the truth?'

'I'm not sure of her intentions or of those surrounding the king. Ealdorman Sigered is a problem as well. The king shouldn't have permitted his wife and his son to determine Lord Coenwulf's punishment. He resents it, yet he shouldn't have allowed such half-cocked evidence to sway him. He has enemies everywhere, and this problem of Lord Coenwulf's children is only part of that.'

'So, the ealdorman sent you here.'

'Sort of,' Wulfheard admits, and now I eye him, aghast. 'The ealdorman bid us accompany the Mercian bishops. We might have taken some other elements upon ourselves. I have my reasons for wanting to ensure this matter is resolved. The rest of the war band are with the bishops,' he adds as though that makes it acceptable. I realise he's talking about his brother. Does Wulfheard feel responsible for Wulfnoth's actions?

'What happens now?' I query.

'We go to Canterbury. Pretend none of this ever happened.'

'But I have no proof for King Wiglaf of whether or not Eadbald went to Winchester. All I know is that Wulfnoth did.'

'Then he'll have to be strong enough to recall Lord Coenwulf without it,' Wulfheard counters, not seeming to notice I mentioned his brother.

'But...' I pause, considering, and then resume. 'There's something happening. I overheard a conversation in Winchester. They named your brother. A man and a woman, in the marketplace, they mentioned him by name, and before you tell me the name isn't unusual, I also found mention of Eamont in the church. He left his name and a large donation of a hundred pence, Wulfnoth of Eamont.'

'What was that bastard involved in?' Wulfheard growls, running his hand through his hair in frustration. I realise I'm right. Wulfheard might have allowed me to leave Kingsholm to go to Winchester, but the reason he's here now isn't just because he fears for my life. He wants to know as well. I can sympathise with that. 'Wait, so what, you think someone in Wessex is involved as well?' His shocked words reflect my thoughts.

'Why else would they speak of him in Winchester?'

Wulfheard paces from side to side while Oswy watches on, arms folded over his chest, his foot tapping on the wet ground. I can tell neither of them are happy about this.

Wulfheard glances over my shoulder, and I sense someone's there. His hand reaches for his weapons belt. I wish my blades weren't in the sack but in my hand. His breathing slows, his body relaxes, as a figure emerges out of the gloom.

The eyes are hooded, a cloak covering much of them. Unintentionally, I take a step back and then recover myself. I'm not a child any more to shy away from a possible fight, even if my back and left arm sting from the earlier attack.

The single figure isn't alone. I'd gasp with shock, but somehow it makes sense that these men have trailed us from Winchester. We've hardly ridden as hard as we can. Instead, we've taken it somewhat easy, just keen to reach the road that runs towards the River Thames before darkness made it impossible to go further. We relied on the rain to prevent others from following us.

'I told you I wanted to speak to you,' is aimed at me. It comes from the man I spoke with in the church. 'I want that horse.'

'But Heardlulf's dead,' I counter, remembering his explanation in the church. 'Why do you still need his brother's horse?'

'You don't need to know that now, do you, my annoying Mercian friend. Give me the horse, and this can all go away.'

I don't relish the thought of another fight, but I've grown strangely fond of Bicwide. I've no intention of allowing him to fall into enemy hands. Whatever it is they want with him, and I don't understand what it can possibly be, he's mine. I paid for him with Wessex coins. He belongs to me. These men can't take what's mine. Yes, it might be more sensible to hand him over, but I'm in the middle of Wessex. I don't believe sensible is an option any more.

'I don't think so,' Wulfheard interjects. I'm unsure why Cenred hasn't warned us of the Wessex warriors. I spare a thought for him and hope he's not dead. 'We need the horse.'

'We need it more,' the man counters. It would be good to know his name. It's evident that he leads these men. I don't miss that he no longer stands as though he's merely a warrior. He commands here. I wish I'd realised that earlier.

'Sadly,' Wulfheard huffs, 'he's not for sale.'

'Then we'll take him from you.' And with that, the figures move into the gloom, lit only by the moon and stars overhead.

I look to Wulfheard and Oswy and spare a glance back towards the rest of our party. I hope Cuthred's holding his own. Perhaps he knows to keep his mouth shut.

And then a blade flashes through the air, an opportunistic throw, but one that has me shouting. I reach for my weapons belt, only to remember I don't have it. It's going to be fists and feet, I realise.

Oswy rumbles with anger, seax and war axe to hand, as he meets the attack of the Wessex commander. The two are of similar height.

Wulfheard, on the other hand, faces two men, both armed with seaxes and shields. I feel as though I've brought nothing but a feather to the fight, and it won't end well.

Hastily, I glance down and spy the only thing to hand, and not really something I think a warrior should use, but fists and a rock will kill as well as a seax. Momentarily, I remember the fight in the woodlands when my uncle lived and how one of those Viking raiders died, hitting himself with one of the rocks. Let's hope this is as simple as that.

The warrior who comes towards me growls low in his throat and has a white beard that assures me he's a skilled man even before he tries to jab at me. I can hear Oswy and Wulfheard's impacts on the shields of those who fight them. My warrior has a shield. He holds it loosely, his eyes on my curled fists.

'It would be easier to hand the horse over, you Mercian scum,' he mutters, his tone belying the intent behind his words.

'It would, yes, but the horse is mine,' I counter, readying myself, both hands fisted, although the one holds the heavy stone.

He thrusts his seax towards me. While I jab, I withdraw my

right hand quickly. I don't want to dent my knuckles on his wyvern-daubed shield.

Oswy's swinging his seaxes as though he were a windmill. I'm not sure it's having any effect other than to wear him out. But my foeman's shield hits my arm, and I'm recalled to the fight. I move backwards, mindful I can't see the ground well enough to ensure I don't put my foot down an animal burrow. The shield sends a judder along my arm. I snap my mouth closed to prevent biting my lips.

I step to the side and aim a blow at the man. He's quick, for all he's white-bearded and older than many men I've met in my life. I'd hoped age might have slowed him down, but it hasn't.

His seax jabs out now. I feel a cut on my right arm. This damn tunic wasn't worth the money I paid for it after all. It's ripped in more places than my old one. A shiver of fury has me punching with my left fist, trying to land a blow on his nose or under his chin, but he's swift. He dances out of my way and knocks my hand aside with the shield. Now it's bleeding and it bloody hurts as well.

He wears a helm, byrnie and has a shield. I have a tunic, a damn stone and my fists. But he thinks he's going to win, and I have the confidence of knowing that I probably won't. And this is all over a damn horse. I consider why they want the horse so badly, they'll kill for it. I aim my left hand with the stone in my palm at his helm. It hits with a resounding thud. The man staggers from side to side, but he's far from down although it knocks his helm askew.

'Crafty bastard,' he glowers, showing me his grimacing mouth, which is missing quite a few teeth. He might yet live, but he's lost fights in his time. Just not ones that would have led to his death.

He's angry. He jabs and stabs, using his shield and seax as though they were fists. I dance backward and sideways and even get so close to him that he can't get enough force behind the action to jab out with his shield. I manage to punch through his guard and feel the crack of his nose, but then his seax is against my belly. He's not stabbed me, but again, I feel the burn of a cut as I move out of the way.

It feels like when I fought Eadweard and his allies. It's almost impossible for me to win, but I did live through that attack. I plan on doing so again. I'd welcome a blade, but Oswy and Wulfheard are busy. Whatever Cuthred and Cenred are doing, they're not coming to help, which has me worrying they've already been apprehended or, worse, killed.

A shrill neigh fills the night air. We all pause, looking towards the sound. Do they already have Bicwide? But it seems not. The thunder of his hooves is the first indication that he's as angry as we are. The sound of his crashing approach resounds, birds taking flight and other small animals scurrying away, but so far, none of us has moved. It's difficult to know what direction Bicwide's taking. He's certainly coming closer and closer.

I look to the warrior and, resolved to not knowing what Bicwide's doing, he resumes his swinging. I lift my left hand, stone showing to defend against his seax strike. The two weapons meet with an uncomfortable grating sound. I feel the scrape of his blade on my wrist but no hot burn of blood. I punch with my right hand, not straight towards him, but rather under and upwards. I get behind the guard of his shield and into the hardness of his belly, although much of the force has gone from the attack by the time it reaches him. All the same, he seems to lift upwards, his face coming ever closer to mine. I use my forehead to smack his face. His helm's entirely reversed now, the chinstraps either failing or not secured in the first place. The sound of Bicwide's screaming is ever closer.

I pause, listen, and hit out with the stone to the side of my enemy's face. This time, I know I've struck him, as his cheek erupts alongside his nose. There's no time to take advantage of my advance because Bicwide's arrived. First, one of his giant hooves appears beneath the undergrowth, and then the rest of him follows. It takes all of my physical prowess to jump aside, and grip his flowing mane. I'm on his back and advancing into the press of the other warriors before I can even think about turning him.

The unmistakable crack of broken bones and a cut-off shriek of terror assure me that Bicwide has been deadlier than I've been. Using my knees, I bring him under control, turning him so that he can once more run through our enemy.

I thought they'd have moved, but three of the men are rooted in place. Bicwide rides through them, the splinter of broken bones making me wince. But not everyone is dead. Oswy still fights, as does Wulfheard, although Oswy has only one foeman now.

I'm panting heavily, looking at the man who's sprawled on the floor, a hoof-shaped hole in his belly visible in a slant of moonlight. I reach down to rub my hand over Bicwide's shoulder, my legs springing forward, and it's then that I realise what it is the horse carries, and these men are so desperate to find. Or rather, I know where it is.

15

I don't even look at the dead men but instead direct Bicwide back to where we left Cuthred, Brihthild and her brother. Oswy has his enemy on his knees. Wulfheard will be victorious soon. The three of them – the man's awake as well – watch me as I arrive, fear etched onto the pale faces of Cuthred and Brihthild.

'I sent Bicwide,' Cuthred hiccups in fear.

'My thanks. But where's his saddle?'

Cuthred clearly doesn't expect my response. For a moment, I think he won't answer. I can't see well, what with the glow from the fire and the darkness closing around us.

'There,' and he points. 'Why, are we going?' I can hear him moving towards me. I shake my head and then realise he can't see it.

'No, but I need to check something.'

I run my hand along the saddle, feeling for what I hope is there. When the trader in Southampton sold me the horse and his saddle, she ensured these men would come after me. Not by telling them of my presence but rather by including the saddle in the sale price. Provided what I think is here actually is, then it won't matter. A few cuts. A few bruises. None of us are dead, and many of them are, and we still might find what they were seeking. I thought his saddle was uncomfortable, but I didn't examine it carefully. Now I do.

The saddle's well constructed, padded in places and stinking of horse and my sweat. It's far from pleasant. Bicwide stays at my side. His chest rises and falls too quickly. He needs to catch his breath. Then I'll let him drink and eat again. But not yet.

My fingers quest all along the leather of the saddle. Whoever Heardred was, he was either wealthy or had someone wealthy who kept him. I imagine it was the latter.

I hear footsteps in the undergrowth but don't need to look to know Oswy's returned. That reminds me.

'Where's Cenred?'

'He went that way, there was someone there.' Cuthred points in the opposite direction to where the fight took place. I need to check Cenred's well, but then I feel it. My hands close around two items. I smile in delight, even while I curse myself for a fool for not realising sooner. No wonder, I realise, the saddle was so bloody uncomfortable.

From the pockets beneath the main part of the saddle, where my arse has been sitting, I pull out two items, one is hard, the other crinkles. I think it's the crinkly bit I want, but the hard rock might be valuable.

'Where's Cenred?' Wulfheard booms, arriving as well, as I turn Bicwide and take him back towards the fire. I hold the vellum tightly in my hand. Its texture is surprisingly smooth. I wish it were light enough to see by.

'He went that way,' Cuthred repeats.

'What are you doing, Icel?' Wulfheard's words are filled with exasperation.

'I've found what they're so desperate to get their hands on,' I offer, holding out what I've found. He nods, but he's not as happy about it as I am.

'We need to find Cenred,' he urges me and Oswy. Oswy's breathing is laboured, I realise.

'They're all bloody dead,' Wulfheard complains, just as another voice calls to us.

'I'm here.' Cenred stamps into the clearing. Even in the darkness, I can tell he's furious.

'Bastards tricked me,' he complains, rubbing one hand over his arm. 'I missed all the fighting.'

'I doubt that, from looking at you, but never mind. They're all dead, as I said. Now, Icel, what have you found?'

I hand the vellum over to Wulfheard and the heavy stone as well. Wulfheard's interested in the stone. I eye Cenred. He has some cuts but nothing that's life-threatening. I'm surprised anyone got close enough to land a blow on his cheek.

'It's amber,' Wulfheard speaks, holding it towards the fire. 'I'm sure of it. A great lump of amber. That'll be worth a few horses,' he chuckles. He peers at the vellum too, getting closer and closer to the flames. His face clouds. He meets my eyes.

'This is a letter sent to Lord Ecgberht.'

'The king of Wessex?' I exclaim.

'So it seems. I don't know of many other lords of Wessex. And it details all they're going to do to kill the children of Lord Coenwulf, and how much they expect to be paid for it.'

'But he never received it.' I can feel my forehead furrow at this new revelation.

'No, clearly the payment of amber wasn't enough to make sure the previous owner of this horse made it safely to the king's side. Unless the amber was from the king to whoever this letter came from.'

'So, who killed him?' I'm astounded that this conspiracy is so far-reaching. I suspected Mercia's queen, as it seems does Ealdorman Ælfstan, but if Wessex's king is involved as well – well, what has Lord Coenwulf done to earn himself so many enemies?

'Who's it from?'

'It doesn't say, but look, the way they write that marks them as a Mercian.'

I peer over Wulfheard's side, but it's not easy to read in this light. But I'm happy to take his word for it.

'I think we have your proof, Icel, but it also means that while those Wessex warriors are dead, their deaths won't go unnoticed.'

'We should return to Mercia,' Cenred's quick to announce. I sense that Oswy thinks the same.

'But we'll be followed back to Mercia, I'm sure of it, and that will put the children in danger once more. Lady Ælflæd's warriors guard the children while we're absent. Ealdorman Ælfstan believed the risk was to Icel, not the children. But, this conspiracy is far from over if these Wessex warriors were seeking this letter and the amber. There will be others as well. If we keep it in Wessex, then the threat remains here. No, we resume our intentions of travelling to Canterbury. Perhaps this Mercian traitor will show their hand, or we'll find even more proof of what the Wessex king was involved in.'

'What's happening?' A harsh snap recalls us all to the presence of Brihthild and her brother. I hope they've not heard what we've been saying about the amber and the letter.

'Nothing. We won't have any more problems with the Wessex warriors,' Wulfheard reassures.

How Brihthild feels about Mercians killing more West Saxons isn't clear. Instead, her brother coughs and Cuthred hastens to his side, reminding us all of why Brihthild and her brother are with us. But Wulfheard beckons me closer.

'Icel, we still need to work on your strength.' His words don't dismay me. I know he's correct. 'Every day, we train and we compete, and hopefully, you'll be able to fight with more than just a bloody stone next time we encounter some West Saxon bastards.'

* * *

Cenred sleeps, and I take the middle watch, as Wulfheard ordered before the fighting. We've ensured the dead are just that and taken from them what we can use. I've also safeguarded that I have my warrior's belt, byrnie, seax and other weapons returned to me from the sack upon which the Wessex man was resting his head. I'm not going to be caught out again. He murmurs his name to me as I do so. 'Brihtwulf.' I nod my thanks, while Brihthild relieves herself in the darkness. I consider Wulfheard's words. I don't deny I shudder to hear them. If he's noticed how weak I am, then the others will have done so as well. I resolve to build my strength. I will become the warrior I used to be.

In the near distance, we can hear the nicker of horses, no doubt left by the riders, but we leave them for now. Wulfheard has the lump of amber and the vellum. He's welcome to them. I know that if I held them, I'd spend the night trying to determine more information from them. But a lump of amber has no way of speaking to me. The written note, unless I recognise the handwriting, is no good to me either.

I feel once more as though we have only half the answers. I came to Wessex to see if Eadbald had ever been to Winchester, but I'm leaving with the unnerving feeling that perhaps he did come to Winchester. Perhaps he was sent on Lord Coenwulf's orders, but not for the intention implied. Perhaps Lord Coenwulf knew of the conspiracy surrounding his children. Maybe the queen's hatred of him isn't just directed at his children.

The thoughts keep me awake even when I should be sleeping through the third watch. In the morning, my head pounds with lack of sleep, my fists hurt from where I used them to pummel our enemy and my back twinges from where the skin is already starting to heal. That doesn't even include the small cuts I have on both arms. I make no mention of my weakness.

I'm not alone in being in a foul mood. Wulfheard grunts and glowers at all, and even Oswy is out of sorts, nursing a livid bruise to his face and also some grazes on his left leg. Cuthred's quick to offer his assistance. I take what I need, ensuring Wulfheard doesn't see what I'm doing. If Cuthred notices my furtive movements, he makes no mention of them.

We make our way to the dead, their pale faces judging us. I remind myself that they wanted to kill us and that, sometimes, the only way to live is to kill. It's not an easy justification when I'm always so much more eager to heal people. But it's the life I've now chosen, no matter my regrets when I watch Cuthred and his assured skills in helping others.

Cuthred also asks Wulfheard if he can look at the letter, and while he does that, Oswy, Cenred and I dig a large hole and throw the bodies into it, the cold, marbling flesh thudding with an unwelcome reminder that one day that'll happen to all of us. I realise my arms are shaking as I shove the soil aside and move the men. My weakness worries me.

The men had some good seaxes, swords and shields with them. While Wulfheard and Brihthild venture to investigate the horses, we pile together the supplies and add them to my now almost empty sack. Brihtwulf waits by the fire, a borrowed seax in his hand, should anyone think to attack him. To my eyes, he already seems better. He's not cured, but he's able to take deeper breaths, and the blue tinge around his lips has disappeared.

Admittedly, that could just be from not having to breathe the smoke of the many fires in Winchester that foul the air.

'Icel,' Oswy huffs to me as we fling the man I killed with the rock into the shallow hole. 'I really wish you were better at making friends.'

His words might normally have me cracking a smile, but my head continues to pound. Time and again, my thoughts return to the children of Lady Cynehild. With Ealdorman Ælfstan's men either here with me or escorting the bishops to Canterbury, I'm fearful for them all over again. Especially now I know to suspect the king of Wessex, and the queen of Mercia. Who, I think, doesn't want the children dead?

'Icel,' he repeats when I make no reply.

'What?' I glower, even as we retrieve another of the dead men, this one having been killed by Bicwide's rampage through the line of warriors. Bicwide himself is in need of a wash on his long legs. They're splattered with blood.

'You're a grumpy shit this morning,' he offers lightly, somehow cheering up thanks to my temper. I grunt, and he relents, his eyes glinting with amusement. 'I was telling you that Lady Ælflæd has trebled the guard at Kingsholm now that we've been brought south. I hear that Gaya and Theodore are also to be summoned to her side.'

Such news startles me from my doom-laden thoughts. 'Is that true?' I question him. I asked Wynflæd to get Theodore and Gaya to help her while Cuthred was absent. I'll berate her for that oversight when I see her next.

'Why would I lie to you?' he queries, and another body hits the ground. I'm sweating, and my tunic, which I've not changed, is little more than thread and stitches now. I'd welcome a bath in warm water and not the stream that beckons to me and from which we've all been drinking. I'd also be grateful to have some time to rest my weary body.'

'I'm just surprised,' I counter.

'Well, the lady's taking the safety of her nephews and son seriously. She's banished the queen from visiting. She says the woman upsets all the boys.'

'The queen, tell me, you used to be her special guard.'

Oswy nods. I've not asked him about this before because he was unhappy about it, but perhaps now is a good time to learn more about her. 'I did, yes, she always demanded that the biggest warriors protect her.'

'Why, what did she fear?'

'No idea. Of course, she was never meant to be queen. She and her son were content on their estate, but then Wiglaf was elevated to the kingship, and she became queen. I can't say that she enjoys it.'

'Well, if she doesn't, she certainly ensures that others don't enjoy her being queen either.' I frown as I speak. The body we're moving has been attacked during the night. We've been forced to kick small creatures aside and a bloody huge blackbird. The buzz of flies is adding to my general feeling of needing to wash.

'She's always been conniving, as far as I can understand,' Oswy continues. We've just one more body to go, and Cenred's already moving away. I can hear Wulfheard and him in the distance. I wonder what we're going to do about all the horses. 'And, of course, she never liked Lady Cynehild. She and her son were always a bit too close to one another.' He shudders as the final body goes into the ground. I look down at those who're dead, remorse hardening as I eye them. These men meant to kill us. I have to remember that.

'Were she and the king ever happy?'

'No, not that I could tell. It was a political union, nothing else.

He had land and no title, and she had a title and no land, or so the servants told me.'

'And did she have any connection to Wessex? To King Ecgberht?'

Oswy pauses, wiping his hands on his arse, as I use one of the shields to scoop the earth over the bodies. 'I don't know the answer to that, not conclusively. But, she did speak of King Ecgberht with more than grudging respect in my hearing.'

'So, perhaps they did know one another.'

Again, he shrugs, and I'd demand he helps me, but while my questions are being answered, I hold my complaints. 'Her father, well, he held land in Berkshire.'

I perk up at this. This might mean something. 'But Wessex claimed that during the reign of King Beornwulf.'

'They did, yes. So, perhaps she did have contact with Wessex after all.'

The news isn't as surprising as it should be. I know, thanks to Wulfheard, that Mercia was once much larger than it is now, encompassing some Wessex-held territory. Perhaps then that's from where the connection comes, if there is one.

'How long does it take to bury ten men?' Wulfheard's querulous voice can be heard through the trees, and with a final glance to ensure we've gathered together all we wanted, we make our way back towards our camp. We've left foot marks, disturbed earth, and a stain over the woodland floor which means everyone will know there was a fight here, but at least they won't find the slowly decomposing bodies on display.

Back through the trees, I make straight for the stream and startle on finding so many horses drinking thirstily, even as I move downstream and plunge my naked body into the cold water. It just about covers me while Wulfheard looks on, exasperated.

'What will we do with them all?' I ask, surfacing and eyeing the animals. They're all high quality, the breeding easy to see in the firmness of their stances. One of the animals is particularly resplendent, no doubt the commander's horse, complete with a black coat darker than night, shimmering in the daylight.

'We'll take them with us. That way, we can pretend to be traders.'

'But, if men recognised Bicwide, then won't they also recognise these horses?'

'Perhaps,' Wulfheard muses. 'Maybe not. We'll see how we manage,' he offers, and I think he should give it more thought, but ten horses, without men to claim them, will fetch a good price. We could all be rich from this, or we could all have new horses. Not that I need any more. What with Wine, Brute and now Bicwide, I feel as though I gather horses as I do scars on my body.

'Come on then.' Cold but clean, I dress hastily, wearing my better tunic and consigning my purchased one to the sack for when we might need some rag for something. I mount up and realise that everyone has a good horse. Brihthild and Brihtwulf sit as well as they can, while Cuthred has kept his original horse, for all he could have chosen a better one.

The other horses are held in a loose line, their lead ropes tied one to another. They all have saddles, and some are marked with the twirling shape of the Wessex wyvern worked into the leather.

As one, we head eastwards, with Oswy and me keeping a guard to the rear and Cenred and Wulfheard to the front. Cuthred speaks to Brihthild, Brihtwulf is slumped in his saddle, for all he does seem better. Not that he was going to be healed with one bowl of pottage and a good night's rest.

Cuthred hands the piece of vellum to me, a gleam in his eye. 'I recognise the handwriting,' he informs me, and then rides away without telling me more. But I think he means for me to make my own decision, so I don't demand an answer but instead study the words.

They're blunt and to the point, for all the script is flowing.

My lord of Wessex. The children will be brought to Eamont. Payment to be made on arrival of fifty mancuses.

The words speak of a holy man and his education. The only slight reservation is that the message isn't written in Latin. Surely, a holy man would have used Latin as it would have been less easily read by anyone who discovered it. Although, perhaps this lord of Wessex can't read Latin. All the same, I'm astounded by the audacity of the plan. If we'd only known of this letter before, then we'd have understood the intentions of whoever is behind the failed attempt to take the children. Not, of course, that we knew to look for the answers in Wessex.

'Here, let me look.' Oswy reaches across and turns the vellum over, looking for answers on the side that shows no writing, as well as at the writing. 'I recognise the hand,' Oswy comments. I eye him. That's both Cuthred and Oswy who've said this. How might they both have seen someone else's handwriting? It's not as though Oswy spends time in the Mercian king's scriptorium or that Cuthred would be in there either. But Cuthred has been helping Wynflæd with Ealdorman Tidwulf's collection of remedies.

'Who?' I demand because I don't recognise the script, not even a little.

But Oswy's face has clouded. Instead of answering, he urges his horse to great speed, and makes his way along the line towards Wulfheard. I huff with annoyance, the vellum taken from me so that I can't even try and determine who wrote the letter fragment that survives.

I watch the two arguing frantically, as we make our way out from the trees and into the open. The river isn't close enough for us to hear, but the burbling sound of other streams is almost pleasant, for all the wind is biting now we're free from the cover of the trees. I keep alert, but I'm also brooding about this conspiracy against the children of Lord Coenwulf. Does it extend only to them, or do the conspirators also mean to direct their attention towards the son of Lady Ælflæd and Lord Wigmund? I recall something Wynflæd told me about King Offa and his need to remove all other potential claimants to the kingship. Is this what's at play here? In which case, who might have a good claim?

Of course, there's this Lord Beorhtwulf, perhaps related to my father, or perhaps not. Only a brave man would claim to be a relative of a failed, dead king, and yet it could still make Beorhtwulf worthy of consideration. There's Lord Wigmund, but I'd have expected his mother, the queen, if she's involved, to want to ensure his kingship and one way of doing that is to safeguard her son's life.

I consider, in the grand scheme of things, who has the better claim. Lord Wigmund, with his father currently king. Young Coenwulf and young Coelwulf, whose grandfather was king, as was their grandfather's brother. Or Lord Beorhtwulf, who some say claims descent from a man who ruled briefly between the reigns of Kings Æthelbald and Offa nearly eighty winters ago and might or might not have been related to my father.

Is there someone else that I don't know about? Other than me, of course. Did my father perhaps have a child with another woman? Am I his only son, or is there another? Or is it no one within Mercia at all but rather an attempt by the Wessex king to claim Mercia through other means than war? Might it even be King Athelstan of the East Angles? He's forged an alliance with King Wiglaf, but does he mean to keep to it?

My thoughts are interrupted by Cuthred.

'What's up with him?' He juts his chin towards where Oswy and Wulfheard continue to argue.

'He says he knows who wrote the letter,' I inform him. 'But, just as with you, he's not told me of his suspicions.'

'Ah, then I wonder if he says the same as me?'

'I wouldn't know,' I reply archly. I wish one of them would tell me.

'Now, Icel,' and Cuthred chuckles. 'There's no need for such ill feeling. I didn't tell you because I wanted to know what you thought.'

'Well, I have no idea. Why don't you tell me?'

'Very well, but first, did you notice the way the words were written? Not what they say, but how they're formed.'

'Tight and cramped,' I mutter. It's always the way. Vellum is too expensive to waste. Admittedly, the monks inside the church in Winchester had taken that to a great extreme. It was hard to make out much of the small writing.

'Yes, tight and cramped, but neat,' he confirms.

'And what does that mean?' I question when he says nothing further. Ahead, I can see we're coming close to a settlement, the smoke of the cookfires and forge starting to cloud the sky.

'It means that it was written by someone who knows minuscule,' he eventually states.

'Minuscule?'

'Ah, Icel, I thought you knew this. There are certain types of writing. Some minuscule, and some not. The other is even more cramped than minuscule.'

'And?'

'Minuscule is favoured by the Mercian king's scriptorium. Some monk, or holy man, created it at the court of Charlemagne, and King Offa thought the Mercians should adopt it as well.'

'And?' I wish he'd get to the bloody point.

'So, it must be one of the king's scribes or someone taught in the same way.'

'And?' Bloody hell, it's like pulling teeth.

'It means that the conspiracy originates in Mercia.'

'Or in Wessex, by someone who writes the Mercian way,' I counter, just to be argumentative.

'Ah, yes, I hadn't considered that.' His face clouds. 'But unlikely, not in the way they wrote some of the letters.'

'Cuthred, just tell me who wrote the damn letter.'

He huffs softly, and I think he'll continue filling my head with information I don't need to know. 'One of Bishop Æthelweald's scribes. A priest, called Heca.'

I shake my head. 'I don't know him.'

'But you would. He's known by another name much of the time. Brother Sampson.'

And now I do know who the man is. And I also know that not only is he one of Bishop Æthelweald's scribes, he also spends much of his time helping the queen with her correspondence.

'The queen again?' I murmur, and he nods.

'Yes, whether he wrote this for her or not, I don't know. But that's why Oswy recognises it. I'm sure of it. But don't tell him. Wait for him to tell you his thoughts.'

I nod. The queen. I've suspected her for so long, it's almost anticlimactic to have something else confirm her involvement. 'But with the Wessex king?'

'We don't know that was for the Wessex king. It was addressed to a lord of Wessex, not to the king.'

'No, we don't,' I admit. 'Perhaps Wulfheard jumped to that conclusion too quickly. But look at the horses. At Bicwide. If it's not the king, then it's someone with as much wealth at their fingertips and as great a reach. It must be the king, one of his ealdormen or one of the bishops.'

'Or his son,' Cuthred interjects softly.

His son. I'd not considered that. He already rules what was Mercian Kent and is now Wessex Kent. He's a warrior, like his father. I saw him in Londinium. I was brought before him to answer for Ecgred's complaints against me.

With the aroma of cooking meat and the distinctive sharp-edged metal smell in the air, we come closer to a settlement. No one pays us much heed, apart from a woman who calls to us. The dwelling she stands before stinks of ale. No doubt, she hopes to offer us food and drink on our journey. Wulfheard surprises me by riding towards her.

'Warm pottage?' he questions. She nods, licking her lips, which I note are dusted with fine hairs in the bright daylight. 'Then a bowl each for everyone here.' He indicates us with his arm. 'But we'll eat outside and just an ale each to accompany the meal.' I'm aware that Wulfheard speaks with a West Saxon accent. I wish I had the knack to converse as he does.

I dismount, as the others do, and lead Bicwide to a water trough. The huge animal drinks thirstily. When Wulfheard brings his horse over as well, I eye him quizzically.

'We need to act as though we're horse traders, remember? Horse traders would eat hot food where it's offered. Now, ensure the stock animals are well-tended.'

'But would horse traders be as well-armed as we are?' I ask him.

'Yes, we have valuable stock. It's only right that they're guarded.'

I arch an eyebrow and move aside. I notice then that Brihtwulf and Brihthild are speaking to the tavern keeper.

'Do we need to watch them?'

Wulfheard shakes his head.

I don't believe they know about the letter or the amber, but I'm unsure. More than once, I've been aware of Brihthild's interest in my discussions with Oswy and Cuthred. Not, I admit, that there's much else to do while riding.

'No, I've told them they can have four horses, provided we make it to Canterbury in one piece. That's more wealth than they've ever had before. It'll buy their allegiance, as will the promise that you can help Brihtwulf.' I hope that's enough to keep them loyal, but I don't question Wulfheard. It's my fault they're here. And it's my fault they know as much as we do. I wish I didn't feel guilty for Brihtwold's death, but I do. Even though he tried to kill me first, and I didn't make the lethal cut.

We eat hastily. We're back on the way just as another group of travellers arrives in the settlement. I eye them, but they're genuine traders. They have the look about them of Benedict and his companions. They have carts that bulge with odd-shaped sacks and wooden boxes as well.

I join Oswy, as he's not spoken to me during our stop.

'Who wrote it?' I ask him, without preamble. For a moment, I don't think he'll tell me, but then he does.

'Heca. I'm sure of it. Or Brother Sampson, whatever he chooses to call himself.'

Cuthred eyes me with a raised eyebrow as he hears the answers. They both agree on this.

'And who's he working for?'

'The bishop, the queen, the queen's son,' Oswy offers, his lips thin, showing his displeasure. 'It could be any of them.'

'The queen's son?' Is he involved as well? I want him to be, but I'm sure he lacks the political guile to plan the murder of his wife's nephews.

'The little runt will do anything his mother tells him to do. We know from Eadweard and his cronies, he thinks nothing of allying with the biggest arseholes there are.'

I nod.

'What does Wulfheard say?'

'He says not to tell you anything, Icel, and to keep quiet about it all until we reach Canterbury.'

I growl at that. I don't like being excluded. Admittedly, I do have too much invested in this. The children of Lady Cynehild are mine to protect. I've already shown that I'll risk death to do so.

I eye Wulfheard angrily. He rides ahead, gaze focused on the road we must take to reach Canterbury. I wish we were going back to Mercia, but we're not. Wulfheard has more on his mind than just young Coenwulf and Coelwulf. I consider those who died last night. Perhaps it would have been better to keep at least one of them alive. They might have known more. Although, maybe not. They were desperate to find the contents of Bicwide's saddle.

Aggrieved, I return to the rear of our line of horses. Oswy stays where he is, speaking with Cuthred. The day turns cooler, the wind springing up once more. I watch the swaying backs of the horses, the slumped shape of Brihtwulf, and then Brihthild is at my side. I startle, surprised to find her there without me noticing.

'Tell me, Icel, what do you know of healing?'

'As much as Cuthred.'

'And why is that when you're obviously a warrior?'

I allow a small smile. 'My destiny was to be a healer, not a warrior. But, I was left with no choice.'

'Will your lotions and potions truly help my brother?'

'They'll ease his difficulties, even if they can't entirely cure him. When we reach Canterbury, we should be able to purchase more of the correct supplies as well. At the moment, we have only some of the ingredients. Some are better than none, but all of them will be better yet. Then you can return to your home.'

She nods, but doesn't seem convinced by what I'm saying. 'Why are you helping us? You have much more to accomplish than mending one of your enemies.'

I'm not sure how to respond. I could tell her of my involvement in the death of her brother, but that wouldn't help matters. Not at the moment. Yes, a sliver of guilt gnaws inside my mind. 'I don't like to see people holding out for religious intervention when a little bit of knowledge could help those who are sick.'

'You don't think much of the church and its teachings?'

'I don't think much of its love of wealth,' I retort. 'I don't think much of its strictures that men, women and children should give more than they can afford when they're clearly wealthy enough.'

'And yet we're going to Canterbury? The birthplace of Christianity upon our island.'

'Yes, and you'll see for yourself how wealthy the bishops and archbishop are,' I snap. I'm pleased not to be talking of healing, but I don't wish to discuss religion, either.

She makes the sign of the cross as though to ward off evil, and I chuckle.

'I say my prayers,' I inform her. 'I have my faith, but there's a lot of difference between faith and the men and women who tell us what we must do.'

'Perhaps,' Brihthild admits.

I find myself drawn into her gaze. She's not much older than me, I don't think. Life has clearly been less than kind to her, evident in the ravages that mark her face – lines where there should be none. Not yet. There's something about her that makes her striking.

'Just as there are with those who rule us?' I think she taunts me. Or maybe she has no love for the Wessex king either.

'Maybe.' I can't say too much. I can't reveal who I really am. It's enough that she knows I'm a warrior and used to be a healer. She also knows my name and the names of Wulfheard, Oswy and Cenred. Whether or not four horses will be enough to buy her silence, I don't know. But it's Cuthred's fault that we have the two with us. Well, it's not. It's mine. If I think about it logically, it's truly King Wiglaf's, and Wynflæd's. He sent me here. And she made me bring Cuthred. But really, I know this is all my doing. I'll have to contend with the consequences.

16

As we make our way towards Canterbury, I find myself trying to decide whether I recognise where I am.

The roadway is liberally splattered with horse and ox shit. I consider where these people came from. One moment the roadway was only slightly covered in shit, the next it's almost impossible to sidestep it and I realise why we're catching them. They're moving at a much slower pace than our horses.

'The ford at Laleham Gulls,' Oswy offers, as though hearing my thoughts.

'If there was a bloody ford then why didn't we use it two summers ago?'

'The river was running too high. I don't know why. It should have been passable. It usually is in the summer months. And, anyway, it would have involved us going backwards to go forwards, so King Wiglaf might have discovered our intentions. And we'd have needed to spend a lot more time on Wessex soil,' he replies quickly. It explains a great deal.

A day later, the settlement of Londonia passes by to our left, shrouded in a haze of smoke. I can just make out the fort of

Londinium, its walls shimmering in the weak sunlight. We've spent enough time riding along the River Thames, looking for Viking raiders and Wessex warriors from the other side of the river. Now those landmarks come into focus more clearly. I'm surprised when, at the end of the fifth day from Winchester, we find ourselves not far from where we crossed the River Thames to save Lord Coenwulf. I consider how easy it would be to just go back to Mercia now but Wulfheard won't allow us to discuss it. He should be with the bishops, and now we must meet up with the Mercian bishops. I can understand his determination.

The memories of rescuing Lord Coenwulf have me considering my thoughts concerning our current endeavours. While we might not be rushing to liberate someone from Viking raiders, is what we're doing really any different? We're working to ensure Mercia remains safe from all her enemies. It's just unfortunate that this time, our enemies don't come with seaxes and blades but rather with scraps of vellum and lumps of amber and with access to people they shouldn't.

I wish I could be confident it was all the work of this lord of Wessex, or Mercia's queen, but I'm not convinced. There are already too many people involved, who shouldn't even know one another, let alone be trying to deprive Mercia of its future king when King Wiglaf is dead.

Brihthild and Brihtwulf keep much to themselves. His cough has eased with the continuing use of the pottage and other healing potions. He can sit more easily in the saddle. I don't miss the look both of them turn on Londinium. They know their brother died there. They just don't know who was responsible for it. They speak more to Cuthred than me, although he whispers to me at night if they say something he thinks I should know. I listen, but I'm tired and exhausted. Wulfheard has been true to his word. Each night before we sleep, he makes me fight him, or lift my shield four hundred times before me, or squat down to pick up weapons from the ground. He merely grunts at me. We've not spoken of anything else.

Wulfheard joins me at the rear of the line of horses. His eyebrows knit together. He's unhappy and uneasy.

'Icel,' he begins.

'Ah, you're talking to me now?' I growl. He reciprocates, his chest rumbling. Then we both look to one another, shrug our shoulders, and forget all that's gone before.

'We'll meet the others soon, I'm sure of it. They were leaving not long after us, and we've been following this trail of horse shit that must belong to them.'

'And what then?'

'I don't know. We need to determine what's truly being attempted. Now that Wulfnoth's dead, I don't know if the conspiracy is at an end. After all, your man Heardred's been dead for long enough that his horse has been sold. It might be that it's all over.'

'I doubt it,' I murmur. 'I can't imagine something of this magnitude being placed in the hands of only one man. And, if it were all over, then those we killed wouldn't have been so intent on reclaiming Bicwide.'

Wulfheard nods unwillingly. 'Which means we need to be alert to everyone at this bloody religious council they've called. It's a perfect opportunity for men and women to converse with those from other kingdoms. That's why I'm so determined to go to Canterbury. They should never have revoked permission for the archbishopric in Lichfield. Then we wouldn't have to worry about our bishops in enemy-held Kent, and we wouldn't be deep in Wessex-held land.' His anger thrums.

I only know of the attempts to found an archbishopric in Mercia thanks to Wynflæd and Wulfheard's many lessons.

'Surely it comes down to loyalty?' I counter.

He mumbles in agreement.

'For those who don't wear weapons and blades, an oath seems to be something that's more negotiable than forged in blood. Perhaps we should arm them all and let them fight it out?' I query, eyebrows high. He chuckles bitterly.

'Keep alert, Icel, keep alert. You seem to attract trouble like flame to wood shavings.' I could say the same about him, but I hold my tongue.

Later that day, a great cloud of churned dust assures us that the roadway is busy. We've passed trees and fields that I fear I know intimately. The roadway is tight, but the hedgerows that protected us two summers ago are yet to be filled with greenery, and instead bend and twist, the brown branches brittle, needing the sun and more rain to make them hardy.

Wulfheard rides ahead, with Cenred, the two of them determined to know who's in the advance now that we can see them. We wait behind, keeping to a steady pace, although we gain on those ahead.

'It's the Mercian bishops,' Wulfheard confirms.

'Is Bishop Æthelweald with them?'

Wulfheard nods. 'As well as Eadwulf of Hereford and Heahbeorht of Worcester. Rethun of Leicester has been delayed, or so they say.' Wulfheard's dour tone speaks of his unease. I agree with him. I don't find Bishop Æthelweald of Lichfield to be much of a friend to Mercia. He's only interested in one thing, and that seems to be himself. Eadwulf and Heahbeorht I know by sight. 'The rest of Ealdorman Ælfstan's warriors escort them alongside Commander Eahric and some of his men. We'll remain here for now. Kyre and Maneca are sharing the command and are content to continue to do so.'

I nod. I should find it more comforting to have so many more

Mercian warriors close by, but all I can think is that Mercia is currently denuded of many of its most accomplished fighters. The children of Lady Cynehild might well be protected by Lady Ælflæd's most loyal warriors, but they don't have the skills of Wulfheard and the rest of Ealdorman Ælfstan's men. I'd feel much better if we were in Mercia. Yet I can't deny that my curiosity drives me onwards. I must know the true power behind the conspiracy.

* * *

Two days later, we finally ride into Canterbury. I'm not sure what I was expecting, but it's not what I see. I anticipated somewhere as old as Canterbury would have some ancient ruins, as in Londinium and Winchester. I also expected there to be many churches. But I didn't expect it to be so small or for two churches, large churches, to be in such close proximity to one another – although, one is outside what remains of the walls. Why would they build a church outside the main walls? Admittedly, it has its own walls, but it makes no sense to me.

We're led not towards the church outside Canterbury, but towards the other, inside the walls, and through a gateway which is watched by a collection of men. I'd call them warriors, but they don't truly have the look of men who could kill.

'Archbishop Ceolnoth's a young man,' Oswy informs me conversationally. 'Perhaps not as young as you,' he hastens to clarify. 'It caused something of a scandal when he was elected, but it means, provided he doesn't fall foul of the Mercian or Wessex king, that he should rule for some time.'

I nod, but I'm really looking all around me. Canterbury. It's one of those places that everyone on this island knows about. Here, the first Christian emissaries came, and here the first church was built. I can't entirely see why. It doesn't seem to be any different than many other places I've visited. In fact, it's quite insignificant. Smaller than Winchester, even.

'We're to join the traders,' Oswy comments, jolting me from my thoughts and forcing me to follow him and not the rest of the mounted men and women ahead who are being welcomed to what I assume is Archbishop Ceolnoth's home in the heart of the settlement.

'And then what?' I question. Oswy doesn't reply. We're just to wait and see what Wulfheard wants us to do, apparently. Of course, Wulfheard joins the rest of the holy party, entering the archbishop's palace complex. I imagine that they're being greeted with fine food and long speeches. Unlike us. We've no canvases and have been sleeping rough on the side of the road, eating what we can find from the settlements we've passed through. At least here, with the smell of baking bread scenting the air, we can find something tastier.

I laugh at myself. I'm not normally one to complain about such things, but I feel dirty and bedraggled. My wounded back itches, although the scratches on my arms are almost healed. I miss the comforts of Kingsholm. Only that thought reminds me of why we're really here. To discover the truth behind the allegations against Lord Coenwulf. I've found no evidence that supports whether Eadbald visited Winchester, but I've discovered that whoever is behind the attempts to kill the children, it is more than just one person. And some of those people are or were in Winchester and might just be connected to the Wessex royal family.

'Help me,' Brihthild calls, her voice filled with fear. I turn from my musings to find her brother falling from his horse. Cuthred's quick to react. I'm even quicker. I hold the man carefully, wondering what's happened to him. He seemed well enough this morning when we struck out for Canterbury. He's been improving daily thanks to Cuthred's ministrations. The last day or two, there's even been a welcome glow to his gaunt cheeks and thin lips.

'Did you see anything?' I ask her as we find a space to lie him on the ground to the side of the road. His face is pale, and his breathing shallow. My forehead furrows. This shouldn't be happening. He should be improving, not getting worse.

I look more closely at him, running my hands down his body, for all Brihthild batters me aside to get closer to him, anguished sobs coming from her open mouth.

'Ah,' I mutter, my hand coming away bloody from the inspection. Still, it makes no sense. 'He's been stabbed.' I'm not sure how such could have happened. He's not cried out. He didn't alert us to any attack.

'What?' Brihthild demands furiously.

I pull his shirt upward, revealing the welling blood on his chest, below his shoulder, and to the side, not far from where his heart should beat.

'What?' she pleads again. I'm as perplexed as she is. Why would someone stab him, and how did it happen? I'd like to think I'd notice if he'd been involved in a fight, but he's been mounted all morning, riding with Cuthred and Brihthild.

Quickly, I take the rag of my old tunic, offered to me by Cuthred, and hold it against the wound. It's deep, and I fear mortal. His breathing's growing even more shallow.

'I don't think I can help him,' I cry, not wanting to admit it. 'See, the blood bubbles, it doesn't just flow. It's pierced him deep inside.' A sharp slap on my face and I rear backwards, only just remembering to keep my ragged tunic held against the wound, not that it's doing much good.

'You said you'd cure him,' Brihthild shrieks. 'We came all this way because you said you'd heal him.'

'Not from a bloody stab wound,' Cuthred explodes with shock.

'How did he get it?' she whines, breath coming too fast. We're all watching as Brihtwulf slowly dies, his eyes thankfully closed so that I can't see his panic, while his sister grips his hand. He murmurs soft words I can't hear. I feel useless and really bloody angry. How has this happened? It shouldn't have been possible, not when we were all so close together.

'Look.' Cuthred draws my attention to a livid mark around his neck. I try to recall if he wore an emblem there.

'Did you steal it?' she asks, her hands everywhere. I sense her frustration, fury and deep grief. She slaps my hands aside, and the wound doesn't bleed at all, well, no more than a trickle. But it doesn't matter, for he's dead all the same.

He didn't even open his eyes as his last breath left his body. She begins to sob, the sound desperate and filled with sorrow.

I look to Cuthred, my hands bloody. He shakes his head. This is so unexpected and so very wrong. 'How?' I form the word, but he shakes his head more violently, tears running down his cheeks, while Oswy stands beside him, looking on. His presence is a comfort and also a concern.

We've come to Canterbury to determine what's been happening, and yet somehow, amongst all the men and women we've travelled this way with, Brihtwulf has been stabbed, and clearly, something stolen from around his neck.

'I don't understand,' I mumble, head bowed, swallowing against the sudden and unexpected grief. 'I don't understand,' I repeat, and from the silence of my companions, it seems they don't either.

17

Not that we have time to grieve. A shout breaks through my reverie, and I realise we're under intense scrutiny. I look up and then hastily glance away once more.

I don't recognise the man before me, but it's impossible to miss that he's a Wessex warrior. His tunic is decorated with the wyvern emblem, and his weapons belt engraved, in leather, with a similar symbol of a wyvern in flight.

'What's this?' the man asks gruffly. 'And where the hell did you get these horses from?'

I don't think we're capable of speech, not after the sudden and horrifying events of the last few moments, yet Oswy recovers himself first. He meets the other man's gaze.

'We're horse traders. These animals are ours.'

'No, they're not,' a gruff voice counters. 'These are of good royal Wessex stock. I'd recognise them anywhere. My own horse looks alike. They're from the Wessex royal stables.'

This is a huge problem. We have a dead man and now someone else who means to start a fight about the bloody horses. Wiping the tears from my eyes, I stand beside Oswy, Cenred doing the same. I'm aware we're causing a massive obstruction in the roadway, but our horses stay together thanks to familiarity and the ropes that bind them. The rest of the traffic moves around us. If they were giving us a wide berth because of the dead man, now they're almost moving into the next street to avoid the armed Wessex warrior as well.

'You'll have to prove it,' the Wessex man counters. I already hate him with his wide stance and healed but clearly once-slit nose. He has more hair up it than on his shimmery bald pate.

'As will you,' Oswy announces calmly. I'm surprised he can be so placid when the man has more and more of his allies joining him. I swallow heavily, my throat constricted by grief. Perhaps these weren't the first men to notice the quality of the horses. Maybe that's why our friend is now dead.

'I'll get the ealdorman.' He juts out his chin as he speaks.

'Very well. I'll get the reeve. They won't like knowing that you've spoken to traders in such a way and cast such aspersions on them. This is, I believe, a market settlement?'

A flurry of emotions covers the warrior's face, but he holds his ground. 'I'll get him immediately. You better get out of the way. You're causing an impediment.'

At that assertion, Brihthild surges to her feet, face red with fury, tears and sorrow. 'My brother isn't an impediment,' she howls, and only Cenred's swift intervention stops her from pummelling the other man's chest with her fists.

'Keep her under control,' is his unsympathetic response as he peers down his nose at Brihtwulf's lifeless body. He appraises the horses for one last time before marching away. He's quickly swallowed by those waiting to get past us, their angry cries making it sound like we're in the shield wall and not Canterbury.

'Bastard,' Cenred mutters, releasing the sobbing woman from his grip. Her sorrow has been replaced with fury, but I look to

Oswy. We've another obstacle now. Especially, if the Wessex warrior does fetch the ealdorman. We don't know which ealdorman he means, and if it's one that I met inside Londinium, it'll cause even more problems.

'Come. We need to find a church that'll allow us to bury him.' Cuthred's the more practical of us all. I'm impressed by his maturity.

'Where?' Brihthild asks, and I don't know, but I step out into the street, noting the curious eyes of a man there, who walks with a limp and has a scar on his chin. Maybe he was once a warrior.

'Good sir,' I call to him. 'We've endured a terrible tragedy. Tell us, where can traders seek burial within this fine place?'

I think he won't answer, but then his eyes soften on seeing Brihthild's evident distress.

'Not the archbishop. Go to Saints Peter and Paul, outside the walls. They'll take him. It's the closest as well. All have to be buried outside the city walls.'

'My thanks,' I reply and offer him a few pennies from my purse.

'No need for payment.' He refuses my coins and turns aside instead.

'Saints Peter and Paul outside the walls,' I inform Cuthred. 'We need to take him there.' I'm attempting to reorientate myself to all that's happened and trying to do so quickly.

'Oswy and Cenred, you take the horses and set us up as traders. Take Cuthred with you, let him do all the talking. I'll take Bicwide and Brihthild to the church.'

When no one argues, I bend to collect the dead man's body in my arms, wincing at his weight and heat. He's not yet cold and marbled. Oswy aids me, and in no time, he's slung over the saddle of Bicwide, and I walk with Brihthild, away from the marketplace, outside the walls once more and towards the structure of Saints

Peter and Paul. I think I'll have to argue with the monks watching the entranceway, but they take one look at the dead body and hasten to our side. The man spoke the truth. This must be where the dead are buried.

'Come this way. You can be assured he'll be tended to, and tomorrow, he'll be interred.' They leave out the expectation of a fee, but I know we'll have to pay. At least they don't argue about taking a stranger into their midst. As we remove Brihtwulf from the horse's back, I ensure his stab wound's covered. I'm confident they'll discover it, but by then it'll be too late for them to refuse to bury him.

Brihthild's being spoken to by one of the monks, her soft sobs punctuating our furtive movements. When Brihtwulf's laid out, in the house of the dead, and not at all the only marbled body there waiting for burial, I realise she's gone.

'The brothers will care for her,' a soft-spoken monk assures me. 'Take your horse, and return tomorrow before sext, and you'll be able to join the short ceremony.'

I open my mouth to say more, but instead merely offer him the pennies the man on the street refused and more besides. If I don't get back to Mercia soon, I'll have no coin left. Perhaps we should sell the horses?

With Bicwide, it's easy to make our way back the way we came, through the open gateway in the ancient walls. His size means people move aside, some mothers even pulling their small children close for fear they'll be trampled.

The sound of the cries of traders, as well as the scent of fresh-baked bread, has me at the market street in no time at all. Unlike in Winchester, the space here is far more compact. I can hear the shouts of men and women from Wessex, Mercia and much further afield. It's not only the holy men who've journeyed to Canterbury for the bishops' conference.

Not that Cenred and Cuthred are part of the main run of stalls. The animals seem to have their own particular area and have been moved to where there's more space for them. I look for the Wessex warrior who wants to claim the horses, but he's not returned. Not yet. Thankfully.

'Where's Brihthild?' Cuthred queries.

'The monks said they'd care for her until the funeral tomorrow, before sext.' The news seems to settle him, but I can tell what's happened that has upset him. 'Did you see anything?' I query. 'Because I didn't.'

Oswy and Cenred join us. The horses have been untied from their line and now mill about in a small enclosure, water and fodder for them to eat and drink. I eye them. They do look like fine specimens compared to the other horses on display. They are higher quality than Bicwide and the other animals we have. Maybe we shouldn't have brought them to Canterbury.

'I saw nothing,' Oswy confirms.

'Or me,' Cuthred echoes, but Cenred isn't so quick to speak.

'There was something this morning when we broke camp,' he says unwillingly. 'I thought nothing of it, but he was speaking to a hooded figure, and it wasn't friendly.'

'Then it's nothing to do with what we're trying to do?' Oswy queries.

'I don't know what it was about. But that's the only person with whom I saw him speaking. I just assumed it was one of the bishop's men or those who've ridden with them. When they parted, Brihtwulf was jostled from behind but mounted easily enough. I mean, he was quiet on the last part of the journey, but I didn't think more of it.'

The thought fills me with unease. If our friend was stabbed and died slowly throughout the morning, we could have done something to help him, if only he'd said.

'He would have thought it was his ailment,' Cuthred speaks confidently. 'He wouldn't have realised what was happening to him. Not until it was too late. The symptoms would have been similar. Feeling breathless, feeling pain in his back. It makes sense why he didn't think he'd been wounded.'

'If you see the man again, Cenred, you must tell us,' I inform him. He nods, his face puzzled. It won't be easy to decide if it's the same person, when all we have to go on is that he was hooded and cloaked.

'Bastard,' he murmurs. 'What are we to do about the horses?' he questions, no doubt keen to be distracted from thinking about how he could have prevented Brihtwulf's death.

'We'll see if the Wessex warrior does what he says. But we'll have to be careful. If he does bring a Wessex ealdorman, then we're sure to know him. I'll seek out the reeve. Inform him of the difficulties. Much will depend on what sort of man he is.' The solution is far from ideal, but Oswy strides out all the same while we attempt to make the best of what we have. Despite the death of the Wessex man, I'm still hungry.

'Cuthred, do you want to find us something to eat?'

He shakes his head. 'No, you should go. With your size, they won't try to overcharge you.' His tone's martyred. 'Here, without Wynflæd to ensure they don't have me paying too much, I know exactly what will happen. And that's if they'll even sell me food without checking all the pennies to ensure the silver content is pure enough.'

I don't really want to leave, not with Oswy already gone, but I'm hungry enough to eat a horse.

'Shout for me if anything happens,' I urge Cenred. He nods absent-mindedly. I can tell he's still thinking about what he might or might not have seen earlier.

I work my way back towards the market street, alert. I don't need my eyes to find where food can be purchased. Along the way, I see something that catches my attention. A trader, wearing clothes that aren't from any part of Britain that I recognise because they're far too diaphanous to be any use against the wind and rain, has before her a collection of stones and silver and gold pieces. There are also some wooden items. She has men watching her stall as she talks to customers. Not that I want to buy anything, but I'd like to know how much the glowing jewels with orange amber at their heart might cost. I don't miss that there are also jewels that seem to contain something similar to amber, but without its fiery heart.

I make my way amongst the few other customers looking at the silver and gold. The far end of the stall is busy with people looking at wood-carved crosses, hammers and other symbols, some of them fishes, others more animalistic. A twirling snake darting in and out of what seems to be an apple arrests my attention.

I can see the stall is laid out in a simple way. Cheapest to most expensive. The wood carvings are of a stunning variety. Some very basic, others so lifelike that I think I'll be stung if I put my hand on the depiction of a bee. There are also bone carvings, perhaps whalebone, and even some that seem to be another substance. Marble? Again, amongst the silver and gold, there are simple pieces and then far more elaborate ones. These are even small beads of dazzling aquamarine. But it's the amber I'm interested in. As is someone ahead of me.

The woman's dressed in great finery, a thick cloak covering her shoulders, white fur at the collar. She has a servant with her. I also think two of the guards are hers, as they watch her and those who might get too close. Perhaps she's the reeve's wife, or related to the archbishop? She reaches out and gently runs her fingers over some of the jewellery and the trader woman is giving her all of her attention. There's a younger woman contending with the other end of the stall, where the goods aren't as expensive. She's wrapped more snugly inside a thick cloak.

'Finest amber,' I can hear her speaking softly. 'Traded from the far north and brought to my attention via a transaction conducted in Hedeby in the lands of the Danes and then crafted into this delightful necklace.'

It's beautiful, I won't deny that. I imagine it would cost more than a horse. Perhaps more than two horses. Yet it's quite plain compared to other delicate items. I think of the eagle hidden beneath my tunic. I've never doubted what the sigil represents. Looking at the goods before me, I appreciate its great craftsmanship. An unskilled artisan didn't create it. Far from it.

Abruptly, I realise they're discussing payment. I listen more carefully.

The stone is less than a quarter of the one that I found in Bicwide's saddle.

'Five mancuses,' the prospective buyer repeats, as though the sum isn't actually all that great. But such an amount staggers me. That would make the piece we found worth over twenty mancuses. That would be enough for a man to live on for many a long year. Certainly, he could build a home with it or set up in trade. Wulfheard assessed it enough to buy a few horses, but it might have greater value.

'Yes, my lady. People will realise it's great worth from the fire at its heart. Some will try and carry off the much less valuable type of amber, missing the fiery heart. But you, and I, will know the true value.'

With the cost known, I move aside, eager to find bread, cheese and something warm to fill my belly. It's been a strange day so far. I fear it will only get stranger as it wears on, and we're visited by the ealdorman and no doubt the reeve as well. It'll be better for us all if we're fed. Still, I mull over what I've discovered. There is expensive amber, and less valuable amber. I consider which sort we have.

With an armful of food, and four bowls of a meaty pottage from the tavern, which I have to return or forfeit another silver penny, I make my way back towards the horses. Oswy has come back and his glum expression tells me all I need to know.

'The reeve is in the pocket of the Wessex ealdorman?' I ask, suspecting the reason for his downcast appearance.

'No, the reeve is in the pocket of the archbishop, and so it'll be for him or one of his minions to decide.'

'Not so bad then,' I counter, offering the bowls to my friends. Oswy takes his more eagerly than his face implies. We eat hungrily, silence falling between us apart from the noise of horses eating and pissing. This part of the market is much quieter than along the main street, but then, not many people visit a market to buy a horse, ox, donkey or goat. These are the once- or twice-in-a-lifetime purchases and not a daily requirement. Well, apart from the goats. They may be bought with more frequency.

That said, there are people with coins to spend eyeing up the horses. Perhaps, I think, we'll get lucky and sell them all before the Wessex warrior can return and make more of a nuisance of himself.

My thoughts turn to Brihthild and her dead brother. I still don't understand how Brihtwulf could have been fatally stabbed and not cried out or even noticed until it was too late. And why? We came upon them in the church in Winchester entirely by chance. Or so I believe. How then, in the space of a few days, could he be murdered, for that's certainly what's happened to him. Poor sod. Once more, I think of Brihtwold. He was no older than I was at the time of his death. Since then, summers and winters have passed, and while I know it's not my fault he died, I still feel guilty.

I was supposed to protect him inside Londinium. I swore to Tyrhtil that I would. But they're both dead now. As is Brihtwold's brother, Brihtwulf, and Brihthild is alone.

'Tell me about this fine beast,' a voice calls to us. We all look, one to another, unsure who will speak. Cuthred surges upright first, all smiles and bows, but his joviality falters as he realises who the man is interested in.

'My lord?' Cuthred leaves it hanging but the man doesn't offer his name. Discomforted, he's still quick to reply, 'Alas, Bicwide isn't for sale. He belongs to us,' he counters smoothly. 'But, we have horses as big and as well bred.'

'Come now.' The man who speaks is dressed well, his gloves removed to reveal long fingers, adorned with rings. He likes to reveal his wealth. Many wouldn't be so foolish when bartering for a horse. 'All is for sale here.'

'But not Bicwide,' Cuthred murmurs demurely. I'm impressed once more by his presence of mind.

'But he's just what I'm looking for. In fact, I'm sure I once owned a horse just like him. Not that his name was Bicwide.' I groan at the change in the man's tone. This then is our ealdorman. Not only does he mean to imply the horses are from the king's royal stables, now he means to say we're liars.

'The horse is ours. Purchased in Southampton, some weeks ago,' Cuthred argues. 'The woman there assured us the horse was hers to sell, as were all the mounts in the stables.'

The Wessex ealdorman's eyes narrow. I keep my head low, for I recognise him. I'm sure he wasn't an ealdorman when I met him inside Londinium, but many men died during those days. No doubt, he's replaced one of the dead. I try to recall his name, or if I ever heard it. I'm sure it starts with an H, but the rest of the name eludes me.

I don't want him to see me. The others won't be known to him, not as anything other than Mercian traders. But for the time being, the man is more concerned with Bicwide. I consider if he's the one behind the message on the vellum and with the amber rock. Is he the lord of Wessex the letter is addressed to? He can't be, I'm sure he's Ealdorman Hunberht, or something like that.

'Southampton, you say.' He strokes his long beard while thinking. 'Was the woman's name Heanflæd, by any chance?'

'Perhaps, my lord...' Again, Cuthred leaves it hanging, and the man takes pity on him. It helps that Cuthred doesn't know the horse trader's name. She never told us. All we knew was that her assistant was named Wulfthryth.

'Ealdorman Hereberht,' he offers.

'She drove a hard bargain,' Cuthred confirms graciously.

'Yes, I imagine she did,' he concurs. 'Then I hope she sold you the saddle for Bicwide, as you call him. I should like to buy that from you for, say, fifty pennies?'

That's a huge amount for a saddle. My eyes narrow as I move so I can see the man more clearly without giving myself away.

'We need the saddle. We can't ride him without it.'

'Then why not two hundred pennies for the horse and the saddle combined?'

It's a huge amount, the equivalent of five mancuses. If Brihthild were here, the bargain would have already been struck because she's been promised four horses to sell in exchange for her silence. I don't think which four was ever discussed.

'I'm afraid I must decline, my lord.' The Wessex lord looks unhappy but doesn't labour the point, which surprises me.

'These other horses were not from her, were they?'

'No, my lord, we gained them elsewhere in Wessex.'

If the ealdorman offers a sharp look to Cuthred for such an evasive answer, he says nothing further and instead turns aside, his shoulders tight with anger.

'He'll be back,' Oswy complains. I think he's right. The ealdorman will return, and I wouldn't be surprised if he brings others with him.

But it's Wulfheard who arrives first when it's getting dark and people are either considering drinking more or sleeping.

'Bloody holy men,' he complains and then looks around sharply. 'Where are they?'

He doesn't need to elaborate on whom he means, and so Cuthred informs him of what's befallen them both.

'So now we have a bloody murderer in our midst as well.' If Wulfheard looked bored by the tediousness of a holy ceremony, now he looks furious. 'And none of you saw anything?' This he directs to us all, and as Cenred has already told of what he saw, there's nothing else we can add. 'Bloody Wessex,' Wulfheard continues. 'I can see why the ealdorman didn't come here again. It's filled with more conspiracies than Mercia.'

I eye him, considering what he'll order us to do next.

'The others will join us shortly, all apart from Landwine and Kyre. They'll keep an eye on the bishops. I mean, the only way they're going to kill one another is with too much bloody arse-licking.'

I chuckle at that, feeling the tension from the day draining away. Wulfheard glowers at me, eyebrows high, and then joins me in laughing as well.

'It's bad enough when there are Viking raiders and our enemy to kill,' he offers softly, for fear he'll be overhead. 'It's ten times worse when it's all back-stabbing and arse-licking. And, I don't even know why we came, for the king has told the bishops they can agree to nothing that the archbishop suggests if it concerns Mercia. He says that the archbishop can get his arse to Mercia if he plans on making changes to boundaries or services or whatever it is these lot feel so passionate about.'

I have no idea what the bishops and archbishop might discuss either, so I hold my tongue.

'Tomorrow, two of you attend the interment and bring Brihthild back here. Then we'll decide what we're going to do.'

'What of the Wessex ealdorman?'

'Hum, indeed. We can sell him some of the horses, if we must, but I don't like it. And if he brings the king's son to demand reparation of the horses, I'll like it even less, but we won't just hand them over.' It's news to me that the king's son is in Canterbury, but perhaps that shouldn't surprise me. He rules Kent, after all.

And then I remember the woman selling the trinkets.

'The amber is worth at least two hundred silver pennies,' I inform him.

'That's more than I suspected,' Wulfheard speaks quickly. Again, the thought of such a conspiracy doesn't fill him with the desire to fight, but he is curious. I think we all are. He must be considering his brother's part in all this. I'm thinking about everyone from Queen Cynethryth to Eadbald.

'There's also less valuable amber, without the fiery heart,' I murmur, and if they're surprised that I know this, no one says. I think we all realise that the amber we have is the more prized sort.

'Right, we'll keep a guard tonight. You can argue amongst yourselves how to divide it. I'm getting some sleep, as is Cuthred here. And don't wake me when the others arrive. The daft sods are keeping watch while the bishops hold some bloody feast.' Wulfheard grumbles himself to sleep while I turn to Cenred and Oswy.

'Third,' I say before the others can. Oswy glowers, while Cenred shouts first. Daft git should have been thinking about what watch he wanted as opposed to being angry at me for taking the best one.

We all settle, where we can. There's not much room with the horses and no canvas. We could have sought shelter in one of the taverns, but then our horse stock would have been vulnerable to theft. No, it's better here, I think.

I regret that much later, when the church bells have rung and people have been singing and drinking, and the rest of the warriors have returned. I feel as though I've only just closed my eyes when Oswy wakes me for my watch.

He's foul-tempered, as he shakes my shoulder. I've half a mind to smack him in the face for his rough ways, but he comes closer, pulling me upright as though he means to headbutt me, only he whispers.

'The damn Wessex ealdorman has his men watching everything we do. Be alert. If you fall asleep, they'll take the horses and that saddle. Where's the amber?'

I have the amber in my money pouch, but I don't tell him that. 'It's safe,' I growl, pleased he's managed to cover our conversation, although I'm angry that he's made my back itch by doing so. 'Get some sleep.' I indicate my spot as I stand. He slumps into it. I'm reminded of when I was wounded, and everything ached. He looks like I imagine I did. All bones and no muscle to support them.

Standing, I yawn and look around me.

The night isn't as dark as beneath the boughs of trees in a woodland. The stars are bright, the moon already waning, and thin clouds hang high overhead. The usual noises of animals and people sleeping greet my ears, as do the soft prayers from one of the churches. I wouldn't expect them to travel so far but, clearly, they do.

I move to Bicwide, and find him sleeping while standing, leaning heavily against part of the wooden fencing erected to keep the animals secure. I leave him and, instead, make my way around the small campsite. It's not light enough to see the rest of Ealdorman Ælfstan's warriors, but I've spent many a night with these men. I recognise the prone positions, snores and farts of those sleeping and stifle another yawn. I walk quietly, but my eyes are alert.

I might be able to see more here, thanks to the lack of cover overhead, but with so many people in one place, it's not easy to determine what's out of place.

I consider Brihtwulf and whoever stabbed him. Was it one of the Mercians? After all, we travelled this way together, having met the Mercian bishops. But there were more than just Mercians in the group. The archbishop had sent Wessex warriors to escort the bishops as well.

I can't help thinking everything is connected to the conspiracy to murder the children of Lord Coenwulf and Lady Cynehild. I thought it was a Mercian plot orchestrated by the queen, or her son, or Lady Ælflæd, and certainly with the involvement of Lord Beorhtwulf, but now I'm really not convinced by that. Perhaps, I think, there's a lot more at play here than just the need to kill the children. I consider Lord Coenwulf. I hope he remains safe in Frankia. I also hope the king allows him to return. I can find no evidence of Eadbald visiting Winchester, and I've also found, or believe I've found, evidence of others being involved. All we need now is for the Viking raiders to reveal their involvement alongside the Welsh kingdoms and Athelstan, king of the East Angles, and Mercia will find itself just as beleaguered as before King Wiglaf managed to oust King Ecgberht from Mercia.

The theories revolving around my head make it pulse. I try to clear it, thinking only of what I'm supposed to be doing, which is watching the camp. I'm grateful when everyone starts to wake, and I can prepare myself for the funeral of Brihthild's brother. The bishop's conference is only set to last three days, so after today, there's only two more to contend with until we can return to

Mercia if we are indeed returning to Mercia. I will the time onwards.

More and more people come to see the horses, and there are some who can clearly afford the beasts, but most of them, I'm convinced, are Wessex warriors, appraising the horses and deciding if they've been stolen or not. The Wessex ealdorman doesn't return, and when sext is upon us, Oswy and I make our way towards the church, leaving Cuthred and Cenred in command of the horses. They also have the aid of Osmod and Uor, the others having gone with Wulfheard to attend upon the Mercian bishops.

The market's once more in full flow. The sound of people haggling floods my senses, and the church's quiet is a welcome balm. Brihthild's waiting for us at the entranceway, her face tear-streaked. A monk stands with her, dressed in a long tunic, his tonsured head bowed as he prays. Together, we make our way to the gravesite. Brihtwulf's not the only one to be buried today. I can see where some of the graves have already received their occupant, and the soft noise of sobbing seems to flood the area.

I swallow my sorrow, as the words are uttered, and the body covered with earth, before turning aside. It's a poor excuse for a funeral, but at least there were people here to honour the dead.

'You're to return with us,' Oswy informs Brihthild in his gravelly voice. She nods with understanding, and we walk once more through the gate and emerge into the marketplace. Somehow, it's even busier, the cries of traders louder and tinged with urgency. Perhaps those who've not yet covered their costs are desperate for people to purchase goods from them.

When we're at the horses, I expect Brihthild to take herself away and continue her grieving, but instead she stops and looks at us.

'I've been offered three hundred pennies for Bicwide and the saddle and another hundred if I can ensure the transaction runs smoothly.' She's defiant. Oswy's face twists with fury and Cuthred's mouth hangs open in shock. Wulfheard bid me protect the warriors and the horses last night, but none of us considered Brihthild. After all, she was in mourning in the church outside the city gates.

'Who by?' I question.

'The ealdorman of Wessex.'

A grimace touches my face. 'He's not for sale,' I reiterate, 'and nor is the saddle.'

But Oswy steps towards me, and whispers into my ear. Unwillingly I nod. I've grown fond of Bicwide. I want to take him back to Mercia with me. But Oswy has thought about this more than I have, and his idea is a good one.

'Fine, you may conclude the sale,' is all I say. Cuthred glowers at me. He too is fond of the horse. But Oswy has convinced me of something important. There's too much interest in Bicwide, and while we have our suspicions, we don't know for sure why. But if we allow Brihthild to sell the horse, we can follow the buyer and see what they do. Then we might have our answers. Brihthild will have four hundred pennies, and I can get Bicwide back.

She nods with satisfaction and turns aside. It's as though she expected no argument from us.

'When are they coming for him?'

'Twilight,' she murmurs. We have much to do before the sun sets. I can't think that Wulfheard will be happy about any of it. I'm certainly not.

18

It feels like the longest day I've ever endured by the time the sun begins to set. It's even longer than that spent inside and then escaping from Winchester. We've not sold any of the horses. There's a lot of interest in them, but it's because people are coming to see if they believe the ealdorman: that these horses have been stolen, and are now brazenly being hawked in the marketplace.

Not that we really want to sell them. After all, we don't want the Wessex warriors using them against Mercia again. It would be better to take them with us to Mercia, and use them against the West Saxons.

If Brihthild's stunned we've agreed so readily to her request, she doesn't comment further. I'm unsure if she's even aware of our sudden change of heart. I assume she must realise how many of our problems can be put down to Bicwide. But perhaps not. Grief for her brother makes her a sullen, wraithlike creature. I'm not surprised. Cuthred has tried to speak with her, offering her remedies and food to ease her heart. He's been soundly rebuffed and skulks around as though a kicked dog. I feel more sympathy for him than I probably should. Bloody women. Always so eager to win the hearts of men and boys and so careless of them when successful. I've seen this many times before. Unbidden, an image of Lady Ælflæd enters my mind. I dismiss it quickly.

The Wessex ealdorman, Lord Hereberht, comes himself, which astonishes me. Oswy's decided to take command of the sale. He waits with Brihthild and Cuthred. Cenred and I have been banished to the extremities of the street, armed with seaxes and our wits, to follow where we need to go. It'll be a problem if they take Bicwide from Canterbury, as we don't have horses waiting for us outside the gates, but none of us think that's what will happen. Especially as, Wulfheard informed us angrily, Lord Hereberht's attending upon the archbishop and bishops this evening.

As such, amongst the archbishop's complex, Waldhere waits. All being well, one of us will be able to keep track of what they're doing, and where they're taking Bicwide. I hope we finally get some answers.

From my vantage point to the side of a long line of carts and wooden tables erected over barrels and boxes, and indeed, anything the traders can find to aid them in displaying their goods that isn't just the dusty floor, I can just glimpse the front of our trading area. It's there that the Wessex ealdorman appears promptly, just as the sun's brightness begins to fade. I move around the stallholders, packing away their goods for the day. They're hungry and grumpy. It's difficult to stay out of their way and remain hidden.

I bite my lip and stop myself from gripping my seax. I'm tired and fed up. This isn't how I thought I'd be spending my evening when I woke this morning.

Brihthild handles the exchange, alongside Wulfheard; Bicwide's ready and saddled. Oswy, who I'm beginning to realise is an even more devious bastard than I thought, has managed to get hold of a piece of vellum, and has had a message written on it by one of the monks inside the archbishop's complex, not dissimilar to the original one. He's slipped it inside Bicwide's saddle, alongside a rather similarly shaped rock, resembling the amber. I have the two original items in my money pouch. The rock, Oswy tells me, is from the woman selling the expensive goods. She informed him it looks enough like amber for most people to be fooled, but is worth a twentieth of the cost.

I huff softly and move backwards again as the woman packing up her stall of badly constructed pots purposefully gets in my way once more. She might as well be earning pennies from Lord Hereberht. She's certainly bloody assisting him.

I can hear nothing of what's being said during the transaction. I witness much of what's happening. They're far enough away that I can't see everything. I watch Lord Hereberht, or rather one of his warriors, inspect Bicwide, running his hands over the animal and, I think, lingering on the saddle. There's then an exchange between Brihthild and the ealdorman. I hope he doesn't stint her or give her poor-quality coins. Bicwide cost me a lot. I don't like selling him on like this. I don't like selling him regardless of how much he cost. I've come to like the huge horse.

Quickly, the transaction's completed. Lord Hereberht and his new horse begin to make their way towards me. He's not being ridden, but rather led by the reins. I watch them carefully. I've already decided on how I'll keep myself hidden when they come closer, if they come closer, with my cloak around my shoulders. Cuthred would have been good at staying hidden, but we're not risking him. If something should befall him, Wynflæd would kill us all. And take pleasure in doing so.

But the woman with the pots is a problem.

'Move away, you great big lug,' she hisses at me, eyes flashing, fire in them. 'You're getting right in the bloody way,' she continues. I scowl at her and step away, keeping hidden behind more of the stalls. It's not as easy as it sounds. They're all odd shapes and sizes, some little more than a man or woman with an open wooden chest before them. The larger stalls, those selling pots or clothes, offer more hiding places. Those from which people are serving pottage or cooked meat are more difficult because I have to avoid the heat of their fires and those queuing to eat at the end of the day. If I didn't know better, I'd think Lord Hereberht knew exactly what he'd planned and was determined that we'd not follow the horse or him.

Eventually, we reach part of the street where the traders who live within Canterbury have their homes and businesses. It's a little easier-going here. With the hood of my cloak over my head, I can meander between those stalls, remaining open while listening for the distinctive sound of Bicwide's hooves over the cobbled street.

Eventually, I manage to linger long enough around a queue of people waiting for ale to be served, that I can follow them, as opposed to trying to follow while being in front. I have an idea I know where they're going, and indeed it's no surprise to watch them make their way into the archbishop's residence. Bicwide's slow, as though he doesn't want to be escorted inside. Lord Hereberht, I realise, has more than one man with him. Others are tailing them, trying to look as surreptitious as I am. I hope I'm doing a better job of it than they are. They might as well be wearing bright red clothes, and not just any red, but thrice-dyed for brightness.

I expect problems at the gate, but Kyre's there, watching those coming and going. He allows me entry without really looking at me. I slip behind him when he moves forward and resume my progress. Oswy, I'm sure, won't be far behind. But it'll not be easy within the archbishop's hall and stables. I hope Waldhere knows his way around better than I do. Perhaps, I realise, they mean to do nothing until after the feast. My belly growls at the enticing smells of pork, chicken and something else, perhaps fish, and as I hasten onwards, the sun finally sets, almost between one blink and the next. Now it's dark as well.

I follow my nose to where the stables are, ducking aside as Lord Hereberht and one of his attendant warriors make their way outside. I wouldn't expect the ealdorman to enter the stables, but his words assure me he's done precisely that.

'We need more light to see by,' I hear him growl, and appreciate that he's found Oswy's replacement note, and, I assume, the amber stone that's not high quality amber. It should mean they're finished with Bicwide. They now have what they need. Indeed, the sound of them leaving assures me that they're happy with their purchase. No doubt, they've gone in search of more light to read the message.

Inside the stables, it's almost too dark to see. I skip aside, only to realise it's my eyes playing tricks on me and not a barrel at all.

'Bloody hell,' I whisper, bringing Waldhere to my side, so silently he startles me.

'They found it,' he huffs. 'Now we need to witness what they do with it.'

A set of confused eyes peers over the stable door. I move forward to run my hand along Bicwide's long nose. I've become too attached to the horse, but I can't help that, not now.

'Stay here, and we'll come back for you,' I urge him. A soft nicker greets my promise, while I join Waldhere at the open doorway. 'What do we do now?'

Outside, brands have been lit, and people rush towards a large hall. The stables are surprisingly quiet, but then, the bishops from all over our island are already here. Anyone else arriving will be from Canterbury itself. Perhaps they'll walk.

'We wait, as I understand it,' Waldhere offers me. 'Wulfheard's inside. Kyre's on the gate. Oswy's just arrived.' And indeed, he has. Oswy surges up before us, a glint in his eye the only thing that gives him away. He must have avoided the light thrown up by the brands.

'They have it?' he questions.

Waldhere nods.

'Then we wait.' I think of guard duty last night and how tired I am of these delays, but we really don't have to wait long.

Waldhere's the most alert of us, standing in the doorway, his eyes gazing out towards the gateway. Oswy and I shelter behind him. But a tug on my arm brings me silently to Waldhere's side.

There's a figure skirting the lit brands that light the extremities of the archbishop's holdings, as Oswy must have done to reach us. People purposefully avoiding the flames make their way towards the gateway. How they plan to escape without being seen, I'm unsure. I take a step to follow, but Oswy forces me backwards.

'What?' I hiss, but he's seen something that I haven't. The man doesn't mean to escape. Instead, he blends into the stone walls, and I squint.

'He's talking to someone,' Oswy confirms, his words almost silent. 'He's given him something.'

I can't make out any of that, so I accept Oswy's description of what's happening.

'He's coming back,' he cautions then. 'To the stables.' And now we have a problem. I scamper aside, slipping into one of the booths, sliding between a small horse eating from its hay net and the wall. I don't see what Oswy and Waldhere are doing, but assume it's something similar.

It's strange that there's no one else here. Where are the stablemen? Surely, they should be looking after all these horses, especially when they belong to the bishops. But they're not.

The man steps inside, pausing, no doubt, to allow his eyes to adjust to the gloom. It's no surprise that he heads towards Bicwide.

'Bloody thing,' I hear him mutter under his breath. In a parody of the ealdorman, he continues. 'Go and check again. It must be there. Look everywhere.'

I consider what they've not found. Was there something else?

'Out the way, beast,' the man almost shouts at Bicwide. A collection of heads bob up from behind stalls at the noise, the sound covering every other disturbance. The actions mask me trying to get closer to see what's happening.

I inch my way towards the door. Another movement catches my eye. Oswy or Waldhere are there before me.

'It's not bloody here. There's nothing else here,' the man hisses, and the thud of the saddle hitting the floor reaches my ears, just before he marches away again. He's still muttering under his breath. 'It's not there. It's not bloody there. It doesn't matter how many times I look. He'll just have to admit it's lost to Lord Æthelwulf.'

I hardly dare breathe as he strides past me.

'Lord Æthelwulf?' Oswy's beside me. I startle. How he moves so silently when he's so big, I just don't know.

'King Ecgberht's son.'

'And the king of Kent,' Waldhere adds.

We look to one another. At last, we have confirmation that this conspiracy involves the ruling family of Wessex. It might not be the king himself, or it could be. Certainly, his son is enmeshed, if we're correct to assume what this man was seeking.

Not that we follow him, or try and discover where Lord Hereberht has gone. Instead we wait.

Wulfheard finds us in the stables. As we tell him all we know, his face clouds.

'Lord Æthelwulf's attending tomorrow to speak to the archbishop and bishop. To talk of peace between the kingdoms of Wessex, Mercia and that of the East Angles.'

'And while he preaches war, he's trying to kill the æthelings of Mercia.'

'Perhaps,' Wulfheard admits. 'It's a possibility. I wish Ealdorman Ælfstan were here. He'd know what to do.' The admission is telling.

'Is it not enough that we know this?' I question. 'Can we not just leave it like that, return to King Wiglaf, have Lord Coenwulf recalled, and then the children will be protected?'

'If only it were that simple, Icel, but it's not. If the Wessex king's ætheling is involved, then who knows how many others? And for them all to keep it a secret for so long and be embroiling men from Mercia, it's a huge concern. We need to find out who it might be. For all we know, it could be one of the bishops. We can't return until we have answers, or everyone, including the king, might be at risk.'

'You suspect Bishop Æthelweald?' I enjoy voicing my suspicions.

'I mistrust all of them,' Wulfheard counters. 'The others could be in it as well. After all the problems between the holy men and Mercia's kings, they might welcome someone new wearing the royal helm.' I know he speaks of long-running disputes between the religious figureheads and Mercia's collection of previous kings. Why, I consider, can't they understand that Wiglaf is nothing to do with those who ruled before him?

'A West Saxon king wouldn't be better,' I counter. I don't want a Wessex king. My uncle died trying to ensure that Mercia didn't have a king of Wessex presiding over her, as though she were a cow to be milked.

'No, it won't. We know that, but men steeped in political intrigue won't consider the likely outcomes, only the possibilities.

All they'll be looking for is someone different. Consider what they could be offered. They might even have been involved in King Ecgberht's usurpation of the kingship from Wiglaf six years ago.'

'So we have to delay until tomorrow then, until Lord Æthelwulf arrives and we can determine his actions having spoken to the ealdorman?'

'Yes, we need to wait. There's nothing for it tonight. The ealdorman is with the bishops and archbishop. Now, go and get some sleep.'

'Are you staying here?' I question Wulfheard.

'Yes, as is Waldhere. We're going to see what our bishops get up to when the feast's over.'

Waldhere grumbles incoherently, but I don't argue with Wulfheard. I've been trying not to yawn for a long time. After last night's terrible sleep, I feel exhausted.

Oswy and I escape, thanks to Kyre, who's still on guard duty. He's slumped, almost asleep, alongside some of the archbishop's men, who seem to be in their cups. It doesn't fill me with confidence that they'll be able to stop any sort of assault, although where an attack might come from, I'm unsure.

'This is getting complicated,' Oswy confides in me. 'It makes my skin itch. I don't bloody like it.'

'I can give you something for the itching,' I offer, although his words make me want to scratch as well.

'You could do with some yourself,' he offers. He's not wrong. 'Men should stand on the slaughter field if they mean to kill one another. And they should be men. Not small children.'

I don't argue with Oswy because I'm in agreement with him. 'Wynflæd once told me that it was a Mercian king who forced King Ecgberht into exile in Frankia.'

'He did, yes. It wasn't King Wiglaf, though. But King Ecgberht has a long memory.'

'Where was Ecgberht's son, Lord Æthelwulf, born?'

'Wessex, I believe. I mean, King Ecgberht wasn't gone for long. A few winters at most. He's held a grudge for far longer than he was in exile.'

'So what do you think? His son means to remove all possible æthelings for Mercia's kingship. I mean, there are few enough of them left. Wigmund. The two boys. And Lord Beorhtwulf, if he truly has a claim.' Of course, I don't mention mine. I don't want Oswy to laugh at me.

'Perhaps. But they didn't succeed in killing King Wiglaf, or keeping hold of Mercia six summers ago. I don't see how they'll manage it again.'

'Maybe they just want the opportunity to take parts of Mercia by causing chaos. Londonia, for instance? They've already got their claws into Berkshire?'

'So what, kill all the æthelings, cause chaos and then take Londonia? Is it worth it?'

'Well, they might have paid those Viking raiders we faced in the kingdom of the East Angles? Was that really to attack Mercia? I know many doubt King Athelstan of the East Angles.'

'I don't think men see that far into the future,' Oswy says slowly. 'There are so many things that could go wrong. Anyone could tell King Wiglaf what's truly planned, and then nothing would happen.'

'I'm just seeing enemies everywhere,' I admit, as we return to the remaining horses, Cuthred and Cenred. I've left Bicwide at the archbishop's, but I'll get him back when we leave Canterbury. Cenred watches us approach and then nods. He's not alone. Landwine and Maneca snore on the ground. Oswy growls and then kicks Landwine to wakefulness.

'You've got the watch,' he informs him.

'You've got the watch, you bloody arse,' Landwine retorts, turning over and resuming his snoring before Oswy can say more.

'I've got the watch,' Cenred informs Oswy in an aggrieved tone. 'And then Maneca and then Ordlaf. Go to sleep, you grumpy bastard.'

I'd not realised Ordlaf has joined us, but I'm pleased by his presence.

'Did you get Bicwide?' Cuthred asks sleepily.

'Not yet, but we know where he is.' I settle beside him. I'm snoring before the final word leaves my mouth.

I wake to an argument between Brihthild and Cuthred.

Blearily, I watch them, trying to determine what's happening.

'She sold his horse,' Oswy offers by way of an explanation. 'To Lord Hereberht, at first light. Now she's taking those two and means to depart.'

I look and see she has two of the Wessex warriors' horses ready to leave. One of them has a saddle. She's going to ride.

'And?'

'Cuthred says she should stay and that a woman alone will be preyed upon.'

'He has a good point.'

'But she says she can look after herself.'

'So, you think we should let her go?'

'There's no reason for her to stay. She has money, and she's sold two horses and has another two. That was the agreement.' It hangs in the air that we're suspicious of her and her arrangement with the Wessex ealdorman. We kept her close for far too long. It would be better if she left before selling any more of our horses, and while we're still in one piece.

'Cuthred, let her leave,' I call to him. Furious eyes turn my way. 'We can't keep her here. Her brother's dead and buried.' The words are intentionally harsh. 'If she thinks she can make it home to Exeter without being attacked, then that's her decision.'

Now Brihthild flinches. Oswy huffs in appreciation of my tactics.

'I have a seax.' Brihthild shows me the blade, her eyes shimmering with fury and perhaps grief for her brother. I look at it in surprise. I'm not sure I've seen it before. It has a thin blade. Immediately, my thoughts tumble. Could that be what killed her brother? Surely, she's not to blame? Is she? Did she use it to kill her brother and now pretends to her grief?

'Provided you can use it while protecting your horses and your money pouch, you'll be fine,' I offer, hoping my sudden suspicions aren't evident in my voice. She looks from me to the horses, to Cuthred, and then to Oswy and Maneca, who're also watching the argument, eating old, wrinkled apples that I'm sure were for the horses. Does she realise she might have erred here? I find myself reconsidering everything about Brihthild and our time with her.

'This is Wessex,' she counters aggressively, perhaps too aggressively, trying to cover her tracks. 'Wessex is safe. A babe could walk from here to Winchester and encounter no ill will.' I mean, that didn't happen when we rode to Canterbury from Winchester, but I don't say that. I don't know who might be listening to our rather public disagreement. And my thoughts are tumbling in a riot of confusion. I can't formulate an argument to make her stay with us.

'And what of the Viking raiders?' I try, all the same. Perhaps she should stay here.

'What of them? They're on the island of Sheppey. They've no interest in anywhere else.'

'Well, as you've convinced yourself, I bid you a good day.' I half bow, feeling I may have overdone the mockery a little in my attempts to mask my sudden concerns. Brihthild stamps away, the horses following her. Cuthred hastens to my side.

'She won't make it home. She might even be killed, as her brother was.' His words are urgent. I don't say I agree with him or suggest she might have killed her brother. I might be pleased she's gone. My overwhelming thought is that I wish we'd never come upon her in the church inside Winchester.

'But it's her decision. We can't force her to stay,' I mutter. I wish he'd stop attempting to argue with me while I try to consider my new suspicions.

'Wynflæd wouldn't approve of you just letting her go.'

If he thinks that argument is going to work on me, he's very wrong.

He sighs dramatically, and then, to the sound of hooves, he rushes after Brihthild.

'You should follow,' Oswy offers, from where he sits, pretending to be asleep, propped up against a barrel. It doesn't look comfortable, but I can see why he'd prefer it to the hard floor.

'I'm sick of following people.'

'Then don't,' he replies, with a shrug of his shoulders.

'Oh bloody hell.' I bend and grab my weapons belt and cloak, and stumble after Cuthred and Brihthild, to the sound of Oswy's laughter. Damn the bastard.

19

It's early, but that doesn't seem to dissuade traders or buyers. There are more than enough people for me to once more sneak my way along the side of the market street, watching Cuthred and his ongoing argument with Brihthild. She rides, and he walks beside her, but they're both going the same speed. Only once she's free from the walls will she be able to move faster. I should have brought a horse with me, I realise, but with Bicwide sold and in the stables at the archbishop's holdings, I feel loath to try riding another animal. If she goes far, it'll be easier to retrieve Bicwide from the archbishop's complex rather than returning to the market stall for one of the other horses. If she leaves Canterbury, that is. She says she is. I'm unsure why I doubt her, but now I've seen that seax blade, I do.

At the gates, she turns to the guards and speaks to them, words I can't hear but can well imagine about how warm or cold it is, whether they think it'll rain that day. But Cuthred hasn't given up. While there's a queue to gain entry, there's none to leave, and he rushes after her, his long legs almost keeping up with the horses until she encourages the animals on. It's not exactly fast, a gentle trot, while she gets to know the horse, but Cuthred's soon left behind.

I don't follow, but instead find a small space to wait and watch. Cuthred eventually returns, dejected, shoulders slumped, almost sobbing, or so it appears from the movements of his chest. I feel some pity for him. This is his first time away from Mercia. His first time contending with women he's not known all his life. I understand why he's upset and fearful, but I've hardened my heart to Brihthild. I believe she knows more than she's saying. I believe she's not as innocent as we suspected.

I don't call Cuthred to my side but allow him to head back towards the others. I hope Oswy has a good excuse to explain my absence.

The day grows marginally warmer, but I wait. The mystery of what befell Brihthild's brother puzzles me. As does Brihthild herself. Why is she suddenly so determined to leave us, having been so eager to stay with us after the events in Winchester? We told her what herbs she needed to help her brother, but she remained with us. Her excuses, now I think about it, ring hollow. She would have been able to buy the herbs she needed. She would have been able to find a healer somewhere who would have created the pottage and potions Cuthred said were needed. But no, she remained with us, risked riding with us even when we'd already had two fights with Wessex warriors, and when she spoke of her hatred of Mercians. Not for the first time, I wish I'd not allowed myself to be led by her fears for her brother, and by my concern that I'd been involved in the killing of her other brother.

The day advances. I think I should return to the others and determine our intentions for this evening, but something keeps me in place despite my need to eat and drink. It would be nice if Oswy remembered me, but of course, he probably thinks I'm following Brihthild and not waiting by the gate. And then, so briefly if I blinked I'd have missed it, she slides back through the gate. A brown cloak is flung over her hair, and she doesn't have the horses with her, but her walk's unmistakable.

I'm unsurprised when her steps are directed towards the archbishop's palace. I watch her enter without being obstructed by the men on guard duty there. None of them, I notice with a frown, are Mercians. Still I wait, and I'm rewarded when, soon after, there's a clatter of many hooves also entering Canterbury. I obscure my face further. Lord Æthelwulf, king of Kent and the son of King Ecgberht, has arrived. He rides with all his battle gear in place. Is he expecting a fight from the holy men, or is he just being careful?

I remember him far too well from inside Londinium. I recall his arrogance and confidence. I remember standing before him when questioned about my interference with Ecgred's wounded warriors.

Amongst Lord Æthelwulf's riders are the two horses that Brihthild took, including the one she was riding when she left Canterbury this morning. He also makes his way to the archbishop's palace, taking his horses and men with him. No doubt, he'll also be speaking with Brihthild. But, I don't follow them. I don't believe I'd get beyond the guarded gateway now that the king's son is inside. Musing, I return to Oswy, paying little attention to the busy street. Cuthred eyes me with a hurt expression from beside the remaining horses. My mind is awhirl. It can't be denied that Brihthild is trying to win favour with the Wessex ruling family. But did she also murder her brother?

'She's gone to the archbishop's, and not long after, Lord Æthelwulf arrived, with those two horses she took,' I whisper to Oswy. I wish Wulfheard was here. He'd know what to do.

'What's she up to?' Oswy muses. I can see they've eaten well. I reach out to help myself to what's left of the fresh bread and cheese. I eagerly drink a jug of water as well.

'Did you see her seax?' I hiss to him. He nods. Clearly, we both have our concerns about her.

'Has Wulfheard decided what we're doing tonight?'

'He's spoken to Commander Eahric, and informed him that something's wrong. Eahric, he says, is already wound tighter than a bowstring. He's not enjoying being in Canterbury.'

'Neither am I,' I agree.

'We'll be there, no matter what,' Oswy assures me. 'If Brihthild has told Lord Æthelwulf everything, then we'll know soon enough.' I realise then that the Mercians are all armed. While they wear cloaks against the chill and damp, for it'll rain at some point today, beneath them they have their byrnies and weapons belts. Their byrnies and weapons are just about hidden. A man of war would know what the odd shapes and bulges hid beneath the cloaks are, but for those busy about their trading, it seems they don't see what they don't want to see. Our time in Canterbury will come to a bloody end, and soon.

I look at Cuthred, who sulks amongst the horses. He has a seax, and his herb knife, but little else. How, I consider, am I to keep him safe if there's a fight? I'll have to do something. Perhaps I should send him on his way now, maybe he could rush to Mercia and inform the king of our suspicions. Or I could give him more blades from the equipment we took from the dead Wessex warriors and left outside Canterbury before we gained entry. Wulfheard didn't think it would be good for us to be found with their weaponry when we're supposed to be little more than horse traders. Not, I realise, that people probably still think that. Not with all the toing and froing from the archbishop's complex. But Cuthred knows what to do with a knife. He knows how to cut, slice and chop. If I handed him a war axe, I worry he'd do more damage to himself than his enemy.

I ponder the problem. I'm not the only one to be concerned about him.

'Cuthred, you're coming with me.' Wulfheard appears, all bluster and command. He startles me, while Cuthred gives a shriek of surprise, being roused from his sulking about Brihthild. Maybe I should tell him of my growing suspicions. 'Bring your possessions. We won't be coming back this way,' Wulfheard adds more quietly.

'Icel,' he speaks to me next. 'What can you tell me?'

'Lord Æthelwulf has the horses. Brihthild entered the archbishop's complex just before him.'

There's no dismay on Wulfheard's face. It's as though he expected me to tell him this. Cuthred's confused eyes look our way but I ignore him. It's better if he doesn't know.

'Take the rest of the horses outside Canterbury and make camp. Don your battle gear, hide it beneath your cloak, and don't forget your bloody helm. We're not going to miss out on a sale of one of the beasts now. We might need them to escape.'

I open my mouth to argue but snap it shut again, eyeing the animals to decide which one I'll ride. I think of Bicwide inside the archbishop's complex but realise I can't get him back at the moment, although that was my original plan. Instead, I determine on a grey stallion, who reminds me somewhat of Wine, at least in colouring, if not temperament. I reach for my sack and pull forth my byrnie, weapons belt and helm. With effort, I manage to pull my byrnie on, although it's far from inconspicuous. There's no saddle for the horse, so I mount up as well as I can. I wince at the stab of pain between my legs, rearrange myself and my cloak, my helm tied to my weapons belt and beneath my cloak, and then lead the way back towards the gates. The other animals are eager to leave. We've all had enough of being enclosed inside Canterbury's walls.

Once at the gates, though, the guards eye us up.

'Leaving so soon?' the one sneers. He could do with a punch to the nose, but I dredge a smile and incline my head. I'm about to speak, but Oswy beats me to it.

'There aren't those with the wherewithal to buy new horses. We'll go elsewhere.' His words are bland, but the guards are unhappy all the same.

'The market doesn't finish until tomorrow.'

'But we're finished with the market,' Oswy counters. I'm aware that our line of horses has caught the attention of many. I don't miss that one of the guards runs towards the archbishop's complex. No doubt he's gone to ask Lord Æthelwulf or the ealdorman if we can leave. But the question of where the horses came from hasn't been voiced for some time. I'd thought the matter forgotten about.

'We need to ensure you've paid your fees,' another guard announces firmly, indicating we should move aside to make way for others who wish to leave. His belligerent stance is no doubt all bluff, but they still bar our path.

'We paid our fees. The reeve will confirm that,' Oswy says reassuringly. If payments have been made to the reeve, it must have been when I was watching for Brihthild. Or maybe Wulfheard's organised it. Or maybe it's bollocks. Oswy wouldn't think twice about a little evasion in his response.

'What of the fee on the sales of those horses?'

'That was for the women to settle, not us.' Oswy still smiles, but I can sense his patience is being tested. Outside, the freedom of being away from Canterbury beckons. I don't believe Wulfheard envisioned our departure would cause so much trouble.

I don't recognise the guards. They're not the same ones as earlier. I'm not even sure they can do a great deal with the weapons they have to hand. Shields rest against the stonework where the gates join the wall. They have seaxes on their weapons belts and, no doubt, war axes or spears inside their guard room, but they're a random collection of men who all seem to limp, or hobble, or generally show they've been wounded before and never fully recovered. However, between them, they effectively block our exit unless we wish to run them down. I can't imagine Wulfheard intended for us to start a fight.

Whatever the guards' objectives, I turn and groan as I see Lord Æthelwulf making his way towards us, mounted and surrounded by ten of his warriors, his warrior's garb gleaming although his helm is missing.

'They tell me you traders are causing problems. Refusing to pay your market fees.' His words are far from furious, but are edged with iron.

'Not at all, my lord,' Oswy speaks for us. He makes it clear Æthelwulf's identity is known as he bows his head. I try to shrink back on my horse, ensure I'm not in the king of Wessex's son's eyeline for fear he'll recognise me from Londinium. But something, and I don't know if he's already made the connection, brings his gaze to rest on mine, even with my cloak shielding much of my face. A flicker of something crosses his face, be it confusion or distaste for a Mercian warrior.

'Remove your cloak, good man, there, on the grey Wessex horse.' The use of those words assures me that Lord Æthelwulf's certainly looking at me. He means to press the case of where the horses came from, despite the sale of Bicwide and three other horses by Brihthild. I don't look to Oswy for support. I try not to notice that Commander Eahric has hastened to attend the possible altercation from inside the archbishop's complex, surrounded by many of King Wiglaf's warriors as well. I can just picture the look on his face.

For a moment, I'm once more inside the smoky hall in Londinium, with Ecgred complaining about my healing, and Brihtwold standing beside me. I managed to bluff my way then. I doubt I'll be as successful this time. Damn it all.

'My lord.' I bow my head as I pull my cloak down and keep my eyes resting on my hands. It's respectful. I question the success of my evasion.

The sound of hooves coming closer assures me I'm right to doubt my ploy. I keep my eyes cast down, even as Lord Æthelwulf comes closer and closer, a handful of his mounted warriors trailing after him, alert to their lord's interest in me. My heart beats ever louder. Will I need to fight my way free? Will Wulfheard want me to merely acquiesce? I don't know. Then there's no more time for thought.

'A change of profession,' the familiar angry voice demands, reaching out and pulling my head upwards. 'A warrior to a healer to a trader?' Lord Æthelwulf interrogates, with the surety of a man who believes he's invincible, here in Canterbury. 'Or a warrior, masquerading as a trader?' I don't want to look at him, but he holds me firm. I keep my head still, reluctant to start a fight, not yet. Over his shoulder, I see Commander Eahric and Wulfheard moving their hands to weapons belts. I notice Brihthild, mounted, a smirk on her face at my current predicament. I didn't tell her I knew her brother. I didn't explain my interest in her. Somehow she must know all the same.

I realise then that I'm right to suspect it was her who killed her brother. Did she do it so that we'd take her more into our confidence, or because he suspected her motivations? Did she do it as a means of getting into the church with the monks? Does she work for the Wessex king's son? Were they in that church in Winchester waiting for a Mercian to arrive because they'd been alerted of my arrival? Was Ealdorman Ælfstan correct to send Wulfheard to retrieve me and Cuthred, fearful that those within Mercia would do all they could to stop the truth being discovered? I wish I knew.

'Detain him,' Lord Æthelwulf demands, and then all hell breaks loose.

20

The first attack comes from Oswy as he knees his horse to force it between me and Lord Æthelwulf, kicking Æthelwulf's horse at the same time. The animal nickers in pain, a scrabble of hooves, showing its eagerness to get away from Oswy. But the gate guards are also with the king's son, reaching up to my legs, trying to pull me down as I turn the horse aside from Lord Æthelwulf's fight with his horse. His face is almost purple with rage, but the animal refuses to obey his commands.

I catch sight of Commander Eahric as realisation dawns that this is about to get very nasty. His mouth opens, but I don't hear the orders he shouts. Hastily, I release my helm, jam it on my head, and then collect my seax and stab down, fending off the probing hands to my left side. I might be the first to draw iron, but I won't be the last. I have no saddle, and my balance is compromised. I'll see now if my thoughts about the gate guards were true or not. Perhaps they do have some skill other than being able to fill the space where we should be able to exit? Without a saddle, it's difficult to stay mounted, although not impossible.

The rest of Lord Æthelwulf's equestrian warriors are quick to engage, even as outraged shrieks fill the air. The people of Canterbury are running scared. That hardly astounds me.

The man to my left goes down with a shriek of pain as my seax skewers his hand. I only just manage to keep my grip on the blade against the hot rush of his blood. I stare down at the man to my right. I'd kick out, but I'm endeavouring to stay mounted. Moving my foot is a sure way to dismount quickly and abruptly.

I can hear raised Wessex voices and hastily given instructions, even as another equestrian warrior, wearing byrnie, helm and carrying a war axe, forces his horse to rear up before me. I turn the horse with my knees and hear the more satisfying sound of one of the Wessex gate guards absorbing the impact of the animal's hooves.

Oswy's busy menacing Lord Æthelwulf, who, as when I met him before, looks eager to fight, his weapons in hand, cloak flung over one shoulder to reveal his shimmering byrnie. He's finally managed to gather his horse beneath him. He was expecting this battle. That disappoints me. I don't want to do what the West Saxons expect. But there's no time to consider that further. There are more and more mounted warriors streaming from the archbishop's complex. At the same time, Commander Eahric has summoned his Mercian warriors to protect us. I can't imagine he's supposed to get involved in a fight in Wessex, or perhaps he is. King Wiglaf did tell me to seek him out if I experienced problems. And right now, I'm experiencing many.

I catch sight of some of the Wessex guards trying to close the gates instead of just relying on the gate guards to block our exit. I need to stop them. I urge my horse onwards. Suddenly two mounted enemies block my path.

It's not easy to fight from horseback, not when my foemen are also mounted. It's easier to land a blow on a horse than the warriors because they're so much bigger, but I don't like to wound animals.

With my seax, I stab towards them ineffectually. The first warrior, wearing a helm and armed with a spear, thrusts it at me. I veer aside, using my knees to direct my horse, hoping that the sharpened edge of the spear doesn't score the animal. I'd welcome Brute right now. His violent tendencies would ensure these warriors didn't threaten me. But this horse is no Brute. Yet, it's also battle-hardened. It doesn't shriek or shy away from the attack. That speaks to its breeding in the Wessex king's stables.

The other Wessex warrior leers towards me. He has no spear, which is good. He does have a seax, which he slashes from side to side, making his objectives known. The horse he rides is wide-eyed and difficult to control. He remains mounted with the aid of some straps around his legs.

I take one look at them and, with half an eye to the spear coming towards me, bend and slash through the ties on the seax-holder's right leg. His arrogant grin disappears. He starts to slip. I take a risk, grip my horse's neck, and boot him. He slides quickly down the far side of his horse, hands flailing for purchase on the animal. The horse, unused to being grabbed in such a way, bucks, and the man thuds heavily to the ground and his struggles cease with a sharp crack.

The spear-wielder shrieks in anger, and now I'm stuck. The dead man blocks my way forward, his horse, all terror forgotten about, nudging the lifeless man in confusion. I can't go backwards because of the Mercian men who fight the Wessex warriors, while Oswy and Lord Æthelwulf are engaged in a bitter fight.

I realise there's little I can do but ride towards the spear, hoping to turn aside at the last moment. I reach over and grab the dead rider's shield from his lifeless hands. I don't have one. With no saddle, there's nowhere to store it, and I'm supposed to be a trader not a warrior.

With the thought, I'm reminded we have more horses than we do warriors. Perhaps I can make good use of them. First, I need to evade the spear. I bend low and place the shield over my head using my left hand. It's difficult to stay balanced with something in each hand. There's little to hold me steady. I tense my legs, almost wishing I could tie them beneath the animal rather than having nothing with which to hold on.

The Wessex warrior doesn't stray from his intentions, directing his horse to ride at me. At the last moment, I see a gap forming where he moves slightly to one side and encourage my horse towards it. The scrape of iron over the shield assures me that without it, I'd be dead or in a lot of pain. But my hand isn't ready for the impact. My stolen shield slips, sliding to the ground, despite my best intentions to grip it.

And the Wessex warrior isn't done with me. With more skill than I want to see, he turns his horse and comes at me once more. And he's not alone. Some of the guards from the gate, now that it's closed, hasten to involve themselves. I have men on foot and a man on horseback, all trying to cut me down. What I want to do is get back to the Mercians and encourage the riderless horses to bolt once I've got the gates open again. Bloody gates. It seems my life is categorised by either trying to get them open or closed, with me on the correct side of them to ensure my safety.

My eye strays to the gates and then sweeps to see the shields to the side. I'd welcome another shield to protect me, the enemy one somehow managing to roll away from me. I couldn't do that again if I bloody tried. Abruptly and with more force than I'd like, I kick the sides of my horse. The animal bolts forward. Not that it's easy to control the direction. Another man tumbles beneath the hooves while a foot warrior manages to jump and grip my arm tightly so that he's dragged along with the speed of the abrupt movement. I nearly unbalance once more.

I turn to punch him, but my focus is on the shields. With a shield that I can keep in my hand, I can fight off the enemy and, if I'm lucky, force the gates open once more. Then, if all that happens in the order I need it to, I should be able to get the riderless horses to bolt.

No sooner have I managed to somewhat precariously snatch up a shield, using it to batter aside my unwelcome passenger, than the cry of my name has me looking to Wulfheard.

The Mercians have joined together, their backs to the archbishop's complex. Oswy and I are on the wrong side of that. But we are close to the gate.

I risk looking at Oswy. He and Lord Æthelwulf continue to fight, trading blow for blow. Lord Æthelwulf's warriors hang back, almost as though they're not to engage. It's a wasted opportunity, speaking of Lord Æthelwulf's arrogance, but it means Oswy need only fight one man.

I gaze at the gates and bite my lip. I need to get them open. But it seems my intentions are easy to decipher. Four Wessex guards, unmounted, stand before the great iron bar that locks the gate tight, their faces menacing. I'm unsure if I'll be able to lift it alone, but to find out, I must kill those men. Shit, I think to myself, why is nothing ever easy?

Directing my horse, and with a much firmer grip on the borrowed shield, I ride towards the gates. The four warriors, helms on their heads, although clearly not the correct helms, as two of them can barely see beneath their edges, menace me with varying degrees of fury, apart from one who looks bloody terrified and not much older than Cuthred. I consider why he's here and not in the king's household warriors but dismiss the thought. It doesn't matter why, only that he either dies or leaves me to the task at hand.

The horse ambles to a gallop. I grip tightly and thrust down, not with my seax, but my shield. One of the men stands forward from the others, no doubt intending to take the glory for halting my advance. He's not there for long. The ache in my arm is painful, but the sound of him hitting the ground brings a wolf-grin to my face.

I jump from the horse, using its momentum to run into the three men still standing. The youngster shrieks but is quick with his shield and seax. I thrust the shield into the man to his left, and my right, absorbing the impact as the warrior ducks. I hit nothing but the wooden gate. My seax is in my left hand. Not my strongest position, but it's enough to counter the remaining warrior. He's old and toothless, but the wiry strength he possesses is visible in the lines of muscle that show beneath his byrnie and along his arms.

He counters my blow with his shield just as I swing mine to hit the exposed side of his body. He tumbles, losing his balance. I don't manage to stab him in the back because the youth, still shrieking and incoherent with rage, has found his stones. With no skill and a helm full of luck, he rushes me, using his shield to knock me off balance, menacing me with the seax that trembles in his hand.

Belatedly, I force my shield between us, but it's not enough to stop him. I go down beneath his weight, landing painfully with something wedged in my back and a wild Wessex man atop me.

I thrust up with my legs, but he's still kicking and screaming, his spittle landing on my face. I want to gag from the tartness of him. It's all I can do to work myself free, digging my elbows into the hard stone floor and walking myself backwards on them. The shields between us mean he can't land a blow on my body, not without standing and casting them both aside. He's too busy bellowing and jerking atop me to think of that.

With a bent knee and a heave of effort, I strike a blow to his face, sending the helm spiralling free. He slumps. I take a breath and eye the other two men.

They're both wounded but seem keen to resume what we started. With casual indifference, I pierce the youth through the back, wishing I didn't have to but understanding there's no choice. The man I thought to kill in such a way glowers at me, face twisted with fury. I consider if the boy meant something to him. I move towards him with wide steps, gathering speed in that small space, so that I can jump above him, seax now in my right hand, my shield lying beneath the dead youth, and stab into his exposed shoulder. His byrnie doesn't fit him. Perhaps it once did.

As he staggers down to one knee, I feel a score along my left arm, where I reach to grip the rim of his shield and take it from him. That leaves me with one man.

I leer at him, not risking looking away to see how Oswy fares. I hope Wulfheard will shout if I'm to be troubled by those protecting Lord Æthelwulf.

'You bastard,' the man glowers, gazing frantically between the two dying men. I spit aside the taste of blood that's filled my mouth.

'Open the gate, and you can live,' I offer, but he shakes his head, stepping to meet my advance with his shield and war axe. The weapon looks heavy. I'd be surprised if he can swing it with any control over where it'll land. Like the youth, his lack of skill makes him almost as deadly as someone with summers of training.

I meet his attack with my borrowed shield. It's heavy and unwieldy. I think it once belonged to a bloody giant. Immediately, the wood cracks, the blade almost impacting my nose. I drop it as though it's burning me, the weight of the weapon and shield combined, forcing the man forward so that he all but impales himself on my seax.

I wrench it free, feeling his stinking blood over my hand, to stride towards the heavy bar that keeps the gates closed.

The angry cries of those outside seeking entry can be heard. They'll run soon enough when they realise what's happening inside Canterbury.

Putting my arms beneath the wooden bar, I strain to lift it. The damn thing is bloody heavy, but I'm beyond angry. Too easily, I lift it free and kick the gates open. A furious face greets mine, hands on hips, a collection of sheep and goats trying to win free from those who keep them in place.

'The market's shut for the day,' I shout. He opens his mouth to argue, but then the gate swings fully open. He gasps in horror, tripping over one of the stray sheep in his efforts to get away from the fight.

I eye the animals and turn back to observe the riderless horses.

Oswy remains locked in a battle with Lord Æthelwulf, and his warriors continue to watch on, offering encouragement, seemingly unaware that their fight may well be lost already.

Dripping gore and blood, I mount my docile horse quickly and urge him towards the collection of riderless horses, swerving around Oswy's fight.

I can see he's enjoying himself, barely even a sheen of sweat on his face. The same can't be said for Lord Æthelwulf, who huffs and pants with the exertion of avoiding Oswy's advance, even as he shouts for his men not to interfere. Arrogant fool.

With a slap to the rump here and a severing of a rope there, the animals rush free, careering around the fight taking place.

I hear a cry from Wulfheard, echoed by Commander Eahric, and now the Mercians surge into the Wessex warriors.

The shouts of those outside the gates and those inside mix with the outraged neighs and nickers of the horses, the baaing of the sheep and the bleating of the goats, but my gaze rests on Brihthild.

An open mouth shows her alarm as I stride towards her. In the background, I hear Mercian voices urging one another to hurry and consider that these might be the bishops and their entourages, hastening to escape from Canterbury before Lord Æthelwulf and his warriors can recover and hold them captive. Or perhaps they mean to take sanctuary inside the church.

The smell of blood and sweat is ripe in the air as Brihthild finally realises my intention to apprehend her. She's quick to encourage the horse she rides, but my mount can keep up with hers. If anything, he's getting better at taking my commands. She weaves a path through Oswy and Lord Æthelwulf's fight.

'Leave it,' I call to Oswy. 'Get out of here.' But he can sense victory as Lord Æthelwulf falters and so persists. There are more and more people in the street as well. Some armed with little more than a hoe or a broomstick. I realise their voices hold the accent of Mercians and also that they're not hindering us but trying to help. Of course, Canterbury was Mercian not that many summers ago. No doubt they resent the imposition of the Wessex king over them.

My focus remains on Brihthild. If Oswy kills King Ecgberht's son, there'll be hell to pay, but it's Brihthild, I believe, who holds all the answers which will ensure Mercia's safety.

She surges through the flock of goats and sheep, the freed horses making a nuisance of themselves between the traders' carts and people who came here with handcarts and little more than sacks on their backs containing precious goods for sale. The sharp crack of broken pottery is greeted with a groan of fury.

Brihthild's able to guide her horse with more precision. She's quick to surge away from the distressed people, seeing their winter work earn them nothing. I crouch low over my mount, but we still find ourselves caught amongst the sheep.

No matter which way my horse goes, the sheep are in the way, kid goats with more bounce than thought, almost reaching my eyeline as I try to fight free.

I spare a thought for Cuthred, hoping he's well, but kick my horse onwards so that the powerful animal bunches its legs and surges over a cart that's in the way. The placid ox lows in concern at what's happening before it, the woman leading the cart shrieking in horror, and falling over, although the horse was never going to hurt her. Now we have clear space to ride through.

Brihthild isn't far in advance, but she's abruptly become a most skilled horsewoman. The animal is eager to follow her instructions. Head low, I encourage my horse to greater speed. I don't want to lose Brihthild amongst the trees. She seems to know this place much better than I do, considering I understood this was her first visit to Canterbury.

'Icel.' The shout of my name almost pulls me up short, but Wulfheard can growl all he wants. I want to discover what Brihthild knows. The thunder of more horses' hooves assures me that he must think the same. I don't look, but I imagine Commander Eahric and his men are fighting free from Canterbury. I didn't anticipate the archbishop's gathering of bishops descending into such violence. No doubt, he didn't either. What King Wiglaf will think when he hears, I've no idea.

Kyre's the first to catch me, his usual mount a fast animal and well used to working with his rider in such a way.

'Hurry up, Icel,' he calls over his shoulder, streaming away from me. At least I'm not alone now in trying to keep Brihthild in sight. Neither is Kyre unaccompanied; Landwine's quick to follow. Both of them wear grim expressions. I hope they don't kill

Brihthild when they find her. We need her. She'll certainly be easier to capture and question about this conspiracy than anyone else.

I'm unsurprised she leads the horse towards the east and not the west. She means to drive us deeper into Wessex-held land. I'd worry about that, but the Mercians who live within Canterbury came to our aid, and the men and women close to the Isle of Sheppey did as well. Perhaps she's not being as clever as she thinks.

While Kyre and Landwine are ahead, my mount's doing well. I can still see Brihthild, and her cloak, rippling with the speed of the horse's passage behind her. Only then, there's a sharp bend ahead, and when I come around it, I can no longer see any of them.

'Damn it,' I mutter, breathing heavily and turning my horse in a tight circle with my knees. I peer all around, but trees stretch in every direction. The road leads straight through a woodland area. The trees are covered in catkins, the bark covered in lichen. I can't hear where they've gone, not above the rapid beating of my heart.

I swallow, try to hold my breath and listen, but it's impossible. Even my horse is panting too loudly. And then, in the distance, I hear the crash of a branch or some such tumbling to the ground, my eyes finally absorbing what's evident. Someone has slipped into the woodland to my right, as though heading back the way we've come, but using the semi-naked trees as cover. There are dislodged branches and even a flash of cloth where Brihthild's cloak has become tangled.

'This way,' I urge my horse just as Waldhere rounds the corner as well. 'This way,' I inform him, pointing where I mean.

There are others behind him, and I sense him pausing, waiting for them to catch up, but I press on.

Where's she going? I muse to myself, ducking low beneath nearly naked branches, the first buds of growth just starting to show but too small to be visible from far away. This is the brown time of year, or so Wynflæd would tell me.

The ground beneath my horse's hooves is soft, and roots protrude upwards. It also smells dank, almost as bad as the River Thames. The animal steps carefully, slowing considerably as both our eyes adjust to the gloom. From behind, I hear the crash of others entering the woodlands, only for cries of dismay to follow as they realise how boggy the ground is. Ahead, I can sense a clearing, and I can also hear the crack of iron on wood. I urge my horse to go quicker, but it takes its own sweet time to emerge from beneath the almost-naked boughs of the trees.

Brihthild's dismounted, her horse standing behind her, breathing heavily, its chest rising and falling, foam around its mouth. Landwine and Kyre face her. Despite their skill, it seems they're evenly matched.

Her eyes flash dangerously as she whirls and slashes with her seax and shield. Landwine and Kyre, perhaps thinking she'll be easy to counter, eye one another, unsure what to do. Brihthild's face is sheeted in flecks of brown mud. She must have fallen from her horse, and there's no other reason for her capture. I'm unsurprised. Quickly, I scout the area. If it was boggy beneath the trees, here it's much worse, almost as though this place should be flooded, and not ground to walk upon at all. Her horse's legs are sheeted with mud up to its knees. Landwine and Kyre's mounts look little better. I can feel my own horse sinking slowly into the marshy ground.

Landwine advances on foot, as I hurry to join them, urging my horse to move before it's chest-deep in the marsh. Once more, I have no shield, having abandoned it inside Canterbury when I forced the gates open because it was about as well made as a moss-built barrier. Brihthild's horse huffs and puffs, its breath pluming before it. I anticipate seeing the animal limp away, but my eyes remain on Brihthild.

She fights neatly, quickly, the fury on her face not matched by the conciseness of her movements. She has a great deal of skill.

The ringing of blades entangling is loud in the air. I expect it to bring Waldhere and the others to our side. And it does, but along with them, emerging behind Brihthild, come a collection of Wessex warriors. And they look furious.

21

'Bloody hell,' Waldhere wheezes, bringing his horse under control quickly enough that a shower of dirt hits the ground behind him, allowing the air to fill with more noxious smells. 'What is this?' he questions, even as the Wessex warriors make their way to protect Brihthild. If they have horses, they've left them elsewhere. I don't know whether he means what's happening to us or what's happening with Brihthild and the West Saxon warriors.

I try to work out where they've come from. Surely, there's little more than woodland and no settlement nearby.

'Come on,' Waldhere urges me, sliding his leg over the back of his horse and dismounting with a wet sucking sound that has him grimacing. If we try and fight from the back of the horses, I fear, as he clearly does, that we'll do more to damage our allies than our enemies. It'll be easier to find somewhere to stand on two legs, not four. Kyre and Landwine have already realised this.

'Do you have a shield?' I question, but he shakes his head.

'Not a spare one.' Looping his hand through the handle on his eagle-headed shield, he rushes towards Landwine and Kyre, his eyes everywhere as he ensures the ground beneath his feet can take his weight. I hesitate, but only for a moment. With or without a shield, I can stop my friends and allies from becoming overwhelmed by the Wessex warriors. I hope the rest hurry and join us.

With a glancing look at the ground, mirroring Waldhere's actions, I rush to join the fight on foot. Brihthild's holding her own, but the Wessex warriors are about to engage Landwine and Kyre, and distract them from Brihthild. That'll leave Brihthild free to run or fight, depending on what she wants to do. And we can't let her run. Not without some answers.

But first, one of the Wessex warriors walks towards me confidently, almost as though he's fought here before and knows which parts of the brown- and green-covered marshlands will take his weight. He's one of the best-dressed warriors I've ever seen. His byrnie fits well, his weapons belt glinting with many blades, and not just a seax, sword and war axe. But it's his helm that draws the eye. It's as though it was made for him, which it's possible it was, although rare apart from for those with the coin to spend. It would cost a great deal more than the lump of amber I have.

Whenever he turns his head, the helm moves with him. He doesn't need to worry about it covering his eyes, or knocking his nose, as the poorly equipped gate wardens needed to do. The iron, or silver, or whatever it's made from, is highly polished. I decide it must be iron with silver embossed onto its surface, for silver would be too soft to provide much protection. It's impressive. Not as impressive as Mercia's king's warrior helm, but notable. And so, too, is the man's sweeping sword, which he levels at me with an arched eyebrow, his wyvern-branded shield in his other hand. He knows his strength as he grips the shield tightly. I imagine he's an ealdorman, or someone oath-sworn to Lord Æthelwulf. Perhaps he's been paid with great big lumps of amber as well.

But I'm a wolf of Mercia, a warrior of Mercia, and I'll protect my fellow warriors and discover the truth of the conspiracy against Mercia's king and her æthelings. I've not sweated and trained on my journey to Canterbury to not make use of my renewed strength. I've not spent the entire winter pushing my body to heal and rebuild just to falter now.

With my seax, I rush into his attack, left fist bunched to thrust against his chest or shield arm, should I get the chance. The shimmer of his sword slices the dank air, but I scamper to the right and into his shield. The metal boss of the shield hits my body. I manage to punch his arm, for all my seax swipes entirely miss. Breath leaves my body at the force of the blow.

He grunts in frustration, growling, and tries again. This time, I don't punch him but rather grip his shield arm as he swings it, ready for the next intended blow. My hand just cups half of his forearm, the strength in my fingers holding him steady enough that I can slash with my seax across the top of his byrnie and into the small gap before his elaborate shoulder guards attached to his helm cover him.

My blade makes no more than a dulled clang. He shrugs my unexpected grip free. I can smell him now. There's no fear to him, only determination. He's not the only one.

His shield pivots perilously close, far too close. I rush around it, swinging into his body, almost a loving embrace so that his sword hits nothing but air. I knock my head back against his chin guard and feel the impact in a pulse of pain along the top of my head. But I sense the air expelled from his body, an explosion of shock. I grip his sword arm again, but he recovers too quickly, bringing his shield in tight, gripping the boss with his sword hand to pull it closer and closer to me so that I can hardly move.

And still he pulls the shield tighter against me. Unbidden, horrifying memories of Horsa's attack close to Hereford flood my mind. I remember the feeling of weakness, the terror, the shock that I couldn't overwhelm him. For a moment, I can't think straight. I know I'm weaker since my injuries. I know I'm not yet the warrior I thought I was before being set upon by Horsa and Eadweard and his cronies. While I panic, forgetting my belief that I'm a wolf of Mercia, a warrior of Mercia, the training I've endured in the last weeks, my foeman's grip grows tighter and tighter.

But I have my seax to hand, even if it's almost held down by my leg because my arms are clamped to my body by the horror of his embrace. His breath makes me want to gag. It's hard enough to breathe as it is without the air being contaminated by his rankness as well as the stink of the marsh.

Grunting, fighting for breath, I close my eyes and summon all of my remaining strength to crash my head backwards, recalling myself to what I've accomplished in the past and what I'm still capable of performing. At the same time, I increase the grip on my seax, coiling my fingers ever tighter. I strain to stab upwards, forced to hold my arm out to bring it closer and go around the man's arms. I gasp at the pain of once more knocking against the man's chin guard as I buck to win free.

Momentarily, my foeman's grip falters. I must have caused some damage. My seax may have scored his upper arm. It's impossible to tell with the unnatural movement. It's all the excuse I need to win free from him. I push outwards with both arms, back pressed against him, mindful of my seax, forcing his shield to open, puffing through my cheeks. He can't hold against me. I'm using his body against him. His sword hand slips away from the shield boss. Before he can recover, his grip's also weakened, the sword falling to the ground. Hastily, I win free, bending and turning with the sword raised before he even realises what's happening.

The sword slashes against his shield, taking with it much of the paint in a shower of coloured scraps, revealing the bare, stretched wood beneath it, the shield boss and its housing. I spit blood from my mouth as I glower at him.

'Bastard,' I offer, shaking my shoulders and body like a dog to reassure myself that nothing is broken and I can fight on. My weapons jangle with the exertion.

With a roar of rage, I rush him, sword held directly before me. It's not a move I've ever tried before, but I plan to use it like a spear. I'll stab him, no matter what. His shield comes up, but the sword isn't as long as a spear. At the last possible moment, I redirect it. It slides to the side of his shield. I think it'll glance off his byrnie, so I push it higher, towards his neck. My seax strike was ineffective against his byrnie, but it's different with a sword.

He watches me, taunting, but the damn fool, thinking to clatter his shield against me now we're so close, doesn't realise he's already dying as my blade slices deeply into his neck, passing his byrnie and shield as though they're little more than soft butter.

I hawk in his face and turn aside, ignoring his flailing attempts to seek revenge. He'll be dead soon. I don't need to know who he is. I might come back and take more of his equipment. He won't be needing it again.

My focus rests on Landwine, Kyre, Waldhere and the others who've made their way into the fight. Brihthild's still battling and hasn't tried to escape despite the arrival of the Wessex warriors. I take one step towards the fight, only for Wulfheard to shout my name. I don't know when he arrived, but he rides a horse that looks like it's galloped far above its usual speed, chest heaving, foam coating its mouth, and mud splatters marring his fine coat.

'Icel, quickly, mount up.' His words confuse me until I see that those with horses have reinforced the foot warriors of the Wessex force. There are ten mounted warriors. Damn them. I'm not eager to battle while mounted, but I will.

'Do you have a shield?' I demand, even as I'm running towards my horse.

'Take his,' Wulfheard orders me. I appreciate I've overlooked a dead man's shield, too focused on keeping his sword. He's on the ground now, body jerking in its death throes.

'I'll take that,' I menace, but his eyes see nothing. I doubt he hears me. I've overpowered him. I feel a surge of resolve flooding my body. I've been weak since my beating by Eadweard and his allies. Wulfheard has been driving me hard, even harder than I've worked my body. But I need to remember who I am and just what I can accomplish and not let minor setbacks strike sudden fear into my heart.

I mount up without kicking myself or the horse, the lack of a saddle still causing us both problems which my long legs just about compensate for. It doesn't help that the ground's soft and unstable. I grimace as mud flies into my face from my swinging boot.

Wulfheard advances without me, not prepared to give me a moment longer. He thunders through the battling foot warriors, his focus on the enemy horses and their riders.

My mount follows along, but at the last moment, I feel him faltering on the soggy ground. He realises it, too, stretching out his front legs to counter the problem with the rear ones, and then doubles his speed.

'Landwine, move,' I bellow breathlessly when I'm close enough. He does so without question so that, with a sickening crunch, my horse ploughs through the Wessex warrior he was fighting.

'My thanks,' Landwine calls in his deep voice, but I'm focused on the enemy warriors and Brihthild.

Oswy's joined Wulfheard, as have Wulfgar and Godeman. I can hear the rush of other hooves behind them. I'd like to know why it's taken them all so long to get here, but perhaps the fighting inside Canterbury was more difficult to win free from than I might have thought. Commander Eahric has undoubtedly instructed the Mercians to hold their own against the West Saxon warriors. But I consider Lord Æthelwulf. Will he come and involve himself in this as he did inside Canterbury or does Oswy's arrival mean that Lord Æthelwulf is injured, dead, or has realised this isn't his fight?

With a crash of wood on iron, I encounter my first mounted warrior. Unlike the man I've just killed, he wears only a byrnie, his helm askew, but his shield is huge, much larger than I'm expecting. It almost hides his entire body. With the dead man's shield, I set about overwhelming him. His grey horse, head down, shows no concern at the thundering noises. I won't be able to scare him into making a bid for freedom.

The shield feels cumbersome in my hand, but I hold it, lashing out with the sword in the confined space. I can't use it like a spear here, although I wish I could. Indeed, the shield I face doesn't allow me to watch my enemy, even as I battle against him. He uses the shield as a weapon, jabbing at me, and it's all but impossible to avoid it. I feel it hit my thigh, wincing at the pain and holding my legs tighter to remain mounted.

Around me, I can sense the intensity of this fight increasing. The shrieks of Brihthild echo above the duller tones of the men. I growl. I'm not getting anywhere with this arsehole. With a sharp kick to my mount, I move on to the next man. The shield carrier can follow me if he wants. I've got others that I can overwhelm.

I realise then that these mounted warriors have taken command of what seems to be a small island of firmer footing amongst the marshes. Belatedly, I recognise the surrounding trees, alder, which enjoy the wet conditions. I should have made the connection sooner. While Wulfheard, Oswy, Godeman and Wulfgar attack our foemen I eye the other five mounted warriors who've yet to get fully involved in the fight, and could cause us huge problems when they do. At the same time, I hear the frantic efforts of the shield-carrier to turn his horse to face me. But he's too slow.

With another encouraging tap to the horse's right flank with my heel, he obeys my instructions, picking his hooves carefully over the uneven surface. The enemy watch me. All five of them. They have hard eyes behind rounded helms. It's evident they're warriors of some skill, so their refusal to engage speaks either of confidence in their comrades who do fight or of knowing something that I don't. That concerns me. We're a small force deep in the heart of Wessex-held Kent, and a long way from home. If Lord Æthelwulf has apprehended Commander Eahric and his warriors, then we're even more alone.

'Hurry up, Icel,' Wulfheard roars, wanting me to join the fight, but my focus remains on the other Wessex warriors. The five mounted men should be able to intercept me but none of them come to counter my intention. Only then I realise why.

The island they've found is entirely that, separated from the rest of the stinking marshlands by a gap my horse can't just crest at a steady walk.

'Bollocks,' I complain, already turning my horse away from Wulfheard and the rest of my allies. I leave my back unprotected for that brief moment, but I don't think my enemy will attack me. They believe the contest is between the other Mercians and the Wessex warriors who fight. I'm aware that my intention isn't sure to succeed but I'd rather attack them now than have them overwhelm us when the rest of their warriors have been overpowered.

Only when I'm far enough away that I think the horse can amble to a fast enough speed do I turn. My fellow warriors are so far winning. There are three dead West Saxon warriors. Brihthild has blood sheeting down her face, but she still holds her own against the Mercians.

'Icel, what are you doing?' Wulfheard roars. I ignore him, directing my horse with more and more frantic kicks, holding my shield before me and to the side, fearful of overbalancing and aware that if my horse makes the leap, which is doubtful, I need to stay mounted or be entirely defeated.

The rush of cool air against my face as the horse leaps is pleasant but sobering. I consider what I'm doing is folly, and then, with a thud, the horse lands on the flat ground, the grasses low from the winter.

I feel the jolt of impact through my shoulders and along my belly scar from last year, and my back wound from Winchester. I desperately try to stay mounted but realise there's no chance. I can fall, or I can jump. There was never really going to be any debate about that. I jump.

In my mind, I see myself landing upright, weapons ready, startling the enemy. But with a clatter and *ouff* of expelled air, I lose my footing and fall onto the churned ground, hillocks rising upwards, arresting my forward momentum immediately so that I'm lying on my back. My eyes, shutting without thought, open to see a horse's face examining me, and above that, all the way above it, one of the enemy Wessex warriors. I don't see my horse, but neither do I hear an animal shrieking in pain. He's either made it and is free, or the bastards have killed him.

Hastily, I shuffle backwards, reaching for my shield because my sword has fallen ahead beneath the enemy horse. My movements feel cumbersome, too slow. At any moment, I expect to be impaled on an enemy sword, seax or spear. But I'm not. Panting, I get back to my feet, wincing at the collection of aches and pains reawakened by my far-from-elegant fall. Behind me, the cries of battle rage on. I'm focused on the five men before me. So far, only the one horse and warrior have truly noted me. I feel as though an entire afternoon has passed since I fell, but it seems not.

Slowly, I watch my foeman's mouth open, no doubt to alert his fellow warriors of my arrival. I surge upwards, hand extended, as though I can punch him from here, which of course, I can't. His horse, bedecked in shimmering iron, with the design of the Wessex wyvern on its harness and equipment, doesn't even move aside at my ineffectual attack, but I can just glimpse the sword's hilt beneath its front legs. With a swift word of thanks to the animal, I bend and in the same movement thrust the weapon upwards, coming around the right side of the horse and impaling the warrior beneath his chin.

His mouth falls slack as blood pools down his chest. His words of warning stutter. I yank my sword back. He falls with the movement, the horse moving two steps forward and then two steps backwards, assisting the dead rider to the ground. I eye the animal, almost convinced I see respect on its long face.

But the crash of the dead man brings the attention of the four remaining mounted warriors, although he sounded no more loudly than when I fell. I slap the spare horse's rump, so that the animal bunches its legs and jumps back over the gap between the drier land and the marsh. At least there's more room now. And I'm going to need it, for my horse has also run from the island, and four mounted Wessex warriors are looming their way towards me.

My gaze rests on a foeman, who rides a tan mare with wise eyes and a coronet of white between her ears. I quickly bend and wipe the dead man's blood on his tunic. The cloth is fine, perhaps made from nettle, not flax, its colourful green, at least three times dyed. A lot of labour went into that item, and I've just smeared it with the dark red of a dead man.

'Bastard,' he glowers, unable to tear his eyes away from my action. He's pulled his shield before him and has a spear to hand.

'Good to see you intend to make this a fair fight,' I mutter. He'll be able to protect himself and stab at me from much further away than I can. Quickly, I grip my weapon. I've stabbed and jabbed with this sword, but I've not truly tested its weight. And then there's no more time.

The shimmering iron of the spear point comes close. I thrust the shield between me and it, but all the same, the advantage of his height and reach almost lifts me clear from the ground. I manage to keep one foot level, but the blow turns me, and for a brief moment, I see how my allies are faring. They're doing well, Wulfheard, Oswy, Godeman and Wulfgar are whittling their way through the Wessex warriors. Brihthild's still fighting viciously. Whoever trained her ensured she knew how to use her lighter frame and agility to good against taller and more powerfully built men. I admire her skill even as I fear for my fellow Mercians. I wish I'd known of her skills. I could have trained against her on the way to Canterbury.

Not that there's time to be considering all this. Hastily, I pivot, keeping my shield and sword close to my body. I can't allow the spear to pierce me. My shield keeps the spear at bay, and now the longer reach is an impediment to the mounted warrior. He can't move his weapon quickly enough to stop me from forcing it aside. Ideally, I'd like to pull it from his grip, but my hands are full. I can hold it downward with my shield and work my way closer and closer to him. I recognise the warrior as one of those who came to examine the horses inside Canterbury. If they've made it here so quickly, then surely Lord Æthelwulf and the ealdorman will be along shortly. Before that happens, we need to apprehend Brihthild and learn the truth of the events of the last few weeks.

The Wessex warrior watches me fearlessly as I draw level with the animal's tall shoulder. I could lash out with my sword and take the horse's life, but it's the man who's trying to kill me, not his mount. Now, so close to him, I'd welcome my seax, not my sword. The spear is too long for the man to attack me, but my sword is too long as well. Two of the mounted warriors are even closer now, one of them preparing to threaten me with his spear.

I'm forced to move my shield from where it holds the first rider's spear away from my body. Quickly, I raise my weapon to strike at his unprotected legs, but he's quicker. I sense the spear falling to the ground, the wood of the long shaft bouncing upwards to hit my knee, and he has a seax ready for my throat.

'Damn it,' I murmur, moving three steps aside to avoid the glittering blade, which I quickly realise allows me the room I need to impale him with my sword.

Now our position is reversed. I have a longer reach than him, and I use it. He can't utilise his shield to protect him because it's on the other side of his body. Neither is his fellow warrior close enough, but instead he's hiding behind his shield and using the spear to try and skewer me.

With a sweeping movement, my sword slices into his leg, just below his knee. It doesn't sever the lower leg, but enough blood wells for me to know it was a close thing. Only my desire not to wound the horse stays my hand. His shrieks of agony echo in the confined space of the marshlands, louder than the cries of raven or eagle, and in that moment, I skip forward into the breach between the second mounted warrior's spear and his horse. I thrust my sword upwards, behind his shield, held loosely to allow his horse to move, and feel the soft give of flesh.

He screams as I dance backwards. I'm caught between both wounded men, the one howling like a fox in heat and the other with glazed eyes to hide his pain. I know which one will give me the most trouble.

Quickly, I bring my shield up before me to counter the blow from the second mounted warrior. His eyes glow with the red of his rapidly draining blood, his teeth gritted around the shudder of pain. I don't know where I hit him because he still holds his shield before him, but it's done enough damage.

I expect him to reach for his seax or sword, but instead, he thrusts the shield at me. I feel the uncomfortable thrum of agony along my sword arm. I try to keep my grip on the weapon, but it's impossible. My hand opens, and the weapon falls. The shield hits my face, my nose guard protecting it but not my chin. My mouth fills with blood, and my rage explodes.

Bending to grip the sword, ignoring the humming lack of sensation along my lower arm and into my hand, I rush to the far side of the horse, bending beneath the animal's long neck, turning the sword as I go, so that I pierce the inside of his upper thigh, assuring myself that he'll die now. Without pausing, I rush towards the final two warriors, ignoring the thundering rush of more hooves. I don't know if they're my allies or more of the enemy; these mounted warriors need to die.

From behind, I hear the clatter of another lifeless form hitting the ground, but my focus is entirely on the two remaining uninjured foemen. The one licks his lips behind his chin and nose guard, watching me come closer. The other has his head turned away from me, no doubt deciding whether to flee. I rush at him, shield batting aside the horse's head with a soft whinny of pain. I don't want to stab the animal. They're too valuable, but my enemies will die this day. I extend my reach and leap upwards, using the firm footing to almost draw level with my enemy. He shrieks as his eyes greet mine, unaware of my approach. Once more, I recognise the man as one of the ealdorman's warriors who've been eyeing the horses up ever since we arrived in Canterbury.

My sword offers a glancing blow to his byrnie, but as with the other men, he's well equipped. He doesn't carry a spear, but instead a shimmering seax, his shield protecting the left side of his body.

I feel the tug of his blade on my byrnie, but not the hot swell of blood. That's all in my mouth. I hope I've not lost a tooth in the fight. I land on my back foot, preparing to surge upwards again, but the warrior's kicking his horse, tugging on the animal's reins. I see I'll not be given the same chance again.

With my right foot, I step on his left, where it rests in the stirrup. His eyes bulge, and the creak of the leather assures me it won't hold for long, but I don't need it to. Kicking upwards with my left leg, I knock him askew so that he has to redouble his grip on the rein. With a touch back on the ground with my left foot, just for impetus, I lift my knee once more, but not to kick him. Then I'm sitting on the horse's neck, uncomfortably close to my enemy, with my sword about to impale him, already slipping beyond the protection of his padded byrnie and through the shimmering links of his mail shirt. He bucks forward, still determined to kill me first. My chest heaves, and my rage pulses. I feel the glance of his seax against my chin guard, but it's too late. He slumps forward. I lift my right leg to kick him from the horse.

There are two men for me to kill now, as I right myself on the horse, who doesn't seem to notice the change in rider. My gaze is torn towards where Brihthild still fights. My allies are doing their best, but the thunder of horses' hooves I heard wasn't from more of the Mercians, but rather a huge influx of Wessex warriors to the back of the clearing.

The Mercians are spread out, embattled in small groups against the surviving initial Wessex force, and now there are more and more enemy warriors who could separate us, and some of them are already moving to close in behind Landwine and Kyre. If we're not careful then the two men will be lost to us.

'Wulfheard.' I bellow his name, hoping to gain his attention and warn him of the problem, and where he needs to order the others to protect their allies, but he's engaged in a bloody battle with three of the Wessex men. He prevents the other men from reaching Landwine.

'Landwine,' I roar instead, hoping to alert him, but he's focused only on Brihthild, as is Kyre.

'Bastards,' I mutter, looking frantically for Oswy. About now, we could do with Commander Eahric arriving with the rest of the Mercians, but I imagine his only concern is to keep the bishops safe inside Canterbury.

'Bollocks,' I murmur, effortlessly countering the blows from the final uninjured warrior. He didn't want to run. He seemed keen to fight me. Now I have other problems and could do without his attention.

'Kyre,' I cry, encouraging my borrowed horse backwards so that we can run at the divide between this island oasis and the marshlands. I might be able to get over there, but it's not as simple as just aiming my horse where I want to go. The ground's uncertain, and there are Wessex warriors everywhere I look, moving to surround us, and worryingly few Mercians.

This time Kyre hears my cry. His head swivels, noticing the warriors coming closer. I tear my gaze away, focusing on the leap the horse must make, only for the animal to rear backwards. It's all I can do to stay mounted, my feet luckily in the stirrups. My eyes catch a growing line of red on the animal's backside, and I know what's happened.

With a sweeping cut, I slice across the enemy's hands, where they rest on the leather reins and reach back to slap the animal on its backside. The animal bolts. It's enough for the Wessex warrior to thunder to the ground. I jump free, following him down, taking my sword with me to thrust it through where his heart should beat. His leg lies at a strange angle, his face bleached of all colour, apart from where his blond beard's coated with blood. His breath bubbles. I know I ease his agony when I kill him, but he needs to die. I'm not cruel enough to slice a horse. I'm not evil enough to allow a man to choke on his own blood. Even if the bastard was trying to kill me.

Now, there's only one enemy left on the island. I've already wounded him. If he lives through this, which he won't, he'll have only just more than half a leg. His howls have grown weaker, but his eyes are furious as I turn to face him.

'You bastard Mercian,' he menaces. His spear is on the ground, abandoned there when this fight began. He can't jump down and get it, not with his leg hanging by sinew and little else. His trews are stained with so much blood, they're blacker than a five-times-dyed piece of cloth. But he has his horse and his seax. And his shield. His pain and fury will also assist him.

'Same to you, you Wessex arsehole,' I glower, stamping my way through his dead allies to rear up before him. I could mount up and meet him at an equal height, but that would remove my advantage. He's wounded. In all honesty, he's bloody dying, but until then, he means to fight.

Casting aside my shield, I grip the seax in my hand. Lifeless bodies are scattered around me, everything they held dear in this life gone from their grips. If they were Norse, they might have made more effort to die with a blade in hand.

With a seax and a sword, I step towards him. He tries to turn his horse to meet my attack, but the animal's used to two feet to kick it. He only has the use of one, the other one flailing lifelessly at the end of his knee. If he's not careful, it'll fall without me having to do anything. Then, only a hot flame and the stink of a cauterising knife will aid him. That's not going to happen. Not here. I don't believe anything could burn in this dank place.

His seax has cut me once, but I don't fear it, not this time. The sound of my fellow warriors fades away. There's only my breath, and his breath and the huff of the horse. The animal sounds as though it could do with some herbal remedies to ease its congestion, and he and I mean to kill one another. The horse has no interest in what's about to happen.

Only then, the rumble of hooves draws near, and despite myself, I flick a glance over my shoulder to see a Wessex horse, eyes wide, being urged onwards by its rider. They're coming this way, the name Ælfwold on the lips of the man. My lonely, wounded warrior has someone who means to save him. I can't allow that to happen.

With quick steps, I jump again, using one of the dead men's bodies to boost me higher, hoping my foot doesn't crack through his ribcage. Almost level with the Wessex warrior, I kick out, urging myself higher, using my left hand to stab into his arm with my seax while I menace him with the hilt of my sword. His eyes narrow, his seax ready to stab me, but he can't stop his body from trying to veer away from my sword, and at that moment, neck exposed, I reverse the grip on my seax and slice through it. Blood rains down on me as I land, winded, beneath the animal.

With no thought for whether the man lives or dies, aware of the rider coming on behind, I push his body to the side and clamber into the saddle, feeling his heat and slickness with a grimace.

Both feet in the stirrups, which are too short for my long legs, I knee the animal aside, encouraging it away from the stink of blood and piss. While the Wessex warrior howls in fury, coming towards me, I dash towards Landwine and Kyre, who are still fighting Brihthild, only with West Saxon warriors hastening to assist her.

I need to get to them. I must stop them from being entirely overwhelmed by the Wessex warriors under Lord Æthelwulf's command, and I might just be too bloody late.

22

The horse stumbles on the rough ground. I fall forward. Better to ride without stirrups than ones that are too bloody short. I don't have time to ensure the stirrups are comfortable. My grip falters, and before I even realise, I'm watching the clouds and the sky pass in the wrong direction, only to land with all the air driven from my body. Once more, I feel the sharp pulse of all my old hurts, especially along my belly and back. But I need to get up. I must protect my friends.

With the horse's breath in my face, I roll sidewards, reaching for my discarded blades.

'Icel, get over here.' Wulfheard's cry reaches me. I stand, blinking the stars from my eyes and the thud from my head, to see that they're becoming overwhelmed again. Lord Æthelwulf and Ealdorman Hereberht have more men to direct than I could imagine. Where they've been hiding inside Canterbury, I don't know. They send them towards the fight. My eyes flicker from Landwine and Kyre who continue to fight Brihthild to Wulfheard, and witness the arrival of Æthelmod, Maneca, Uor and Ordlaf, who manage to evade the Wessex force by using the path we must have taken from the road. They quickly assess the situation. While they aim their mounts towards Landwine, Kyre and Brihthild, I pull myself back into the saddle of the horse that threw me and direct it towards Wulfheard, who's also in danger of being routed.

The Wessex warrior that tried to stop me from killing Ælfwold has turned his horse. I know he'll chase me. I must reach my fellow warriors first. Lord Æthelwulf stays mounted, watching from the side of the clearing, his eyes everywhere as he assesses the battle. He has three warriors surrounding him. I don't believe they'll join the fight. Their job is to protect the king's son. And Lord Æthelwulf seems confident of victory. A wise man should never be assured of anything until it's actually happened but he does have the numbers to overwhelm us. The ealdorman is beside him.

I consider what happened between Lord Æthelwulf and Oswy. Both men still live. I can't see that Lord Æthelwulf appears wounded in any way. Perhaps the Wessex warriors protected their lord after all, and that's why there are only three of them, and not the seven from earlier. Although how Oswy escaped so many is worth considering. Maybe he just understood it wasn't his fight and bolted through the open gateway.

The horse I ride is more alert than me. As it rolls to a canter, I realise it's looking where it goes. The animal's well trained, and seemingly used to fighting in such conditions. Either that or it knows that failing to be careful will result in a broken leg. Already, I can hear the screaming of a wounded animal which hasn't been so observant. Someone needs to put it out of its misery. It won't be me anytime soon.

Wulfheard and my allies face double their number. Oswy's battling two men. Godeman and Wulfgar face three to their two.

Wulfheard's the most at risk. He has three foemen alone. I watch as a sword, seax and a war axe all try to inflict a final blow on him, his mount taking the lightest of touches from his knees to evade the enemy.

My horse canters too slowly. I'd urge it to be quicker, but the smell of the marshlands assures me that beneath the tufts of grass lies treachery. Finally, I'm close enough to land a blow on the Wessex warrior wielding a sword. He's the greatest threat to Wulfheard as he's able to attack from so much further away.

Snarling lips turn to face me as my sword pricks a thin line of blood above his byrnie. The man's huge, with the neck of an ox. The score I raise is the length of my palm. I meet his gaze with a curled lip and cry of fury. His eyes widen, but his reactions are fast as he ducks aside from the stabbing motion of my sword. He doesn't entirely evade the sharper edges of the blade. They're already dented from the ongoing fight. A thin shard of dislodged iron shimmers close to my eye. I jerk aside to avoid it, but he sees a chance. Now his blade is too close to my neck. However, the short stirrups give me an idea. I've jumped to fight my enemy warriors. Now I can tower over the man even though he's huge and my horse isn't.

With a heave of effort, I stand, trusting the animal to stay firm-footed. Using my sword's hilt like a war axe, I hit the warrior's helm, his eyes momentarily losing focus as the sharp ring of iron chimes too loudly in his ears. It's all the opportunity I need. Before I retake my saddle, my seax stabs into his open mouth. I grip it tightly to release it from the warrior's teeth. He's dead already.

Urging the horse onwards, I reach the warrior with the war axe. It's a vicious-looking thing, blackened in the heat of the fire to make it look as though eyes peer at me from its haft. I veer aside from the first blow, my foeman prepared to meet my attack before I am.

'Is that all you've got?' he spits, long hair flowing beneath his warrior's helm. His gloves aren't just leather, but seem to have iron rings around them as well, no doubt to protect his fingers. They catch the glow from the late afternoon sun, momentarily blinding me, as I think how to counter his attack.

Again, the war axe sweeps an arc too close to me for comfort. I'm lying almost entirely against the long neck of the horse to evade it.

'Bastard,' I glower, aware he could better me here if I'm not careful. His weapon is almost an extension of his arm. He's used it many times before and knows how to kill. I'd like my shield in hand right now, but I don't have it. He comes towards me, closer and closer, the sweep of his war axe making it impossible for me to sit upright and make use of my blades. The horse I ride seems reluctant to move as well, my feet kicking against its belly not its flanks, the short stirrups, so useful only moments ago, now a hindrance.

My view closes to one of horsehair and the edge of that blade, coming ever, ever closer, if only he'd lower it a fraction. Does he mean to spare the horse, who'll surely die alongside me, should the weapon finally reach its mark, or does he mean to kill me in some other way?

I inhale the familiar scent of hay and horse sweat, of my stinking exertions, and the choking stench of the marshlands. As his war axe seeks for my neck, the animal lurches forwards, not of my doing, and we're both free from the menace.

Surprised, I see Oswy's smirking grin, his foot still extended where he booted the animal aside. His smile only widens as his seax stabs into the axe wielder's arm. The warrior roars with rage. While he looks towards Oswy, I lash out with my seax, a sweeping arc across his left thigh. Blood wells immediately. Oswy slashes again. I force my seax point further up our enemy's leg, seeking where the lifeblood thrums through his body. The animals are close together. Hooves and legs tangling with our own. The man's fury bellows from his lips, as Oswy launches himself across the divide to drive his seax upwards and into the man's nose, evading the nose guard.

My blade pierces his upper leg simultaneously. He's bleeding and dying even as his war axe sweeps towards Oswy, who's not quick enough to retreat. With a slap of my seax, the horse spurs to freedom, desperate to be away from the smell and stink. Oswy's unhurt. The war axe thuds to the ground, remaining upright, the wooden haft forlorn, abandoned by its warrior, whose horse rides towards the Wessex warriors protecting Lord Æthelwulf.

'Bollocks,' Oswy huffs, pleased to have prevailed. Wulfheard joins us, all of our eyes on the terrified horse. The Wessex force can't stop the animal, which only increases its speed as it senses safety despite the flailing body on its back. As the Wessex warrior is finally flung free, the horse surges through the defensive line surrounding Lord Æthelwulf and the ealdorman.

Oswy and I direct our horses towards Landwine and Kyre, fighting our way through the press of horses and mounted warriors trying to kill our fellow Mercians. Protected backs face me. I stab and slash at them so that when they turn, I can slice my blade along their exposed faces or necks as Oswy fights his way closer, kicking and hacking with his blade. Heat grows, the stench of fear and the marsh making it impossible to get a clean gasp of air. I choke on men's blood and sweat, damp swinging hair beneath helms, and the thrusting punches and stabs of fists and blades bringing the scent too close. But we're prevailing. We're getting closer and closer to Landwine, Kyre and Brihthild. A woman's high shriek of fury assures me that she's about to be overwhelmed. I'd know some pity for her, but she's played us all for fools. We must know what she knows.

Closer and closer. I can see Landwine, where he turns his horse in a tight circle, stabbing with his seax and punching with his shield, his horse nipping and biting with its huge teeth. The Wessex foeman try and prevent him but the whirling fury is impossible to counter. And then he's beside Kyre, and between the backs and faces of Wessex warriors, I see Kyre engaged in a bloody fight with Brihthild.

'Come on,' I urge Oswy and my mount, as the gap closes around them. I keep my gaze on where they were, only to be distracted by a blow to the right of my head, coming from nowhere, stunning me so that a seax point just misses piercing my eye. I jerk to the side, only to collide with another blade; this one glimpsed from the corner of my vision, the sharpened edge glinting with menace.

With my knees drawn up too high, I don't have the means to move as much as I'd like, rotating the horse as Landwine did, but I can overtop most of these warriors. Surging upwards, seax to hand, I stab down and knock aside the helm of the man who tried to blind me. Blood surges upwards, but I'm already standing, using his body to hold me upright, as I seek out Landwine and Kyre amongst the press of bodies.

'Get down,' Oswy roars to me, echoed by Wulfheard, but I've seen what I need to do, and I must do it. Landwine's overwhelmed, and Kyre needs his assistance, or Brihthild will kill him. Already, blood smears Kyre's left shoulder. His face is pale and bruising, his helm knocked askew in the press of bodies.

'Bollocks,' I exclaim, but there's no choice. With a swift prayer, and a thought for King Wiglaf, and how this can only be his fault driving my anger, I vault forwards onto the back of a tan horse. It startles at my added weight, the cry of its rider echoing that shock. But I'm not stopping. I jump forward again, this time landing on the rider, facing the way I'm coming. His thin face and drooping moustache twist in fury. I feel the cold press of iron on my thigh, but I don't stop.

The next horse is black as night, a nick of blood behind its saddle, showing it's been wounded. I wince as I feel its legs falter, but I'm onto the next animal, this one so pale that to call it sandy would be incorrect. It has the coloured of bleached cloth. Just two horses away, I can see Kyre and Landwine.

Only now, the enemy have realised my purpose. The rider of the bleached horse reaches for my legs. I knee him in the face, so that he recoils and falls backwards. His horse shuffles forwards and backwards. As I spring towards the final animal, I feel hands on me and stumble from the air like a bird caught by a falcon, tumbling to the soggy mass beneath me. The air leaves me, the scent of shit and piss overwhelming me as I flail with an eye full of something green and stinging. I pitch upwards, gasping for air, wiping the muck from my face and reaching for my lost weapons. Once more, curious horse eyes look at me, while above the cries of frustrated Wessex warriors try to sight me. Ahead, I see the familiar legs of Kyre's horse. I scamper to all fours, plunging my hands into filth and crap as I finally emerge close to the most bitter fight of all. Kyre and Brihthild.

With a cry of fury, her seax connects with Kyre. I see him wobble, and his arm waver. A flood of blood begins to bubble from his chest. I reach up and grip Brihthild around the waist, pulling her to the ground beside me, holding her tightly no matter the stink on my hands, and the way she bucks and strains against me.

'Stay still,' I menace. 'Stay still, or this seax blade will end your life.' Not waiting for a reply, I open my mouth wide. 'I've got her,' I cry. 'I've got her,' I call again, unsure if anyone can hear me, but Oswy is at my side, and then Landwine, but not Kyre, although Wulfheard's arrived too.

'Tie her up,' Wulfheard instructs. More and more of the

Mercian warriors force their way to us, Wulfheard threatening all Wessex warriors who mean to come closer. Only when Oswy assures me that I can let go of our squirming prisoner do I release my grip, bending to suck in much-needed air, rushing to Kyre's side to stem the bleeding. From close by, we hear the rumble of more hooves coming.

'It's Commander Eahric,' Oswy announces, and I don't think I've ever been more pleased to hear those words. Although, a momentary panic for Cuthred has me concerned. Where is the boy? I hope he's with the Mercian bishops. Or Commander Eahric. He'd better not be fighting. Or dead. Wynflæd would kill me.

'Show me,' I demand from Kyre, trying to lift his byrnie and tunic, for all he feebly batters me aside. 'Show me, you damn arse,' I repeat. This time, I have more success. Wincing, I eye the wound, only to reach out, forced to grab him to stop him tumbling from the back of his mount. 'Help me,' I push through tight lips. The strain of keeping Kyre from dropping is telling after such a long fight. I've felt weak and then strong, but abruptly I'm weak. Despite all my training with Wulfheard, despite my growing arms and thighs, what I lack is the ability to endure over long periods.

Luckily, Oswy's quick to assist me. Together, we lift Kyre free. Well, we let him fall without hurting himself, would be a better description. I lift clear his tunic and byrnie, hoping to staunch the bleeding before it makes him even weaker, but whatever's happening around us, it's not going as well as I'd have liked. I can hear angry voices. Some of them are sharper and speak with the Mercian tongue, others roll with that of the Wessex-born, but no one seems to be disarming.

We may have Brihthild, and I might be on the ground, tending to Kyre, even while blood drips from my cut chin, but the Wessex force continue to surround us.

'What's happening?' I huff through tight lips, trying to stay focused on Kyre. My eyes keep straying to the legs of the Wessex horses, and the shiver of iron raised in anger that thrums through the air.

'Nothing good,' Oswy assures me. He's not really any help, but no doubt, since he aided me after my beating, he thinks himself half a healer.

'Get your damn hands out of the way.' I slap them aside, noticing the blood on his gloves. I've pulled my hands free, needing to check the skin close to Kyre's wound and to assure myself he has no more wounds. His skin's slick with sweat and blood, the smell of him noxious, although it could be the horse shit that still smears my face or the smell of the marsh.

'He won't be able to ride,' I announce, wishing I had my supplies with me and could pack the wound with moss and honey as a temporary measure. I could use Cuthred and that bloody huge sack of healing supplies Wynflæd lumbered him with.

'He's going to have to,' comes Wulfheard's gruff voice. 'Lord Æthelwulf doesn't want to let us leave, even though Commander Eahric matches his numbers. We need to make a run for it.'

I sit back on my heels at that, feeling the dankness of the marsh through my trews, and knowing it sticks uncomfortably to my skin. I move my head from side to side, and lift my shoulders to my ears, anything to banish the tension that floods my body.

I look to Oswy. He grimaces back at me. When I was wounded last year, my fellow warriors had time to help me, but we're to be denied that and yet I need to ensure that Kyre lives.

'Do we at least get to keep the woman?' Oswy demands, but I don't hear the answer, not above the shriek that comes from Brihthild at his words. She's a feisty bitch. I suspected it, but she's been so placid, so keen to learn and help her brother – until he died, that is. She's excellent at artifice. I even believed her grief, although I suspect it now. For all we know, she might be a lord or lady.

Thinking of Brihthild reminds me of why I'm here, in Wessex, and my thoughts tumble back to the children, Coenwulf and Coelwulf, and their father, exiled in Frankia.

'We tie him to me,' I inform Oswy quickly. 'Help me mount, and then we tie him to me, and I'll ride like that.'

'On what?' Oswy questions. 'The horse you have is too small. We need an animal to take the weight of both of you.' I grimace at the reminder Brute isn't here with me. I wish I had Bicwide, the beast that started all these problems. I should have given him to the Wessex warrior back in Winchester. My stubbornness on the matter has led us to this. Yet if I'd not been so stubborn, we would've never come upon all the information, and hold the suspicions, we currently have.

'Do they have Bicwide and Cuthred?' I question Oswy. He rolls his eyes, opens his mouth to argue, but then stands and marches towards Wulfheard through the press of Mercian warriors. He slaps those he sees, no doubt pleased they yet live. I turn back to Kyre. His face is clammy, but his fingers grip my arm uncomfortably tight. He's unaware of what's happening around him, but that's not allowing him to give up. A tight smile touches my cheeks. He's a fighter. He won't die, no matter how far he has to ride, wounded and bleeding. At last, I realise, the wound has stopped flowing. I might be lacking all I need, but I have my knowledge.

'Yes, Bicwide's here. I've told Wulfheard we need him. Commander Eahric's protecting us, but Lord Æthelwulf, the Wessex ealdorman and him are having a proper war of words. It's a close-run thing, even though we've won for now. Cuthred's with the bishops.'

The knowledge that Cuthred lives is reassuring. I might

survive this, and the lash of Wynflæd's fury. 'I thought the bishops had permission to enter the kingdom?' My body's exhausted but my mind remains sharp.

'We're hardly holy men,' Oswy counters aggressively. His argument is valid.

'We're at least three days' ride from returning to Mercia.' I resume my reasoning. 'We can't be chased for all that time.'

'Then what would you have us do?' Kyre mumbles. I'm impressed he's alert enough to be following the discussion.

'We need to join up with the bishops and Cuthred. Then we can move more slowly and without fear of being attacked. It's not as though we're a threat to Lord Æthelwulf. All we want is Brihthild.'

'For now, that's all we want,' Oswy glowers. 'But he's not going to allow us to take her without a fight. I suspect he knows what she knows.' I hadn't considered that and I should have done. If Lord Æthelwulf is involved in this, he's going to want to make sure that Brihthild can't be forced to tell us the truth.

I sigh, hands busy as I try to make Kyre comfortable. For now, we're not going anywhere.

'Water,' Kyre requests. I turn to Oswy because I don't have any.

'Here,' he thrusts his water bottle towards me.

'Help me,' I urge him. Between us, we get Kyre upright enough that he can take small sips, for I won't allow him more than that. While we're busy, the thrum of violence dissipates in the air, all apart from Brihthild, whose shrieks never cease.

'Someone gag her,' Kyre mumbles, when he jerks awake once more. I still don't know if we're going to get Bicwide, and Wulfheard hasn't returned either. Whatever's happening between Commander Eahric, Wulfheard, Lord Æthelwulf and the Wessex ealdorman, it's taking a long time. If we're not careful, it'll be bloody dark, and we won't be able to go anywhere. Only then I detect a new voice.

Unable to stop myself, my head bobs upright, and I stand, focusing on a young man – well, older than me but still young – bedecked in his religious finery, which shimmers in the daylight. Before him, a monk carries a silver cross high in the air, almost like a war banner.

'That's not light,' Oswy murmurs at my side. We can both see where the poor monk sweats from his exertions, but it's what the archbishop has to say that draws my attention.

'Lord Æthelwulf, Ealdorman Hereberht.' His voice is rich with assurance. I'm impressed, despite myself. I've not yet caught sight of the archbishop despite our stay in Canterbury. 'The Mercians are here at my invitation.'

'Not all of them. They mean to take that woman as their prisoner.' I'm still standing, surrounded by my fellow Mercian warriors, and it's not that easy to see between horses' heads and arses, but Lord Æthelwulf's words of denial carry easily.

'Ah, the woman. Will we really cause more bloodshed just because of one of God's children?' All have fallen silent to listen to the archbishop speak. He's a voice of reason when all we can think of is violence.

'She's a woman of Wessex and should be protected.' Lord Æthelwulf's stubborn in his resolve.

'She's a child of God, as is everyone here. We should all be protected, but I hear worrying rumours of her involvement in a plot to wound small children with no mother or father to protect them. The sin of murder is a grievous one, especially if it imperils the kingship of one of our fellow kingdoms, and so she'll come with me. I'll decide on the merits of the accusations, dependent on her oaths and those who would speak for her, with words, as opposed to with iron.'

I consider who's had the time to inform the archbishop of all this. Perhaps it's Cuthred. It must be Cuthred. I doubt Commander Eahric and Wulfheard had the opportunity to apprise him of the truth behind the violence.

The words are reasoned, but a murmur of dismay ripples from my mouth. I'm not alone. However, of everyone there, it's Brihthild who screams the most against such an idea. A smile tugs on my lips. I don't like this, but in such a situation and so far from home, it's better if Brihthild is held accountable to the archbishop. I know he's eager to be seen as a bridge between the Wessex and Mercian kingdoms. This could be his chance to perform some much-needed diplomacy. Provided he discovers Brihthild's conspiracy and that of Lord Æthelwulf's involvement in it.

'Is Cuthred with the archbishop?' I mutter to Oswy in the sudden silence, but there's no reply, and I can't see him. Cuthred must still be within Canterbury, with the Mercian bishops. That boy, I think, has always been able to talk quickly.

'My lord,' Lord Æthelwulf eventually argues, but Commander Eahric agrees first. His words are echoed by the Mercian bishops, who I realise have escorted the archbishop. They seem incongruous, in this marshland in all their finery. They also look horrified at the wounded and dead warriors. Some of their number look desperate to tend to the dead and dying, but they're too fearful. I stifle a smirk. I see Cuthred. He looks bruised and battered, but not at all afraid. If anything, he looks angry to have been left with the bishops and not be joining the fight.

'Then it shall be so,' the archbishop confirms.

Commander Eahric speaks once more. 'Wulfheard, ensure the prisoner's handed into the keeping of the archbishop on our return to Canterbury.' I don't hear Wulfheard's agreement, but it must be given, for slowly, the West Saxon warriors unwillingly begin to disperse. I catch sight of Lord Æthelwulf, his expression surprisingly bland for a man who might just have lost a great deal. Brihthild's held tightly on a horse, with Wulfheard to one side, and Commander Eahric to the other. The Wessex ealdorman is also with them, no doubt there to ensure nothing ill befalls Brihthild on her journey to Canterbury.

I turn to Oswy.

'We need to discover the truth before she makes it back to Canterbury.'

'And how should we do that? We have to make sure Kyre's well.'

I've not forgotten the wounded man, and neither has Wulfheard, for Bicwide is being brought towards us, the animal placid although his eyes perk up on seeing me. I consider who rode him from the archbishop's stables. Who has no horse to ride now? But I'm just pleased to see him. I need him.

'If Lord Æthelwulf insists on being there when she's questioned, we'll never discover anything,' I hiss. This was the task laid at my feet by King Wiglaf, to discover the truth about events in Winchester. It's not at all what we suspected, but Brihthild, I'm convinced, is the key to it all.

'I'll see what I can do, but you must stay with Kyre,' Oswy announces unhappily. He mounts up quickly, and moves away, leaving Landwine and me to attempt to wake Kyre and get him seated on Bicwide. Cuthred also rushes towards us, bringing Bicwide with him. Perhaps Cuthred rode Bicwide. Not that it matters. All that's important is that I have Bicwide at my disposal.

'Let me help.' Cuthred's on his knees, inspecting Kyre. He does so quickly, his hands seemingly everywhere at once. I'm relieved to see him.

It takes a long time, but eventually, mounted, and with some of Commander Eahric's men as our companions and one of the Mercian bishops there to remind the Wessex contingent left by

Lord Æthelwulf that we're essentially under a truce, we move away from the woodlands. Taking the route the West Saxons must have used to arrive so quickly. I'm consumed by thoughts of Brihthild and who'll speak in her defence. We must find out what we can from her, and I'm not at all convinced that Oswy is the right man for the task.

23

As we near Canterbury a short while later, I'm tending to Kyre, where he slumps before me. We could have tied him prostrate over the horse, but that would only have made his wound bleed again. Cuthred is beside me, trying to do more, but until we've stopped moving, there's little more that can be done. We use a different gateway to gain entry, but few watch our arrival. My concern is all for Oswy and his endeavours to get to Brihthild, and for Kyre and how we'll heal him. What if Wulfheard won't allow Oswy close to Brihthild, or the bishop? I've realised that we have not only a Mercian bishop escorting us, Bishop Heahbeorht of Worcester, but a Wessex one as well. These holy men keep their sharp gaze on all of us as though wanting us to defy the decree of their archbishop. Aside from whatever Oswy's doing, we all behave ourselves.

We're taken, as I suspected, to the archbishop's complex. Cuthred scampers off to find his supplies. With Landwine's assistance, and he's sporting a few wounds himself, I manage to get Kyre off the horse and settled in an area of the stables that's free from horse shit. Kyre groans, and his eyelids flutter open again. But his mind's razor-sharp.

'Where's Oswy?'

'I don't know,' I complain, turning as though he'll just appear. We were the last to arrive back inside Canterbury. I don't like the feeling of the walls closing around us. Cuthred's eyes are alive as he tumbles to his knees, his retrieved sack in hand, still stuffed with Wynflæd's supplies, busy as he reaches for the items he needs to tend to Kyre.

'Oswy waylaid me. He told me to tell you to be alert. These walls have ears.'

'Did he say anything else?'

'No, just that,' Cuthred announces. He's already examining Kyre's injury with a fascination seen only on Wynflæd's face in the past. He truly is intrigued by how to heal and tend to the sick and injured.

'So, we don't know if he spoke to Brihthild then?' Kyre whispers. I don't think it's because he's feeling weak but rather because he's heeding Oswy's caution.

'She's been taken into St Saviour's, and I saw some of the monks rush towards the other church, where we buried her brother. They mean to find people to speak on her behalf.'

'But we must determine what she knows?' Frustration makes my voice squeak.

'Or, perhaps we don't,' Oswy announces, arriving at that moment. He casts a look over at Cuthred's endeavours. 'I couldn't get close to her,' he mutters darkly. 'The archbishop had her ride beside him, and none of his guards would let me through. And now Lord Æthelwulf has demanded an audience with the archbishop. We won't be getting any answers from her. And we'll be lucky if we make it back to Mercia. I imagine that, even now, Lord

Æthelwulf has sent for reinforcements.' The news isn't unexpected.

'What does Commander Eahric say?'

'He's pissed at being caught up in all this.'

I sit back on my heels, trying to absorb all that Oswy's telling me.

'Surely it's enough that one woman is causing all these problems,' Cuthred murmurs.

'The archbishop's determined he's the only one who can resolve this problem, but Lord Æthelwulf's yapping at his heels like a damn dog. The Mercian bishops and Commander Eahric intend only to ensure we make it back to Mercia without further problems. We won't be getting our hands on Brihthild, not again. So, we've lost our chance to discover the truth of her involvement in this.'

Gloom settles upon us all. We're all bruised or bleeding, although none as bad as Kyre. We've not managed to accomplish what we need to do.

'We might as well have stayed in Mercia,' Oswy offers with a shrug. I glower at his defeated tone, but he's right. If anything, all we'll have done is make the discord between Wessex and Mercia worse.

'Can we prove she killed her brother?' Cuthred questions, sitting back to eye his handiwork. He's stitched Kyre's skin together; the need to cauterise it long since passed. I eye the stitches, wishing he'd been there instead of Oswy to bind my belly back together. I don't even want to consider the uneven scar that marks me now.

'How would we do that?'

'We could look at his body?' Cuthred offers. 'We didn't look that closely when he died.'

'No, we didn't,' Wulfheard muses. 'But it's not as though the monks will allow us to dig up a body.' But then I'm struck by a thought.

'Do we still have his tunic? He was buried without it, wasn't he? If so, we might see some mark on it to show how he was murdered.'

'But how would that help us with Brihthild and the archbishop?'

'I doubt he'd want a murderer in his holy complex. There's a difference between being suspected of trying to kill some children in another kingdom, and murdering your own brother. Isn't there?'

'I still don't see how it would prove her guilt.'

'No, perhaps not.' I deflate, wishing there was something else that might assist us. All these half-thoughts and possibilities are a far cry from any sort of solid proof. 'Tell the bishop,' I direct at Wulfheard. 'Tell him that she's the murderer. We've seen her seax. We suspect it was the blade that skewered her brother. See what happens then.'

Wulfheard meets my gaze, holding it for a moment too long, and then nods sharply.

'You really are invested in this, Icel. It would be better if you weren't, but we've come this far. We may as well see what can actually be accomplished.'

With that, he leaves us. The soft snores of Kyre remind me that I'm just as exhausted. We've not been told where to sleep or eat, but right now, sleep is more important. I'm not alone in that. Oswy's slumped against the wall of the stable. Landwine's already sleeping, standing against the same wall. Cuthred's alert, as is Maneca.

'Wake me as soon as something happens,' I inform Cuthred, and take myself to where Bicwide stands in a stable. He has another horse for company. I might fear being trampled, but I'll try my luck. Better than cramming myself in the other stable with the rest of the Mercians.

* * *

It's a probing nose that wakes me. I can still just about see in the gloom, but Bicwide clearly thinks I'm in his way. Lumbering to my feet, I run my hands along his body and all four legs, assuring myself that he's hale. I eye him. This all began with him. Well, not with him. This all started with King Wiglaf's demand, but it all became very interesting when Bicwide was sold to me. We've been chased since then. We've killed, and Brihthild has hoodwinked us. And yet, all we know is rumours and half-whispers. Is Lord Æthelwulf involved, as we believe he is? Where did the amber come from? How did any of these people gain access to the Mercians who are also involved in this? My mind spins with the possibilities. Are we wrong? Is it nothing to do with Bicwide and the Wessex warriors who wanted his saddle? Am I seeing a conspiracy where none exists?

No, I berate myself. There are too many coincidences. Neither, I realise, am I the only one to have perceived them. My thoughts turn to Bishop Æthelweald. He wasn't one of the Mercian bishops who came into the woodlands to assist the archbishop. Indeed, his absence was conspicuous. And he has the best access of all to the king's wife and her son, and, indeed, to every member of the king's court when he resides at Tamworth, as well as Brother Sampson, or Heca, who wrote the vellum letter. Further afield, at Worcester, it would be the other bishops, but not in Tamworth, and Tamworth is where the men employed by Wulfnoth went to receive their payment.

Possibilities whirl in my mind. The queen. Wulfnoth. Brihthild, even King Ecgberht and Lord Æthelwulf. And then a commotion outside rouses me from my thoughts. With a slap for Bicwide's backside, I amble out of the door, keen to see what's happening in the growing daylight.

There's someone at the closed gateway commanding to be admitted. I can hear their loud demands to be allowed inside, and equally, the muffled responses of those who mean to deny them. I consider who it might be as I walk closer. I feel the cool breeze in my sweat-dried hair and beard and shudder at how filthy I feel. I'd welcome bathing or just some cold water to throw over my face.

I'm not alone in striding towards the gateway. I see Wulfheard there, as well as Lord Æthelwulf and Ealdorman Hereberht. Commander Eahric has also been roused. He looks exhausted. And I also notice Bishop Æthelweald. How strange that I've just been thinking of him.

'Allow them entry,' Lord Æthelwulf shouts to the men on guard duty, but they seem unwilling to do so.

'Commander?' I recognise the Mercian voices as they call to Eahric. This then is perplexing. Lord Æthelwulf wants to allow whoever is outside to enter, but the Mercians on guard duty are less keen. My heart thuds dully inside my body, a hollowness in my chest assuring me that this development isn't a good one, not for the Mercians.

'Allow them entry,' Lord Æthelwulf huffs, but Commander Eahric doesn't echo those words.

'We were told no one is to enter, on the archbishop's order,' a voice refuses.

'And I'm the king of Wessex's son, and I vouch for them.'

'No one is to vouch for anyone who's not already involved in this mess,' Commander Eahric retorts. I rush to catch Wulfheard.

'What's all this?' I demand to know. He shakes his head.

'They're loyal to Lord Æthelwulf, or so the man who came to

the archbishop's hall informed us. We can't ask the archbishop. He's praying.'

'Then surely they should just wait,' I offer.

'Yes, they should, but Lord Æthelwulf's strangely unprepared to be patient.'

By now, we've reached the gateway, and I nod at the belligerent-looking Mercians standing there, with their weapons drawn, not against those outside the gateway, but those inside. Commander Eahric, wearing a perplexed expression, has taken himself to the gateway.

'Open it,' he instructs the Mercians. 'But only a little. I wish to see who demands admittance.'

I reach for my seax, but I don't even wear my weapons belt, having dropped it beside Bicwide so I could sleep. A mistake, and one I vow never to make again.

'Who are you?' I hear Commander Eahric's familiar voice query, only for a recognisable sound to fill the air. One just as well known to me but very unwelcome, as the gateway crashes open and mounted warriors erupt into the archbishop's complex.

24

These men aren't Mercians and it's not just the look of triumph I see on Lord Æthelwulf's face that assures me of that.

'Run,' Wulfheard calls, and he doesn't just mean me, but every Mercian there. While we've been making ourselves comfortable in the stables, many of the Mercian horses have been left outside to drink from deep stone troughs and eat the hay that's been liberally left in piles on what was probably once quite a nice herb garden.

I dash towards the stables, while Wulfheard veers to the side. I've lost sight of Commander Eahric, but I can already hear the telltale wet sounds of people being wounded, their cries of agony and pain muted beneath the rush of horses' hooves. My breath puffs before me, my chest tight with fury, rage and, I confess, fear. We're trapped.

'Mount up,' I roar to my fellow warriors when Oswy's head appears through the doorway. He turns quickly, pulling Cuthred with him, as I surge into the dark space. All of the men are on their feet, in various stages of wakefulness. 'The bastard has summoned reinforcements. We need to get out of here,' I call, hurrying to see

Kyre staggering upright with Landwine to one side. 'Can you ride?' I bark at him.

He nods mutely. I notice how pale his face is. Cuthred's already fiddling with bits and pieces left out of his sack of supplies for future use.

'Hurry up,' I urge him, reaching for Bicwide, and thrusting the saddle over his body. The horse is alert, his eyes bright in the gloom. 'We're going to have to make a run for it after all,' I call to any who'll hear.

Maneca has taken himself to the doorway, his horse ready beside him, his weapons gleaming. I thrust my byrnie over my head. I wince as it touches bruises from yesterday's altercation, as well as my cuts from Winchester. Not for the first time, I wish it was easy to put on in a hurry. My hands shake as I fumble for my weapons belt, not helped by the growing rumble of the fight that seems to draw closer and closer.

'Arseholes,' I hiss through tight lips, turning to ensure that Cuthred and Kyre are mounted. 'Have you got your seax?' I call to Wynflæd's young apprentice. He nods, and for once, I see real, stark fear on his face.

'The bastards,' Oswy huffs, heaving himself into the saddle. We have what weapons are to hand. I have my uncle's seax, and the sword I took from the dead Wessex warrior. I don't have time to fumble and find the rest of my equipment.

'Where's Wulfheard?' Kyre calls to me.

'He ran the other way. I don't know why. Maybe he's gone for the bishops?'

'Won't they be safe with the archbishop?' Landwine questions, but I only shrug. I don't know the answer to that.

'He'll join us, don't worry about him. I've seen him fight his way out of a nest of vipers. He'll do it again,' Oswy growls. It's evident he's not about to let us go after Wulfheard.

'What about Brihthild?' Cuthred questions. And that is a problem.

'We can't do anything about her. These Wessex scum have come to kill us despite the fact we have safe passage here. We need to stay together and head north.' Oswy's taken nominal command in the absence of Wulfheard. Not that he really needs to. We're warriors. We know what needs to be done. And, we're more than aware that our strength is as a unit of fighting men. Between us, we can keep Cuthred and Kyre safe. 'Come on then,' Oswy encourages, and Maneca mounts up and leads onwards. Outside I shudder in horror. The Wessex warriors aren't all equestrians. There's a contingent of at least thirty warriors fighting their way through Commander Eahric's Mercians.

'We need to help them,' I call, but Oswy's either not listening, or cares not to heed their difficulties. He's not alone.

'This way,' Maneca urges, turning aside from the gateway.

'Is there another exit?' I demand to know, my eyes never leaving Commander Eahric's. Either by some trick of the light, or because he truly does see me, I think Eahric waves his hand as he fights one of the enemy, encouraging us onwards. As we race around the side of the archbishop's complex, I see the archbishop, his face blackened with fury, rushing towards the fighting. He's surrounded by his monks and bishops. I'm surprised by how many of them carry blades and wear helms. They're a militant lot.

From inside the church itself, Wulfheard rushes towards us, escorted by Uor alongside the Mercian bishops. Æthelmod stands ready, with enough horses for all the men, and I also see another figure, bucking and twisting. Wulfheard has thought to capture Brihthild from under the archbishop's nose. I consider how he managed that. I'm sure the archbishop will be furious. He thought to end this peacefully. Not, I realise, that it's our fault there is to be no peace.

'This way.' Wulfheard echoes Maneca's words. I appreciate they know another way to leave the menace of the fighting inside the complex. I turn to ensure Cuthred and Kyre are with us, my gaze lingering on Lord Æthelwulf. He's mounted and thunders towards us, flanked by many of his warriors. He was ready for this. I hate him even more. He has no honour. None at all.

'They really want this bitch,' Oswy confirms beside me, mirroring my thoughts, as we race after Maneca and Wulfheard. Brihthild has been roughly thrown over one of the horses' backs, her hands tied to the reins so she can't get free despite her flailing. Not that I would. The grey horse is fleet. If she falls from the beast, she'll be dead in no time at all.

And then I'm ducking low, forcing my horse through a hedgerow, bare of its new growths, but rife with sharp thorns. It's almost as impenetrable as a stone wall.

'Bloody hell,' I murmur, my byrnie snagging repeatedly, but once I'm free, I can see why Maneca and Wulfheard were so eager to come this way, for ahead is another gate in the ruins of the wall encircling much of Canterbury. It's open and men and women move freely in and out of the settlement, although they shriek and dash aside as we thunder towards them. They're early to be about their daily tasks. Not that we stop when we're outside. Instead, if anything, Maneca redoubles his entreaties to his horse, and Bicwide keeps up easily. I can't say the bishops look comfortable, jumping up and down on their saddles, thorns snagged in their clothes, and I spare a thought for Bishop Æthelweald, who looks like he sits on himself every time the horse stretches out its long legs, but it's either that or face the wrath of the Wessex warriors.

I turn, desperate to see if we're being followed; unhappy when I'm sure I catch the slightest glimpse of racing warriors.

'We can't keep this up,' I call to Oswy, but he ignores me. I direct Bicwide towards Kyre. He offers me a bloodless smile. His face is fevered and dripping with sweat but he makes no complaint. Cuthred's beside him. He too shows no enjoyment in our escape. We all know we've got a long way to go, and that at some point, we must stop, for the horses already endured a great deal yesterday, as did we.

A sullenness infects us all. Quickly, I count, naming my fellow warriors, wanting to ensure they're all there. I've left the wounded behind before and not noticed. I won't do that again. Maneca and Wulfheard lead. Æthelmod and Uor are keeping pace with the bishops, as though they'll leap in to assist them if their horses should stumble. Goðemon and Cenred are to the rear, protecting our retreat, while Wulfgar and Ordlaf remain close to Cuthred and Kyre. Waldhere stays beside Oswy and Landwine's trying to catch Wulfheard, although why, I'm unsure.

'What of Commander Eahric?' I call, but there's no response. Loud hoofbeats behind have me turning, fearing the worse, but I recognise the horses and the men. It seems that Eahric has managed to force himself free as well. That cheers me. I don't wish to leave Mercians for the Wessex warriors to overpower.

Not that they catch us, but instead we move in two groups, pushing the horses on, stopping only when there's no choice throughout the lengthy day. Neither group is very large. Eventually, the sky reddens and then darkens. Beneath me, I feel the gait of Bicwide falter, and I'm unsurprised. We've been riding in near enough silence since leaving Canterbury. It's been a long day.

'We stop here.' Wulfheard finally calls a halt.

I can't see why this place might be better than anywhere else. It doesn't offer us higher land or any protection from long-abandoned ditches or even a tangle of trees to protect our heads.

'Icel, Oswy, Waldhere, you take the first watch,' he calls before I can question his decision. I slide from Bicwide's back, a thump of appreciation for all he's accomplished, and lead him to a small stream. Overhead, the moon's bright, so bright that it'll not be difficult for our enemy to find us. I'm amazed that they haven't caught us already. The others dismount with pain-filled protests, the bishops complaining of aches, but I ignore them all. I don't want to ask them if they'd rather be captives. Neither do I seek out Brihthild. I refuse to be anywhere near her.

I hear Cuthred speaking to Kyre, and then I'm tense, listening to the approaching horses' hooves on the roadway, only relaxing when I see Commander Eahric is at the fore.

He nods on seeing me, and is quick to offer his own instructions.

'We lost five men,' he grumbles unhappily to Wulfheard. 'But the archbishop intervened to stop the madness. He was furious. He called down no end of complaints against Lord Æthelwulf. He's forbidden him to chase us on pain of excommunication. But we're being followed, I'm sure of it. Probably by the ealdorman.'

The news isn't good, but as I note the size that Commander Eahric commands, I feel better. Our numbers have doubled.

'Get what rest you can,' Wulfheard urges Commander Eahric. 'It'll be a bloody early start.'

I hear the men settling to sleep, the horses as well, beside the soft prayers of the bishops, and the complaints of Bishop Æthelweald. Not that I think any intervention with our Lord God will stop the Wessex bastards if they catch us. I stare into the vivid moonlight, determined not to let my fatigue claim me. We've made it this far. Another three days, at the worst four, and we'll be back in Mercia, or at least close to the River Thames. The thought isn't the comfort I hoped it would be.

I walk the impromptu camp perimeters, eyeing the exterior, not the interior, until I hear a voice I know well. Bishop Æthelweald. I strain to catch all of his words, but it's not easy above my soft breathing. I want to know if he's talking to Brihthild, but hope that Wulfheard has considered that and kept her far from him, perhaps under the personal guard of Cenred. I dare not move, and yet I still can't decipher his actual words. Is he merely praying, or is he up to something else?

Yawning widely, I clench my fists as though that'll make my hearing better, but I still can't quite decipher the words. If I move, he'll know that I'm close by and listening to his conversation.

Only when I can't hear him any more, do I move on, Æthelmod coming to relieve me so that I can get some much-needed sleep. I find Bicwide, and settle beside him. I'm not going to risk being far from his side. My belly rumbles, but I ignore that. I'd rather be hungry than dead.

A hand on my shoulder wakes me, my seax blade almost piercing Cuthred in the eye as he veers backwards.

'Sorry,' we say at the same time, but the worry on his face has me scrambling to my feet in the greyness of dawn.

He leads me to Kyre, and I glance down at him. He's still pale, but his breathing is even more laboured. I can smell the foulness of his wound.

'Bollocks,' I exclaim. 'Do we have honey?'

'I've used it all,' Cuthred worries. I'm not surprised. The wound is turning pink, and green, red in some places. It's infected and we need time to make a poultice and clear it. I'd also welcome heat to cauterise the skin, but I'm not going to be allowed to start a fire. I can tell that Cuthred's worried, but there are always other items to hand.

'Get some moss,' I urge him. The night has been damp and cold, but I'm not shivering in my cloak. Instead, I eye Kyre and his wound. It could prove deadly. I'm not about to lose another of my fellow warriors. Enough men have died in recent years. I'll save him. Somehow.

I pull my seax clear from my weapons belt. With Cuthred

gone, scampering away to find some spongy moss, I know what I need to do. I just don't want to do it.

Taking to my knees, mindful of those on guard duty and those who sleep, I slide the edge of my blade beneath the tight pig's-gut stitches. Cuthred did well, but the wound has swollen and now strains against the stitches. The best thing to do is to remove the stitches, cut away the infected skin, and then pack it with moss if not honey. I need to keep him alive until we reach Mercia, and then I'll be able to add honey and make the poultice.

Kyre groans, and I wrinkle my nose at the noxious smell as the mottled flesh bounces free from the confines of the stitches. I look to him, but if he's awake, he keeps his eyes closed. I take that as all the permission I need to continue.

Around me, I can feel the camp waking, men and horses relieving themselves and hunting for food, the bishops' prayers thrumming through the impromptu arrangement. Any moment now, I expect to be hurried but I keep my hand steady and my actions firm. I try not to notice the coating of blood on my hands, or the filth in my nails. They're not going to aid Kyre, but I can.

Cuthred returns with enough moss to wad a foot-long cut, but I welcome it. He nods as he watches me, his tongue protruding from his worried lips.

'Get me another tunic,' I urge him, 'or at least some clean cloth.'

'That I can do,' he assures me, reaching for his sack, looking for whatever he has. I'm aware of more voices. Of Commander Eahric and Wulfheard discussing the intention for the coming day, of horses' hooves and the single female voice of Brihthild as she's led away to relieve herself.

With the moss in place, and the wound bound as tightly as possible with a covering of linen and then a longer piece of cloth tied over the whole thing to keep it in place, I throw the cut strips of flesh to one side. They land with an unsettling whiteness to the ground. I fear I might gag at their resemblance to worms. But I don't. And now Kyre opens his pain-hazed eyes.

'We need some ale, or wine,' I call to Wulfheard, who's come to see what I'm doing.

'And I'll summon some from up my arse, shall I?' he glowers.

'Ask the bishops. They're always drinking in the name of our Lord God,' I glower. I think he'll argue with me, but he doesn't, turning quickly to do as I ask, I assume.

'What's happened?' Kyre huffs.

'Our journey is doing you no favours,' I offer. 'I've cut free the stitches. Your body didn't appreciate them. You'll be able to ride, but be careful. Don't move suddenly. I don't want to have to gather your guts together.' I offer a smile, but it hardly touches my cheeks let alone my eyes.

Wulfheard returns with a small silver container, which he thrusts towards me. I lift the cap to smell the contents and veer aside.

'That'll put hairs on your chest,' I inform Kyre. 'Drink it sparingly, but keep yourself a little bit pissed,' I advise him. He whimpers. As I hand it to him, I wince at the trickle of blood that drips beneath the linen, but that's all I can do for now.

'Shall we tie you to your horse?' Wulfheard queries, his eyes everywhere. He must sense that the Wessex warriors are close. I too feel the need to hurry from this place.

'Yes.' Kyre's admission is telling, but sensible. With the aid of Oswy and Landwine, we settle him on his horse. At least the animal is familiar to him, and then, with the thin edge of dawn growing on the horizon, we're once more rushing northwards.

I can't help thinking that we've done this before. Last time we triumphed. There's no guarantee of success this time.

25

By noon, we can sense our pursuers. We've been followed since leaving Canterbury, but now the enemy warriors feel confident enough to make their presence known. I keep my eyes focused on the way ahead, staying close to Kyre, or taking the rear guard, protecting us from the attack, which must surely come soon.

Commander Eahric seems beleaguered by the Mercian bishops. I'm determined to watch everything that Bishop Æthelweald does. Brihthild is once more kept tied to her horse, close to Wulfheard who won't let her out of his sight.

Our pace is much slower than yesterday.

'It'll take us days to reach Mercia,' Oswy complains, when he joins me at the rear. The air we pass through is cold but far from clean, stinking of the horses' farts and piss. Kyre lolls in his saddle. Landwine and Cuthred don't leave his side.

'It will,' I admit, once more refusing to look behind me. Whoever thought it would be a good idea to send Mercian bishops to Canterbury was a bloody fool, unless, of course, it was all a mask for some other nefarious plot. The men aren't seasoned riders. I wince every time I see Bishop Æthelweald lose his steady rhythm. He'll be black and blue when we return to Mercia. If we manage to do that.

As the weather's better than in recent weeks, there are men and women who watch us with disinterested gazes from their homes and fields, the lambs more fascinated by us than anyone else. They don't call to us, or try to stop us. I'm grateful for that. I don't want to have to stop. Our pace is slow enough as it is.

'The enemy will catch us,' Oswy continues.

'They will,' I reply. It's impossible not to consider that. Is our headward dash a waste of resources, and the strength of the horses? Probably, but what else can we do? The archbishop tried to intervene, but Lord Æthelwulf was having none of it. Once more, my eyes rest on Brihthild and Bishop Æthelweald. What do they know? Do they understand they're probably both in this up to their necks? If we question Brihthild, will she say the names of those she's involved with, or will it remain a secret?

'And then what will we do?' Oswy questions. I turn to meet his gaze. He shows no fear. Indeed, this just seems to be a problem for which the solution hasn't yet presented itself, but it certainly will in good time. I admire such confidence. I personally think we're well and truly buggered.

'Fight them?' I question. I don't think we have any choice. Not that we're guaranteed to have success.

'Well, of course we'll bloody fight them,' Oswy growls, as though I've lost my mind. 'But how will we overwhelm them and make it back to Mercia?'

'If I knew that,' I grumble, 'I'd have already suggested it.'

He lapses into silence. The landscape passes not so much in a blur, as just quickly. I can see where, in my time in the south, the hedgerows have begun to turn green, just the faintest hints, and men and women are busy in the fields, the cows and sheep enjoying being free from their winter confines. I wish I could relish it, but the thrumming of Bicwide's hooves merely makes me strain harder to hear those who're following on behind. Not that we've seen them yet. But we know they're there.

'We could do with King Wiglaf sending some reinforcements,' Oswy eventually says.

'How would he know to do that?'

'Well, he wouldn't, but perhaps Ealdorman Tidwulf has been told to rescue us if we're in Canterbury for too long.'

'But we haven't been. The bishops were only supposed to finish their meeting yesterday. They'll wait a good few days yet before they believe we've been apprehended.'

'Well, thanks for the positivity,' Oswy huffs, moving away to complain to Wulfheard instead. I watch him, although really I'm looking to Brihthild. Perhaps, if we just abandon her here, for the enemy to find, they'll leave us alone. But no, we must first discover what she knows.

Although, well, we have the vellum, and we have the amber, so we can prove that something was being plotted. My gaze turns to Bishop Æthelweald. I so want him to be involved in this that I fear I've already labelled him as the traitor without more than the knowledge that he had access to the queen, Lord Wigmund and Brother Sampson.

And, of course, we can all speak to Lord Æthelwulf's overenthusiastic attempt to claim back Brihthild from us.

My thoughts turn to how we could prove she was the murderess of her brother, but again, we have no proof of that. Indeed, we have little to prove anything, only hints and half-formed ideas. I huff to myself, lifting myself out of the saddle to stretch my legs, aware my arse rides high over the back of Bicwide. The smell of my body disgusts me, but I'll not be getting a bath any time soon, not until we return to Mercia.

We're not travelling the way we went to Canterbury. Leaving

through the gate closest to the archbishop's complex has meant we're on another road. I don't think we've rejoined the original one. This way, we won't see the Isle of Sheppey, or indeed, any of the routeways we took to rescue Lord Coenwulf. Thinking of him has me considering the two children. I hope Coenwulf and Coelwulf are well and protected inside Kingsholm. The swirl of politics and threat that surrounds them astounds me. Not for the first time, I'm grateful that no one other than Wynflæd knows of my true identity. I wouldn't wish to live in peril as the small children do. This game of kings and kingdoms is too contrived for me. Everyone thinks to gain, but only ever at the expense of others.

I sigh, the sound filled with sorrow for the days when I was merely a boy who wanted to be a healer. How my life has changed since my uncle's death.

But thinking of the children reminds me of Wulfnoth. I still know too little about him. Wulfheard won't speak about him, and no one else will either. But I've heard more than enough about him. Even the seamstress in Winchester knew of Wulfnoth. My eyes narrow, taking in the tight shoulders of Bishop Æthelweald and Brihthild. Perhaps, after all, there might be a way to prove the conspiracy surrounding the children, and perhaps even Lord Coenwulf's actions.

When Commander Eahric calls a halt for the night, we've still not sighted our enemy, but we know they're out there, somewhere close. I'm not instructed to take first watch, or second, or third, and I should welcome a night of sleep, but instead I fix my gaze on Brihthild, and then on Wulfheard. I need his help to accomplish what I want to, but if I tell him my plans, he'll refuse it. Instead, I turn to Oswy.

'You trust me, don't you?' I question him.

'Yes,' he offers, his eyebrows high, revealing his confusion.

'Then, come with me, and remember, I'm doing this for a good reason.'

'Doing what?' he asks, but I allow his words to fade away without an answer, as I make my way to Wulfheard.

At that moment, he's close to Brihthild, and also Bishop Æthelweald, although the bishop does seem to be trying hard not to notice his proximity to our prisoner.

'Wulfheard,' I call roughly, when I'm close enough that not everyone will turn to observe our exchange.

'What is it, Icel?' My tone has Wulfheard reaching for his weapons belt, but it's not the Wessex warriors who are about to assault him.

'I've had enough of this,' I call, my voice cold as ice. 'I've ridden from one bloody end of this island to another, and I still know nothing about your damn brother and his place in all this. Now, tell me about Wulfnoth, and why he's involved.' I consider shoving him for good effect, but decide against it. I need him to be where I can still see Brihthild as well as the bishop. Already, I'm aware of her interest at the use of Wulfnoth's name. I'm hoping that Oswy is paying careful attention as well.

'Icel, now isn't the time.' Wulfheard's words are heated, in contrast to mine. I know he won't appreciate this discussion. He'd sooner keep his brother a secret. He doesn't want others to know about him. 'We're trying to make it back to Mercia in one piece.'

'But now is the time,' I continue, furious. 'Kyre's more dead than alive, and we're being chased down by the Wessex ealdorman's warriors, and all because of something Wulfnoth set in motion.'

Again, I'm aware of Brihthild's interest, although she tries to hide it, and also the bishop's. I realise, just before Wulfheard angrily rears up before me, that I could have perhaps achieved the same without involving Wulfheard, but it's too late now.

'He took all that coin, from whoever it was, and he was going to murder the children, and we don't know who ordered him to do so.'

If Commander Eahric is perplexed by our discussion, he makes a good effort to hide it. Bishop Æthelweald's suddenly a man with no skills at all in concealment. His mouth opens in a smirk. His eyes rest on Brihthild. I don't think he could be any worse at pretending he doesn't know who she is.

'We have the slip of vellum, from Bicwide's saddle, with all the details upon it. We heard Wulfnoth of Eamont's name spoken in Winchester, and written in the church records. We know amber was part of the bargain, because we still have it in our possession.'

Brihthild's soft sigh sounds loud in the air, but Wulfheard's face is flecked with fury. I think he'll hit me; only abruptly it clears. With his back to both Brihthild and the bishop, he winks, surprising me, before reaching towards me.

'Why, you little shit. I taught you everything you know. I'm the reason you're alive to this day. I've trained you to fight twice. Now you stand here and accuse me of treason against the Mercian king.' His hands are tight on me, but not too tight that I'm uncomfortable. I pretend I am all the same. I should have realised he'd be a willing accomplice. I grip his hands with mine, but only enough that it looks like we're fighting. I don't truly want to feel the force of his fists on me, but it might come to that.

'I speak of Wulfnoth's treason, not yours,' I counter, but then catch sight of Wulfheard's lips moving once more. I can't determine what they say, but I hope I'm correct when I open my mouth once more. 'Unless it was you and not Wulfnoth. After all, you knew everything there was to know about the children. And we don't know anything about you and Wulfnoth, because you won't talk about him. Is it because you were in this together from the beginning?' Once more Wulfheard winks, as we pretend to fight. Only then Commander Eahric is there.

'Break it up, you two. This is for another time and place,' he glowers, but his eyes rest on Wulfheard, who takes the opportunity to cuff me across the face so that I taste blood as I stagger backwards. Wulfheard's forcibly removed by three of Eahric's men, grunting and complaining as he's dragged away, although even I can tell he's going easy on them.

I open my mouth to retract my words, but Oswy grabs me, pretending to keep me upright after the blow I've received, all the while taking the opportunity to whisper in my ear.

'Leave it. He wants this.' I appreciate that what started as a last-ditch attempt to uncover the truth has become something else entirely. While Wulfheard fights the Mercians trying to restrain him, I see the gleam in Bishop Æthelweald's eye, and the knowing look on Brihthild's face. I'm unsurprised when Wulfheard finds himself trussed up beside our prisoner.

'Leave it,' Oswy urges me, as I think to inform Eahric it was all just a sham, but perhaps Commander Eahric knows because he comes to me, under the pretence of ensuring I can still stand after the blow, and speaks.

'Let's hope this ploy works,' he murmurs, and then lifts his voice. 'Oswy, you have command of Ealdorman Ælfstan's warriors. We'll leave it for him to deal with the treason, or not, of Wulfheard.'

26

But while Oswy and Commander Eahric might realise this is all a ruse, the rest of Wulfheard's men are slower to understand.

'Arse.' I'm kicked awake at some point when darkness still coats the land by Godeman. I'd like to think he knows me well enough to appreciate that not all is as it seems.

'I don't have a guard duty tonight,' I grumble, trying to turn over in my cloak.

'You do now Oswy's in charge,' he replies gruffly. I'm sure Oswy wouldn't have punished me when he knows what's happening, but as I sit upwards, prepared to argue my piece with Godeman, Oswy's voice drifts to me.

'Get over here,' he calls, and others murmur for quiet in their sleep. I sigh and stumble to my feet, trying not to trip over Cuthred and Kyre who are close by. I've half a mind to kick them.

'Tell him,' I urge Oswy, after the leg of Maneca threatens to trip me as well.

'No, it's better this way. Now, keep an ear out for what she's saying to Wulfheard, but don't get anywhere near them.'

I open my mouth to argue, considering how I'm supposed to

do that, but Oswy's already walked away. It seems we both have the night watch, and indeed, as I travel the circuit of our campsite, this time on a small rise that lifts us above the dampness of the ground close to a stream, I encounter Commander Eahric. He meets my gaze, and nods sharply.

'Nothing yet,' he assures me in a voice so quiet I have to lean far enough forward that his moustache tickles my ear. 'But if this is going to work, it'll be tonight. The enemy will catch us in the morning.'

His words are as comforting as a wet sock. Moodily, I resume my patrol around the sleeping men and horses. The Mercian bishops have been quiet throughout the day, their complaints worn down by yesterday's exertions. But I've heard their soft prayers, and hope they beseech our God for a safe return to Mercia. I've half a mind never to leave the place again. Every time I do leave, I encounter an enemy, and always end up in a fight. Not, I realise, that I can be assured of peace when I'm in Mercia either.

The sounds of farts and snores fill the air, the scent redolent of the latrine and not the open air. The moon's hidden behind clouds that promise rain eventually, and I don't welcome that either. My boots are already damp from the wet grasses as the night draws on. I'd appreciate hot water, and clean clothes. What I get instead is the murmured conversation between Brihthild and Wulfheard.

I stay still, not wanting to draw attention to myself.

'Why didn't you tell me?' Brihthild whispers towards Wulfheard. I'd allow a grin, but my white teeth might reveal my location. She's made the connection. But it's also clear she's ignorant of the estrangement of the two brothers.

'Why didn't you tell me?' Wulfheard responds, aggravation in his voice, in just as hushed a tone. His words sound a bit whistly. I consider if he's had a few punches for his alleged treason. I wouldn't be surprised. Commander Eahric's warriors are fiercely

Mercian in their outlook. They won't welcome an enemy in their midst.

'I didn't know you'd replaced your brother. Not that it matters. You have the vellum and the stone?' she evades instead.

'I do, and what of it to you?'

'I want to be paid,' she rejoins. 'Without them, Lord Æthelwulf refuses to accept my involvement and has withheld all funds until I can find out what went wrong with his carefully laid plans.'

'And what of the bishop?' Wulfheard questions.

'What bishop?' Brihthild prevaricates.

'The Mercian bishop?'

'I don't know more than Wulfnoth's participation and some damn fools named Eadbald and Eadweard.' I feel my eyes open wide at those names. 'But I know the queen was embroiled. She and Lord Æthelwulf have been on friendly terms for many years.' Her words have turned sly. I suspect she's not supposed to know that.

I could almost shriek with joy at her admission. I've long suspected the queen's involvement. Why else would she have been so determined on Lord Coenwulf serving his punishment away from Mercia?

'But the children are safe,' Wulfheard counters.

'For now they are. Once we know where the original scheme faltered, Lord Æthelwulf will make another attempt. All we need to do is find a way back into Mercia, and that, my friend, seems to be where you're involved. A man in your exalted position is sure to have access to the children.'

'But only if we live through this,' Wulfheard quickly clarifies.

'Oh, we will.' Brihthild oozes confidence. 'The Wessex warriors are merely toying with the Mercians. Making them believe they'll make it home, with me and you as their prisoners, and then they'll attack. I imagine that, even now, Lord Æthelwulf's determining on the assault. I know he has a ship as well, ready to venture into the River Thames. He told me as much. I'll ensure you live.'

This is all news to us. I wouldn't have expected a Wessex ship to risk journeying anywhere close to the Isle of Sheppey, but perhaps the Viking raiders have long since left. Maybe they gave up the settlement. And, of course, so close to the winter that's just past, the waterway will still be passable, as opposed to during the summer months, when they'll be dried out.

I want to tell Oswy of all this, but Brihthild, so determined to say nothing to the Mercians, has finally let her tongue loose, and I'm not going to leave until I hear all she has to say.

'Lord Æthelwulf has assured his father that Mercia will be deprived of all its æthelings, and then, when King Wiglaf falls prey to an unwelcome accident, the kingship will naturally pass to him.' I want to argue with that, but snap my mouth shut. There are others, me included, who could rule in Mercia, but best not to say that out loud. And I know that the Mercians would rather have anyone else as their king than bloody King Ecgberht of Wessex.

'But what of the queen's son?'

'She thinks he'll rule after his father, but she's misinformed about that.'

'You know a great deal for someone that Lord Æthelwulf won't pay,' Wulfheard complains. I don't see her response, but I imagine it well enough, the gleam in her eye revealing all she knows.

'I've managed to make connections, even where others have failed. And, after all, a man will say many things to a woman in his bed.' The taunting chuckle that fills the air speaks of passion and desire, and I grimace to realise how Lord Æthelwulf has fallen foul of that most base desire. Yet I'm also grateful. Without Brihthild, we'd have little to base our suspicions upon, despite our time in Wessex.

'And what, you think to rule at Lord Æthelwulf's side?'

'Good God, no. I'll take a stake of Mercia, and be rewarded with land and riches. But enough of that.' Her words turn sharp. 'Tell me, how will you get to the children? If you tell me, when the Wessex warriors attack, I'll ensure you live to conduct your plan.'

Wulfheard's voice drops even lower, and the sound of someone close by taking a long piss obscures all of his words. When I can hear again, the two have lapsed into silence, and I only hope I've not missed something important, for Brihthild is surely correct. The Wessex warriors under the command of the ealdorman or Lord Æthelwulf will attack tomorrow. And we need to ensure Brihthild and Wulfheard return to Mercia, the one to denounce the other. How we're going to do that, I still have no idea.

I yawn. I'm tired and uncomfortable. Not only do I fail to hear the end of the conversation between Brihthild and Wulfheard, but so too does Oswy, when I eventually resume my patrol, the pair of them having fallen silent.

'What did he say?' Oswy whispers to me when we cross paths.

'I didn't hear the end of it. The bloody bishop was taking the longest piss known to man,' I growl. 'And why didn't you hear it?' I question.

'One of the horses had come loose. I had to grab it.'

'Bloody wonderful,' I expel, my fury tight and constrained for now. 'What are your instructions for the morning?'

I sense Oswy startle at my words, while his mouth opens and closes, emitting nothing but stale air to give away his actions.

'I...' he starts. I glower at him, for all he can't see it.

'Wonderful. We don't know what Wulfheard agreed with Brihthild and now we don't know what to do come the morning.'

'We ride,' Oswy stutters.

'To where? We won't make it to Mercia tomorrow.'

'No,' and I feel his resolve stiffen. 'But all we need to do is evade the Wessex warriors.'

'That won't be easy,' I say slowly, thinking him a fool for not realising this.

'Well, Icel, what would you have me do? It seems you have all the answers, so I suggest you offer a solution now.' His words thrum with frustration and urgency.

'I...' I start, only to pause as well. 'I'm not a bloody commander,' I growl.

'Oh, and I am?' Oswy retorts, and I shush him with a touch of my hand on his arm. Our conversation has grown too loud. 'Bloody hell,' he expels more softly. 'How are we going to get out of this?'

I share his worry. It's not as though we have allies close by. We're still in Kent, and while it might once have been Mercian, and there might be those sympathetic to the Mercian cause, we don't know who they are. Or whether they're likely to have a fighting force to assist us against the ealdorman's warriors.

'I don't know, but we're going to have to,' I mumble. I feel a thrum of unease in my body. I'm unsure how we'll escape. When King Wiglaf sent me to Wessex, he told me to seek out Commander Eahric in Canterbury if I encountered problems. I can't believe he realised how complex the situation we'd find would be, or even the calibre of those involved. And yet, perhaps he did. I bite my lip, tasting blood, and then turn to Oswy.

'We use the bishops.'

'Use them how?'

'They must offer us protection, and that way Lord Æthelwulf and his warriors won't be able to attack us.' For all I jut out my chest and speak with conviction, the only response is a low rumble of laughter from Oswy.

'Surely, young Icel, by now you appreciate that the church has no means to protect anyone. If Lord Æthelwulf was determined to ignore the bloody archbishop, then he's certainly going to do the same to Mercia's bishops. Even if he fears excommunication he has the ealdorman to fulfil his wishes. No, lad, that won't work at all.'

I open my mouth to argue, but then snap it shut once more. From close by, I can hear the murmur of voices, and grimace, detecting the telltale sound of hooves over the road. The enemy are coming. They've caught us during the night. I imagine that Lord Æthelwulf and the ealdorman have warriors throughout his kingdom upon whom he can call at such times, although, well, they had no success against the Viking raiders on the Isle of Sheppey.

'Get everyone up,' Oswy menaces. 'Before we can think of how to get back to Mercia, we need to evade the Wessex bastards for another day.' I mumble my agreement, going to wake Kyre first, as he'll need the longest time to mount up, then Cuthred who'll aid him, and then the others. But all the time, I feel as though I'm being watched, not unlike my experience close to the kingdom of the East Angles years before. The enemy perhaps surround us, and of course, they know where we need to go. And as much as I'd like to prove them wrong, we must return to Mercia with our prisoner, and the knowledge she carries. Or die trying.

27

Stifling a yawn, I help Wulfheard into his saddle. His hands are tied together, and I'm forced to secure his legs to the stirrups. All the time, I can sense he wants to say something to me, but Brihthild's gaze is fierce on both of us. Perhaps, I realise, it would have been better to get her mounted and moved aside, and then I could have spoken to Wulfheard.

I growl angrily as he puts up a pretence of being difficult, my head thick from lack of sleep and my fingers fumbling with the knots.

'A pleasant evening,' Wulfheard huffs to me, and I shake my head, miserable at what I've put in play, although I can't deny it has told us what we need to know. Provided we can take our information to King Wiglaf.

'Not so you'd notice. Some of the bishops can piss for Mercia,' I glower, hoping he'll understand I missed some of the conversation he shared with Brihthild. But it seems not.

'Be ready,' he hisses down to me when I've made the best attempt I can to make it seem as though his hands are bound to the saddle when they're not.

'For what?' I retort, but a sharp instruction from Commander Eahric drowns out my words. 'Bloody wonderful,' I mutter to myself, stamping some life into my feet as I make my way to Bicwide. The sense of being watched hasn't gone, and yet I can't see any of the Wessex warriors through the grey haze. The bastards are hiding behind a line of trees, no doubt aware of how powerful it can be to toy with their enemy, especially when that enemy knows it's been watched.

Before I'm settled, Commander Eahric orders his warriors onwards, ignoring the complaints of the bishops and their bruised arses from riding at such a fast pace. I hasten to hurry but still find myself to the rear of the line, Cenred at my side.

He glowers at me. 'Happy with yourself?' he growls. I have a mind to tell him to take a short walk over a high cliff, but keep my temper in check.

'Sleep well?' I offer instead. 'Always good to have someone with a good night's sleep at the rear of our force.' His silence tells me all I need to know. Damn them all. I wish more than just Oswy and Wulfheard knew of our ruse.

I ride sullenly, my back itching with the feeling that we're under surveillance, as well as from the disturbed cuts. I'm trying not to pick at the scabs. I'd like to hurry Bicwide, but the bishops are even slower today, despite Commander Eahric's exhortations that they hurry. I've half a mind to overtake them all and see how they cope when the Wessex warriors do attack, screaming their defiance and with seaxes and shields to hand.

I constantly find myself looking at Wulfheard and Brihthild, wishing I knew what he had planned for the day, or if it will even happen today. He rides morosely, head low, while Brihthild carries herself as though she were the bloody queen. It would be impossible to depict two people in such counter positions to those I'd expect. And, when I'm not glaring at Wulfheard, my gaze settles on Bishop Æthelweald. I know he's involved in this.

Commander Eahric has men sent ahead, to scout the landscape, and even though I realise we're too far from Mercia to reach it today, I confess, I feel deflated when they arrive without the information I hope for. Not, I realise as the sun climbs overhead, that the enemy has attacked us yet.

'What are they doing?' I mutter to Oswy when he joins me at the rear, yawning just as widely as me, glowering at Cenred who offers him a 'don't get too used to it' jibe as Oswy sends him to ride closer to the bishops.

'Bloody arse,' Oswy mouths at his back. 'And as to the Wessex warriors, I imagine they mean to trap us somewhere. It's a pity we don't know exactly where.' The thought is as uninspiring as Wulfheard's demand I stay alert. We're riding as quickly as we can, but the horses are tired, and the bishops, no doubt hoping that they won't be slaughtered by our enemy, and not fearing if we're caught because they won't be expected to fight, ride too slowly.

Every so often Godeman turns, lips downcast, to glower at me.

'Keep your eyes forward,' Oswy roars at him, only to earn himself a glare as well.

'Good to see we're making friends,' I mumble. Oswy surprises me by smiling, standing upright in his saddle to rest his arse.

'Aye, lad. It's all well and good riding with men who'd do anything for you, but doing so when they want to murder you is another matter entirely.'

We fall into an easy camaraderie, both of us tired from the lack of sleep, and overly alert to what our enemy might do. Only when another scout rushes to Commander Eahric, who beckons Oswy forward imperiously, do I realise that while we've been chased, it's only been to exactly where the Wessex ealdorman wants us to go. For, as the sun starts to set in a welter of dull yellows and mauves, I see the valley through which we need to ride and which the Wessex ealdorman, and no doubt Lord Æthelwulf as well, has sent his warriors. We can't go forwards, and we can't go backwards, for no sooner have I had the thought than those following on behind emerge as well.

We're trapped. Night is upon us, and I have no idea how we can possibly escape.

'Weapons,' Commander Eahric instructs, as Oswy echoes the cry. Lord Æthelwulf and the ealdorman walk their horses towards us. Lord Æthelwulf holds his hands to either side, as though he's the one who'll need to surrender.

'Come now, my lord bishops. We don't wish to fight with Mercia's bishops. We merely want Brihthild returned to us.' I can hear Commander Eahric's muttered complaint from where I try and hold Bicwide still, having turned him to meet the attack from the rear. My seax is ready in my hand.

'Bastard,' Oswy mutters. By appealing to the bishops, Lord Æthelwulf implies what will happen isn't for Oswy or Commander Eahric to determine. I consider how much he's prepared to risk to get Brihthild. Does Lord Æthelwulf believe the archbishop won't excommunicate him? He's taken a huge risk if that's his thinking.

'My lord.' Brihthild's voice rises above the grumble from the Mercians, and prevents Bishop Æthelweald from speaking. She sounds assured and far from panicked. 'They've not harmed me yet, my lord,' she continues.

'Return the Wessex woman to us, and you may leave, with an escort, of course.'

'You're most gracious,' Bishop Æthelweald manages to say before Oswy interrupts him.

'Lord Æthelwulf. The woman is guilty of treason against Mercia's kingship. She'll be taken to Mercia to face King Wiglaf and answer for the charges. We have those who will testify against her.'

Lord Æthelwulf's face unexpectedly breaks into a smile at those words.

'What could a woman such as her have done to the Mercian kingship? She's little more than a whore.' His tone is disparaging. I feel Oswy bristle, but he holds his tongue, while Brihthild shrieks in defiance. I think she's much more than a whore. A whore wouldn't be able to fight as she does. She's a better warrior than her brother ever was.

'She's to face justice for her crimes. After all, why else would you be here if you didn't wish to ensure that didn't happen?' Oswy argues. The mocking smile slips from Lord Æthelwulf's face just as Brihthild shouts again.

'I demand to be kept in Wessex. I'm a woman of Wessex.'

'A whore of Wessex,' I hear one of the Mercians mutter. Brihthild must catch the words as well, for she shrieks again with outrage.

'We should consider the offer,' Bishop Æthelweald speaks almost simultaneously. It's difficult to keep track of what's happening between the Wessex and Mercian forces. Only suddenly, it really doesn't matter any more.

While I've been keeping a wary eye on Lord Æthelwulf, from behind us, a woman's cry of rage is abruptly cut short. I see Lord Æthelwulf's confusion laid bare on his face, but I feel the same. I turn aside, trying to determine what's happening, only to be greeted with what seems to be a scrum close to the centre of our party where Wulfheard and Brihthild are kept prisoner.

'This must be it,' I inform Oswy. He nods, his head flicking from the Wessex warriors, to whatever it is that Wulfheard's doing, because we can't see.

Bishop Æthelweald's voice rises in a roar of indignation, immediately followed by other equally angry shouts, but my ears are alert to something else, and it comes quickly.

'Get to him,' Oswy informs me in a gruff voice. 'Cenred, get your arse here. Take whoever you can convince to go with you and just keep up with Wulfheard,' Oswy instructs.

Eagerly, I encourage Bicwide forward, calling to Maneca, Uor and Landwine. Angry faces greet mine. I see Cuthred's confused expression, but he must remain with Kyre to ensure Kyre makes it back to Mercia alive.

'Hurry up, you damn fools,' I order them, finding it surprisingly easy to surge through the Mercian warriors, who all have their eyes locked on the Wessex lords, and not on what else is happening. They're better trained than me, I reason, or perhaps Commander Eahric ordered them to do this when whatever was going to happen happened.

Not that I make it to Wulfheard's side, for he's already veered off, his hands – unbound, as are his feet – gripping the reins while Brihthild appears lifeless before him. At least he's stopped her from talking. I glance up, urging Goðeman and Æthelmod to join me as well. I realise that while the Wessex warriors have surrounded us, there's one small gap in their defence, and Wulfheard crashes towards it. It's narrower than the horse's shoulders, and yet Wulfheard disappears quickly between the side of the stream and the overhanging branches that dip into the water. It's easy enough to follow his movements, as Bicwide hurries to keep pace. I risk a glance behind me. Oswy and Commander Eahric have engaged Lord Æthelwulf in conversation while we make our escape. None of the Wessex warriors even seem to have realised we're escaping now that Brihthild's been silenced.

A sudden jolt and Bicwide dips a hoof into the stream but quickly regains his footing. I can hear the huff of Maneca behind me as his horse tries to avoid the same.

'What's happening?' he questions, but I have no response to that. I just know to keep close to Wulfheard. I expect the Wessex lords to realise what's happened and chase us, but quickly, all sound of events behind us fails, as we're entirely covered by a growing band of thickly packed trees, the river growing wider beside us. I can't imagine that Wulfheard knew of this. He's been damn lucky.

'Just keep up,' I urge Maneca and the rest of the men. The horses haven't been overly tested today. But they were already tired, and I realise that Wulfheard's intentions are simple. We're going to break away from the rest of the group and dash for Mercia in the hope that the Wessex warriors might not realise what's happening or even try and chase us.

As dusk falls, highlighting everything in strange shadows, I finally win free from the trees and see Wulfheard up ahead, haloed by the dying glow of the sun. His horse is steady beneath him, but the weight of him and Brihthild will take its toll. I wish I'd brought another horse with me, even as I hurry to join him. Wulfheard doesn't look over his shoulder, his focus only on going forward, and neither do the others question what's happening now. It's obvious, as our horses stumble to a full gallop, and we race into the dying light of the day.

28

We don't stop, even when the sky grows even darker with rain clouds and a fine drizzle drenches us. Whatever Wulfheard's done to Brihthild, she remains immovable before him. I catch him but don't speak. Every so often, when I glance at him, I see a shadow on his face, which can only be a bruise. I realise I should have done something different rather than accusing him of being involved in his brother's treachery before everyone. I'll learn that lesson and hope never to repeat it.

My eyes grow gritty with lack of sleep, but I don't urge a stop. If we have to ride until the horses can go no further, then that's what we'll have to do, regardless of how we feel. The rain makes it more difficult to see. It's a relief when the clouds move away from the moon, lighting our path once more. And still, we race onwards.

I don't know if this is a track known to Wulfheard, or if he's just been lucky to find a path northwards. I'm not going to argue against our luck, or his planning. Only when dawn once more threatens to break through, does Wulfheard call a halt. As his horse comes to a stop, he fixes me with a broad grin that highlights the bruises on his right cheek.

'Bloody fools,' he crows, leaping from the saddle and flinging a rousing Brihthild to the ground as well. She's trussed up like a bundle of furs, ropes covering her every which way, as she opens her mouth to scream in fury, only to be met by the implacable expression on Wulfheard's face. 'Scream all you want,' he offers her, taking himself off to have a piss. I eye her. She has no bruises, unlike Wulfheard, but she's furious.

'I need to,' she demands. I nod, and haul her upright, and take her away from the scrutiny of the men, although I don't undo her hands. I allow her to crouch against a tree, lifting her skirts above her knees, and while she vents angrily, I watch her, wishing I didn't have to, but after all we've been through, I won't let her out of my sight. At least her shouts drown out the noise of her water hitting the ground. When she's done, I return her to Wulfheard without a word. He offers her water, while I see to my own needs, and those of Bicwide.

'Not far now,' Landwine offers conversationally, as he stands beside me on the banks of a small stream, flooding with water after the rain during the night.

'Good,' I grumble. Without Bicwide to keep me upright, I feel exhaustion tugging at me. 'Let's hope the others manage to evade Lord Æthelwulf and the ealdorman's men.'

'Without the woman, they've nothing to fight for. They'll let them go. Wulfheard's considered all that.' There's respect in his voice. I nod. Wulfheard has done well, but whether it's enough, I'm unsure.

'Right, half of you can sleep until full daylight,' Wulfheard orders as we return, eyeing the surroundings, which are exposed. There are no trees to protect us here. 'The rest can sleep on their horses later.'

At his words, I yawn widely, unable to help myself. Wulfheard takes pity on me.

'Æthelmod, Maneca and Uor, you stay awake, and Uor, you keep her tied up and watch her. Don't let her move from this position.' Brihthild lies on the ground. She can't even sit up without something to support her. I feel a moment of pity for her but dismiss it. Her intent is to kill the children of Lady Cynehild, and I can't allow that to happen.

Wulfheard slumps to the ground, away from Brihthild, and is asleep before I can join him. I tumble to the ground while it seems to move and sway around me. I take a deep breath and then another, letting them out slowly so that my eyes close, and I'm asleep as well.

A boot in my belly wakes me, Maneca leering down at me. I wince at the bright daylight and try not to complain that I'm still too tired because his face is bleached with fatigue, and from close by, I can hear either Æthelmod or Uor retching with exhaustion.

I'm tasked with assisting Brihthild to the tree once more. When I return her to Wulfheard, he takes one look at her and jerks his head to have me haul her over the back of his mount. The animal seems refreshed. While she bucks and strains, landing a kick on my shin, I soon have her in place, and Wulfheard mounts up. His eyes are clear, even as he yawns.

'We make it back to Mercia today, or they'll catch us,' he announces, his words flecked with iron. By the time I'm ready with Bicwide, Brihthild is motionless over the horse. I consider how Wulfheard's accomplished that, but I don't ask the question. I can imagine well enough.

The horses amble to a canter, and then a gallop, allowing those who kept watch no time to sleep, but it's more important to cover the distance home to Mercia. We don't stop, not as the sun rises all around us and the day advances. And then, when I fear exhaustion will have me sleeping on my horse, I detect the welcome glint of the sun over a vast expanse of water. I can hardly believe we've made it back to the River Thames, but my elation dies on my lips, for ahead, I can also see a force of Wessex warriors, and they far outnumber us.

'Bollocks,' Wulfheard explodes, while Maneca's eyes open from where he's succumbed to sleep. 'So bloody close,' Wulfheard continues, his eyes alert to our surroundings. Ahead lies a small quayside. We must be much further to the west. There are a collection of ships just waiting to transport us over the river, although I'd welcome the water over my stinking body if we did need to swim, but before them, twenty Wessex warriors watch us with the enjoyment of a wolf that's found its prey.

'We can go around them,' I offer, looking to the expanse of the River Thames.

'We need the ships,' Wulfheard counters. 'She won't swim away from Wessex, and we can't pull her. She needs to make it back alive.'

'Then we'll just have to bloody fight them, and win our way to the ships,' I huff, fatigue making my words snap with fury.

Wulfheard rounds on me, his lips curled in a snarl, highlighting the purple bruise on his cheek, but whatever he's going to say dies on his lips as we all hear the thunder of fast-approaching hooves.

'Icel has the right of it,' Wulfheard calls. 'We attack and make our way to the ships.' That he doesn't argue with me is more worrying than the thunder of so many approaching hooves.

The enemy blocking the river aren't mounted but instead have already formed up before the walkway to the quayside. Why they've not removed the ships, I'm unsure. It speaks of their supreme confidence in overpowering us. But only one of us needs to get to a ship with Brihthild, and we'll be able to escape. Unless, of course, the enemy tumbles into one as well.

The smell of the river brings with it the scent of the far-distant sea. The tides have no doubt been high throughout the winter months, ensuring any residual stink of those using the river as a latrine or midden have been banished for now.

'Icel, ensure Brihthild makes it into the ship. We'll protect you.'

I don't like that order and want to argue, but there's no time. The Wessex warriors are advancing, and the horses that have chased us here are even closer. Growling, I tie Bicwide's reins high, and grab the straining woman and haul her over my shoulder. She's heavier than I remember, but that's because she's fighting. We're so close to success, and her to failure, it's given her extra impetus.

Redoubling my grip on her, I move within the protective circle of my Mercian warriors, eyes fixed firmly on where I need to go. If Wulfheard and my fellow Mercians can clear a path to the furthest boat, a small thing with oars in its belly, then I should be able to escape into the river's current. Or so I hope.

'Give us the woman, and no one needs to die,' a gruff voice calls, but if he thought there wasn't going to be a fight, he was very mistaken.

The crash of iron on wood resounds in the air, as Wulfheard and Landwine lead the charge. Our horses have all been abandoned on the riverbank. I spare a thought for Bicwide. I don't want to leave him, and my fellow warriors won't want to leave their mounts either, but it'll be for the horses to follow us into the water if they expect to come to Mercia with us.

It's as though we move as one, despite there being six of us. A shuffle forward, a crash of iron, a huff of outrage from our enemy, and another step forward. Brihthild is no help at all, twisting in my arms so that I wish I was fighting rather than tasked with ensuring she makes it to the ship.

I can only see the feet of my warriors who surround me because Brihthild's dress has wrapped itself over my head in her struggles. I can't risk letting go of her to move it. If I do, she'll be on the sodden ground in no time. Another step forward and then a hasty one back again. The sound of the horses is coming ever closer. Wulfheard's growling in his fury, his instructions sharp to his fellow Mercians, but it's impossible to predict what will happen. I step over the bloody remains of a suddenly sightless Wessex warrior, and feel the wooden quayside shift beneath my feet.

I allow a slither of hope to embolden me and strengthen my arms, only for Uor and Maneca, who are behind me, to collide with me as they're overwhelmed. I struggle to keep upright, not wanting to drop the twisting bundle.

I can smell spilt blood and the foul breath of everyone in close proximity. I regain my footing, and abruptly, I can see again as Brihthild twists in my grip. I grimace, tighten my hold on her, and realise that the way ahead is blocked by only four warriors. I wish I knew what Wulfheard did to her to leave her senseless. I'd welcome the same.

'Knock them into the water,' I growl. It's probably not deep enough for them to drown, but it will distract. Wulfheard rushes the enemy warriors, Landwine joining him, but the men hold firm, only one of them overbalancing with a loud splash.

'Keep your damn mouth shut,' Landwine complains, and I know he means me.

Still, there are only three against two now, although there are certainly more and more behind me, as I'm jostled again and again, Brihthild doing her best to buck herself free from my grip. If she's not careful, she'll fall into the water and drown there because with her hands and feet tied, it'll be impossible to swim away.

'Go,' Wulfheard urges me. Suddenly, there are only two enemies against my fellow warriors, another splash assuring me one of our foemen has also fallen into the water. I wobble forward precariously. The quayside is only wide enough for a barrel to be rolled along it, not for three warriors abreast, one of them with a woman slung over his shoulder.

The boat comes closer and closer. I can see it, as Wulfheard shoves me roughly, urging me onwards, turning with me to protect my back from the Wessex warrior. Landwine still faces the other way. My legs are shaking with the effort of keeping upright, and Wulfheard's encouragement doesn't help. And then I'm falling, one of the bastard enemy hands tripping me, but it's too late. Brihthild lands heavily in the boat and I scamper to follow her in, reaching for one of the oars while she twists and turns like a snake in the bottom of the dirty bilge water, unable to right herself.

With a huff of effort, I feel the boat float free into the current, even as I reach for the other oar, my elbow impacting Brihthild at the same time, unintentionally, so that she slumps back down, for the time being, unaware of what's happening around her. I'm grateful that she's still.

I remember the ship close to the Isle of Sheppey, and how awkward we all were with oars and sails. I fumble the oars into position, so that I can make my way deeper into the river. I don't relish the thought of crossing alone, but the others still fight. My eyes narrow, seeking out the enemy and trying to determine how my fellow warriors fare, even as I hear another loud splash. With the oars both finally in position so I can row instead of circling around, I see something moving towards me. I almost drop the oars, only to realise it's Bicwide surging into the water, followed by the remainder of the horses. I grin with pleasure at seeing them walking deeper and deeper until they can finally start to swim. A cry of outrage from the quayside stills my heart as I witness Wulfheard stumble and fall, landing in the water.

With fumbling hands, I try to turn the boat around, determined to find him, but unexpectedly, I sense another ship at my back and turn, terrified once more, only to be greeted by the grinning face of Ealdorman Ælfstan.

'I should have known you'd cause trouble in Wessex,' he offers, a smirk etched into his cheeks, even while he watches the fight taking place just out of reach. 'Who do you have there?' he questions, jutting his chin towards Brihthild.

'A woman who can tell us all there is to know about the conspiracy, provided we can get her to talk. The Wessex ealdorman and King Ecgberht's son are desperate to get their hands on her,' I caution him.

Ealdorman Ælfstan's grin doesn't falter, but he watches those still fighting with concern. 'You've done well, young Icel,' he compliments me. 'But we'll end this fight. Go,' he urges me. 'Go. I'll get the rest of the men. Eadred, help Icel.' And at those words, a sudden weight joins mine in the ship, bright eyes above a thick black moustache, and the words, when they're spoken, are hoarse and high with amusement.

'Give me the oars, you damn arse, or you'll be back in Wessex in no time.'

I hasten backwards, tumbling over the prostrate form of Brihthild, Eadred's chuckle assuring me that he'll be telling this story for many long years to come of how one of Mercia's best warriors is about as useful with a ship as a fish out of water. But my gaze remain on Ealdorman Ælfstan and the contingent of warriors he commands, men from Ealdorman Tidwulf, and also on the horses swimming across the river. I've fought many battles for Bicwide. I hope the big bastard can swim the River Thames and make it safely to Mercia.

29

Brihthild's sullen where she sits, facing the glowering faces of Ealdormen Ælfstan and Tidwulf inside Londinium's high walls, in the very place where her brother met his death. She's been questioned before, but Ealdorman Ælfstan has determined on a new way of extracting the truth from her which she refuses to share. I shudder to be in this place once more, but I know its relevance. As of yet, Brihthild has no idea, but it won't remain that way for long. Kyre and the others from our Wessex expedition have finally returned to Londonia. It's four days after our arrival, but the extra time has given no new information. Not yet.

There are fewer wounds than I might expect amongst our allies, but the men are tired and hungry. Even now, Lord Æthelwulf and the Kent ealdorman prowl the far shore of the River Thames, seeking out our small force and Brihthild. They don't believe we could evade their reach when we were so deep within Wessex-held territory.

Some call for Brihthild to be taken before King Wiglaf, and deprived of her life. Word has been sent to King Wiglaf to come to Londonia. It'll take a few days yet, but when he arrives, it's to be hoped we know all there is about the conspiracy against his kingship and the future of Mercia. If Ealdorman Ælfstan is proved correct in his new ploy, then that might even be today.

Ever since Brihthild woke on being brought ashore in Mercia, slung over the wide shoulders of Eadred, she's said nothing. She's drunk and slept and stayed tight-lipped about it all. She's also remained bound, or under lock and key.

'Brihthild, this is Londinium,' Ealdorman Ælfstan begins, his hand indicating the stone building we're inside. His eyes are hard and I wince to see the lack of sympathy in them. 'My men tell me that your brother died here, fighting my warriors. They say his name was Brihtwold. Is that correct?'

Brihthild flinches. I see her eyes take on a crazed fear. I've not been inside this place since I showed King Wiglaf where much of the fighting took place. I'd rather not be here now. If I close my eyes, I can see everything as it was on that long-ago day. I can see Brihtwold, and I can remember his fury and I recall how he died. I was supposed to keep him alive, but he fought me, nearly killed me, and Frithwine came to my assistance, killing the boy.

'It was, yes.' She spits the answer, perhaps not wanting to but needing to know all the same. Her words are belligerent. I'm not alone in startling to hear her speak. I've almost forgotten what she sounded like when not shrieking like a fox in heat. Ealdorman Ælfstan hides his relief that the tactics are working.

'I can tell you where he's buried,' he offers.

But she shakes her head, teeth gritted.

'I can tell you who killed him.'

This has her trying to win free from her bindings, teeth lashing together. 'You bastard,' she cries.

'Tell me what I need to know, and I'll tell you what you need to know.'

I think she'll argue. I believe she'll say nothing. Instead she nods sharply.

'So, you came upon my warrior, Icel, and his companion, Cuthred, in Winchester,' Ealdorman Ælfstan states. He's been patiently questioning her every day since our return. While to begin with, all those who travelled to Wessex attended, there are fewer and fewer every day. Even Ealdorman Ælfstan's men have lost interest in listening to her confession. They already know she's guilty. They know that she killed her brother. They know that she conspired against Mercia. But I find I can't pull myself away. I need to understand everything she knows or suspects.

'What if I did?'

Ealdorman Ælfstan takes her answer as though it was to be expected, swiftly moving to the next of his many questions. 'Did you know to find them there, in Winchester, in the church of Saints Peter and Paul, or was it luck?'

'I knew,' she confirms. Defiance thrums through her body. Her arrogance, bound and apprehended by her enemy, astounds me. 'I was told to seek them out.'

'By whom?'

That's greeted with silence. Ealdorman Ælfstan beckons me forward. I stand reluctantly. I don't like where this is going.

'This is Icel, as you know.'

There's no response.

'Icel was there when your brother was killed.'

'You bastard,' she roars. 'I knew I hated you the moment I laid eyes on you.'

'I didn't say he killed him,' the ealdorman clarifies. 'But if you want to know everything, he is the man to ask.'

I nod to show I do know everything, and then clear my throat. 'It was in this very room,' I offer, joining the ealdorman in trying to entice the answers from her.

Her lips are pressed tightly together. For a woman who cares so much about what happened to Brihtwold, she showed very little care towards her other brother. Still, it's a weakness to be exploited.

'I saw it all,' I murmur, aware than Ealdorman Ælfstan needs my help. 'I can tell you of his last moments.'

'Did he die a proud West Saxon?' she demands with a shriek.

I open my mouth to answer, and then snap it shut, looking towards Ealdorman Ælfstan.

'The answers will be given, when you answer our questions,' he reaffirms.

'Lord Æthelwulf, of course, you damn fools.' Her voice echoes inside the stone-built building. I wince at the sharpness of it.

'When were you told this?'

'Weeks ago. I had more than enough time to reach Winchester from Canterbury and wait for them to arrive. Now, tell me of my brother.' She watches me, eyes almost pleading.

Ealdorman Ælfstan's pause is momentary. Perhaps only I see it. Whoever sent word to Lord Æthelwulf knew almost before I did about what the king intended. We need to know who that was.

'To what purpose?' Ealdorman Ælfstan continues, waving me aside. I'm to say nothing more until we know everything.

'To ensure that they didn't learn the truth of who was behind the decision to implicate Lord Coenwulf as treasonous and then to have the children killed.'

Her words chill me. I didn't think a woman would speak so coldly about children. It's as though they're little more than an inconvenience to be dismissed. There's no thought for their mother and father. There's no consideration for the lives that would have been denied them.

'It was unfortunate that they found the amber and the note. That was out of my control. While the death of the messenger was suspected, nothing had been proven. It would have been better if his damn brother hadn't become involved. Heardlulf was a damn arse. Good riddance to him.'

I nod. I can't believe that everything that happened to me and Cuthred was pre-planned and this proves that some of it was, but much of it wasn't.

'Tell me of my brother?'

'So you knew of Lord Æthelwulf's involvement in the abduction of the children of Lord Coenwulf.'

Brihthild's eyes narrow and I think she'll refuse to say more, but she doesn't. She must realise that the ealdorman is implacable in his resolve. 'I did, yes. I've long been in his service. He knows I'm a woman who can look after herself. He's paid me well over the years.'

'He sent you and your brother to intercept the Mercians?' This is the bit that has plagued me since having the time to consider all we endured.

'He sent me. I brought my brother along to help me. It was easier to linger in the church if all thought I was seeking a miracle to cure him. But he was useless to me. His illness wasn't faked. He was dying. I knew it.' Her words are edged with scorn. 'I just helped him on his way. I couldn't allow him to recover and tell Cuthred what he knew. The damn fool suspected me and wanted to voice those suspicions.'

'Tell us what you know of the wider conspiracy? Who else was involved?'

Bishop Æthelweald's also sitting, listening to this discussion. He's complained repeatedly about the necessity of it, and yet he can't keep away, even though escorts have been provided to return him to his bishopric in Lichfield. He wishes to know if she'll implicate him.

'The Mercian sell-sword, Wulfnoth, was to arrange for the children to be taken northwards. Once there, they were to be handed to another who would arrange to have them killed and buried. It was important that no one knew where their bodies would lie. Far to the north would mean they'd never be found.'

'How did Lord Æthelwulf know of Wulfnoth?'

'All within Wessex know of Wulfnoth's predilection for involving himself in the ruling of Mercia. Lord Æthelwulf was convinced that Wulfnoth would happily interfere once more, especially if enough money was offered as compensation.'

'What did you know of Heardred?'

'Nothing, other than what I've learned since. He was a go-between moving between Mercia and Wessex. Lord Æthelwulf was convinced he'd run off with the amber, not that he'd been killed. We don't know who murdered him. Lord Æthelwulf was angry that he'd been killed. It's made him fearful that more of his plans are known.' Ealdorman Ælfstan lets this pass, more focused on who is the ultimate instigator. I want to know what else Æthelwulf has planned.

'So, who gave Heardred the amber? King Ecgberht?'

She smirks, and I don't like to see it. 'Tell me of my brother,' she counters. 'I will say no more until you tell me more.'

Ealdorman Ælfstan allows her words to hang in the air. 'So who gave Heardred the amber?' he repeats, but Brihthild says nothing else. He beckons me forward.

'Your brother was a loyal West Saxon to the end,' I say blandly.

A smile of triumph lights her face. 'Did he wound you? Make you bleed?'

I say nothing further.

'How did he die?' she demands. 'How did he die?' she repeats when I say nothing else.

Ealdorman Ælfstan shakes his head, ensuring I know to hold my silence. 'Who gave Heardred the amber?'

'Not King Ecgberht,' she grudgingly admits. 'It was his son, who was the West Saxon power behind the conspiracy.'

'So, who offered up the amber? Lord Æthelwulf?'

She smirks again, shaking her head from side to side, her eyes once more turning to me. 'No, it wasn't Lord Æthelwulf. He wasn't the one ensuring everything was done as was wanted. He wasn't the money behind the conspiracy. He was merely a willing participant. The amber was for him, not sent by him.'

As she speaks, a chill shudders its way down my spine. I find my gaze drawn once more towards Bishop Æthelweald, yet I abruptly know that's not going to be the name that tumbles from her cracked lips. She's been refusing food since being in Mercia. And she only drinks sparingly.

'Tell me of my brother, and I will give you the name.'

Ealdorman Ælfstan nods for me to speak.

'He didn't wound me. We were friends, but we became enemies. He died protecting Ealdorman Wilfhardi. He died at the hands of a man called Frithwine.'

'I'll kill him,' she rages. I don't tell her that Frithwine is dead. 'The amber was sent by the queen of Mercia, Queen Cynethryth,' she eventually announces.

A gasp runs through those assembled within the hall. I note the look that passes between the two ealdormen, and the grin of delight on Brihthild's face.

'So, Heardred, as you understand it, was to deliver a letter and amber into the hands of Lord Æthelwulf, and both were sent by the queen of Mercia.'

She nods, licking her lips again, not breaking eye contact with me.

'She wished to ensure her son's kingship. She was prepared to pay heavily for that. It was she who told Lord Æthelwulf of Icel's trip to Winchester.'

'This isn't the story you told me.' Wulfheard stands, and walks towards her, his eyes narrowed. She eyes him with contempt, directing a similar look my way.

'I told you what you needed to hear. You wanted to believe it was a Wessex conspiracy. I told you that it was. You would have helped me to escape provided you believed the Mercians weren't involved. I was asked for the truth by these two ealdormen, and so, I'm providing it in exchange for knowing how my poor brother ended his life. I'm glad he died fighting the Mercians. That's what he'd have wanted. He hated the Mercians. All of them. Just as I do.' Once more, she bucks against her restraints.

Silence settles within the hall. There are so many things I want to know, but abruptly, I realise something. I've spoken a kind of truth to her. Has she done the same to us?

I realise we can't trust her words, not at all. She's cast the guilt on Wessex, as Wulfheard told us, and on Mercia, as she's now revealed in exchange for knowing about her brother's final moments. If we give her the opportunity, she'll denounce the Welsh or the kingdom of the East Angles. I can tell that the ealdormen are quickly realising the same.

'Lock her up,' Ealdorman Ælfstan announces abruptly, standing and walking away from where Brihthild is closely guarded by Ealdorman Tidwulf's warriors. 'Lock her up until the king arrives.' And so spoken, he indicates I should join him, Wulfheard as well.

Outside, I blink in the bright daylight, enjoying the welcoming heat from the sun overhead.

'This isn't over,' he announces slowly, face tight with fury. 'This isn't over, but we're getting somewhere, slowly.' He nods as though trying to convince himself that progress has been made. While we stand there, I hear the aggrieved cries of Brihthild as she's returned to her captivity by Ealdorman Tidwulf's warriors.

I shut my ears to her outrage. I see Cuthred, watching, his expression inscrutable. What does he think of her now? What do I think of her? All I do know, as Ealdorman Ælfstan says, is that this is far from over, but slowly, piece by piece, we're starting to assemble the layers in this conspiracy. What started with Lord Coenwulf's trip into Wessex, and ended with his children being abducted, is merely the most obvious of the parts of this ruse to deprive Mercia of her æthelings, in which Mercia and Wessex both seem to be complicit. Why the queen would ally with Lord Æthelwulf I don't know. Why Lord Æthelwulf would ally with her, is also unknown.

'We'll protect them, Icel, never fear that,' Ealdorman Ælfstan assures me, but what remains unsaid is that we still don't understand, with certainty, who we're protecting them from. Is it the queen of Mercia? Is it the king of Wessex's son? Is it from this woman who might or might not be telling us the truth? Wulfnoth's dead. Eadweard and his cronies are also dead, but there are many who still live. And they aren't yet finished with the children of Lady Cynehild. I remain bound by my deathbed oath to Lady Cynehild. Will I never be free from it?

HISTORICAL NOTES

Saxon Medicine – the cure for lung disease is taken from *Bald's Leechbook*, a compendium of remedies which survives from the era. There is a version easily available on the web. The translation reads as follows.

> Make a pottage for lung disease: take betony and white horehound; wormwood, wood sage, the lower part of lesser celandine, lupin, garden radish, stemless carline thistle, [and] wild carrot. Pound all very well and boil in butter and wring through a cloth. Scatter barleymeal into that juice. Stir into a bowl [that is] against a flame until it is as thick as pottage. Eat three morsels with a drink of the warm [pottage]. Afterwards, boil white horehound alone in honey. Put a little barley meal in [it]. Eat after a night's fast and then you should give him either the drink or the pottage. Give it hot to him and afterwards let the person rest for a period of time during the day on the right side and have the arm extended.

I have asked many people about wild carrots and no one seems to know what they are – and I know many more gardeners than I thought I did. Although, I've now discovered you can find out all about them on the Kew Gardens website – so I was not asking the right people.

Winchester – is perhaps one of the best-understood cities in Saxon England in terms of its historical past. While I've often relied on the John Speed maps of the early 1600s to get a sense of what the settlements my characters visit might have been like in the Saxon era, where Winchester is concerned it's known that the John Speed map portrays much of Winchester as it would have been in the later 800s, after King Alfred rearranged some of it – seemingly in a planned settlement that even saw eight thousand tons of distinctive knapped flint cobbles made use of. Luckily, a great deal of research has been undertaken on Winchester since the time it was a Roman settlement, *Venta Belgarum*, which at the time was the fifth-largest settlement in Roman Britain. It appears that the early Saxon settlement was not based on the Roman street plan. For those interested in Saxon Winchester please consult the work of the Winchester Excavations Committee and also the article by Martin Biddle in 'The Land of the English Kin', which was available freely when I downloaded it some time ago. As with Canterbury, below, there is also 'An Historical Map of Winchester' available, which I made great use of in orientating myself and getting a feel for buildings that might have been there in the 830s. It does seem I might have made a mistake and there might not have been a St Mary's in the 830s, but I can't correct that now having used it in the previous book as well. Apologies for this oversight. The Nunnaminster, founded by the wife of King Alfred, by c.902 was dedicated to St Mary as were later churches.

Accents – just before I began work on this volume of Icel's tale, I attended (virtually) the International Medieval Congress held yearly in Leeds, featuring thousands of papers presented by academics and some independent researchers (which I think fits me well) into the past. There was a particular thread on Mercian Studies (I know, I was in heaven). This alerted me to something I didn't know. There are – and it has evidently been known for many, many years – Mercian dialects in the written records. There was a discussion on how often these dialects are written out of translations at the request of modern editors. This then, is something to consider, and I've included it by referencing Icel's Mercian accent in Wessex – which I've included before but now I know was actually evident between the two kingdoms. This is but a small attempt to ensure knowledge of the past makes it into the wider public consciousness. For those who might be developing an interest in Mercia, I recommend the following resource, which is very much just beginning to take shape. https://www.st-andrews.ac.uk/~cr30/MercianNetwork/ For now, it has very useful bibliographies, including some articles on the written Mercian or Anglian language, as opposed to the West Saxon or Saxon language.

Archbishoprics – while King Offa attempted to found an archbishopric in Lichfield, Mercia, he was ultimately unsuccessful, and that meant that the holy men of Mercia were still under the nominal authority of the archbishop of Canterbury. We know there was unease during the reign of early ninth-century kings, and the Councils of Clofesho had occurred intermittently throughout the eighth and ninth centuries. Religious councils would continue to be called by the archbishop, which would mean the bishops would need to travel into enemy territory, as it were. Canterbury, as with Winchester, had been a settlement since before the Roman era, with evidence of Iron Age occupations. During the Roman era, it was known as *Durovernum* (the stronghold by the alder marsh). As with Londinium, the Roman settlement acquired its walls many years after it was first constructed. I have used 'An Historical Map of Canterbury from Roman Times to 1907' when trying to imagine what the settlement might have looked like at the time. I did find a wonderful reconstruction image but, alas, it was from the 600s, and not the 830s.

Writing and reading in the Saxon era – I appreciate that some might argue with me allowing some of my warriors to be able to read and write, but I think the lack of surviving documents is often used as a means of arguing that people couldn't read or write. I suspect that more than just the monks/nuns would have been able to write. And if people couldn't write themselves, they would have been able to make use of those who could. And they would really want to know that their words were correctly recorded.

Historically, there is not much to say about the year 835 in the *Anglo-Saxon Chronicle* with reference to Mercia. There are also no surviving charters from this year. But Wiglaf was certainly still king, King Ecgberht was in Wessex, and the Viking raiders were still sniffing around.

While working on this novel, I've been reminded that horses could only travel so far in a day and that, indeed, they needed to spend up to six hours eating. Wowsers. I've tried to ensure my journey times fit with this. I think twenty-five miles a day would be the topmost, at a steady gallop.

I have also found an old resource which lists the prices of everyday items. I've made great use of this, and hopefully, I'll track down the original resource so that I can add those details here. Coins, money, costs – these would all have been something that our ancestors thought about just as much as we do.

I'm entirely grateful to the fabric specialist I met on my post-excavation week with the Bamburgh Research Project for teaching me all about fabric and how it was made, and for informing me that brown sheep would have allowed the monks to have robes of brown as opposed to them being an expensive commodity. I'd not considered that. And also to the whole team, and my fellow attendees, who made the experience so interesting. I will never make an 'on your knees in the dirt' archaeologist, but I very much appreciate the work they undertake in reconstructing the past.

The name of the Wessex ealdorman is taken from Charter S280, with thanks to PASE and the Electronic Sawyer. There is some confusion there, as another Æthelwulf is listed, but I've decided that one Æthelwulf is enough.

ACKNOWLEDGEMENTS

As ever, my thanks to my editor, Caroline Ridding, for allowing me to continue to write the story of young Icel. I would also thank my copyeditor, Ross, and my proofreader, Shirley, for ensuring this story is as free from error as possible. It really isn't that easy to get the Old English names correct – the thryth's have a habit of rearranging themselves.

And to the whole team at Boldwood, with a special mention for Claire Fenby, for all they do in providing fabulous covers and marketing my books. It is wonderful to see the company growing.

Huge thanks to my support authors and my family, especially EP and AP who help me and keep me focused, and to MP who provides just enough incentives with cooked breakfasts to keep me on track. And to Duke, who sometimes sits quietly while I work, and sometimes demands a long walk, both of which can be very helpful (he is the dog).

And to my readers. As ever, sincere and genuine thanks for enjoying my stories set in the Saxon era.

ABOUT THE AUTHOR

MJ Porter is the author of many historical novels set predominantly in Seventh to Eleventh-Century England, and in Viking Age Denmark. Raised in the shadow of a building that was believed to house the bones of long-dead Kings of Mercia, meant that the author's writing destiny was set.

Sign up to MJ Porter's mailing list here for news, competitions and updates on future books.

Visit MJ's website: www.mjporterauthor.com

Follow MJ on social media:

X x.com/coloursofunison
instagram.com/m_j_porter
bookbub.com/authors/mj-porter

ALSO BY MJ PORTER

The Eagle of Mercia Chronicles

Son of Mercia

Wolf of Mercia

Warrior of Mercia

Eagle of Mercia

Protector of Mercia

Enemies of Mercia

The Brunanburh Series

King of Kings

Kings of War

WARRIOR CHRONICLES

WELCOME TO THE CLAN ×

THE HOME OF
BESTSELLING HISTORICAL
ADVENTURE FICTION!

WARNING:
MAY CONTAIN VIKINGS!

SIGN UP TO OUR
NEWSLETTER

BIT.LY/WARRIORCHRONICLES

Boldwood

Boldwood Books is an award-winning fiction publishing company seeking out the best stories from around the world.

Find out more at www.boldwoodbooks.com

Join our reader community for brilliant books, competitions and offers!

Follow us
@BoldwoodBooks
@TheBoldBookClub

Sign up to our weekly deals newsletter

https://bit.ly/BoldwoodBNewsletter